The HAUNTING of Suzanna Blackwell

A Novel by Richard Setlowe

A SIGNET BOOK

NEW AMERICAN LIBRARY

It was only the memory of desire ... yet it was a passion beyond time ... beyond imagination ... beyond reality itself.

Most women would envy Suzanna Blackwell. The beautiful, privileged daughter of a high-ranking Navy officer, she has a handsome, exciting new lover—a dynamic, successful young TV newsman who attracts her more powerfully than any man alive.

Yet there is another man ... a seducer of more-than-human beauty and exquisite sexual genius against whose will Suzanna is powerless ... until little by little she discovers the true nature of his dark and irresistible secret. . . .

The
HAUNTING of
Suzanna Blackwell

Recommended Reading from SIGNET

To Beverly
With Love

"Death signifies nothing. For us believing physicists the distinction between past, present, and future is only an illusion, even if a stubborn one."

—*Albert Einstein*

"Myth embodies the nearest approach to absolute truth that can be stated in words."

—*Ananda Coomaraswamy*

PROLOGUE

1958
Charles City, Virginia

SUZANNA WHISPERED GOOD-BYE TO HER MOTHER as Grace Blackwell's coffin was lowered into the wintry Virginia loam. Still, the twelve-year-old was not really frightened when her mother appeared to her two weeks later, materializing out of the lacy curtain in the bedroom of her grandparents' house.

Suzanna knelt, as if waiting, in the same antique fourposter bed in which her mother had dreamed during another childhood. Gradually the girl became aware of a faint floral smell, strange to that place but somehow familiar, deeply familiar. She recognized the delicate fragrance of L'Air du Temps, her mother's perfume.

There was a tingle of static electricity along the fine hairs of Suzanna's neck, and a sound not quite heard teased her ear. A figure hovered in the corner of her eye, just out of sight. The child cried out.

Her mother then swirled into view, as if she had been there to see all the time, but a lens in front of Suzanna had suddenly focused. The indistinct sound became fuller, though still vague, as if the background noise on a radio had now tuned to a lovely, wordless song. Her mother sat on the bed beside Suzanna, and her smile, her lullaby, her gentle caress told the child that she was loved and not alone in the world.

Suzanna woke the next morning in the empty, sun-filled bedroom. She realized that such a visitation was not to be taken lightly. She immediately ran to her grandparents' room, bursting in on her grandmother, who was in the midst of dressing.

"My mother. She's a ghost or something. She came to my room last night." Suzanna's words erupted in an excited rush.

Her grandmother stared at her for a long while, then smiled and said in a very gentle voice, "Sugar, you had a dream about your mother."

"No, it wasn't a dream," Suzanna insisted.

"Yes, it was," her grandmother said firmly, and there was a no-nonsense admonition in her voice.

"No, it wasn't."

Her grandmother continued to smile, but there was now a tightness to her mouth and brow that seemed to squeeze the warmth right from her face. "Then why didn't she appear to me too, *her own mother*?"

There was a sharp edge to her grandmother's voice that made Suzanna sense she was on dangerous ground. The girl remained silent.

In life, Suzanna and her mother had always been each other's main companions. Her father was a naval officer and the family hopped from base to base, faithful fleet followers alighting temporarily in a succession of stark tract housing for the military. Suzanna attended a half dozen different elementary schools, indistinguishable in memory one from another, jerry-rigged for the post-World War II baby boom.

To Suzanna, Grace Blackwell seemed a beautiful and wistful princess ever pining for her faraway lover. At first, in her innocence, Suzanna had assumed that the absent lover for whom her mother yearned was her father, who seemed always to be away at sea. Gradually she became aware that her mother longed for another, a poignant infidelity that, in the end, caused her death.

Often at night the last thing Suzanna would hear as she fell asleep was the sweetly phrased crooning of Frank Sinatra and the plaintive, sentimental brass of Tommy Dorsey's trombone, as her mother sat alone, sipping bourbon, playing one old record over and over and over like a threnody, working her way through sorrowful remembrances of joys past to the oblivion of sleep.

> *"I'll be seeing you*
> *In all the old familiar places*
> *That this heart of mine embraces,*
> *All day through."*

The long, lonely nights, the transience, and the social doldrums of service life were beyond Grace Blackwell's endurance. Her drinking—a genteel, discreet nipping—became another secret that mother and daughter shared. Only Suzanna was sensitive to the intensification of Grace Blackwell's vapors, as the bluesy depression and the giddy upswings of her natural temperament were fired up by alcohol.

Finally, one night in Norfolk, when Suzanna's father was off on maneuvers with the Sixth Fleet, somewhere in the Mediterranean, Grace Blackwell's bottle had run dry at the moment her cup of painful memories had overflowed.

> *"In that small cafe,*
> *The park across the way,*
> *The children's carousel,*
> *The chestnut tree, the wishing well."*

She had left Suzanna alone, asleep, for just a few minutes. She hurried into the wet winter night in search of an open liquor store. Her insensate foot pressing the accelerator, Grace Blackwell had taken a corner too fast and too wide; slewing out of control on the wet asphalt, she crashed into a truck. The long, slender, graceful neck had snapped.

     *B*ut Grace Blackwell had not deserted her daughter. Her love, perhaps her guilt over abandoning Suzanna that night, transcended death. All during the funeral and in the days afterward, Suzanna felt her mother's presence about her, hovering protectively, the hint of a touch, the suggestion of a sound not quite felt or heard but there nevertheless, trembling on the threshold of perception.

Exactly a week after the funeral, Suzanna had her first period. She had been nervously anticipating it for months and had, in fact, secretly taken possession of her mother's tampons and sanitary napkins in preparation. When the cramps had begun, she felt excited and proud, but also, in a confusion of emotions, oddly shameful and secretive. There was only one person with whom she could share this momentous event. She went to bed early, not even feigning sleep but kneeling in the center of the four-poster, terrifically excited and expectant.

Suzanna suddenly felt weak, as if she were dissolving, and a trembling mist permeated the room. It coalesced into a fleecy plume, and from it Grace Blackwell materialized, her smile and expression a reflection of Suzanna's own secret glee.

1

1976
Mare Island, California

*T*HE GREAT HORNED OWLS OF MARE ISLAND were a separate species—blacker than the other horned owls that stalked California, and larger, with wingspreads of five feet.

They inhabited the most inaccessible ledges, radar platforms, and bridges of the old derelict World War II warships mothballed at the north end of the Navy Yard on the island. The horned owls preyed on the rats on the base and the frogs and snakes in the nearby marsh. But mostly they ravaged the pigeons that roosted below them in the eaves and gun turrets of the old warships.

Every morning, when the maintenance crews came aboard the ships, they found bundles of feathers, fur, and bones strewn about the decks. But the owls had horrible whims. There were mornings when the workmen clambered aboard and found the skeleton of a dog picked clean, or the corpses of two dozen decapitated pigeons, their plump bodies untouched, but their brains fastidiously tidbitted.

The horned owls were so dusky as to be invisible against the night, and they were silent, their soft feathers making no sound as they flew. But they had a bone-chilling cry, like a demon's laughter. Decades before, the immigrant Irish shipbuilders who lived on Mare Island had gone dumb with terror at the sound.

To them it was the wail of banshees announcing that someone was about to die.

Now the hideous cries of unseen owls pierced the black skies over the navy base, resounding every night over the docks of nuclear submarines, through the classrooms of the electronic-warfare school, and in the pillared mansions of the senior officers along Walnut Avenue.

"It is an odd thing, but everyone who disappears is said to be seen in San Francisco. The city must possess all the attractions of the next world."

Wally Adams had told Suzanna that when he drove her to the Leonardo da Vinci Airport in Rome to catch the jet to San Francisco. He had quoted Oscar Wilde. Whenever Wally was hurt or grieved, he became a little pretentious. It was his reaction to pain. He had been the resident faculty painter at the Academy in Rome, Suzanna's teacher, her good friend, but never her lover. It touched Suzanna that he should be so distressed at her leaving, but perhaps Wally sensed something in Suzanna that she herself did not then recognize.

Seated now on the parade ground at Mare Island, the sprawling navy base and shipyard in the northeast corner of San Francisco Bay, Suzanna felt as if some essential part of her was indeed disappearing into the next world. She shifted her weight and sighed impatiently, a discreet complaint against the heat, the boredom, and all the pompous circumstances of a naval change-of-command ceremony.

Suzanna's father, Captain John Blackwell, was replacing another officer as C.O. The two men, along with Rear Admiral Warren Doyle, who was the ceremony's featured speaker, the admiral's lady, and a passel of captains and commanders whom Suzanna did not know, occupied the shaded bandstand, a whitewashed, Victorian-aged cupola. The deposed navy band blared away in the unshaded sun on the bandstand's right flank.

The towering Monterey pines and eucalyptus of Alden Park encircled the parade ground like pillars, creating a sunlit amphitheater. At the west side of the little park an honor guard, a platoon of marines in sparkling dress blue uniforms, stood at a stiff parade rest. Directly facing them at the east end were ranks of navy petty officers in white short-sleeved shirts and dark slacks. In contrast to the resplendent marines, the navy enlisted men looked like a bloc of office clerks. The park's most prominent exhibit, a three-story-high Polaris missile, loomed behind them, throwing a long black shadow across their ranks.

It was for this ceremony that Suzanna's father had summoned her from Rome. For a while, at least, she was to play mistress of the three-story Colonial home that was the captain's official residence. This new post was her father's "twilight tour," his last before retirement. He had been passed over again for promotion to flag rank. Admiral Doyle's presence underlined that rejected status. Doyle and her father had been classmates at Annapolis.

One of the marines in the front rank suddenly buckled, silently collapsing like a marionette whose strings had been cut. He was quietly dragged out of line from the rear and another marine stepped forward to take his place. Hardly any of the spectators noticed.

Suzanna had been placed in the front row center of the spectators, seated on folding chairs in precise lines facing the bandstand. It gave her an unobstructed view of the parade, but no shade whatever from the broiling sun. It was unseasonably hot for the San Francisco area even for June, hot enough to fell a marine.

Suzanna studied the shady woods beyond the bandstand with longing. Two huge naval artillery shells, painted black, flanked the path through the park like sinister sentries. Rows of low concrete blockhouses squatted among the trees. They had originally been built during World War II as air-raid shelters. Now, thirty years later, they were weathered, ivy-covered, and bore a macabre resemblance to the ancient crypts of Rome. Peering into their shadows, Suzanna felt strangely chilled despite the heat and suppressed a shiver.

"I relieve you, sir." Suzanna was yanked from her reveries. On the bandstand her father saluted Captain Hailey and with that terse, official phrase took command in a heartbeat. The speeches, the remarks, the minutiae of the reading of the orders were all over.

The Catholic chaplain strode forward and the official party and spectators all rose on cue. The base's Protestant chaplain had given the invocation, and now the padre gave the benediction, thereby ecumenically covering all divine bets. He beseeched the blessings of the Holy Ghost and "a fair wind and a following sea." The band exploded into "Anchors Aweigh."

Suzanna rose to greet her father, Admiral Doyle, and his wife as they came off the bandstand.

Mrs. Doyle was a bleached and bosomy woman, sporting a white, low-cut dress that accented the deep cocoa tan she'd cultivated during her husband's recent Pearl Harbor duty. She looked closely at Suzanna and her eyes widened in astonishment. She stopped and the blood drained from her face. As her knees faltered, she clutched at the admiral's arm for support. Her eyes never left Suzanna's face. Her mouth quivered and she whispered one questioning word: "Grace?"

Suzanna took her hand and smiled. "No, I'm Suzanna."

"Suzanna?" Mrs. Doyle's brow knit in puzzlement. "Suzanna. Oh, my God. *Suzanna.*"

To Suzanna's embarrassment, Mrs. Doyle suddenly clutched at her and hugged her to her ample, browned bosom. "I thought I'd seen a ghost." She thrust Suzanna at arm's length and studied her face avidly. "Oh, you're the image of Grace." She pulled Suzanna to her once again and kissed her wetly on the cheek.

She turned to the admiral. "You never said a word about Grace's daughter being here," she admonished him.

"I didn't know." The admiral in turn wheeled on Captain Blackwell for an explanation of this dereliction.

Blackwell shrugged. "I wasn't sure myself until the last minute." He hesitated, then offered uneasily by way of explanation, "She's been in Europe."

Mrs. Doyle dismissed the two officers and turned back to Suzanna. She held her by both hands and looked into her eyes beseechingly. "Oh, honey, do you remember me? Shirley Doyle. You were so young then. Just this terribly frightened little girl. Your mother was one of my best friends."

Suzanna nodded and smiled reassuringly, but she remembered nothing of this blond, beefy woman. At the west end of the park a reception area had been cordoned off, and the guests were now assembling impatiently into a receiving line. Suzanna was the official hostess.

"I went to live with my mother's family," Suzanna explained. "Since Dad was away."

Shirley Doyle sighed deeply, and her eyes misted at the memory of that terribly frightened little girl. "Oh, yes, I remember. The Halls." Mrs. Doyle nodded mournfully and then added, "The Halls of Virginia." There was a change of voice, and she continued cheerfully. "But you're married now. Another Annapolis man." Her head bobbed with approval, and she turned to Suzanna's father. "I remember Jack at least sent us an announcement about *that*." She turned back to Suzanna. "Is your husband here with you?"

Suzanna took a deep breath. "No. Robert and I separated. We're divorced now." She glanced at her father. The immediate pain and distress was etched for a moment in his face.

Mrs. Doyle frowned and then gave a short laugh. "Well, I'll bet that shook up the Halls of Virginia more than anything since the burning of Washington. No wonder you took off for Europe."

Suzanna squeezed her hands. She was suddenly very fond of this buxom, blond admiral's lady.

"Honey, you greet your daddy's guests." They were at the reception area. "We'll have lunch soon. Or better yet, have ourselves a day on the town in San Francisco."

"I'd like that very much," Suzanna agreed.

The base public-information officer, a lieutenant junior grade, very deferentially positioned Suzanna's father and Suzanna herself, then took his place at Captain Blackwell's right to introduce the guests. He leaned forward deliberately at each introduction to include Suzanna, the movement a courtly but somewhat comical bow in her direction. The aide was young, almost smooth-cheeked, and overweight, and his flushed, sweating face and neck swelled out over the tight white collar of the dress uniform like a sausage bursting its rind.

Suzanna had been very anxious about the reception. She was once again being compelled to play out a role meant for her mother. That morning she had completely dressed and undressed three times before committing herself to a coral silk dress she had bought in Rome. It accentuated her flowing chestnut hair and green eyes. If they saw her as the dangerous divorcée who had deserted an Annapolis man, she thought, then she might as well make the most of it. But the moment she stepped into the glaring sun of the parade grounds amid the other proper navy wives, her bravado instantly evaporated. Everyone treated her with great hospitality and politeness. She was, after all, the captain's daughter.

Yet several times that morning she saw in her father's

eyes a pain and disappointment so deep and primal
that it had shocked her when she first sensed it. This
day marked the final post in his career.

The band broke out into a brassy arrangement of the
Beatles' "Yesterday," apparently part of their pop rep-
ertoire for official receptions and sailings. Suzanna could
never hear a navy band without feeling the pain of
standing on a pier watching a ship leave. First it had
been her father aboard, and then it had been her
husband. She found herself intently studying each male
face that presented itself and then discreetly checking
the left hand for a ring. The majority of faces and
hands belonged to navy officers, who returned her
smile with bright male interest but then quickly de-
ferred their eyes to her father. There were a few civilians:
longtime civil-service employees of the base, a state sena-
tor from Sacramento whose district encompassed Mare
Island, and the mayor of nearby Vallejo.

The band struck up "Some Enchanted Evening," the
overture of a medley from *South Pacific*, possibly inspired by their proximity to a Japanese human torpedo,
a one-man kamikaze sub captured in World War II.
Alden Park was in fact a gallery of such artifacts, reeking of blood and history. Behind Suzanna was a fat-
breeched, black iron cannon. A bronze plaque identified
it as a pivot gun from the *Kearsarge*, the sloop that
savaged and sank the Confederate raider *Alabama* in
the famous sea battle of 1864.

To her right was the figurehead from the U.S.S.
Independence, the man o' war that cowed the Barbary
pirates on the shores of Tripoli. Both ships had ended
their days here at Mare Island, the latter being burned
for the copper in her hull.

Suzanna studied her father, standing very straight
and handsome in his formal white uniform, his chest
blazing with the medals and campaign ribbons of three
wars. As he stood by her side at that moment, he

seemed once again the romantic, mythic hero of her childhood, the father she had rarely seen and still hardly knew.

In her teenage years, Suzanna had deeply resented her father for having abandoned her. It was only during her own frustrating marriage that she realized the only alternative would have been for her father—then at mid-career—to resign from the navy and flounder in a civilian job for which he was untrained. In the end she would have become the object of his resentment.

Instead he had given her a secure home and compromised his career for her sake. He had restricted his assignments to ships operating out of Norfolk, and to shore duty in the immediate area. The limitations had had a dampening effect on his advancement. It was not until she married that he had arranged for duty in the Far East, with a destroyer squadron in the Gulf of Tonkin. But by then John Blackwell had missed too many opportunities.

A great emotional upwelling brought a flush to Suzanna's face and tears to her eyes. She impulsively reached out and kissed him on the cheek. He was startled by the sudden embrace, but pleased, and gave her hand a quick squeeze before dropping it to greet his next guest.

"This is Mr. Edward Riley, the TV reporter and anchorman from San Francisco." The public-information officer now presented a tall, gaunt man with the deeply lined but handsome features of an aging actor.

"I'm frankly surprised you'd come up here to cover a dull navy family affair," Captain Blackwell said.

"Not at all. Admiral Doyle's comments on the post-Vietnam military cutbacks are newsworthy." The voice was deep and resonant but had a harsh, gravelly edge to it, the result of years of too much alcohol and too many cigarettes, which Suzanna recognized as well in her own father's voice. "But, hell, I'm an old warhorse who loves a parade. The jingo that recalls the great battles of our youth, the war that forever flavors life thereafter with the stale taste of anticlimax. Eh, Captain?"

The exaggerated bravado of Riley's speech made Suzanna suspect that the man had been drinking.

"But I had to drag my hotshot young producer here." Riley indicated a younger man standing behind him, and there was an almost paternal affection in his voice.

Before the PIO could make the introduction, Riley's companion took Suzanna's hand. "I'm Michael Lowenstein," he said. He glanced at Riley, then shared a bemused smile with Suzanna at his colleague's theatricality.

It was an attractive if not a handsome face, lean, with a high-bridged nose. The hair was longish and shaggy. But the features weren't what caught Suzanna's interest; it was his vitality and then, in his eyes, a contradiction, a touch of melancholy. This face might not have been exceptional if she had seen it in Rome, but here on Mare Island, amid the brutally barbered faces with shaven sideburns, it seized her attention, and somehow moved her.

"I understand you've been studying art in Rome," he said. "What sort of work were you doing?"

Suzanna was surprised. "Painting. That is, at first. But then I started doing commercial art."

He nodded and smiled, looking at her curiously, as if he had more personal questions he wanted to ask. "Any TV work?"

"No, but I'm fascinated by the way you routinely use graphics in television. I haven't the foggiest notion how you create the effects you do."

"It's actually not very complicated. I'd be happy to take you on a grand tour of our shop so you can see how we put things together." He gazed at her with that intense, disquieting interest.

"Why, thank you." A question suddenly struck Suzanna. "How did you know I had been studying art?"

"There was a line at the end of your father's official press biography." Michael Lowenstein cocked his head and there was a twinkle of amusement in his eyes, the slight pursing of a smile about the lips. "It's the only thing I remember."

"I take it you don't share Mr. Riley's interest in the navy?" Captain Blackwell interrupted. He had been following the conversation with mounting impatience, and a hint of curtness edged his voice.

Michael Lowenstein turned to Blackwell, and something in those dark eyes dulled. He seemed to take in and address the rows of campaign ribbons and the gold-braided uniform rather than the man. "It's not the navy in particular, Captain. It's this whole machinery of war that I don't share Ed's romanticism for. It terrifies me." There was neither apology nor deference in his manner, and the gesture of his head seemed to take in not only the bloodstained artifact of Alden Park but the entire base and the wharves beyond.

Blackwell's eyebrows lifted in consternation, then frowned.

"But I want to thank you and your staff for your cooperation and hospitality," Lowenstein added formally.

Suzanna had never before seen a look of instant and mutual contempt flash between two men who had apparently never met before. It was as if they had immediately recognized one another.

In a moment the anchorman Edward Riley and his "hotshot producer" with the melancholy eyes passed on. Suzanna stared after them, both fascinated and disturbed by the brief confrontation.

A chief, one of the few enlisted men to brave the reception line, shook her hand perfunctorily. He turned to her father, stopped, and took his look. Then he spoke, hand outstretched. "Master Chief Damage Controlman Slade, sir. We served together back in World War II."

Captain Blackwell gave a slight start. He seized the chief's arm, gold-braided from wrist to elbow with a dozen hash marks of service, and stared into the lined gray face, searching for the man he had known thirty years before. "Slade. By God, Slade. How are you?"

"Fine, sir. Thank you. It's nice to be serving with you again, sir." The old chief hesitated a moment and then, as if compelled to reveal something fearful, he added, "The old ship, sir. She's still here."

"The *Santa Cruz* is here?" the captain exclaimed, genuinely astonished.

"Yes, sir, in the mothball fleet. With all the other old ships. On the pier at the north end of the base."

Blackwell's eyes narrowed. "All these years," he whispered, suddenly moved.

"It'd be dangerous to go aboard. I wouldn't advise it, sir," the chief said, his voice sharp with alarm. "What I mean, Captain, is that she was never completely repaired." The last was said in a secretive voice. The chief peered about over his shoulder, as if expecting someone eavesdropping. He gave Blackwell a direct look and a nod in farewell, then moved on quickly, as if he had been obligated to deliver a message but said more than he had intended.

Captain Blackwell stared after him, then glanced uneasily at Suzanna. She had no idea what to make of this strange encounter. She turned back to the next smiling face and outstretched hand in a seemingly endless and anonymous line.

2

THE FIRST THING AT THE OFFICE THE NEXT morning, Michael tried to call Suzanna Blackwell. She was out, and the base switchboard took the message. Michael repeated his invitation to visit the station.

He had been strongly attracted to the girl and he wanted to see her again, if it was possible. She was lovely and his reaction was natural enough. His reaction to her father was another matter. He had thought he had his anger in better control than that. Apparently not. There were times when he was still as unstable and explosive as old dynamite.

Michael headed reluctantly to the videotape editing room to work on the footage they had shot at Mare Island the day before. What perversity of his soul had ever possessed him to agree with Riley to do this show? Everything about it made his flesh shrink.

The tape editor was a slender girl, pale as a consumptive. The multicolored images flashing on the video screen were reflected on her face in a ghastly flush, as if her flesh had no inherent life or color of its own, but only that emitted by the cathode-ray tube.

On the screen, the towering bridge and steel ramparts of an old warship were silhouetted against the distant brown hills, the massive turrets and heavy-caliber guns resembling a lonely, ancient fortress. The only sound was the wind bassooning through the smokestacks, whispering eerily through the spiderwork of masts and antennas.

The camera panned down to reveal a great desolate armada—aircraft carriers, battle cruisers, assault transports, destroyers, and submarines—all packed stem to stern in tight rows along the length of a narrow, bleak pier.

"This is the ghost fleet of Mare Island," a stentorian voice intoned.

The picture now cut to Ed Riley on the deck of one of the warships, the wind rustling his hair, his feet astride as if bracing against the roll.

"After the titanic sea battles of World War II, the great Pacific armada sailed home. Battle-scarred but triumphant, the ships steamed through the Golden Gate, its spans still ringing with victory, and into this quiet backwater, this most remote tentacle of the Pacific," Riley narrated.

"Here they were mothballed, their guns corked, their machinery coated with Cosmoline, their pipes flooded with rust preventive. The ships were dehumidified and sealed up, preserved so that they might be quickly readied for battle in the next great war. Some were. Thirty were reconditioned and served in Korea. A handful in Vietnam. But most were bypassed by the accelerating technology of the sixties and seventies, the new sophisticated electronics and guided missiles.

"But the warships still wait here in their forsaken moorings, their obsolete guns and radar antennas poised against the sky, great haunted galleons riding at anchor in their historic warp of time."

Riley paused for the dramatic effect, but then was suddenly seized by a cough, a hoarse rattling of phlegm whose sinister sound once again alarmed Michael.

"Boy, he can make the phonebook sound like the

Gettysburg Address," the videotape editor said to Michael.

Michael nodded. "Yes, he can." He did not say that Riley had been half in the bag when he had narrated that. But it did not matter. Michael remembered now why he had consented to produce and direct this special about derelict ships, forgotten heroes, and titanic battles fought before he was born.

Drunk or sober, Riley still had the power to stir and move him. Riley was the real thing.

The phone suddenly rang. It was Jerry Adler. Would Mike please meet him immediately in Don Spaulding's office?

Michael's antenna, finely tuned to the changing frequencies of station politics, was suddenly up and scanning. Adler was the news director and Spaulding the station manager.

"What's up?"

"We have a rather serious problem. We'd rather discuss it with you here."

"I'll be right down."

Spaulding's executive suite was two floors below. Michael took the stairs rather than wait for the elevator, which ricocheted between floors at its own eccentric electrical whims, answering rings in no particular sequence.

Adler's voice had been curt, without even a mumbled pretense at cordiality. Michael suspected he was about to plunge into a major territorial battle with the news director. Adler, a thin, intense, balding man in his early thirties, had recently joined the station from Los Angeles, where he had been the assistant news director at the network station there. He was energetic and competent, but it was Michael's impression that he was not a newsman but a manager. It was not the drama, blood, shock, and tears of news that stirred his passions; it was power. And Michael somehow threatened his.

Michael's title was officially Executive Producer, a deliberately ambiguous nom de guerre that seemed to trigger departmental infighting. Michael was independent of the news department, producing and directing his own specials and documentaries. He did not have a full-time camera crew assigned to him, and he had to commandeer whomever and whatever he required from the news department. He made a point of cooperating so that the news operation never lost a story because he had a crew tied up. In fact, Michael often got stories they might not otherwise have covered. But that did not assuage Adler, who felt constantly invaded.

The scene that confronted Michael as he walked into the station manager's office only heightened his expectations of trouble. Spaulding sat behind his desk, playing distractedly with a pencil, and Adler sat slumped glumly in a chair at his right. Both wore the expressions of men who had received word that the station had been sold out from under them to a conglomerating chain of pizza parlors that had decided to diversify.

"I'm afraid we have some rather bad news," Spaulding announced in a gravely sincere tone. Like most TV station managers, he had come up through the ranks of sales, selling one-minute and thirty-second spots to advertising-agency time buyers. He was handsome in a beefy way, smartly tailored, meticulously groomed, and always gravely sincere, as though this were some requisite for those whose careers are made selling abstractions like time to hucksters.

"It's about our friend Ed Riley," Spaulding added after a pause.

Michael felt his flesh turn to stone. Riley was dead, Michael thought. He had finally drunk himself into a fatal stupor. But then he thought—a bolt of hope, really—that Riley had woken up coughing blood again, and was in the hospital.

"The coast guard found his body this morning," Spaulding continued in a hushed, sepulchral voice.

"The coast guard?" Michael was confused.

Spaulding nodded to Adler for amplification.

"He was found in the Bay near Richmond."

"What the hell was he doing in Richmond?" Michael wondered aloud, rubbing his temples. It was another world on the east side of the Bay, two bridges and twenty-five miles from San Francisco. He had a mental image of the smoke-belching Standard Oil refinery, bleak, small boatyards framed by busted-up wooden fences, ancient diners that looked like rusting railroad cars.

"Damned if I know. He's in the Contra Costa County morgue in Martinez now," Adler said. "The sheriff's department called me immediately because he had a press card in his wallet." Adler's voice was somber but businesslike, a demonstration to Spaulding that he was wired into the most forsaken nooks of the Bay area where a story might break. "They need to know the next of kin. Who was he closest to?"

"The bartender at Mallory's."

Spaulding frowned, and a beat later Adler also frowned at Michael.

"He has a daughter living in Los Angeles," Michael said.

"Did he have a wife?" Adler interrogated him. "I really don't know much about his personal life."

You did not want to know anything about the man, Michael thought. You only wanted to shitcan him. "No, there's no wife. Only ex-wives."

"What kind of Irish Catholic has ex-wives?" Spaulding's eyebrows arched in disapproval.

"A very bad one." Michael stared down at the carpet, a decorator rug with subtly varying shades and plushes of blue wool, handwoven into an irregular, barklike pattern. The numbness was returning. The numbness had once been like a thick callus deadening his heart and mind, and he had never wanted to feel it again.

"They need someone to identify the body."

Michael stood up. "It'll give you a wonderful opportunity to make contact with all those stalwart fellows in the Contra Costa County sheriff's department."

"Could you take care of it, please?" Adler asked. The brisk machismo of the news director's voice softened noticeably.

Michael looked him directly in the eye. "No. They called you. You follow up on it." He turned to leave.

"Mike, please. You've got more experience with this sort of thing."

Michael turned back to him. "What sort of thing?"

Adler glanced sheepishly at the station manager Spaulding, then back at Michael. "You know. Bodies." His eyes were distressed, pleading. "You're used to it. I'm just not."

It had cost the news director a great deal to say that in front of Spaulding. Michael nodded. "Okay, I'll handle it." He knew he would have no problems with Adler for a long time. Even in death, Ed Riley had given him another boost.

*M*ichael drove across the Golden Gate Bridge, up Highway 101 through Marin, and then across the San Rafael—Richmond Bridge to the East Bay. He lead-footed the car, a '65 Mustang convertible, deliberately driving fast, passing all traffic, weaving in and out of lanes, forcing himself to concentrate on driving and not think about Riley for the moment.

Michael had bought the Mustang several years before for $450. Its top and paint job had been flayed by the San Francisco weather, its fenders rusted, its transmission and engine burned out on the hills. Michael had, to date, invested more than six thousand dollars in restoring the car, twice what it had cost new. But this was not just a car. It was a fantasy that Michael had deferred for ten years. The 289-cubic-inch engine gave him a rush of power, and the four-speed stick shift provided the illusion of control, at least in that narrowly defined part of his life spent on the road.

Ádler was wrong. Michael had never gotten used to the bodies. He never would. He had just choked off the feeling and the pain. When he had choked it off too long, too many times, bits of him had died until one day he had found himself sitting on the edge of a hotel bed, staring at a forty-five, finally ready to blow away the little bit of him that was still left alive.

A blaring horn and the piercing squeal of brakes shattered Michael's reverie. He had a flashing glimpse of a dilapidated Buick sedan, with a fat black woman at the wheel, slewing into the intersection as he barreled through. He looked into the rearview mirror, checking for a light or a stop sign he might have missed.

> *Here lies Michael in dismay.*
> *He died defending his right-of-way.*

His father's voice, echoing silently in some cerebral fold—a driving lesson when Michael was sixteen—was suddenly triggered into consciousness. *His father.* That scar tissue was the last thing Michael needed to rip open right now. If he could just get through with Riley, he might be able to make it.

Michael, in another era, had been Riley's protégé. Lately he was the only one who had stood between Riley and the destitution of being canned at that awkward age when he was too young for a pension and too old for the brave new electronic world of TV news. But booze, not age, had been Riley's primary problem. It was, as Riley frequently quoted Eugene O'Neill, "many a good man's failing." And it was certainly Edward

Riley's. He had failed three times as a husband, twice as an anchorman, and once as a news director.

If it had not been for Michael hustling the occasional offbeat news feature for him, and insisting that Edward Riley narrate the documentaries and specials that won awards with extraordinary regularity, he certainly would have been canned.

Michael protected him with fierce, filial devotion. He fought with management, arguing that the old correspondent brought a "great personal authority" to his reports that no one else could touch. But for the most part Riley sat, half crocked, in a dark broadcast booth, employing his great personal authority to voice promos for the news ("The rape squad—live at eleven."); station IDs ("KSF, Channel Three. Your bay window on the world."); teasers for old movies ("At three this afternoon, it's *Love in the Afternoon*, your rendezvous with Gary Cooper.").

His voice was a trained instrument that performed independently of either sobriety or passion. Between the electronically amplified Olympian pronouncements, he wandered about the new station, aghast at its chrome and plastic hightech decor and its abstract art, lurching through the halls like a ghost out of time and place.

Michael slowed down, weaving through the dusty, industrial back streets of Richmond to pick up the freeway to Martinez. What the hell had Riley been doing down here?

He was a drunk and anything was possible. A half-dozen possible scenarios unreeled in Michael's mind. Awash on a wave of boozey nostalgia, as Riley often was, he had floated across the Bay to visit "one of the dives from the good old days."

Riley had a romantic mania for waterfront gin joints. With a few belts under the belt of his trenchcoat, he thought he was Humphrey Bogart. The danger that Michael saw in the faces of the laid-off, the unemployable, the ex-cons, petty thieves, and pushers bent over a drink, stoking their anger, never quite existed for Riley. Riley shared their rage. But down here his Cadillac Seville would be a magnet for muggers.

By the time Michael rolled down the freeway off-ramp into Martinez, he was reasonably sure how Riley had died. Bludgeoned, rolled, and dumped in the Bay.

The Contra Costa County morgue was a one-story white stucco building next to the community hospital. Both buildings had slanting roofs of blue-splashed clay tile, giving them a sunny Mediterranean look. They sat atop a hill, and the surrounding slopes were wooded with oaks. There was a scattering of large two-story ranch-style homes, and on the next hill, horses grazed among the trees and manzanita bushes. The sign identifying the Central Morgue must have given the patients at the adjacent hospital a sharp jolt.

A deputy sheriff named Morrison, wearing plain clothes, was waiting for Michael in the coroner's main office. "The feller, Adler—is that his name?—called to say you'd be here. I'm sorry about Mr. Riley. I never met him personally, but I watched him on TV a lot. I really liked him. I felt he was giving us the straight skinny. None of this cutesy-pie shit most of the stations hand out nowadays."

"I think Ed would have liked to hear that," Michael said. The deputy had an accent, not quite Southern, not quite Southwestern, probably Arkansas or Missouri, something he would never lose.

Morrison led Michael into an adjoining smaller office furnished only with a desk, a chair, and a leatherette couch. A gold brocaded curtain covered one wall. It seemed out of place in the stark, utilitarian room.

"You know what happened?" Michael asked.

The deputy shook his head. "Some fishermen from Richmond hooked into him this morning, and they called the coast guard. That's all we know so far." He opened a file on his desk and withdrew several four-by-five color Polaroid photos. "I suppose we might have identified him, but a close acquaintance or family member had to make the ID officially. Besides, I guess people look different on TV than in real life. Or, you might say, real death in this case."

Michael looked at the photographs. The face was swollen, the skin inflamed and mottled. It did not seem real. It might not be Riley. "Jesus, what happened to him?"

"We don't know yet. The coroner made a preliminary examination. He hasn't performed an autopsy yet. But there were no signs of foul play. The only unusual thing is the skin and the swelling. It's like a burn, but not quite. There's no scorching of the skin." He looked up from the photos directly at Michael. "Can you identify him?"

Michael shook his head. "I can't tell from these pictures."

The deputy nodded, his expression thoughtful and concerned. He was a beefy, balding, avuncular man, conducting an unpleasant business as delicately as he could. He took a breath and let it out as a sigh. "I was afraid of this," he said. "We really don't like to ask close friends to view a body, especially if it's in bad shape. It can be pretty traumatic. You up to it, you think?"

Michael nodded but said nothing.

Morrison rose heavily and stepped to the curtain. He hesitated a moment, then very gently drew it open.

The curtain concealed a large display window that looked into a cramped alcove. A gurney was parked right against the window, and the body laid out on it under a glaring overhead light was shrouded in a white sheet. Only the head was exposed.

The photos had not prepared Michael for the shock. The face was red and bloated, as if it were one huge blister. The outer layers of skin were shredding. Fish

had fed at the cheek and chin. Michael turned away,
his stomach heaving.

It took him a moment to catch his breath and quell
the gagging. The shock was much worse than he had
imagined it would be. The horror was multiplied by the
very things that made the face familiar—the aquiline
point to the nose, the sharp widow's peak in the sandy
hair turning to steel gray, and the indented gnarl of
the ears. It was like a grotesque caricature of Ed Riley,
a rubber death mask that had been blown up to the
point of bursting and then obscenely mutilated.

Why could Riley not have died in his sleep, his craggy,
baggy-eyed, aging-matinee-idol looks laid to rest in state?
Then Michael might have kissed the pickled cheek with
its bloom of red vessels, and wept. For this horror he
could only steel himself and try to erase the picture,
knowing that the image was already blazed into his
nightmares.

He turned to the deputy and nodded, reluctant to
speak.

With an almost delicate touch, as if the body beyond
were sensitive to the slightest movement, Morrison drew
the curtain shut. Then he gestured to the couch, offering Michael a seat. "I'd like to clean up a few routine
questions. That is, if you're up to it."

Michael nodded again.

"When did you see him last?"

"Yesterday, about noon. We were at Mare Island,
shooting a story." Michael felt a sharp pang. His last
words to Riley had been in anger, insulting.

"He didn't come back with you?"

Michael shook his head. "I rode back with the camera crew. He had his own car there."

Michael told the deputy what friends he might call to
trace Riley's whereabouts. There were not a lot of people to call.

The deputy walked Michael out to his car, tagging

along as if something was still bothering him. When they got to the car, Michael reached into his wallet, pulled out a business card, and handed it to the deputy. "I want to know what happened. As soon as you have the autopsy report or any news at all, will you please call me? Personally. I'd greatly appreciate it."

The deputy studied the card. "Michael Lowenstein. Executive Producer." He enunciated each word as if it were a key to some mystery that was baffling him, and then looked curiously at Michael, as he had done several times during their meeting. "Berkeley. Seven, maybe eight years ago," he fingered Michael.

Oh, Christ! That's all I need right now, Michael thought. To refight the wars of Sproul Plaza.

The face now studying his own with great interest was unrecognizable to Michael. The deputy would have been younger, slimmer, and as mean as a shotgun then, but anonymous behind a helmet and plastic face shield.

"You weren't one of the regular newsmen."

"I was one of *them*."

The deputy snapped his fingers. "Gotcha," he exclaimed happily. "The *filmmaker*. The one always shoving his camera in our faces."

Michael felt an ancient anger flare somewhere in his chest, but he said nothing.

"I knew I knew you from somewhere," the deputy said with satisfaction. He tapped his right temple with a blunt trigger finger. "A cop's memory." Then his expression changed to one of regret. "Things got a little rough sometimes." It was an apology.

"It's all blood under the bridge now," Michael said, but he did not reach out to shake the deputy's hand.

When Michael opened the door to the apartment, the phone was ringing. It was Rita.

"Michael, how are you?" Her voice sounded hesitant, strained. "Are you all right?"

"I'm all right, Rita." He took a deep breath. "It's Ed Riley. He's . . . he's had an accident. He's dead."

"Oh, oh, oh." The sound on the phone was a series of deep, plaintive moans. "That lovely man. That beautiful man." She sighed deeply, the mournful sound resonating over the phone line and in the small earpiece, a lamentation. "What happened? Was he drinking?"

"I don't know, Rita. Probably. He was always drinking."

She sighed again. "Michael, come over to my place. Come talk to me."

"I'm all right, Rita. It's okay."

"I know you're okay. But come over anyways. You're a stranger. I haven't had you over in a long time. I'll cook something special."

"Rita, I already have heartache. I don't need heartburn."

"Don't be a wise guy. Come over. At a time like this you should be with family."

Rita Cohen-Delaney was his mother's sister. He never called her Aunt Rita. Ten, almost eleven years younger than his mother, she had been more like a big sister, the permissive babysitter of his childhood, the savvy counselor of his adolescence, with advice on topics from girls to grooming.

When Michael walked through the door of Rita's apartment, she immediately covered him with several wet, smacking kisses. Her dark eyes searched his face anxiously, like a mother dog probing a puppy that had returned to ascertain he was all right, then kissed him wetly again to confirm her examination before she spoke a word. "Oh, Michael, that lovely man. That lovely man. He couldn't have done more for you if you had been his own son."

Michael nodded, suddenly unable to speak, his throat constricted.

"They don't know what happened to him yet?"

He shook his head. "I just went over to the East Bay to identify his body," he said with difficulty.

Again Rita searched his face. "Was it very bad?"

"It wasn't good. It wasn't *what* it was, it was *who* it was." The grief he had been checking all day suddenly spilled from his eyes, and it was moments before he could talk. "Oh, shit, Rita, I keep thinking about the last thing I said to him. I was pissed off and insulting because he had blown a story on the air. He was half bagged."

"That's all right," Rita crooned. "He knew you didn't mean anything. He had his problems. He knew that. Don't be ashamed to cry for him, Michael."

"Christ, I haven't cried since my father died." Michael took a deep breath, snuffling like a child. "How'd you know to call? Was something on the radio?"

"I didn't hear the radio. I just *knew*."

"Your gift?"

"Some gift. If someone gave it to me, I'd take it back and exchange it for earrings." She sighed, the sigh conveying the *tsoris* not only of her own problems but of the multitude to which she was unwillingly privy.

Michael's maternal grandfather, Sam Cohen, had, in one instance, become so disturbed by his younger daughter's insights that he consulted a rabbi. The rabbi, a bearded Brooklyn Chassid, had probably not entirely believed the excited, voluble father, but consoled him that since Rita was—from all he had been told by Cohen—a good Jewish girl, her prophetic talents were undoubtedly a small gift from God. The father should not distress himself. Thereafter, Sam Cohen often boasted of his dark younger daughter's "gift," insisting, "If you don't believe me, go ask the rabbi."

At length Rita asked, "Would you like a drink or something? On second thought, forget the 'or something,' we only have drinks here."

"I'll have a very dry martini."

"You'll have white wine. We're eating Israeli tonight."

"Israeli. What's Israeli?"

"It's stuffed grape leaves. And *kibe,* which is ground lamb and cracked wheat."

"It sounds Greek to me."

"It has similar Mideastern origins, but it's definitely kosher."

"They don't eat chicken soup in Israel? For Chrissakes, Rita, I came here for chicken soup and comforting."

She handed him a glass of white wine and stared in that disquieting, probing way she had, all the more unnerving to Michael because he knew she was seeing more than was apparent to the eye.

"The gypsy." That had been her affectionate nickname within the family. Partly it was her Romany coloring: pale olive skin and black glossy hair, the opposite of Michael's mother, who was fair. Partly it was the flair for bright colors, peasant blouses, and full skirts she had favored as a teenager. But predominantly it was the unsettling prescience she had demonstrated as long as Michael could remember.

But Rita Cohen-Delaney's psychic foreknowledge was by no means infallible, certainly not in her own *affaires d'amour.* The hyphen had been adopted after the heart-breaking dissolution of her marriage to a sometime advertising copywriter, incomplete novelist, and steadfast rogue in New York.

Rita abruptly broke off her disturbing gaze, pirouetted, and stepped off toward the kitchen. "Come talk to me while I cook."

"Where's Bridget?"

"At a friend's. She'll be here. She wouldn't miss a dinner with her cousin Michael for a date with Shaun Cassidy. Actually I'm worried about her."

"Why?"

"The other day she asked me why it is that first cousins can't marry."

"What are you worried about? I think she's showing great taste for thirteen. What did you tell her?"

"I told her all about recessive bad genes and drew little pictures of Mendel's peas until she got bored."

"Mendel's peas. Where the hell did you learn about Mendel's peas?"

"From Peter. He explained it all in great detail to me once in a restaurant in Greenwich Village. Even drew charts of the white and black peas on the napkins to convince me that we couldn't help but have beautiful children. Whereas, if I insisted on marrying a Jew, the swarthy, hooked-schnoozed recessive genes that were lurking in both of us would eventually get together and pop up in the children."

"Oh, that's wonderful." Michael laughed, the sudden release from depression and tension so explosive he almost spilled the wine in his glass. That was why he had come here eagerly. Here he could hold his wake for Riley, alternately mourn, laugh, drink, weep, eat, and curse the man unself-consciously, and there would be no impiety.

"My ex-husband was not without his charm," Rita said, turning to Michael with a sly smile. "Besides, he was right. Bridget *is* beautiful. She looks just like Elizabeth Taylor as a child."

"To all the beautiful Cohen girls," Michael toasted, raising his wine at Rita.

Rita, in her mid-forties, was an arresting woman. Her bust and hips had fleshed out from her voluptuous youth, when she had studied to be a modern dancer, a fledgling Martha Grahamnik grounded by marriage and motherhood. But Rita's waist was still a tight pinch in an overflowing hourglass, a marvel of nature, aided by regular yoga exercises.

She and Michael's mother looked totally unrelated

until one noticed the same sultry-lidded sloe eyes and the nose, a pert triangle almost as long on the underside as from bridge to tip. The effect in Michael's taller, slender, cream-complected mother was haughty, almost aristocratic. In the Mediterranean, shorter-limbed, bountiful Rita, it was sensual. Both women, in their separate fashions, had been beauties. Only a tourist from China would have mistaken either for a WASP.

Michael poured himself another glass of wine and watched Rita stuff a grape leaf with some unidentified glutinous substance. "Why do you always experiment on me?"

"I'm not experimenting. I just like to try out a new recipe on a sympathetic but cultivated palate before I serve it to gentleman callers."

"What's this *Yiddische mama* kick you're on now? Are you done with your fettucine Alfredo period?"

"Italian food and red wine lead to misunderstandings, if you must know. Sharing a nice meal, traditionally Jewish but with panache, served at home with me and my daughter, quickly separates out the men who are interested in a meaningful relationship from the boys who are only after my body."

"My God, I didn't realize family honor was at stake here. Indigestion is a small price to pay."

Rita did not respond, and Michael noticed she was staring out the window. The apartment was on the north flank of Telegraph Hill. The kitchen and dining area shared a sumptuous view of the Bay from Alcatraz to the Golden Gate. The evening fog was pouring in under the bridge in billowing clouds. Somewhere at Lands End a foghorn moaned, answered by another in Marin, the two sounding like great, hideous monsters secreted in the mists and signaling one another.

Rita suddenly shuddered, an involuntary spasm that seized her whole body for a moment and then evaporated as quickly as it had gripped her.

"Rita, what is it?" he asked, alarmed.

"I don't know," she said after a moment, in a small voice. "I don't know what it is. I'm suddenly very, very terrified." She turned to him, the blood drained from her face as though on the verge of a swoon. "And it's for you, Michael. It's for you."

3

*A*T FIRST THE FOG ENCHANTED SUZANNA.

As she chatted over cocktails in the officers' club, set high in the hills over the shipyard, she watched the fog seethe up the Mare Island Channel in a solid white wave. It swarmed through the hills, spilling over the darkening piers, and slowly enveloped the stark ironwork cranes that reared up through the mists like the skeletons of dinosaurs until they too were smothered.

By the time dinner was served, a romantic haze cloaked the four-mile-long waterfront of grimy workyards, bleak machinery shops, foundries, and gaping concrete drydocks below. Suzanna was perched in an eagle's roost above immaculate cloud tops.

The dinner at the officers' club marked the end of two days of unrelenting tours, luncheons, inspections, meetings, coffees, teas, and cocktails—all in the wake of the change-of-command ceremony the previous day.

After dinner her father had to leave immediately for a meeting in San Diego the next day. He insisted on arranging a military escort home for his daughter. The marine captain of the guard, a young officer named Bill Bingham, as strapping as an Annapolis linesman, drove her home.

Suzanna thought with amusement that her father was being outrageously protective. But driving down from the bright aerie of the officers' club into the thick, ominous fog, she was oddly grateful for the solid, reassuring convoy beside her at the wheel.

The fog now frightened her, as though something alien and threatening had crept in with it. Suzanna felt it as a charge of electricity coming through the dank black night. The dark curls at her temples and the fine hairs on the backs of her neck and arms prickled, as if galvanized by a mystic current.

Perhaps it was just her closeness to Bingham. He looked almost courtly in his marine dress blue uniform, but he was attractive in that athletic, comforting way of American men, which she had almost forgotten. Lord knows, she was vulnerable enough, susceptible to that muscular sexual attraction. Was that what frightened her? She trembled, but not from the chill in the air.

Her father's official quarters, a cavernous, three-story Colonial home, were a twisting, mile-long drive down through the hills from the officers' club. The house suddenly loomed up in the headlights, isolated in the mists like a mansion in a dream. It was one of a dozen similar homes, reserved for the base's senior officers, that lined the west side of Walnut Avenue. Across the way, fronting the east side of the street, stood the dark cathedral columns of eucalyptus, deserted bandstand, and the brooding war relics of Alden Park.

The house had a large front veranda overlooking the park. Veils of smokelike vapors drifted through the pillars and railings as Suzanna and Bingham mounted the front steps. She flirted with the idea of inviting him into the empty house. But a navy base such as Mare Island was a small town, close-knit and rank with gossip. She might not particularly care what this provincial community thought of her, but she would not do anything that would hurt her father. This was his world.

At the door she shook the captain of the guard's hand with coquettish formality and said good night.

Immediately inside the commodious, walnut-paneled hallway, she regretted her decision. A loneliness, so deep and piercing that it twisted her stomach and nearly brought her to tears, engulfed Suzanna. It was the house. It uncannily resembled her grandparent's home, Grey Knolls, in Virginia. She could have been standing in that great front hall where she and her luggage had been abandoned after her mother's death.

This house on Mare Island had been built at the turn of the century, but it was of another era, another place. The entire line of homes appeared to have been conceived, transported, transplanted, and built by a past generation of naval officers. Their concepts of architecture and the privileges of rank had been framed in homes about Chesapeake Bay, in parlors in Norfolk, and on verandas overlooking the James River.

To Suzanna's left, a linteled doorway led to the great parlor, and to the right, an alcove in the hall harbored a fireplace flanked by built-in bench-chests. At the rear of the hallway a wide switchback stairway, with banisters of birdseye walnut, led up to the bedrooms. A large stained-glass window framed the middle landing. Suzanna glanced through it, but in the fog she could not even see the house next door, only twenty-five yards away. Her father's house was wrapped in a white cocoon that insulated it from the sight and noise of the outside world.

Suzanna wearily climbed to the second landing, toward her bedroom. She felt edgy, exhausted. A few moments earlier, flirting with Bill Bingham at the door, she had been exhilarated. But suddenly the hectic events of the day had caught up with her. A dank, enervating chill permeated the house. It sucked the energy right out of her, as if drawing it through her pores.

Her bedroom was at the front of the house, next door to the large master bedroom in which her father normally slept. There were a half-dozen rooms and several baths on the floor. The rear quarters, in fact, could be partitioned into a separate apartment by a door in the hall. This was a house conceived on Victorian standards and built for an officer with a litter of kids and a squad of servants. Back stairs and passages led up from the kitchen and pantry; paging buttons in each room were connected to a signal box in the kitchen to summon the servants. Idly, she fingered one.

But Suzanna was alone in the house, in the echoing spaciousness. The page rang out in the deserted kitchen.

What she needed at the moment, she decided, was a hot, soaking, sybaritic bath, the perfumed oils easing the aches and nervousness running through her body. She undressed quickly, carefully hanging up her plum-colored cashmere dress, but leaving her bra and silken panty hose in a heap on the floor.

There was a sharp creak in the hall, the sound as loud and explosive as that of a stick snapping. Suzanna's heart lurched. She bolted for the connecting bathroom, grabbed a towel, and hurriedly wrapped it around herself. She listened for a moment, heard nothing, then tiptoed silently in her bare feet to the door and peeked out into the hall. It was empty. She crept to the stairs and peered nervously down into the shadowed stairwell, her ears straining as intently as her eyes.

Behind her there was suddenly another creak. A footstep. Suzanna spun toward it. There was nothing there. It was only the sound of an old, sun-dried house expanding with the humidity. The explanation did not entirely comfort her.

She retreated to her room and quietly shut the door, locking it. The bolt slid in place with a heartening thud. The door itself was solid oak. It would take three bosun's mates with sledgehammers to knock it down.

Suzanna stood back, her lips set firmly together, and gazed at the massive wooden and brass barrier that stood between her and whatever menace, real or phantom, lurked outside. She felt herself relax. It was just her imagination, overwrought and fueled by that feeling of vulnerability which came upon her again and again, ever since her divorce. She retreated into her bathroom, like a creature seeking the most remote nook of its den for protection. Another door. She shut it and bolted it.

She drew her bath. This was, for Suzanna, an act that was as ritualized as a church baptism. She poured *L'Air du Temps* bath oil into the steaming water. The deep aquamarine oil diffused evenly until it had tinted the water the blue of a crystalline sea. At that moment she recalled Grace Blackwell's smile the first time she'd poured from her own flask for her daughter's bath. As the color filled the bath, she looked at Suzanna: "This is the blue of the Mediterranean. That very color." Even Suzanna's common bathwater was enchanted, part of a fabled romance.

At her mother's death, Suzanna had taken possession of the ritual as her own, along with Grace Blackwell's French perfume, powders, bath oils, and eau de toilette, caching the flacons of Lalique crystal and using them so discreetly that her grandparents never noticed, or perhaps they subconsciously thought of Suzanna as their daughter rather than as a granddaughter with an alien adult scent. As a lonely, abandoned child, Suzanna had fervently clung to the artifacts and memories of her mother, and as she metamorphosed into a woman, they had eventually possessed her.

With an elegant gesture she raised the flacon of eau de toilette and dripped it slowly into the water. Immediately the mists about her had a delicate floral scent and she was enveloped in a cloud of luxury. Now she felt safe enough to drop the protecting towel and step naked into the pillows of fragrant bubbles. They swathed her, the hot, slippery oils soothing her taut skin, melting her tense muscles, quieting her humming nerves.

She washed herself with a flower-patterned cloth, not scrubbing herself, really, but rather gently massaging the long muscles of her arms and shoulders, and then her breasts, and finally she gave up that pretense, dropped the cloth, and caressed herself lightly across her breasts, stomach, loins.

She lay back, buoyant and totally relaxed, drowsy with the heat. Her fingers played gently with her clitoris. How long had it been? Rome. She didn't want to think about the last time—the ugliness in the morning, the taste of ashes, and the sick, hollow feeling of using and having been used.

By an act of will she thought of the marine captain who had seen her home, his clean-cut, not-quite-handsome face. But that athletic stolidness was of no use; he triggered no excitement or desire, and her thoughts drifted off in the drowsy twilight between daydream and sleep, conjuring up images of other men she had known in Rome, men who had wanted her, pleasant romances of wine and laughter, games played over tablecloths checked like chessboards. Somewhere in her memories there was a face to match her fantasies.

Rap! Rap! Rap!

Suzanna sprang straight out of the water. Her cold feet dripped on the tile. She faced the sound, the door.

Rap! Rap! Rap!

The bathroom door shuddered visibly under the sharp blows.

"Who is it?" Suzanna's voice was shrill and choked with terror. She felt suddenly encased in ice.

"Who is it? Dad, is that you?"

There was total silence. Not another sound.

Suzanna took a deep breath. "Whoever you are, you'd better get out of here. My father will be back any second. I'm going to scream out the window and get the base police."

She waited, transfixed, shivering in her nakedness, staring at the door.

Bam!

"Oh!" Suzanna screamed and recoiled in a leap from the sound, now *behind* her. She whirled about.

There was nothing there. The room was empty. Suddenly the door of the medicine cabinet above the sink swung slowly open, hung open a moment, revealing packets of razor blades, bars of European soap, and a bottle of Vanquish—then it slammed shut again with a violent bang.

Suzanna watched in horror as the medicine cabinet door opened a third time, held a moment in the grip of an unseen hand, then was thrown shut.

"Is that you?" she wailed.

The door opened and closed angrily.

"Talk to me. Let me see you."

The cabinet swung open and crashed shut again.

Suzanna dropped to her knees in supplication, tears spilling down her cheeks. "Stop it. I haven't done anything wrong. You're frightening me. Please. I haven't done anything wrong!"

4

MICHAEL STOOD AT THE BOTTOM OF THE
stairs, sweat pouring from him in rivulets that coursed
down his face and dropped from his chin. He was
frightened, the fear a painful knot in his gut. The long,
narrow staircase led up to his apartment.

Outside, a foghorn bellowed, and he started, his head
jerking around, eyes staring through the still open door
behind him. The world outside was enveloped in clammy
mist, dreamlike, a realm where the once solid lines that
demarked reality had dissolved.

In the dark at the top of the stairs, Michael's nightmares waited for him. He thought—he prayed—that
they were finally over. But now he could feel the familiar throbbing in his temples, the twitching under his
left eye, the tight, dull aching in his neck. It had been
there since the moment he willed himself to look at
Riley's burnt, swollen corpse. Now the nightmares were
all going to begin again. They awaited him in the sleepy
shadows just beyond the hall light.

He fled out the door, into the fog, into his Mustang.
He jammed his foot down on the accelerator and blasted
straight up the mountain-cliff slope of Divisadero, first
gear and eight cylinders defying gravity, accelerating
slowly like a rocket lifting from the pad, horn blaring

all the way to warn fellow suicidal fools hurling blindly through the fog.

The Mustang crested Pacific Heights, broaching the clouds, and leveled off in the clear air at the top of the hill. Bright stars salted the southern sky ahead, and there were trees and substantial concrete-block apartment buildings about him. Michael's panic eased. He slowed the car and turned east on Broadway.

The Pearl was ensconced in a neon-lit alley off Stockton Street, the marginal area where Chinatown ended and the climb up Nob Hill began. Here the new wave of refugees had set up shop. The restaurant and bar were almost empty. One party of three was finishing dinner, and two black guys sat at the bar. They were about Michael's age. They looked up as he entered and their eyes engaged and held for a moment of inquiry, then one of the black men made a brief nod of recognition, although they had never met. Michael sat down alone at the other end of the bar. He waited.

"Buy lonely girl a drink?"

Michael turned and smiled at the girl. He fingered the long, black, silken tresses, looked into her face, and wondered how old she was. Somewhere between twenty-five and forty. Once they became women and were no longer girls, they became ageless. "I dream of you and me lying on a white sand beach, palm trees, a gentle ocean swell, the warm sun on us, making love," he said.

"You really have dreams like that?"

"No, never. But I'd give my left ball for dreams like that."

She reached up and stroked his cheek.

"You know everything by reading faces?" Michael asked.

"Long time I don't speak English. Only know six, maybe seven words. So I learn read faces."

"What does mine say?"

"You feel very bad tonight, Mikey."

"I need a happy dream, Gigi."

They walked to her apartment, a block and a half away. "What you want?" she asked after they had stepped into the bedroom.

"Hold me. Just hug me for a while."

They lay down on the bed with their clothes on and she put her arms around him. They stayed that way, her face muffled in his chest and his smothered in the silky, fragrant hair, for a few minutes. Then she disentangled herself, smoothed out the creases in her dress. "Undress," she said. "It be better."

She reached for the light and Michael stopped her. "No, please leave it on."

She stared at him a moment, then nodded and undressed. There was nothing coy or seductive in her disrobing. She stripped so quickly that Michael was still fumbling with his trousers when she came to him and helped him take off his pants and shorts. Without a word she guided him to lie back on the bed and she laid all her weight directly on top of him, their thighs and bellies pressed together, her breasts burning against his chest with a candescent heat of their own greater than that of normal flesh, her face nestled in the crook of his neck, her arms and hands hugging him to her.

There was a primal healing power in the feminine flesh, the soft, yielding weight kneading against his taut muscles, the warmth flowing into the chilled hollows of his body. Michael felt his face and limbs twitch as his body gave up its resistance and released the energy cramped in the tensed nerves and muscles. They lay quietly until desire again flowed in him and swelled between their bellies, a throbbing phallic presence.

She rolled off onto her side. "You want something first for beautiful dreams?"

"What do you have?"

She shrugged noncommittally.

"Thai stick."

She rose from the bed and crossed the room to a large bureau, returning with a thin, deftly rolled, brown paper joint. She lit it for him and he took a long, deep drag, then offered it to her.

"Very strong shit," she said.

"I believe it." Little soundless pops of light were already going off in his head. He smoked three-quarters of the stick before he carefully squeezed off the glowing end in the ashtray beside the bed.

The light in the room seemed intensified, the girl more luscious than flesh and blood. She lay back on the bed and her legs embraced him, simply enveloping and swallowing his prick within her. There was something illusionary, magical about the scene. Part of him stood apart, in a space and time outside the here and now, watching himself as if he were the actor in a porno-graphic film and part of him, his nerve ends acutely sensitive, was the magnified participant.

The girl rose and fell beneath him, hips undulant, carressing him like lapping surf. The long black hair and the tawny, full breasts heaved rhythmically. His fantasies and reality flowed together. The lovely native girl made love to him on a moonlit beach. He reached out and stroked the ripe, sensational luxuriance of her ass, lost his mind in the fleshy mound of shining black hair, cupped the breasts inches from his face. Nothing else existed but this girl, their entwined, succulent flesh.

He looked into her face and she changed into an adolescent, a plump, innocent bride, inexperienced but dutifully having sex with him. Suddenly she was an older woman, regarding him with cunning eyes, manipu-lating his desire for some secret purpose of her own. The woman had a thousand faces, each one springing into perception for a split second and dissolving into the next. She was an Oriental, then a lithe young Frenchwoman, then darker, with almost negroid fea-tures. Each, at the instant of her appearance, was more arousing than the last. Michael was being fucked by every woman in the world.

Now he mounted a bored, weary Vietnamese whore, sweating slightly, working to make him come and get the job done. An old lady squeezed and milked him laboriously and then was eerily transformed into a scraggly, bony bag. Then, suddenly, she was Death, the pelvic bone of her skeleton clamping on his boner, trying to yank the life right out of him.

Michael screamed and shoved the horror away from him. She rolled over onto her side and he stared again at Gigi, the spell now broken.

"*Beaucoup* Thai stick, I think," she said.

"I think so." The urgency of his desire had suddenly evaporated, leaving him shaken. But he held tightly to her, drawing comfort from the warm, satiny feel of her flesh against him. It had not been a hallucination, he knew beyond doubt. The drug had given him the power to see beyond the scrim of skin. Everything he had experienced abided there now in her flesh, constantly recreating itself, timeless.

"You want to stay all night?"

"Yes."

She reached for the light, but he grabbed her hand.

"Leave the light on." He gave her a nervous grin. "I'm afraid of the dark."

She looked at him a moment, then nodded solemnly because she knew he was not joking. Apparently there were many like him.

5

SUZANNA AWOKE WITH A START. SHE PEERED quickly about the room, momentarily disoriented, as though waking from a dream in which she had been transported back in time seventeen years to her childhood bedroom in her grandparents' home, Grey Knolls.

But she was now in her father's home on Mare Island. What happened the night before had not been a dream.

The visitation that had terrorized her in the bath had ended as abruptly as it started when Suzanna, almost hysterical, begged her phantom visitor to stop banging. Later she had waited in bed, nervous and expectant but not really frightened. It seemed as though another identity, that of Grey Knolls, had latched itself to this house on Mare Island, as if by the sheer force of the older house's personality—or its attachment to Suzanna. She had again felt the sharp loneliness, the chill that had hit her like a perceptible drop in temperature the moment she stepped on the pillared veranda of the house. She wondered if her mother was in the room, hovering perhaps by the black iron hearth, a triste gossamer spirit about to materialize.

Nothing else had happened last night. Suzanna, drained by the day's events, enervated by the hot bath, had simply fallen asleep.

But now, awake, the black haunted shadows of the

bedroom washed out in the streams of white-yellow morning sunlight, Suzanna was very frightened. She did not fear her mother's ghost, but what that ghost now meant.

She was going insane. She was reverting back to the crazed hallucinations of her adolescence.

Throughout Grace Blackwell's funeral service and burial, Suzanna had clung to her father's hand. He held himself with grave formality, almost at attention, as if any ceremony, however personal, required a military bearing on his part. But as the coffin containing the remains of her mother was lowered into the Virginia earth, Suzanna felt her father sob, a silent spasm that momentarily shook him before he regained control.

Later, when they were alone in their bleak quarters outside the base, he knelt and hugged his tear-wracked daughter to him and wept, his voice breaking into breath-catching sobs and heaves despite his efforts to maintain control. Their tears ran together, and in those moments of grief, Suzanna's love for her father was fiercely welded.

But their time together was brief. John Blackwell had to return to his ship, and Suzanna was committed to the charge of her grandparents.

Her father's leaving, at first, seemed natural to Suzanna. It was what he had always done. But when she moved into her grandparents' house, the full impact of her abandonment hit her. A deep resentment toward her father rose in Suzanna, sharpened by a lonely, rivening hurt.

It was then that the haunting of Suzanna Blackwell began. Grey Knolls was, in its way, convivial for a ghost. The brick foundation of the house had been built in 1731, and although the white wood-frame manor was not as grandiose as several of the Georgian plantation mansions in the area, it had been grand enough to attract pillaging Yankee troops who ransacked and shot up the place in 1864. Like the nearby, more famous manors of Sherwood Forest and the Shirley Plantation, Grey Knolls had a proper name, one that distinguished the habitation from the inhabitants. The houses of that area had identities, histories, and even personalities that outlived the brief mortal spans within.

Grace Blackwell had been born and had grown up in Grey Knolls. Suzanna not only occupied her mother's old room, which looked out through the moody woods to the swirling stream of the James River beyond, but she seemed, at times, to be occupying her mother's former life. Her grandfather, in absentminded affection, constantly called her Grace. Her grandmother, stirred by an old memory, would suddenly ask her, "Sugar, whatever happened to Anne Lee?" Or Rebecca Carter, or another of her mother's childhood friends.

But there was something more turbulent stirring in Suzanna, whose early years had been spent bouncing from Norfolk to San Diego to Key West to Seattle. The lonely, haunted child confided her mother's visits only to her sketch pad.

Her mother had always encouraged her drawing and, in fact, had been Suzanna's most frequent model. In her daughter's eyes, Grace Blackwell was a beautiful dark swan with lush chestnut hair piled high and a faultless face poised above a long, regal neck.

Years later, when she was a serious art student, Suzanna dug out her early drawings from a box in her grandparents' attic and was greatly disappointed in the youthful primitives. She had remembered them as the delicate sketches of a melancholy, romantic figure.

As she and her mother had moved about, at each new location, Suzanna had drawn pictures of Grace, the new house, and the landscape, which her mother dutifully had mailed off to Daddy. Suzanna frequently had been the new girl at school, and drawing became the child's way of playing alone until she made friends. She had created a world of her own.

Now, in her grandparents' home, to acknowledge her mother's ghost, she sketched pictures of it. At night Suzanna gazed out the window of her bedroom at the dogwoods stirring and sighing in the moonlight. In the explosion of white blossoms and the silvery path of the river she imagined she saw her mother now united with the spirit of her lost lover, transcendent and flying as if in a dream.

But Grace Blackwell's visitations were never frivolous. Suzanna could not summon her mother out of boredom, curiosity, or amusement. The hauntings were always occasioned by a great emotional need, as if the depth of Suzanna's longing, or anguish, had a measurable voltage. Once a certain level of intensity had been reached, her mother would appear as a picture materializes on a TV screen when the necessary power is switched on, the appearance invariably preceded by the faint but unmistakable aroma of her mother's perfume.

The ghost of Grace Blackwell was not a silent, vague apparition, a fleeting will-o'-the-wisp in the moonlight. She talked to her child, a few whispery words of comfort at first. Then, increasingly, mother and daughter conversed about Suzanna's loneliness, her difficulties with her grandparents, her absent father, and, as Suzanna plunged inexorably into the turmoil of adolescence, about boys, romance, sex.

Grace Blackwell seemed compelled to pass on to her daughter even in death as much wisdom and knowledge as she had acquired in her life. But she spoke from a void beyond time and Suzanna's everyday life. Her reference points were a yesteryear where girls flirted and had romances but not sex.

Living with her mother's ghost, Suzanna discovered, was in at least two particulars exactly like coping with her drinking in life. First, Grace Blackwell's moods were violently unpredictable and, second, Suzanna could not talk about her to anyone. After each of her mother's visitations, Suzanna fell deeply asleep, totally exhausted, as if the emanation had required an extraordinary effort on her part.

On her father's next visit, she tried to tell him about her mother's ghost.

"Yes, your grandmother wrote me about your nightmares," he responded in an abrupt tone that Suzanna envisioned him using on malfeasant sailors.

"I would strongly suggest that you put a rein on your imagination and confine it to your drawings and paintings. The dead are dead, Suzanna. They do not return to us."

For an instant Suzanna thought she saw fear in her father's eyes. It confused her. She could not imagine her father being afraid of ghosts, certainly not of her mother's gentle spirit.

But her father had changed toward her. His visits had always been those of a rowdy, giant playmate who delighted in bouncing her on his knee or tossing her up in the air. As she got older, a gangling tomboy, he had taught her to swim and fish.

Now there was something courtly, almost shy in his manner. The adolescent Suzanna was blossoming, and between her father's shore visits, sea changes occurred in her. Her father was awed by them. On each renewed acquaintance, in a greeting that became a ritual, he would hold her at arm's length, study her until tears threatened behind the glistening surface of his eyes, and then awkwardly give her a shy kiss on the forehead.

On her sixteenth birthday her father had taken her to dinner at the officers' club in Norfolk. It was the first time she had ever danced with her father, and the event was cast in Suzanna's memory in a wistful and touching aura, like the first date with a very shy but faithful suitor.

She never again mentioned her mother's visitations to him. The hauntings became another secret of adolescence, along with nipped whiskey on dates with older boys, the petting, sexual groping, and self-gratification—all the clandestine intimacies of her nights. A few of these secrets she shared with one or two close high-school girlfriends, but Grace Blackwell's eerie shade she confided only to her pencils, charcoals, and paints.

In high school, Suzanna took her first formal art classes. The teacher, Mr. Rubenstein, studied Suzanna's spooky portraits of her mother, the sketches of phantoms gliding over the dark, winding rivers viewed through dormer windows. In his flat New York accent, Mr. Rubenstein muttered something that sounded like "another shuggal."

Suzanna thought it was a comment about the femininity of her work.

For the next art class Mr. Rubenstein brought in several large volumes with reproductions of the paintings of Marc Chagall, especially to show Suzanna. Suzanna stared transfixed at *Bouquet with Flying Lovers, The Apparition, Time Is a River Without Banks.*

Somewhere there was an exuberant, wildly talented child who saw and felt and painted all the things churning inside her.

"Where is this?" Suzanna questioned.

"Paris. Or Vitebsk. A village in Russia where he grew up."

"The river. The old buildings. It looks like here. In Virginia."

"Well, yeah, I guess. That's what makes him a great artist," Mr. Rubenstein declared.

A ghostly hand and palette painted a transcendent, shawled lady rising over a narrow river. Lovers cavorted in floating promenades and soared over cramped villages and the rooftops of Paris. Heavenly fiddlers played, evoking that deep, mystical blue that Suzanna experienced whenever her mother appeared. There were visions within visions, a mysterious world beyond the three dimensions of normal sight.

Suzanna begged Mr. Rubenstein to let her take the books home. That night in her room, her lips parted, her eyes wide, she pored over the Chagall reproductions. She was ecstatic, feeling oddly happy and somehow justified. She decided that night that she would be an artist. She would go to the Art Students League in New York, where Mr. Rubenstein had studied, and then go to Paris to paint, as Chagall had done.

Of course, neither her grandparents nor her father would hear of such bohemian nonsense. In her senior year Suzanna applied to Mary Washington, the women's college of the University of Virginia. It had a well-established department of fine arts, housed in its own triad of buildings on the Jeffersonian campus in Fredericksburg.

The night before she left for college, Suzanna lay awake in bed, neither unhappy nor despondent but charged with a terrific confusion of emotions: a nostalgic sadness at leaving what had become her home, the rush of excitement at the adventure of going off to school. All the hairs on her body once again tingled. A glowing mist gathered and coalesced. And her mother appeared.

In many ways it was like Grace Blackwell's first visitation. She did not say a word but merely smiled at her daughter, a loving smile that was at once proud, encouraging, and yet heartachingly sad.

Grace Blackwell was finally saying farewell.

Through college, her marriage, her study and work in Rome, Suzanna experienced no further visitations. Her memory of her lonely, haunted adolescence at Grey Knolls had softened, assumed a dreamlike quality. Gradually, without becoming aware of exactly when it had happened, she assumed the "adult" view of her grandmother and her father. She regarded her mother's ghost as the desperate creation of a griefstricken, imaginative child who had suddenly and traumatically lost her mother.

Younger, relatively normal children invent imaginary playmates in whom they fervently believe, but they abandon them as they grow older. Suzanna rationalized Grace Blackwell's ghost as a similar invention brought on by the shock of her mother's death.

Then what the hell had that been last night?

The violent pounding on the door, the slamming of the cabinet had happened. She had heard it and seen it. There had to be an explanation.

Unless, of course, she was going crazy.

"What is this call concerning?" the secretary asked in a remote, officious voice.

It concerns my being afraid for my sanity, Suzanna thought, unable to work, between jobs and between lovers, lonely, adrift in body and soul among ancestral ghosts. "It concerns a 'grand tour' of the station," Suzanna said in a businesslike tone. "I'm answering Mr. Lowenstein's invitation."

But Mr. Lowenstein was out and probably would be gone for the rest of the day.

Suzanna handled the call as if it were a professional contact, but her disappointment was acute and personal, a nervous, hollow feeling in her belly. It had nothing whatever to do with work, jobs, the electronic techniques of TV graphics.

Suzanna had been excited when the switchboard operator called just before lunch to give her the messages. In the rushed, minute-by-minute schedule of the previous day, before her father's departure for San Diego, the messages had not been picked up. All but one had been for her father.

The exception had been the invitation from Michael Lowenstein. From the stream of blurred, unmemorable faces of the reception line two days before, his face still remained a vivid impression—a darkly attractive stew of toughness, intelligence, and sensitivity. He had really been more interested in Suzanna—her artwork, her studies, her travels—than in her status as Captain Blackwell's daughter.

There had been that strange, momentary confrontation with her father—all the more bizarre because it seemed to Suzanna entirely unmotivated. Her father and Michael Lowenstein both appeared to be responding to challenges each had thrown at the other, but Suzanna did not understand what they were. In Lowenstein's eyes there had been black flashes of anger and arrogance, but he had conducted himself formally and moved on.

Now there was this invitation.

On appearances, it was merely repeating the polite offer he had made on the reception line. But to Suzanna, distraught and at loose ends, it came as an answer to her prayers.

In her twenty-nine years Suzanna had finally learned that no man, however fascinating and attractive, ever lived up to the fantasies her fecund imagination could weave about him after a fleeting impression. More pragmatically, she convinced herself, Michael Lowenstein was a contact to cultivate if she was to build a new life for herself in San Francisco.

Restlessly she wandered into the dining room. There was a liquor service set up on an antique Philadelphia mahogany side table. She poured herself a whiskey from a blown-glass decanter and was halfway to the kitchen for water when she stopped cold.

She turned and stared at the pier table. The black and white marble top, the carved fretwork, and the decanter with its molded label and elegant geometric patterns, were poignantly familiar. She had a vision of her mother at the same mahogany pier table set up in some bleak postwar housing unit.

My God, it was the same service.

Her father had taken all the old furniture out of storage in order to furnish the large Colonial house. Rather than being touched, Suzanna suddenly felt trapped. She stared at the drink in her hand.

It was all starting again.

In Suzanna's own marriage, she had all too often found herself taking a drink too early in the day. The painting and work had not been enough to dull the isolation, the loneliness and frustration, but especially the fear that she was becoming her mother. Like mother, like daughter, not just in Grace Blackwell's appearance, her tics and scents, but in the empty, lovelorn tragedy of her life.

Despite her talent, her schooling, her passion for work, Suzanna had become an ornamental hostage to her husband's career.

She had been too young, not strong enough, to combat her mother's legacy, her family, her father, her husband, the demands of being a navy wife. So she had fled.

After her divorce, her father had urged her to fly to Hawaii, where he was then on the Pacific Fleet Headquarters staff. Instead she had flown—again, *fled* would be a more honest description—in the opposite direction, to Europe.

Rome!

Midway through her year at the Academy, Suzanna suddenly quit painting, or rather found that there was nothing she wanted to paint. Whatever had possessed her during her childhood, college, and marriage evaporated away in the sunwashed studio on the Janiculum, overlooking the teeming *vicoli* of Trastevere. The ghostly, mystical visions, the fragmented Chagallian images, were the creations of a lonely, disturbed child. They were no longer real to her.

She started half a dozen canvases, struggled with them, then gave up. There was no longer anything there. She was empty.

"It'll come back," Wally Adams counseled her. He was her faculty adviser. "The important thing is to keep working."

She went back to fundamentals, sketching and painting still lifes, Roman landscapes, portraits, rediscovering the world about her.

By the end of her year's fellowship at the Academy, she gravely doubted that she was a *serious* artist. Paradoxically, her technical skills were at their keenest and she developed a flashy style that Wally sardonically dubbed *brio Americano*.

He introduced her to art directors in the advertising and commercial-art field, whom he knew in Rome. With her previous experience, Suzanna was able to hustle enough freelance work to supplement the small annuity her mother had left her. In time she built up a solid portfolio, a variety of free-lance assignments complemented by her own exercises.

Still she lingered in Rome, and the year of study abroad stretched into a peculiar emotional limbo, as Suzanna became a familiar resident, yet an expatriate in a city in which she would never be at home. But to what did she have to return in the United States? And where? Her flight to Rome after her divorce had been frightening enough, but at least she had had an institution and a role to which she was heading.

Roman life threatened to be a succession of temporary assignments, temporary assignations. Suzanna found herself one of a colony of American divorcées, desper-

ately gay divorcées tramping from job to job, man to
man.

She read the letter from her father at a café in the
Piazza Navona. He was being transferred to San Francisco. There was again the invitation to join him for as
long as she liked. Even in the Piazza Navona, San
Francisco conjured up pictures of sugar-lump sky-
scrapers, confections of buildings heaped on the cakes
of the hills rising from the Bay. Suzanna had visited
there once as a child, with her mother and father. In
Suzanna's memories, the city was enchanted.

She sat amid the millennia-stained cobblestones of
the piazza, encircled by honey-colored stone walls and
baroque façades that traced the ancient racecourse of
Domitian.

"I'm going home," she said aloud, as though the
actual sound of the words had the power to transport
her.

Tears started rolling down her cheeks. Until that
moment Suzanna had not realized how tired she was of
Rome. Telephones never worked, electricity and plumbing were haphazard, and the mail was, at its best,
unreliable. She was tired of being pinched and pawed
by strangers, of being followed halfway across the city
by sexually obsessed men she did not know, of constantly being propositioned as though she were a whore.
What had at first seemed colorful, perhaps gallant,
became frustrating, infuriating, exhausting.

The musky smell of Italian men who doused themselves with cologne rather than shower had at first
seemed sexy but now had become merely unhygienic.
Their preening vanity, their hysterical jealousy while
reserving their inalienable right to screw around, their
cramped, untidy *garconières* that they maintained for
affairs while they still lived at home with mama, no
longer seemed Continental but only a tiresome pain in
the ass.

Nevertheless, she was sad at leaving Rome, closing the door on a poignant, rewarding milestone in her life. She had made friends. There were farewell parties, dinners, drinks.

Wally was genuinely unhappy about her leaving. He had been a very good friend, a suitor really. But they had never had an affair. He had a wife and a daughter. Although such things were regarded lightly when in Rome, in this case Suzanna chose not to do as the Romans did.

At the Leonardo da Vinci Airport he had kissed her, smiled with his characteristic sardonic twist of the lips, and said, "Be careful. Remember what Oscar Wilde said. 'It is an odd thing, but everyone who disappears is said to be seen in San Francisco.' "

"Screw Oscar Wilde! I'm going home."

Home!

Her father's new house, a sumptuous Tidewater Colonial, seemed itself to be a ghost from her past that had materialized here in northern California.

In this house, with its heirloom furnishings, Suzanna felt herself at once dispossessed—and possessed. Dispossessed of the independent woman she had fought so hard to become; possessed by her mother's role and—God help her—her spirit.

Suzanna had to work. Anything to focus her mind on the here and now.

She desperately picked up that morning's *San Francisco Chronicle,* skimmed the headlines, and selected a story on the war in Lebanon. She read it quickly, not for information—the facts of the atrocities in Beirut hardly registered with her—but to trigger visual images in her mind. Then she seized her sketch pad and pencil and quickly drew.

She repeated the exercise with two more stories, a

murder in Hunter's Point and the presidential race. By the time she finished sketching a belligerent donkey and an angry elephant butting heads, it was time for the evening news on TV.

She turned it on to check the illustrations the station artists had created to key each story. The first report— that of a body found in the Bay the day before—was not depicted by an abstract graphic but by a photograph, a familiar face with the gaunt, handsome features of an aging stage actor.

Suzanna understood why the secretary had peremptorily informed her that "Mr. Lowenstein is out and probably will be gone for the rest of the day."

It was as if a balloon had suddenly burst. Suzanna's fantasies, her cheerful expectations were shattered in an instant by an irrational tragedy. She doubted that she would hear from Michael Lowenstein. She might call again after a respectful period, but the eager immediacy, that momentum of promise, was lost. And Suzanna suddenly felt lost, adrift again among ghosts.

That evening the summer fog crept halfway up the length of San Francisco Bay and stopped. The bank ended abruptly where Point San Pedro on the west and Point San Pablo on the east shore pinched the Bay like two fingers. The balmy heat of the Napa Valley flowed out over Mare Island. Sloughs and bogs bound the north end of the island, and there the swollen and languid Napa River narrowed to the Mare Island Strait, the base's eastern waterfront, and then disgorged into the Bay. The turbulent boil of hot, dry air, sultry humidity, and the chilled fog bank charged the air with a seething electricity that threatened summer lightning and thunder.

The filmy fabric of Suzanna's nightgown clung to her breasts, loins, and thighs and crackled slightly as she roamed restlessly about the house. The brass knob tingled her finger with a slight buzz of static electricity as she opened the door to the living room. She was searching for the sketch pad in which she had been working a few hours earlier.

It was not anywhere in the room. She wandered into the kitchen, thinking she might have absentmindedly carried it with her when she had gone there to make herself a salad for a light dinner earlier.

Suzanna was very edgy. She couldn't shake the feeling that she was being watched. Twice she spun about, expecting to find someone standing behind her. There was no one. But there was an exotic aroma in the room she had never noticed before, a spicy, distinctive, pleasant scent like that of wild cloves.

The kitchen was one of the largest rooms in the house, a sprawling workroom designed for a staff of servants preparing memorable dinner parties. On the wall was the signal box to summon the servants, rows of numbered black arrows indicating from which room the call for service had originated in bygone days.

To the rear there was an ample walk-in pantry. Suzanna retraced the steps of her solitary meal preparation, peering about for the mislaid pad. Suddenly a bell in the room rang out.

Suzanna whirled. There was a sharp metallic click, and in the signal box the arrow marked with the numeral "1" rotated and pointed down.

Suzanna stared at it bewildered. Number "1" indicated the adjoining formal dining room. But she was alone in the house. Her father was still in San Diego, conferring with navy officials on shipyard business.

She listened intently, her breath stopped, ears straining to pick up the faintest creak. There was no sound from the next room. It might just have been a short circuit, she rationalized, all the while terrorized that the call had nothing to do with crossed wires or corroded terminals. Her heart suddenly froze. She heard foot-steps crossing the dining room.

Who was there? A stream of warnings from her mother, cautions from her ex-husband, horror stories from other navy wives flooded Suzanna's thoughts.

Workmen and sailors wandered about Mare Island at all hours. There were always delinquents, criminals, psychopaths who joined the navy to avoid jail. A base was itself a prison where orders, marine guards, and steel fences confined men, pent up their rage. Alcohol and illegal drugs stoked it. Rape, even murder were not unknown. The uniformed security was an illusion.

Suzanna searched about desperately for a weapon to protect herself. A knife, a cast-iron frying pan. There was nothing in sight.

Double sliding doors of oak separated the kitchen from the intruder in the dining room. Suzanna did not move, but stood very still with her hands pressed against the silky, sheer nylon covering her trembling legs.

Anyone passing outside could have spied her wandering alone through the house. There were a dozen windows in this mammoth house she might have left open.

There was another creak of the floorboards in the next room, this one closer to the door.

Was it a footstep? Or was it just a warped old board contracting, a natural sound magnified by her fears?

She glanced at the signal box. The arrow was pointing down. She had not imagined that. Someone, or something, was summoning her.

Oh, God, it was beginning again.

The house was possessed by her mother's ghost. Was it real, or Suzanna's insane fantasy? Suzanna feared that as much as any drunken rapist.

She finally moved, and there was something somnam-bulistic about the way she walked, with arms rigid at her sides, across the room to the doors. She threw them open and stepped through, expecting to be greeted immediately by the spectral figure of her mother.

The room was absolutely empty. Puzzled, Suzanna peered about and saw nothing out of the ordinary. The sharp, pungent smell of wild cloves was sharper here. Then she spotted one of her missing sketch pencils on the built-in hutch in the corner. She walked over and picked it up, examining it curiously. The drawer immediately below the shelf on which the pencil had been was ajar.

As if playing a game of treasure hunt, she opened the drawer and searched about. There was, at first glance, nothing unexpected, only napkins and table linens. But probing further, Suzanna discovered a spring-loaded lever hidden in the upper left corner. She triggered it.

To her astonishment, the entire top half of the hutch swung out, hinged to the wall at the right side, revealing a large secret compartment behind it.

Suzanna's first reaction was a childish delight. She had heard from Elizabeth Hailey, the previous captain's wife, that the old houses harbored secret compartments, caches built during Prohibition in the twenties to hide bottles of booze. However, this hiding place concealed the errant sketch pad.

The pad was folded open to a fresh page, and across the paper, neatly columned like the stanzas of a poem, was written:

> "I'll be seeing you
> In every lovely summer's day,
> In everything that's light and gay.
> I'll always think of you that way.
>
> "I'll find you in the morning sun.
> And when the night is new,
> I'll be looking at the moon
> But I'll be seeing you."

Tears flooded Suzanna's eyes. The words and music echoed in her mind with the childhood memory of her mother, distraught and grieving for love lost, that last night of her life.

Suzanna's tears dropped on the paper, and she tried to wipe it away, smudging the penciled script. Something struck her as odd, alien, and she examined the paper more closely. It was not her mother's painstaking, graceful penmanship, the handwriting Suzanna would recognize immediately from old cherished letters and notes. The writing on the pad was sharp, heavy-handed, a pressing angular scrawl that almost cut the thin rice paper.

It was the handwriting of a man.

6

TWO NAMES ON THE MESSAGES STREWN ON Michael's desk jumped out and seized his attention. "Kim, please come talk to me," he shouted to the next room.

"In a sec. I'm making coffee for you."

Kim Bradley never made coffee. She had informed Michael the second day on the job that she did not drink coffee and therefore she did not believe her duties included making coffee. Kim was black, the daughter of a minor but senior post office official, a graduate of San Francisco State, and an avowed feminist. This combination of roles, assigned and assumed, swirled like rubbish in a tornado about her refusal to make coffee, as today her voluntarily making him coffee was all mixed up with her soulful-eyed, sincere sympathy over Ed Riley's death.

Kim sashayed in, bearing two steaming mugs, one of which she placed carefully on the edge of his desk.

"When did Morrison call? The deputy sheriff."

"First thing this morning. He said he had some news for you. He wanted to talk to you personally. He wouldn't say what it was even after I told him who I was."

"Who are you?"

"Your executive assistant."

"Does that mean I'm the executive or you?"

"Whatever."

"*Whichever,*" Michael corrected.

Kim pouted.

"What about Suzanna Blackwell?"

Kim cocked her head and eyed him with mischief. "What *about* that lady?" The question was insinuating, suggestive.

"Why, what did she say?"

"She said yawl had promised that little ole gal a grand tour of this little ole station." Kim burlesqued a Southern accent syrupy enough to crystallize a phone's earpiece.

"You be nice to Missy Blackwell. Her daddy's a commanding officer at Mare Island, and we're going to have to go back there and pick up more shots."

"What's she like?" The question was naked feminine curiosity about another woman, and Michael wondered what it was in Suzanna Blackwell's voice, or perhaps in his own tone, that had sparked the interest.

He leaned back in his chair and mused a moment. "Lovely cascading chestnut hair, green eyes to die for, and when the breeze stirred it made this red silk thing she was wearing cling to the smooth curve of her long thighs, the lush swell of her mons pubis, and the assertive cakes of her breasts in a way that made my blood surge."

"I don't want to hear this," Kim exclaimed, and turned to leave.

"You asked," Michael called after her. "Anyways, thanks for the coffee."

"You caught me in a weak moment."

"The coffee too, apparently."

Kim turned back to him, crestfallen, the sassiness instantly evaporating from her face. "The coffee's no good?"

"It's fine. What there is of it gives the hot water a subtle, elusive flavor."

"It must be the coffee. I measured out a teaspoon per cup."

"A *table*spoon per cup," Michael instructed. "And one for the pot."

"Well, I guess that's why I don't make coffee," Kim said haughtily, regaining her composure and sauntering out.

"Gloria Steinem will be so pleased," he shouted at her retreating figure.

Michael stared at the phone. It lay on his desk, an ominous dark hulk like the thick black body of a snake coiled to strike. It took an act of courage to pick it up and dial.

The number was a direct line, and Morrison answered the phone himself. "Mike Lowenstein here. I just got your message."

"I'm touching base with you. You wanted me to contact you personally when I had any news," Morrison plunged in without any pleasantries. "Actually, I don't really have anything. Just the preliminary coroner's report. And that raises more questions than it answers."

"What did Riley die of?"

"Shock, as far as they can tell."

"Shock?"

"That's it. They're still waiting for the results of certain lab tests that take longer—toxicological, blood—that sort of shit. But it won't change the preliminary findings unless something exotic pops up."

"What the hell could have caused it?"

"You tell me. Great pain. Fear. His heart just stopped. Cardiac arrest."

"A heart attack?"

"No, it just stopped. There was no sign of heart damage. In fact, his heart would have outlasted his lungs or liver, according to the pathologist. And nobody hit him on the head or anyplace else. There were none of the usual signs of foul play."

"Drugs?"

"Drugs were negative. There was alcohol present, but not enough to even ticket him for drunk driving."

"What about the burns?"

"Now that's something else. They're third-degree but there wasn't any charred flesh. More of a scalding." There was a sudden silence on the line, but Michael could hear the deputy still breathing heavily into the mouthpiece, as if reluctant to say more.

"Morrison."

"Yeah."

"What the hell are you telling me?"

"You've got all the information I have."

"Yeah, but what it adds up to is that Ed Riley was boiled to death. Like some goddamn crab on Fisherman's Wharf."

"I didn't say that. I can't confirm that." There was something official and stilted in Morrison's voice, and it infuriated Michael.

"Goddammit, Morrison. You're not on the TV news. I'm not taping this and I'm not taking notes. Riley was a good friend, more than a friend, he was like a father to me, and I demand to know what the hell happened to him."

"We're doing the best we can," Morrison snapped, his own restraint now cracking. "Your guess right now is as good as ours. Maybe better. So far as we know, you're the last person who saw him alive," he said ominously. "I checked out all the people you gave me, and none of them saw him that day."

"I told you everything I know."

"Well, we still don't know what happened to him. Or even where it happened to him. Tell me again, where did you see him last?"

"At Mare Island. On the old pier where the ghost fleet is moored."

"The *what?*"

"The mothball fleet. The old World War II warships that are docked there. At the very north end of the yard. We were shooting the ships for background for a

TV special on World War II. We left him there. He had his own car. Did you find his car yet?"

"Not yet. We've got an APB out on it, but so far we got zilch. *Nada.* In fact, if you talk to anyone in the news department, don't mention anything about the car. If someone is riding around in that Cadillac Seville, they can sure as hell tell us something. I don't want them to hear on the six o'clock news that we're looking for the car and ditch it."

"Not a word to them."

"Good. And I'll be back to you as soon as I know anything else."

"Thanks. I'd appreciate it. And Morrison . . ."

"Yeah."

"Sorry if I got a little hot."

"It's all blood under the bridge, Michael. Isn't that what you said the other day?"

"It sounds smartass enough to be me."

"You said it. I didn't. Well, take care."

"You too."

Michael sat staring at the phone, trying to absorb this new horror. But it just lurked there in his mind, irrational, incomprehensible. Ed Riley had become another one of the demons that populated his nightmares. He did not see or hear Kim come into the office again until she placed another cup of coffee in front of him. It looked dark and strong.

He looked up at her. "You hear?"

"I heard your end. That's as much as I ever want to hear. It sounded awful. And it sounded very weird." She sat down on the couch opposite Michael's desk, and neither of them said anything for a while.

He sipped the coffee, savoring the sharp hot bite of it as he swallowed. He nodded approvingly to Kim and gestured with the mug. "You know, there's a whole dark side of life represented by black coffee, blood-red steaks, and strong, straight whiskey. And, my aging flower child, you'll never really be a newsman, a writer, a filmmaker if you insist on staying mellowed out on herb teas, alfalfa sprouts, and Colombian grass."

Kim smiled. "You sound exactly like him when he was out drinking, you know, 'belly up to the bar.' " She tried unsuccessfully to imitate Riley's basso profundo.

"When did you go bellying up to the bar with him?"

"Oh, when I was a young, innocent intern in the news department. He was filling in as anchorman one night. He was very interested in what was happening at S.F. State and what we 'young people' thought about things."

"Was he really?"

"No, not really. I mean he was the total gentleman. In fact, I was a *little* disappointed he didn't make a pass. After all, when I was in school, he had been the big star anchorman in town. But I think all he really wanted to do was go out with a young black chick. To reminisce about the forties, when he was at the network in New York and they all used to go slumming up to Harlem. Groove at the Cotton Club, stomp at the Savoy, smoke tea, and go with black girls."

"Did that offend you?"

"Oh, no. It was history." She gave a small laugh. "I mean I've never known anyone else who really stomped at the Savoy. When he had had a few drinks, his head was totally into the past."

"That it was." Michael studied Kim. She was the color of milk chocolate and wore her hair in a close-cropped Afro set off by large hoop earrings. There was a feline exotic quality about her features, a sensual slyness to her smile that would have sparked the memory of hot Harlem nights for Ed Riley.

"Why don't we go on the town tonight?" Michael proposed. "And go bellying up to a few bars."

She shook her head in a sharp, violent rejection. "No, I'm really not into wakes." She looked up at him and there was pain in the dark liquid eyes, but it seemed to evaporate as quickly as it had appeared. "I'll tell you what I think you should do. You should call that gal."

"What 'gal'?"

"Scarlett O'Hara. If she's half as foxy as you make out, or she sounds, you should really show her the *grand tour.*" She slurred and stretched the words out to six insinuating syllables, making it sound like an indecent and delicious proposal whispered in Michael's ear by a lascivious *demimondaine.*

"I don't think I'm up to *that,* whatever it is."

"Sure you are." Kim bounced off the couch to Michael's desk. She picked up the phone, fingering through the messages on his desk with her other hand, and dialed. She fixed him with an oblique smile, her lips pursed in an oblique way that Michael always found vaguely suggestive.

"Miss Suzanna Blackwell, please." A pause. "One moment for Michael Lowenstein." She handed him the phone, whispering "a grand tour" again in a breathless tone that gave Michael mental images of the voyage of a moist, undulant tongue over nude, writhing flesh. Then she pivoted and exited from the room without a backward glance.

Michael was totally flustered by Kim's caper and the fact that it was Suzanna Blackwell on the line. All he could think to say was, "Hello."

As the maître d' led them to their table, Michael watched how Suzanna gazed about the room with unrestrained curiosity and delight. He had noticed the same uninhibited, almost childlike absorption as he guided her about the TV station. There was no pretense at sophistication, only eagerness to see and experience it all.

It fascinated Michael, because they were the same

age and he had had to learn to put so many checks on what he saw and felt.

They were seated, and she studied the cascading grand staircase, the hand-carved oak panels, the velvet wall covering, and the etched glass skylight, then fixed Michael with a smile that was unadulterated pleasure. "Thank you, Michael. For everything today. You can't imagine what I feel at this moment."

"I did all that?" Michael said, somewhat surprised at her extravagance.

She nodded, then laughed at her own dramatic rhetoric, the laugh a musical ripple of sound. "I don't want to frighten you. It's just that until this afternoon, I was in a terrible limbo. I thought I had made a mistake in coming to San Francisco. Now I know I did exactly the right thing. That's what I meant." She spoke in a breathless contralto, a little rushed and unsure and somehow all the more fetching in her nervousness. There was a lilting murmur of the South in her voice, but not the thick, cloying molasses that Kim had imitated.

She looked at Michael, holding him with shining eyes. "I was terrifically flattered that you remembered I was interested in graphics. We only exchanged a sentence or two on the reception line."

"That's the programming of the journalistic mind. It automatically pigeonholes people's interests and professions." She unsettled him, and he sought calming refuge in chatter. "At the worst, it reduces everyone to a handy cliché. But my work is what I get up in the morning to do. It keeps me sane. Without it I'd just be a bundle of nervous energy, reactions, a craziness that might go tripping off anywhere, anytime."

"That's exactly how I feel lately." She gave a small laugh and tossed her head. There again was the insecurity, an edgy vulnerability about her that puzzled Michael.

"Harvey asked me to bring in my portfolio and show

it to him," she added abruptly. "What do you think?"
Harvey Alexander was the art director of the station.

Michael shrugged. "You saw what they do. How good
is your work in comparison?"

"It's different. It was all for print media. Newspapers,
display ads. But I have as much technical skill as anyone I saw there. Except maybe for the Japanese girl.
She's amazing, the way she whips out the news graphics.
But I didn't see anything I couldn't learn to do very
quickly."

"Is it what you want to do?"

"I don't really know."

"Then show Harvey your work. As my father used to
say, it couldn't hurt. At least it will give you a professional critique of your work. Maybe a few contacts in
the city. He's good. And he knows all the other art
directors."

A tuxedoed waiter materialized at Michael's elbow,
pencil poised to take their orders. They had ignored
the menu up to this moment, and now hurriedly scanned
the pages of legal-size parchment bound in gilded leather
like a historical document.

The waiter suggested several *spécialités de la maison*
not on the menu. Suzanna chose the *terrine aux deux
poissons*, Michael the *veau avec sauce trois moutards*. He
studied the wine list intently, then glanced at Suzanna.
She had been living in Europe, but this was a personal
offering. He ordered the Beringer Fume Blanc.

"A good selection, sir," the waiter responded in a
totally uninterested voice; a domestic wine was certainly
not one he would have selected.

"I love this room," Suzanna said.

They were in a Victorian mansion in Pacific Heights
that had been restored, decorated with antiques, and
refurbished as an intimate restaurant. The room in
which they dined suggested the front parlor of an
elegant turn-of-the-century brothel.

"Some cities sanctimoniously preserve their past, make dusty museum tours of it," Michael commented. "But San Francisco constantly recreates its past, positively revels in it."

Michael looked across the table into Suzanna's eyes, reflecting pinpoints of candlelight. A shadow suddenly fell across her face. It was only the waiter again, but his unexpected appearance at Michael's elbow at that moment startled him.

The waiter formally presented the wine for Michael's inspection. Michael nodded. "That's the one."

The waiter deftly opened the bottle and poured a sample for approval. Michael sipped and nodded. "A young, modest vintage," he commented with mock pedantry, as the waiter next poured her wine.

"Its main attraction," Michael continued, "is that these very grapes were grown just over the hill from your new home on Mare Island. In the cooler, southern portion of the Napa Valley. I thought you might find the neighborhood *vin du pays* amusing."

"I'm impressed."

"Don't be," he said. "It's the journalist's grab-bag mind." He tapped his head. "It's *The Old Curiosity Shop* of scraps and rags from long-forgotten stories. I once did a half-hour special on the wine country."

"No, I'm impressed because you thought of me when you ordered." And the way she gazed at him over her wineglass was delicious.

"Well, to your future here," Michael toasted.

"I'll certainly drink to that."

"What were you doing in Rome?"

"Studying at the Academy." Once again there was that indecisive toss of her hair, the glancing away.

"That sounds like the official reason. Not the real reason."

She looked levelly at him, the green eyes open and vulnerable in a way that touched him. "It is the real reason," she said. "Or at least half of it. One doesn't study painting at the Academy unless one is *very* serious. Art was my major in college. At Mary Washington. It's a very good school, but it's not the Academy. I got married in my senior year. I didn't really pursue a career. I worked at whatever convenient jobs I could get to supplement my husband's salary. I worked on a free-lance basis for an agency in San Diego and for a department store in Norfolk, doing newspaper layouts."

"Your ex-husband was in the navy?"

She nodded. "We were married in the chapel at Annapolis. With the bridal procession under the traditional arch of swords of his classmates."

"Sounds romantic as hell."

"It was the high point of the marriage."

"And that's the other half of why you went to Rome. To get away from all that."

Suzanna nodded, her gaze vague, as if the past were now a blur in her memory.

"Then why the hell did you fly right back into it all?"

Her eyes went wide with astonishment. "What made you say that?"

"The first place I saw you was in a receiving line next to your father and a squad of other navy officers bedecked with swords and all their medals."

Suzanna looked away, acutely distressed. Michael immediately regretted he had blurted it out. "I'm sorry. That was out of line."

She looked back at him, the eyes pained and teary, and shook her head. "No, you're absolutely right. That's the godawful thing."

At that point the waiter brought their salad, fussing with an ornate pepper mill as if the bestowing of fresh-ground pepper were a sanctified rite. Suzanna played with her asparagus, preoccupied. "When you intro-duced me to your secretary, she made a remark, something about my making such an impression on you on the reception line. What did she mean by that?"

Michael laughed, dismissing it. "She was just very curious as to what you were like. Your Southern accent on the phone really caught her attention."

"My accent? I thought I'd lost it in Rome. But what did you tell her?"

Michael shrugged, slightly embarrassed. "Well, as I remember, I said you had lovely chestnut hair, green eyes to die for. And there was a slight summer breeze off the Bay, and the way it pressed the red silk of your dress against your breasts and legs made my blood surge."

Suzanna's laugh was a ripple of delight, and the memorable eyes were wide with pleasure. "You told your secretary that?"

"She's not my secretary. She's my assistant."

"What's the difference?"

"An assistant gets paid twenty-five dollars a week less, doesn't know shorthand, but expects to be promoted to an executive job because she's a college grad."

Suzanna laughed again. She took a drink of wine, then fixed him with a playful, mischievous look. "To change the subject—or to get the subject back on course—tell me, what else makes your blood surge, Michael?" Her lips lightly traced the edge of the crystal and her gaze was so forward and teasing that Michael actually flushed with excitement.

7

SUZANNA HAD NOT MEANT TO BE SO DIRECT, but she was delighted with Michael's reaction. He was at once excited and flustered, as boyish and vulnerable in his befuddlement as if he were sixteen. She had felt sexual tension spark between them from the moment she walked into Michael's office. Yet their afternoon together had been completely businesslike.

The offices of Michael and his assistant displayed the work of a decorator in their streamlined chrome-and-suede furniture, contemporary lithographs, and color coordination. But the original decorator would have had apoplexy over the filing cabinets, typewriters, videotape players, coffeemaker, cups, plates, and stacks of tape, film, newspapers, magazines, and files piled on the sprawling oak table-desk and sleek glass conference table. The offices had the atmosphere of a command post in a siege. There was a darkening in the cloth at one end of the plush sofa, the oily imprint of a head that testified how often the couch had been slept on.

On one wall there were plaques and citations and a shelf with three gold-plated, winged nymphs, Emmy awards. The figurines and scrolls were talismans that gave authority to the clutter in the room, even a magical effect. In this setting, Michael Lowenstein's dark, brooding intensity no longer seemed as alien as it had when she first saw him amid the spit and polish of the Mare Island parade ground. He was an artist in his studio, potent and attractive.

Suzanna mentioned her professional interest in TV graphics. To her surprise, Michael had already arranged for her to "hang out" during the afternoon in the art department. All it was necessary for anyone to know, apparently, was that she was a friend of Michael's. Everyone had been friendly and casually informative. Looking over the harried artists' shoulders, she was able to pick up the matting, photographic, and collage techniques used to produce graphics quickly on TV news deadlines.

Michael then escorted her into the newsroom to watch the artwork being collated with the script. Next he conducted her on a bewildering technical tour of slide chains, projectors, banks of hulking, wall-size video recorders, and, in the chilly barn of a studio, newscasters poised before blank blue backgrounds. He pointed out special cameras and display easels, but their esoteric significance was lost on Suzanna. Finally he led her into the dark grotto of the control room.

A handful of people sat before an electronic console, their faces ghastly, lit by the cathode-ray light of a bank of TV monitors. All communications were uttered in hushed, intense spurts. At every moment cameras were being ordered repositioned, slides or graphics changed, films or videotapes rolled, counted down, taken, sound levels brought up, down, or under. The speed with which it was all executed was awesome to Suzanna, and the fact that the news show was *live*, the mistakes unredeemable, created an electricity that charged the booth.

She and Michael sat behind the console, their shoulders and legs frequently touching as he leaned toward her, his lips almost brushing her cheek, and whispered how each effect was accomplished. Slowly Suzanna became aware of the reason he had taken her on that seemingly incomprehensible tour of electronic hardware. She now had a sense of the place from which each of the dozen video pictures before her was emanating. She understood why the artwork and titles were produced in different modes and how they were integrated with live studio shots, with the remote broadcasts from the field, and with the film and videotape into the final series of images that were transmitted. What had been an overwhelming mystery to Suzanna a few hours before was now not only comprehensible to her but, more important, professionally accessible. Michael had opened up a whole new territory of commercial art to her.

She had a thousand questions. After the broadcast, he took her to a colorfully bohemian bar in North Beach. There he patiently answered her interrogations, until he finally threw up his hands. "Enough. The graduate seminar is over for the day. Let's go to dinner." There had not been a formal invitation or acceptance. What had now evolved into a romantic, candlelit dinner had simply happened.

The waiter served the entrées with elaborate fanfare, and they exchanged bites of each other's dishes. Still, Suzanna might have mistakenly been served the veal and Michael the fish, for all the attention they accorded the food.

They talked. She told him about her girlhood in Virginia and inquired about his family. Michael, she learned, was the son of a lawyer, a man who commuted every working day of his life from their home in the suburban Long Island town of Lawrence to his Manhattan practice. He had wanted Michael also to become a lawyer, a persistent lobbying that Michael escaped by going to the University of California at Berkeley. It was there that he had become interested in filmmaking.

"I'd always been into photography. I got a Nikon for

my bar mitzvah instead of the traditional fountain-pen set. At Berkeley I started working with film. They didn't have a formal program in filmmaking—that was at UCLA—but there was a crowd making underground films, psychedelic light shows, political tracts. I was ostensibly a political-science major, a pre-law student to make my father happy. But in the special program in my junior and senior years, you could do pretty much whatever you wanted—it was, after all, the sixties—as long as a professor approved it. I always found a radical prof who approved my films as academically sound studies of the antiwar movement, the media, contemporary political activism, whatever. I was making 'statements' with film. Although, looking back now, I'll be damned if I can remember what it was I was supposed to be saying."

He narrated the story with a slightly askance smile, a self-deprecating sardonic humor that looked with bemusement upon past ardors. Suzanna had first noticed it at the station. One moment he was intensely serious and professional and the next he would step back and discover some amusement in what was happening in the control room or even in what he himself had just said. It gave his conversation a certain fey charm.

It was during those student days of sound and fury, Michael related, that Ed Riley spotted him scrimmaging with his Bell & Howell on the student side of a riot. "In those days Ed was the news director, the anchorman, and a working reporter. He was in his prime." There was a gleam of pleasure in Michael's eyes, an almost filial pride. "He tracked me down, asked to see what I had shot, and wanted to buy it for the news. I hesitated, pondering the deep moral implications of selling my 'statement' to the media. Ed philosophically resolved them by throwing in a box of film and a frugal charge account at the lab in exchange for a first look at whatever I shot. I became their stringer during what Ed

referred to as 'the troubles at Berkeley.' " Michael said
the last in a burlesque Irish brogue. "And when I
graduated he hired me as a temporary vacation relief."

"What did your father think of your becoming a
cameraman rather than a lawyer?"

Michael shook his head, and Suzanna saw pain cloud
the dark eyes. "He died of a sudden stroke during my
junior year. But it would have been just one more
disappointment for him."

"Why on earth?"

"My father and I were a couple of embattled clichés.
The Generation Gap." Michael intoned it like a title.
"Father versus son. Tough, Brooklyn-born immigrant
son versus the pampered suburban prince. World War
II hero versus antiwar activist. You could even throw in
booze versus pot and my long hair and beard if you
needed minor fronts on which to wage the war." Michael shook his head, his mouth twisting into a sardonic
smile. "Don't totally regret your lonely childhood. Families aren't always what they're cracked up to be in TV
commercials. You can call your father long distance
from college and get kicked in the teeth. My Christmas
vacations weren't memories by Kodak. They were
bloodlettings."

"It sounds tragic."

"It was dumb. It was absurd. But the raw anger and
the emotional pain were very real. When my father
died suddenly in the midst of it all, it really left me
hung up." He shook his head. "Part of me forever
stuck in time."

Suzanna stared at Michael, amazed at the naked,
almost neurotic quality of the revelation. Yet it struck
such a personally resonant chord that she automatically
nodded in empathy. The evening had suddenly taken a
darker turn.

"Well, that explains something that threw me," she
said.

"What's that?"

"The instant tension between you and my father. You exchanged only a half-dozen words, and it was as if you both agreed to dislike one another."

Michael's face darkened, as though a cloud had passed between him and some source of light. He unconsciously rubbed his left temple with his fingertips, drawing her attention to a long, thin scar that followed the line of his left eyebrow almost to the bridge of his nose.

"Where did you get that scar?" she asked in a soft voice.

"The troubles at Berkeley." He flashed a roguish smile.

The answer stirred a question that had puzzled Suzanna earlier in the afternoon. "Were you particularly close to Ed Riley? The reason I ask is that at the station I noticed that people kept telling you they were so sorry to hear about him. It was as if a member of your family had died."

Michael shrugged. "Most of them have heard the story of how Ed gave me my first job. At a station where the average tenure is two years, if that, it's tantamount to epic myth. I don't think either one of us was particularly close to anyone. Certainly not to each other. There was too much difference in our ages for that sort of confidence. But there were times—not to sound too melodramatic—when I honestly don't know what I would have done if it weren't for Ed. Those proverbial forks in the road. Ed gave me a job, made a phone call, a contact, or maybe was just there to talk things out. So the right fork leads to here and now. The left one to God only knows where." There was a troubled expression, a meditative silence. Suzanna had a sharp mental image of a twisting, shadowed road lined with gnarled, leafless trees.

"It sounds like he was a very good friend."

"He was that. But in the last year or two we began to

get on each other's nerves. 'Lowenstein, lad, you are rapidly developing those pushy, irritating qualities to which your race is often, regrettably, heir,' " he quoted.

"Are you?"

"Probably. On the other hand, Ed had a drinking problem. He went from being the *mensch* of the news department to a reader who just recited the script handed him and then to a fill-in announcer." Michael held up his wineglass and again launched into his brogue. "Drink is at best a whore who extracts a price for her pleasures. At worst, it is the Devil himself whose price is your soul.' "

"Did he really talk that way?"

"Somewhere between cold sober and dead drunk was a point where Riley was professionally worthless but theatrically eloquent. Unfortunately it happened on the air a few times where he could no longer read the script, so he creatively ad-libbed it."

Michael suddenly stopped talking and stared moodily into his wineglass, twirling it in his fingers. His hands were large and strong, with big veins and long fingers. But the nails were painfully short, cut—or, more probably, bitten—back almost to the quick. "I think I've just transformed what was a lovely evening to a neurotic dark night of the soul," he groaned.

Suzanna instinctively reached forward and, for the first time, took his hand. "I'm having a lovely evening," she said. "Including your dark night of the soul. God knows, I've had enough of those of my own." She studied Michael. Her attraction to him had, if anything, increased. He was not handsome in any classic, clean-cut mode, but in the course of the evening his face had conveyed toughness, tenderness, humor, intelligence, sexuality, and, strangely, at moments a fearfulness that had risen to the surface of his eyes, like a twilight creature rising to the surface of a lake and then plunging back into the depths again.

"You've a long drive home," Michael said morosely.

Suzanna shook her head and touched her hair, a nervous habit of hers when she was unsure of herself. She glanced away, focusing on a candle on an adjacent table. Suzanna wanted to make love with this man. To hold him and be held. But this evening she questioned her own motives.

Her father was still at the San Diego navy base and not due back until tomorrow. There was something frightening in that big, empty Colonial house on Mare Island. Whatever haunted its shadowed halls, grottolike rooms, and hidden compartments had a distinctively masculine smell and a man's handwriting. She had that sheet of paper with its scrawled lyrics in her purse, a tangible scrap she could hold in her hand as proof that she had not imagined it all. Whatever he—or it—was, *it was not her mother's ghost.* But it knew the secrets of Suzanna's heart, and that made it all the more terrorizing. She would not go back to Mare Island tonight under any circumstances.

She looked back at Michael. "If you hadn't asked me to dinner, I was planning to go to the theatre. I wanted to see the American Conservatory Theatre's production of *A Midsummer Night's Dream.* In any event, I wasn't going to make an hour's drive across a fog-shrouded country road at midnight. The prospect would have made me extremely nervous and ruined the evening for me. My mother died in an accident like that." There was puzzlement in Michael's eyes. "What I'm trying to say in a very roundabout way is that I'm staying in San Francisco this evening, not driving back to Mare Island. I'll be damned if I know why I'm saying all this."

"So I won't take it as an invitation."

Suzanna nodded. "I mean if you have other plans or have to get up at the crack of dawn, I understand."

"No, no," Michael exclaimed. "We'll dance all night.

Watch the dawn come up like thunder in Oakland 'cross the Bay."

"That's a little extravagant. What I had in mind was to buy you a nightcap in someplace colorful," she said. Let's take it one step at a time, she thought.

Michael nodded eagerly. "Terrific." But in his eyes there was a hint of the fear she had glimpsed earlier. "Tonight is one of those nights when I don't want to go to sleep."

How strange, Suzanna thought. Neither do I.

> *The night that Paddy Murphy died*
> *I never shall forget.*
> *The whole damn town got stinking drunk*
> *And some ain't sober yet."*

> *"But the terrible thing we did that night*
> *That filled my heart with fear,*
> *We took the ice right off the corpse*
> *And drank it in the beer."*

Michael stood in the living room of his apartment waving a glass of brandy, reciting the ballad in a broguey baritone.

Suzanna laughed. "And that's the sort of wake Ed Riley would have liked."

"I think so. He had great affection for the outrageous."

"Maybe you should still throw a farewell party for him."

Michael shook his head. "I thought about it. But I'd be the only one who might appreciate the gesture. So few of his old friends are still around. And there are still too many loose ends. I don't even know how he died, let alone why. As far as the police can find out, I'm the last person to have seen him alive. And that makes me feel somehow guilty, that I'm in some way responsible for his death."

"That's absurd. There's nothing to indicate that."

"I didn't say it was rational. I just feel guilty. Hell, I felt guilty about my father's death, and he died of natural causes in New York, when I was at Berkeley."

Michael stared gloomily out the bay window. The apartment was on the third floor of a narrow, gabled Victorian on the north slope of Pacific Heights, near the Presidio. It had a spectacular view, Michael insisted, of the Marina, the Palace of Fine Arts, and the Golden Gate Bridge. They were all now buried under the fog, except for the towers of the bridge, which stabbed through the silver billows funneling into the harbor from the great black void of the Pacific beyond.

The fog had stalked Suzanna and Michael as they bistro-hopped about San Francisco. After dinner they had sat at Enrico's, a sidewalk café in North Beach, and watched a cloud visibly creep up Broadway toward them until the dank chill caused them to flee.

"I've never really seen the city," Suzanna said as they hurried along Broadway. The street was now a strip of sleazy peek-easies ballyhooing topless, bottomless, and live sex shows, punctuated by venerable restaurants and cabarets from less salacious epochs. "I was here once, as a child, with my mother to see my father off somewhere. To a ship in the Pacific. Japan. I've forgotten where. But he took me for a ride on the cable car. And that I'll never forget. It's one of the most exciting, enchanting memories I have. At the time it seemed very dangerous, but my father held on tight to me, so I felt safe."

"Let's go for a ride," Michael proposed. "I promise to hold on tight to you."

"I'm afraid it will ruin my childhood memory."

"It won't. Just be a child again."

They took a cab to the Market Street turntable and struggled through a press of summer tourists just as the cable car began clattering up Powell Street. Michael yelled, and they scampered like two runaways trying to catch a ride on a moving freight out of town. The car was jammed, the wooden benches facing outward all occupied, and Suzanna desperately clutched on to a pole. She balanced on her toes on a running board as the cable car moved in a series of jolting lurches. Suzanna was terrified she might lose her grip and tumble under the steel wheels or the crushing auto traffic alongside. But Michael immediately had his arms about her, holding on to the pole so firmly that she realized she could not fall off even if she let go. They stood immediately in front of a middle-aged couple seated facing outward.

"Can you see all right?" Michael asked them solicitously, although it seemed to Suzanna it would have been impossible for him to budge an inch.

"Oh, yes, fine, thank you," the woman said, then added, "We're from Sioux City," as if that explained her unobstructed vision.

"Terrific," Michael said enthusiastically. "I'm from New York and she's from Virginia. Don't you think we make a good-looking couple?"

The woman studied them a moment as if it were a reasonable question, then answered, "A very nice-looking couple. Don't you think so, George?"

George looked at them, smiled, and nodded.

"Are you getting married?" the woman asked.

"Not yet," Michael said. "I'm trying to talk her into living with me, but she's very old-fashioned."

"Well, you stay that way, dear," she said to Suzanna. "Don't do anything you might regret."

"I'm trying," Suzanna insisted. "But he's very attractive, don't you think? In a beat-up sort of way?"

The lady from Sioux City looked at Michael and nodded. "On the other hand, sometimes it's the things you didn't do when you were young that you regret later," she confided to Suzanna.

"What are you saying?" George demanded.

"I'm not saying anything. But this is San Francisco. And things are different nowadays."

The cable car made a long, clanking haul up Nob Hill and clashed to a stop at the crest. Two people sitting next to the couple from Iowa got off and Michael eased Suzanna into the seat, then spun around the pole and sat down next to her in a single gymnastic movement. He immediately began pointing out the sights: the granite façade of the adjacent Fairmount Hotel, the glittering Top of the Mark, the entrance of Chinatown directly below them, down the precipice of California Street. The car careened down Nob Hill, skirted the western edge of Chinatown, and then climbed Russian Hill with a metallic, rackety clamor. All the while Michael kept up a running commentary, recounting high-spirited tales of legendary railroad barons, murderous tong wars, notorious madams, and luxuriant brothels.

"Are all those stories true?" the woman from Sioux City asked, more in awe than in contradiction.

"Absolutely researched and documented," Michael insisted pontifically, then laughed. "Of course, if the facts contradict the legend, the newspapers here always reprint the legend." To Suzanna, the dark, narrow streets through which they clattered were now romantically haunted, their shadows peopled with legendary revenants.

The cable car mounted Russian Hill, then suddenly plunged down a breathtaking incline as steep as the fall of a rollercoaster, straight toward the Bay. Fifty yards from the water's edge it made an abrupt, body-banging change of direction that defied the laws of centrifugal motion and sent them sliding into the manicured gardens of Aquatic Park.

As the Iowa couple debarked from the cable car, the woman clutched Suzanna and whispered fiercely in her ear, "You hang on to him, honey. He's a live one."

"I will," Suzanna whispered back gleefully. She grabbed Michael's arm possessively and kissed him on the cheek. "You were right. It's still a wonderful memory." There was a strong, chilling wet wind off the Bay, and she snuggled against his arm. Like most visitors to San Francisco, she had dressed much too lightly for the evening, falsely assuming that sunny days made for balmy nights.

The jammed, casual intimacy of the ride made her comfortable with touching and holding on to Michael. He led her across the street to the Buena Vista Café, a local landmark with the dimensions and throbbing crowd of a rush-hour subway, although a more convivial one. He confidently elbowed his way to the bar and struggled back bearing two cream-topped Irish coffees, the house specialty.

"An appropriate drink to toast the memory of Ed Riley," he proclaimed over the yammering of the crowd.

"Was this a favorite of his?"

"Hated it with a passion. ' 'Tis an abomination,' " Michael quoted. " 'The foul ruination of two good drinks, Irish whiskey and strong coffee, to make them palatable to milksops.' "

"To Ed Riley, then," Suzanna toasted. She was still giddy with cocktails and wine, a high reinforced by the hilarity of the cable-car ride.

Through the bar's window Suzanna could make out a pier at the end of the street. A turn-of-the-century ferryboat and a historic sailing ship thrust their prows, funnels, and masts through the fog, as if the streaming mist were time itself flowing by. Michael pointed off to the left of the pier. "That looming dark shadow is Fort Mason, one of the original Spanish garrisons on the Bay, General John C. Frémont's headquarters during the conquest of California. Now it houses such exotica as a Zen Buddhist bakery, the Whole Earth Bookstore, modern art galleries, primal dance troupes, the greater

San Francisco mishmash of avant-garde weirdness. However, its most historic moment came in 1942 when one David Lowenstein sailed from its piers to Guadalcanal and World War II." There was a preoccupied, sepulchral note in Michael's voice, one that had marked the almost manic-depressive ups and downs of the evening as it swung from the frivolous to the funereal in an instant.

Now here it was again, in Michael's apartment—the sardonic reference to his father.

"Tell me about your father," Suzanna asked. Michael was gazing moodily through the bay window.

He turned, his brows lifted in a startled expression, as if she had been reading his mind. "What?"

"You've mentioned your father at least three times this evening. You want to talk about him." It was a statement, not a question.

Michael shook his head. "You mentioned World War II," she prompted.

"The epic event of my father's life," Michael responded. "He was working his way through CCNY, the City College of New York, driving a delivery truck at night, when Pearl Harbor was hit. At that point his life assumed certain mythic proportions. He enlisted in the marines. He was in the Second Marine Division and made his sergeant's stripes on Guadalcanal. A battlefield commission on Saipan, where he was promptly wounded. As soon as he could walk, he jumped the hospital against doctor's orders and hitched a ride back to his platoon. Marines did that sort of thing in that war. They finally caught up with him an amphibious landing and several battles later, and shipped him back to the United States with a chestful of medals, to recuperate and train recruits. He subsequently finished college and Columbia Law School on the GI Bill and lived successfully, if not always happily, ever after." Michael shrugged. "He was a tough man to live with. Or to live up to."

He was silent, meditative for a few moments, and he looked at her, his dark eyes troubled and searching. "I'm sorry. Ed's death seems to have aroused a lot of old ghosts that have come back to haunt me."

Suzanna was chilled by the figure of speech. Were those all her own ghosts were—the neurotic projections of an adolescent psyche? No, her spooks banged on doors, opened and slammed cabinets, wrote her ballads. She had not imagined all that. Not unless she was going insane. She suddenly felt very tired. All the energy and exhilaration that had stirred her earlier in the evening had now drained away, leaving her with a bone-deep craving for sleep.

"Don't go," he said.

"What?"

He looked at her with concern. "You look like you're about to fall asleep. And you want to go back to your hotel."

"I'd better. It's very late. Or very early."

"You can stay here."

She shook her head. "Not tonight." She tried to make it sound promising. She desperately hoped there was not going to be one of those scenes. She was just too tired.

"I'm not talking about sex. There's fresh linen on the bed and an inside lock on the door. I'll sleep out here on the couch. I do it often anyway. It's somehow comforting to hear the foghorns and look out at the sky over the Bay."

Suzanna was truly tempted. At best, it would be a cold, weary ride through the fog back to her hotel. "I don't understand why you want me to stay."

"Just to have you here. Especially in the morning. I make terrific omelettes for breakfast. I grind my own beans and brew ambrosial coffee. And there's a French bakery right in the next block where they are baking incredibly light, flaky croissants at this very moment, while you stand here in indecision."

"I look a fright in the morning," Suzanna pleaded.

He examined her face, a photographer studying his subject. "No, you don't," he decided. "Your hair looks even better when it's tousled. You don't wear very much makeup, and after you wash your face in the morning you're probably at your most bright-eyed and beautiful."

Suzanna smiled at him, the grin of defeat. "Do you really grind your own coffee beans?"

"You have a choice of Guatemalan or French roast."

He gave her his terrycloth robe to wear in the morning, took an old, frayed sleeping bag from the bedroom closet, and said, "Good night," with a sweet, bemused smile.

Suzanna locked the door behind him. She undressed and crawled under the covers, half expecting a soft knock on the door at any moment. She had underestimated her own exhaustion and fell asleep after a minute's musing. But she slept lightly.

She was not sure just what it was that woke her. A soft gray twilight, dawn's first gleamings, illuminated the windows. She became aware of a furtive thumping and scurrying noise outside the bedroom. She listened a moment. The sound came from the living room, distorted and echoing in the narrow hall connecting the bedroom with the front room.

Suddenly there was a loud crash, the sound of broken glass, and then a frantic banging about like that of a large panicked, trapped animal.

Alarmed, Suzanna sprang from the bed and turned on the light. She hurriedly put on the robe Michael had given her and stood with her ear against the door. She heard a soft cry of pain, a moan, then silence.

She opened the door, more confused than frightened, and stepped cautiously into the living room. The light was on, but the room appeared empty.

"Michael?" she called.

There was no reply. She stood on the threshold, listening intently. A few feet away, down low on the floor, she heard strained, harsh breathing coming from behind a chair.

She tiptoed forward and peeked around the chair. Michael, naked except for his undershorts, was on his hands and knees, crouched tensely, like an animal about to spring. His body was drenched with sweat, glistening in the lamplight like a coat of oil, and he was smeared with blood. Blood puddled and stained the floor about him. He peered about with eyes wide with fear. He looked directly at Suzanna. She had the distinct feeling that he did not even see her, but searched for some terror that lurked behind her.

8

MICHAEL SAT STRETCHED OUT ON THE COUCH, his bare legs resting across Suzanna's lap, feeling acutely embarrassed. He was humiliated to be sprawled there, naked except for a pair of scarlet French designer briefs, while she cleaned his lacerated shins and knees with antiseptic and bandaged them. But he was even more ashamed by the circumstances, as if he had been caught practicing some perverted vice.

"This is really a deep gash," Suzanna said with concern. She taped a gauze pad to his leg. "You might need stitches."

"Tape it as tight as you can. Tighter. The compression should stop the bleeding. It's just a meat wound."

He felt stupid enough without having to go to a doctor for stitches. He had knocked over the brandy glasses and crawled over the broken glass. He had not felt a thing.

"I'm amazed it didn't wake you up."

"Where I was, getting my legs cut up was the least of my problems."

"Where were you?"

He hesitated. Where had he been? The A Shau Valley? The Fish Hook? Hoi An? No, he had a nightmare image of a savanna with no place to hide except to crawl under the bodies of the dead. There were mountains in the distance and, about fifty yards away, elephant grass taller than a man, stirring and heaving like water as an invisible army moved through it toward him.

"Where were you?" Suzanna repeated.

"Probably An Hoa." She looked puzzled. "Vietnam," he explained.

She frowned and looked even more confused. "You were in Vietnam?"

"I was a cameraman."

"Oh." She nodded, as if that explained everything.

Was it really that simple? Michael wondered.

"My ex-husband was there. He was a gunnery officer on a destroyer. It was a very good spot to be in for his career." She concentrated on taping his shins, but Michael detected an embittered note.

"We have a lot in common," he said.

"He was Annapolis. A career man. I thought you were a rabid antiwar activist from Berkeley."

"That was in Berkeley. Being in Vietnam was a great equalizer."

There was a long silence. Michael saw a darkness fall across her face that had nothing to do with the light.

After a while she said, "You don't like to talk about it either. Robert never told war stories. I thought, at first, it was because he was on the fringe of it. Sailing around it."

Michael shook his head. "That wasn't it."

"What was it then?"

Michael shrugged. "Maybe he just didn't know what to say. People ask you questions, but they really don't want to hear the answers. They already know what they want to hear. They're committed to what they want to hear. So you never have the right answers. Hell, none of the questions make any sense either."

There was another long silence while she finished bandaging his leg.

"Can I ask what your nightmare was about? Or is that out of bounds?" She did not look up at him but gently pressed the bandage on his thigh where a spot of blood soaked through.

"It was about outtakes."

"Outtakes?"

"The film they didn't show on TV. The shots that were edited out."

"You dream about the film you shot that didn't make it on the air?" She was astonished.

"No." She looked at him curiously. "Not the film. The faces. The people. The dead. The images of them." And there was always something else he could not talk about. The fear that never went away.

"How long have you had the nightmares?"

"Off and on since I've been back. But I haven't had any for a while." He shook his head. "Tonight was the first time in months. But it was different."

"How?"

"I think Riley was in it."

"Did he send you to Vietnam?"

Michael laughed. At least he had meant it as a laugh, an expression of irony because it was really very funny. But it seized his body as a shiver, shaking him, making his teeth chatter, and he could not stop shuddering.

Suzanna was alarmed. She grabbed the open sleeping bag on the couch and threw it over his shoulders like a blanket, hugging it to him. Gradually he stopped trembling. "I'm sorry," he said.

"There's nothing to apologize for."

"It really is very funny."

"What is?"

"Why I went to Vietnam. It's a helluva story. You see, I went to Vietnam to avoid the draft."

"You're kidding."

"No, I'm absolutely serious. As soon as I graduated, my student deferment ended. A few months after I started working at the station full time, I got my draft notice. It was one hell of a moment of truth. I mean, I had burned my draft card. I had my principles. On the other hand, running away to Canada or going to jail seemed somehow *cowardly*. The role of expatriate or martyr held no romance for me. I was my father's son, after all, and the apple doesn't fall very far from the tree. I had to measure up. Fulfill the rite of passage."

Michael couldn't believe he was sprawled out, bleeding and naked, telling this woman his life story.

"You don't want to hear all this."

Suzanna looked at him, steadfast, serious, a shadow across her face. "Yes, I do. I really want to hear all this."

"This is some first date," Michael said.

"So you went as a combat cameraman," she prompted.

"Oh, that's much too simple. I had to jerk off intellectually a lot more than that. I had this Quaker creed I'd picked up on the barricades at Berkeley. I would go and bear witness. A person bearing witness must accept the responsibility for being aware of injustice or inhumanity. He may just stand by, but he may not turn away out of ignorance or fear. Hell, I even paid my own way over. Ed arranged the Defense Department clearances. He even set me up to work for the network on a free-lance basis. Eventually they took me on staff. Then he wrote a personal letter to the draft board informing them that I was on the front lines in Vietnam, wherever the hell they were, and it would be utter asininity—and I'm quoting now—to have me desert my post in order to return to the United States to be inducted to fill a clerk-typist job. And that's how I stayed out of the army."

The tone was bantering, meant to be amusing, but from the way Suzanna looked at him, Michael knew she was not taken in. She reached up and gently adjusted the cloak of the sleeping bag about his shoulders as one might tuck in a sick child.

Michael looked away. Out the window, the rosy dawn silhouetted the hills across the Bay. He looked back at Suzanna and studied her a moment. "I was right," he said.

"About what?"

"You do look beautiful first thing in the morning."

She laughed self-consciously, then reached up and stroked his cheek and chin. Her fingertips made a scratchy, sandpaper sound across his stubble. "And you have this incredible capacity to look absolutely wretched and irresistible at the same moment."

He leaned forward and kissed her. It was an unhesitant, totally committed kiss, and it surprised Michael to realize that they had not kissed until this moment. In the recesses of his mind he felt that they had already been intimate.

They sat quietly kissing, murmuring to each other, necking on the couch like two teenagers. Michael tried to shift his body, but the movement brought a sharp stab of pain, so he continued to sit awkwardly stretched out on the couch.

When they separated for air, he spied a new cause for acute embarrassment. His bandaged legs were thrust out before him, and out of the scarlet waistband of his shorts, the swollen head of his penis thrust up like an inflamed tulip.

Suzanna looked down and then back at Michael's face with an amused glint in her eyes.

"It seems to have a mind of its own," he stuttered, totally flustered.

Suzanna laughed, a throaty chuckle.

He made an awkward grope for her, and the move made him gasp.

"Don't," she whispered. "You'll rip open your cuts."

"It doesn't matter. No blood has gotten past my groin in the last ten minutes," he muttered into her hair. He reached under her robe to caress her, and the movement again made him wince.

"Michael, don't. You'll bleed to death," she said gently, but she did not resist his touch.

"If I don't, I'll die from want of you."

She separated herself from him, but only far enough to study his face. Then she softly kissed his eyes and smiled. "I wouldn't want that on my conscience," she said. "Don't move."

To his astonishment she reached down, plucked both sides of his shorts in her fingertips, and peeled them all the way down, gently easing them over his wounded legs.

Move? Michael was hardly breathing.

She stood up and, still fixing him with a sly look, opened her robe and dropped it. She was wearing only a pair of silken panties, and she stripped them with the same deliberateness as that with which she had stripped Michael.

Suzanna then knelt on the couch and straddled his hips. She reached for his prick and, holding it upright with her fingertips, gently eased down over it. She was moist, open, warm as a mouth, as though she had been ready for him for a while. At first she moved easily, rhythmically, all the while regarding him with a mischievous half-smile, teasing him with her boldness, drawing pleasure from his initial surprise and delight, his mounting excitement.

Then her own excitement suddenly seemed to catch, registering on her face as momentary astonishment. Her eyes went wide and then narrowed, her lips parted and her breath deepened and quickened. Her thighs tensed and squeezed him, she squirmed and pressed forward, seeking to touch some secret sensitive spot within. Her eyelids fluttered, her glazed eyes oblivious to him, but her arousal, her murmurs and muted moans, stirred him wildly and he thrust at her.

Her coming was a heaving convulsion, her hands pressed against his chest, dragging herself, shuddering, up and down the length of his cock, emitting incoherent cries and moans. Her body shone with sweat and her eyes were pressed shut in inner concentration. Gradually her breathing quieted and her movements became more rhythmic, as she slid down from a frenzied peak to a gentler pleasure.

It was then that Michael came, a hot liquid stitch that sprang from the base of his spine, as though the very core of him were unraveling into her. She moved, drawing every last thread into her, then seemed to melt onto him. They rolled onto their sides, her upper leg still hooked over him, holding his softening stalk in her, their sweating bodies hugging one another, now kissing so that Michael could no longer sense where his body and breath ended and hers began.

After a while, her face pressed in the crook of his neck, she asked, "Was I very selfish?"

"You were awesome."

"I'm really not like that. Not very often. Never, really."

"I feel privileged."

"Damn it, Michael, don't be glib. It felt right with you. It just did. I don't know why."

"It feels right with you."

The couch was cramped, and after a few minutes Michael picked her up and carried her like a bride into the bedroom. He almost immediately fell asleep, a peaceful, dreamless slumber from which he woke into morning sunshine.

Suzanna was awake, watching him with sleepy, half-opened eyes.

"You still look beautiful in the morning," he murmured, burying his face in her sprawling hair. The air in the bedroom still held a morning chill, but the air about them under the quilt was warm and provocative, redolent with Suzanna's perfume and the musky, lascivious smells of sex. He nuzzled and kissed her breasts. He had awakened with an erection and now he joined her so naturally that it was as if they had never been apart.

Their lovemaking this time was languid, somnolent, without the searing climaxes of their first time. On occasion she shuddered and sighed from some fluttering, unexplosive release, tensing her lithe, lean body against him, then lay back contentedly, enveloping him until the steadily brimming flood of his excitement pulsed into her.

*M*ichael washed Suzanna's back, and in his careful appreciation of it he fell in love first with that part of her. Her abundant chestnut hair was piled and pinned on top of her head to keep it out of the shower, exposing the delicate, swanlike column of her neck. There was a slender fragility to her neck, shoulders, arms, and back that touched him. It made the fullness of her hips and ass that much more voluptuous to him, and made her breasts, in their nakedness, seem larger than they really were. Sexually spent, he looked at her body and still found deep delight in it.

He turned her around and began soaping her shoulders. She seemed to shy away from his touch. Her averted eyes were troubled and anxious.

"What's the matter?"

"Nothing's the matter."

"Something's bothering you. What is it?"

She shrugged, her breasts rising and falling in the rivulets of water. "All this *intimacy*." She said it as if it were something unpleasant. "It's all too sudden, too fast. I'm just not used to things happening so fast. Maybe it's your lifestyle. Like hot tubs or something.

I'm just not comfortable with it." She stood with her arms pressed to her sides, looking uncomfortable and awkward.

Michael handed her the soap. "Okay," he said, and left the shower stall.

He toweled himself dry quickly. She was still lingering in the shower. "Take your time," he called out to her. "I'm going to run out and get a few things for breakfast."

There was a pause and then she responded, "Do you always treat your one-night stands so well?" The tone was meant to be teasing, but a sharp edge to her voice cut through the drone of the water.

Michael was furious. "Goddammit!" he exploded and slammed a fist into the center of the bathroom door. There was a thin plywood panel at that point, and the force of the blow shattered it, luckily, or he might have broken his hand.

He stalked angrily out of the bathroom, naked, trailing his towel behind him.

9

AT THE SLAM OF THE BATHROOM DOOR, SU-
zanna peeked out of the shower and spotted the shattered panel. She ducked back into the shower for
protection.

She turned up the hot water, hiding in the opaque
cloud of steam. Michael's sudden explosion of anger
frightened her. She had not expected it. She had seen
the bewilderment, then the hurt in his eyes when she
suddenly withdrew from him in the shower.

Suzanna was in an emotional turmoil. The night
before, she had been excited, unusually aggressive, but
suddenly she just wanted to get out of Michael's apartment as quickly as possible. She had not felt this contra-
dictory and confused about sex since she was a teenager.

There was something else that unsettled Suzanna:
Michael's scars. She had become sensitive to them when
they held each other in bed before dropping off to
sleep. She had delighted in their new intimacy, touching the smooth, warm skin, the hard, lean muscles of
his back, the cleft of his spine, the tautness of his ass.
But her exploring fingers had tripped on the alien,
hard slick cords and knots of flesh.

In the morning light, while Michael slept on his
stomach, his breath a soft snore, she had lifted the quilt
and studied them. Red, thick scars ripped Michael's

110

buttocks, back, and left shoulder blade as if his flesh had been savagely torn by a great bird of prey. In the harsh shadowed light there was a wanton brutality to the scars that frightened Suzanna. It was, admittedly, an irrational fear, but it seemed cruel evidence of some deeper wounding she had seen reflected at moments in Michael's eyes. Given his violent swings in mood the night before, the bloodletting nightmares, and now the door-shattering anger, Suzanna was suddenly apprehensive.

She dried herself and dressed quickly. When she emerged she was relieved to discover that Michael was nowhere in the apartment. For a moment she considered writing a note and leaving. Then she noticed the breakfast setting for two on the cocktail table in the living room. Fresh orange juice had been poured, a glass carafe of *café filtre* sat on an electric warming pad, and its dark, pungent aroma filled the room. The fog had burned off with the morning sun, and from the window she could look out over the roofs of the Victorians across Union Street, to the Bay on which sailboats now glided, their canvas radiant in the sunlight like the wings of gulls dipping in flight. She sipped her orange juice and decided to wait.

The west wall of the living room was windowless and lined with bookshelves surrounding a gas wall heater manteled as a fireplace. Suzanna browsed through Michael's books. There were novels, mostly contemporary except for what looked like the complete works of Hemingway and Fitzgerald, apparently purchased and read over a period of time, since no two editions matched. There was a shelf of books on movies— Truffaut's *Hitchcock*, Pauline Kael's *Deeper into Movies*, a textbook called *The Movie Business*—and several large, expensive photography and art books. Curiously, there were no books having to do with contemporary events or politics—as though the passions that had stirred

Michael at Berkeley were now totally absent. Even more surprising were three full shelves, overflowing into a fourth, totally devoted to World War II. There were stunning collections of combat photography—*U.S. Navy War Photographs*, edited by Edward Steichen, and Robert Capa's *Slightly Out of Focus*—as well as stacks of memoirs: *Al Schmid, Marine* by Robert Butterfield, *Admiral Halsey's Story*, and *Reminiscences* by Douglas MacArthur. The books were old, worn by use and decades of dust and dustings. A new book jacket caught her eye by its distinctiveness—*Tarawa, the Story of a Battle* by Robert Sherrod. She opened it and the cover cracked at the fold. It had never been opened before. She replaced it.

There were historical volumes: *The History of the U.S. Marine Corps Operations in World War II*; Samuel Eliot Morison's *The Struggle for Guadalcanal* and *New Guinea and the Marianas*; Gilbert Cant's *The Great Pacific Victory*. Suzanna found the collection extraordinary. Neither her father nor her ex-husband, both professional navy men and Annapolis graduates, had ever had such a library.

She sprawled in the window seat, totally absorbed by the startling black-and-white images in *Power in the Pacific*. In Steichen photographs, the young men at war appeared still alive, vital, frozen in time as if they might become animated again at any moment. Suzanna stared at the picture of one handsome, grinning young navy officer. For a reason she could not identify, it seemed to her heartbreakingly sad. It stirred some forgotten tragic memory, one she immediately knew had to do with her mother, but beyond that her memory was blocked. To her own amazement, she began to weep.

Suzanna had composed herself by the time Michael returned, carrying a paper bag and a bakery box. Their eyes met for a moment of inquiry, then Michael asked, "Would you like champagne and strawberries? There's a mom-and-pop grocery a few doors down from the bakery. They had fresh strawberries. Also champagne on ice. That's one of the great advantages of this neighborhood."

"I love champagne and strawberries," she exclaimed enthusiastically. And no more gratuitous cracks about treating your one-night stands very well, she vowed. She followed him into the kitchen. "I've been browsing through your books. It's really a library. You've got an unbelievable collection on World War II."

"They were my father's," he said. Suzanna thought of the new, unbroken copy of *Tarawa*. The publishing date, she noticed, had been 1973. Michael had bought it himself years after his father's death, even after his own return from Vietnam.

"My father was a great buff on the campaigns in the Pacific," Michael chatted, setting up the strawberries in glasses. " 'Buff' is probably too casual a word. Each of those books was very personal to him. They concerned battles he was in or, in the case of the later ones nearer the end of the war, battles in which his outfit had fought, in which his friends had died. It was a very personal scholarship that my father, the lawyer, pursued. Trying to place his experiences, his horrors, even his heroism, in a historical perspective. I don't think he ever did."

Michael struggled with the champagne, holding the bottle against his stomach pointing away from him, and forced the cork with both thumbs. It exploded open like a cannon shot, the .50-caliber cork ricocheting off the ceiling and walls.

Champagne foamed out of the bottle and Michael frantically poured it. Laughing, he handed a glass to Suzanna. "It's gauche, I know, to pop them, but I still get a bang out of it." He tipped his glass to her. "To us. To the future," he toasted. "May all the shit be behind us."

"I'll drink to that." In Suzanna's own ear her gaiety

sounded forced. The fact of Michael's nightmare—or rather nightmares, since they seemed to be chronic—had, of course, shaken her, but now it took on a darker hue. Was she getting involved with yet another man obsessed by war?

"You know, I really think you and my father would like each other, if you got to know one another."

Michael shook his head. "We do know one another. Your father is every senior officer in Vietnam who demanded I get with the program, or asked me point-blank whose side I was on anyway. They'd smile at us with these clenched teeth and tight, bloodless lips and say something like, 'Our troops are winning the war, but you people on TV are losing it for us.' And we'd all sit there politely, despising each other's guts. I never had a grunt or anybody in the field below company commander ever ask me whose goddamn side I was on."

Michael said it with such heat that Suzanna was intimidated into silence.

Michael began preparing the omelette. He melted butter in a frying pan while he deftly sliced garlic, chives, and mushrooms. "Why did you save your father's books?" she ventured.

"They're the totems of my childhood. I'm going to burn them someday. When I work up the courage," he said offhandedly. He threw in the vegetables to sauté them. "No, that's not true," he reconsidered. He stirred the herbs and mushrooms with a wooden spoon and lowered the flame. "They were my textbooks. I used to thumb through them when I was a child, totally fascinated. The pictures are burned into my memory. Images of marines charging up the beach on Tarawa and hugging the sand at Iwo Jima. George Strock's photo for *Life* of three American soldiers, dead, sprawled on the surf-line of Buna Beach. It was a classic case of the medium being the message. I didn't identify with the marines or the soldiers but with the photographer. I remember thinking that what the photographer saw and felt at that moment, the whole world would see and feel forever."

"That's a very romantic notion."

"Well, hell, if you can't have a romantic notion at, say, thirteen, when the hell can you? Of course, I didn't know that if I felt as strongly about what I saw as any rational, sensitive human being should, I would never get the shot. So when I went over, I was there to see, see everything, but not feel. Perhaps just a twinge to maybe tell me that this was a good shot, one that should totally devastate ordinary people sitting at home in front of their TV sets." Michael fell silent, but his hands kept remarkably busy, melting butter in two saucer-sided omelette pans, breaking, seasoning, and scrambling a half-dozen eggs.

They were sure, sensitive hands with long fingers that seemed to have a quick intelligence of their own. Watching Michael cook had its own fascination. There was a fastidiousness about his work. The paradox was that his deft fingers were tipped by ragged, neurotically chewed nails.

Michael worked silently, as though gathering strength from the preparation of food. He neatly folded over the omelettes, heated them a few moments, then slid them out onto their plates and placed a flaky croissant next to each.

They carried their plates and glasses into the living room and Suzanna preempted the window seat. She moved the book of war pictures she had left there, and suddenly a connection between Steichen's cover photograph and Michael's breakfast plate leaped to her mind. They had both been composed instantly. Michael was by habit meticulous. Even in combat, one did not simply cram film into a camera whose mechanisms were calibrated in fractions of millimeters. Dirt on a lens or in a camera would ruin the shot for which a photographer might be risking his life. Even in the midst of hell, neatness counted for a cameraman. Why was she going out of her way to find something sinister in him? She forked into her omelette.

"Michael, this is very good. You really do this well." She made a sweeping gesture with her fork to take in the whole breakfast.

"It's part of my religion."

"Which religion is that?"

"Hedonism." He raised his glass of champagne and strawberries. "Life here and now, with all its fleshly pleasures. Not life everlasting."

"Hush now," Suzanna said, her mouth full of eggs. "Don't let the chaplain hear you."

"Why? Doesn't he like omelettes?"

"Not with French names. And definitely not strawberries and champagne for breakfast. It's sinful."

"I'll tell the padre the story of my conversion," Michael said. "That'll get him. I'm a born-again Hedonist."

"Tell *me* the story."

Michael shook his head and gave her a bemused, sardonic smile. "It's a story of stark, raving madness. Of dark deeds. And of ghosts. It's a ghost story, really."

"Oh, please tell me."

There was something in her voice that made Michael study her curiously. "I will," he nodded. "But not this morning. It's not a story for breakfast on a beautiful, sun-shining morning."

Again he fell silent, sitting on the sofa with his champagne, and for a moment Suzanna had the suspicion he'd been carried off to a darker side of the planet. But then he suddenly said, "I like you. I'm very glad you're here."

The phone suddenly rang. Michael seemed to freeze. The phone rang again, the noise jarring the silence.

"The answering machine is on," Michael said. "Probably some salesman selling Time-Life Books."

The response tape clicked on and the red signal light began blinking.

"Don't you think you should answer her?"

"Her?"

"The girl selling books."

Michael gave a small smile, shook his head, and silently mouthed, "No."

Suzanna heard a faint beep, then heard the message tape turn on. She wondered who it was calling Michael on Saturday morning, and the thought resonated with pangs of jealous suspicion. The red blinking light of the answering machine was hypnotic, and she had to force herself to look away. "You really do have a wonderful view," she commented. "Last night, when I could only see the fog, I thought your fabled panorama was a myth to lure me up here."

"It was."

They turned their attention to eating, while the tape ran on, silently recording the unheard but disturbing third party in the room.

"Have you ever been to wine country?" Michael suddenly asked.

The tape clicked off.

"No. Where is it, exactly?"

"Just north of Mare Island. There are fifty wineries up there, some of them in ivy-covered stone buildings that date back to the days of the Spanish land grants. They give tours of the presses and cellars, but the real treat is the wine-tasting rooms."

"It sounds intoxicating."

"We'll drive up there this afternoon," Michael exclaimed enthusiastically. "Pick up some French bread, Italian salami and sausages, cheese, olives. Picnic on the local fare."

Suzanna shook her head with sharp regret. "I'm sorry. I really have to get back to Mare Island. My father's due back this morning. And I've hardly seen him at all since I've been here. I really do have to spend some time with him."

Michael nodded and said nothing, but Suzanna saw in his eyes the same flash of angry disappointment she had noted before.

Her father. Was that the cause of her nervousness? In two hours she would have to face him. What would she say about how she had spent the night?

No, she would have to lie, or at least evade the truth. She had traveled halfway around the world to communicate at last with her father, the father she had never really known, and now she had to start off by denying the truth about herself. Whatever that truth really was. She had no idea what this morning's turmoil of feelings meant.

Suzanna studied Michael's troubled face with such a vast uncertainty that she could not think what to say next.

10

OKAY, I'LL BE BRIEF. THIS IS, MORRISON. AL-meda Sheriff's Department, remember? We got Riley's car. And I think we got the guy who did him in. A real loser. Call me for the details."

That had been the call on the answering machine. The details, when Michael called back after Suzanna's departure, had been sketchy.

"An AWOL sailor. Black."

Then, without warning, there had been the jolting question. "There's no point in being coy, so I'll ask you straight. Your friend Riley, was he gay?"

"What? What the hell made you ask that?"

"Was he?"

"No, he was married a couple of times."

"That's no answer at all."

A few minutes later Michael was out of his apartment and into his car. He gunned the Mustang up the hill to Broadway, the byway through the pastel-painted luxury apartment houses and mansions that crowned Pacific Heights like heaps of candied frosting.

"Your friend Riley, was he gay?"

Michael rejected the idea violently, but in his mind he heard a mocking voice respond, "Well, isn't just *every*body?"

It was the voice of Harvey Alexander, the station art

director, one of several of Michael's co-workers who had recently come out of the closet.

Michael braked for the light at the corner of Broadway and Polk. Polk Street, formerly a dying neighborhood, had been recently resurrected by an insurgence of trendy bistros, boutiques, and bookstores. Two men, Michael's age, both dressed in tanktops and jeans, waited on the corner for the light to change, holding hands.

Michael, given to cinematic visions, had a fantasy of a circus staged by Fellini. Instead of the traditional Volkswagen from which emerged a great line of clowns, a lone wardrobe closet stood in the center of the ring. And from it streamed bearded TV newswriters, middle-aged insurance executives, brawny football players, taxi drivers, air force men, and bartenders. They poured steadily out of the closet, overflowing the circus arena and inundating the surrounding hills of San Francisco. *But, goddammit, not Ed Riley.*

He barreled through the Broadway tunnel, the engine's roar reverberating loudly off the encircling tiles, and shot toward the on-ramp of the San Francisco—Oakland Bridge.

*T*he Oakland Police Administration Building was a nine-story black and gray concrete monolith just off the Nimitz Freeway at the seedy edge of the downtown area. The narrow, windowless halls and the succession of locked iron doors through which Michael passed oppressed him. He felt almost as if he were once again a prisoner here. He had spent a night in 1968 jailed in a holding cell in the basement, caged in a foul drunk tank with other bleeding, cursing, and sobbing students and teaching assistants whose militancy had been battered by police truncheons. Even now, eight years later, the memory of the stench of boozey puke and piss made Michael queasy.

"The thing is, we don't know who the hell has jurisdiction, 'cause we still don't know what happened to Riley. Or even where it happened," Morrison explained. "The Oakland Police picked up this beauty last night, cruising around in the Cadillac in an area where only pimps drive Cadillac Sevilles. He didn't look like a pimp to them."

"What did he look like to them?"

"A punk who stole a Cadillac."

"What does he look like to you?"

"A heifer for some bull in the slammer." There was no humor, not even a sadistic note in Morrison's voice.

"What does he say happened?" Michael asked.

"At what moment? This guy's a regular Scheherazade. He's got a thousand and one stories. And he keeps changing each one of them." Morrison led Michael down the corridor. "At first he said some guy he met in a bar loaned him the car. Of course, he couldn't rightly remember the guy's name, or the bar. As a matter of fact, he was cruising around looking for the guy to give him back the car when he was picked up."

"This guy's too dumb to be a car thief."

"Believe me, they're never too dumb to steal." Morrison stopped at a closed door. "But this dummy had military ID on him when we booked him. We ran a check this morning and, guess what, he's AWOL."

"From where?"

Morrison gave a hint of a smile. "An ammunition ship stationed at Mare Island. And, what a coincidence, he's been absent without leave since Tuesday, the day your friend Riley was there with you. Goddamn, but don't I just love it when things are neat like that," he chortled.

Morrison opened the door into a small, dimly lit office, and they walked in and he carefully closed the door behind them. The room was barren except for what appeared to be a mirrored medicine cabinet on the wall. Morrison opened the cabinet and there was a one-way glass panel inside that looked into the adjacent room. In the other room a black youth sat at a green Formica-topped table facing two men, one white and one black, whose faces Michael could not see. They all sat on hard metal chairs under a glaring overhead light, and even from the back, in their shirtsleeves, the two detectives looked intimidating.

"Why are we fucking around with this shithead?" the white man snarled. "All he does is lie to us."

"That's because he's frightened," the black man said reasonably. "Aren't you, James?"

The frightened youth looked fragile. Round pop-eyes stared out of a very black face. His cheeks were sunken and his forehead prematurely creased, like that of an old woman. A homely boy, but he held himself with tense elegance and nervously moved his head and hands with exaggerated delicacy. Michael knew immediately why Morrison had labeled him as the cornhole for a jailhouse stud.

"You've got reason to be frightened," the black cop continued in the same sympathetic, counseling tone. "A man is dead. A very prominent man. Maybe it was an accident. We don't know. But you're caught flat-out driving his car. A stolen car. You can see how it looks, James."

"I want to talk to a bail bondsman."

"No bail for you. This is murder," the white cop sneered.

"What murder? I didn't murder no one. You can't prove nothing."

"I'm afraid they really don't have to prove a whole lot," the black cop confided. "You were caught driving a stolen car. That's a felony. There's a homicide involved. A felony that results in a homicide is murder, even if you really didn't do it. You know a little about the law, James. You've been inside before."

"I never knowed this guy," James wailed.

"Bullshit," the white cop exploded. "You were drinking with him. Boozing it up buddy-buddy."

"No. Never."

"Don't lie to us, you little faggot. We got your fingerprints and his all over that fancy flask."

"What's this about a flask?" Michael asked Morrison.

"Your friend Riley have a fancy leather hip flask that you know of?"

"With hunting dogs and pheasants etched in the leather?"

"That's the one. Riley was a right-fisted drinker. The spade's left-handed. So we got two very distinct sets of prints, like they were handing the flask back and forth."

James sat nervously gnawing his lower lip.

"Maybe it wasn't your fault. Tell us what happened to Riley," the black cop prompted.

"Man, I tell you I don't know this man. I never laid eyes on him. That's the truth. God, that's the truth. I just *found* the car."

"What do you mean, you found the car?"

"I mean it was just sitting there. Wide open. The keys right there. And that there flask, it was just lying there in the glove compartment."

"Where was that, exactly?"

James looked nervously from the black detective to the white detective. His eyes narrowed, his brow furrowed in concentration. "I remember it was in . . . Oakland . . . somewhere. On MacArthur. Yeah, that's it. On MacArthur Boulevard."

"This big Cadillac was just sitting there wide open. On MacArthur. With the keys in it. Liquor right there. But no one around," the black cop reviewed.

"Yeah," James said weakly, as if he did not believe the story himself.

"I've never seen this guy before in my life," Michael said.

"You sure?"

"Yes."

"Not at Mare Island?" Morrison persisted.

"No."

"What about in San Francisco somewhere? Hanging around the station, maybe?"

Michael studied James again, then shook his head. "He doesn't look familiar at all."

Morrison shrugged. "It was just a shot in the dark. It doesn't really matter."

"Let's change the subject, James," the black detective suggested, as if introducing some new pleasantry. "What baths do you go to?"

"Bath?"

"Steam baths or whatever. You know, to meet other guys like yourself."

"Like me," James repeated hopelessly, as if he were a member of some doomed species.

"Yeah, faggots," the white cop snarled so fiercely that James jumped in his seat.

Morrison touched Michael's shoulder and motioned him out of the observation room. "I wanted you to get a good long look and listen to him."

"Sorry, I couldn't help you."

"Like I said, it was just a shot. Here's another. Would Riley have picked up a guy like that? Forget the homosexual trip. Say, if he was hitchhiking?"

Michael pondered a moment and nodded. "If he was in uniform. Or if he was waiting in one of those booths set up to share a ride with a serviceman. I think they have them outside Mare Island. Yeah, Riley would probably stop. Hell, he might even buy the guy a drink to get his views on the problems of the black serviceman." He looked at Morrison quizzically. "I just wrote half the script, didn't I?"

Morrison nodded. The cop stood with his thumbs hitched in his gunbelt, head bowed pensively as if contemplating the thick wad of suet rolling over his pants.

"As banal as all that," Michael said wearily. "Only the way he died is still a mystery."

Morrison shrugged. "We get a guy a month cooked to death in a hot tub or sauna. The combination of a few drinks and the high heat stops their hearts dead. Or they simply pass out and boil away." Morrison snorted. It was meant to be a laugh. "Among you beautiful people, it's the second leading cause of death."

"What's the first?"

"Sideswiping joggers." He patted his thick, hard gut with satisfaction.

Michael drove into a reddening sun, across a steel and concrete track suspended two hundred and twenty feet over the Bay. The San Francisco—Oakland Bay Bridge was two separate bridges, really, as if the two cities it linked had quarreled during the construction and each declared its separate identity. The Oakland section was a cantilever, a graceless industrial steelwork of girders. The San Francisco side was a dramatic and sweeping suspension bridge, smaller but no less lovely in its architecture than its sister, the Golden Gate. Both sections of the San Francisco—Oakland Bay Bridge joined in the middle of the Bay, each anchoring on the navy base of Treasure Island.

The navy dominated Michael's immediate vistas. Just off to his left was the naval air station at Alameda. Its runways, flanked with jet fighters, boresighted directly at him. At the adjacent docks the aircraft carriers *Midway* and *Coral Sea*, state-of-the-art dreadnoughts named for World War II battles, rode lethal and ominous at their moorings. Ahead of Michael, at the Hunter's Point Naval Shipyard on the San Francisco shore, the thicket of towering gantry cranes loomed like a great winter forest, now dead and leafless.

The Bay was the vortex through which men and ships funneled to the wars of Asia. It had been the gate for Ed Riley and Michael's father and, in his own time, for Michael's rite of passage. And the dead always returned here. They no longer were transported on ships riding the incoming tide. Now they flew on jet streams to Travis Air Force Base, north of the Bay. The corpses and pieces of corpses, as Michael remembered from his own desolate homecoming, were packaged in shining aluminum coffins stacked to form a silver beacon for the dead winging in behind him.

Michael had fled Vietnam because he had become terrified that he was being annihilated in a way even more obscene than death. But once back in "the world," he didn't feel he was going to make it. He ricocheted from San Francisco to New York to Los Angeles to Mexico and back to San Francisco, prowling about like a baffled beast.

New environments suppressed the nightmares, at least at first. His life was in chaos, but he could afford to drift for a while. He had practically two years' salary in the bank and unemployment checks every other week.

It was not just the decompression from the war that made him crazy. He did not know where to pick up the threads of his life. He had no desire to be a network cameraman dashing off to wars, riots, strikes, political campaigns—a piece of flotsam tossed by the storms and currents of events. He would become one of those doomed action junkies who always needed the rush of a war like a fix. That would be the final shove into insanity. He required more direction in his life, more control.

In San Francisco he crashed with Riley. He got stoned and wandered about Berkeley, through Sproul Plaza. The lineup of desks where students signed petitions for the legalization of marijuana, against killing whales, for gun control, seemed as permanent as the granite Campanile. The students looked so young that Michael could not believe he had been one of them three years before.

He fantasized about going to law school, tripping in his father's footsteps, and the next day, stoned again, he bounced across the Bay to the San Francisco Civic Center. The neo-Renaissance dome of City Hall, taller than that of the United States Capitol, loomed like St. Peter's above the vast piazza and adjacent government buildings. Michael wandered among the students of Hastings College of The Law, perceiving the law itself as a work of baroque architecture. He knew he would never survive the three-year grind.

He bought the Mustang, battered and marginally operational, and drove slowly down the coast back toward Los Angeles. It was astonishing how many pilgrims one encountered along Highway One if one stopped often enough, picked up hitchhikers, and, of course, had dope to spare. He could not tell the war veterans from the noncombatant casualties of the sixties.

It was while walking on the beach south of Big Sur, contemplating William Randolph Hearst's castle at San Simeon, that Michael had a flash of insight. He had simply been perceiving himself as a grunt, rather than as an officer and future general. Buzzing with cannabis, he gazed up at Hearst's "enchanted hill" and concluded it was a very heavy omen. He cut through the coastal hills to pick up the faster inland highway back to San Francisco.

"I'm going to produce and direct," he announced to Riley.

"Produce and direct what?"

"What have you got?"

Michael then spun one of the gossamer weaves of ideas he had conjured up in pot smoke.

Riley dismissed it.

Michael came back with a second idea. Riley shot it down even quicker.

" 'The Different Drummers,' " Michael announced, making quotation marks with his fingers.

"Very catchy. What the hell does it mean?"

"A cinematic shopping list of our indigenous seekers—EST, Arica, Transcendental Meditation, coitus interruptus in hot tubs. A visual menu of the human-potential movement. Heavy Eastern philosophy, insightful interviews with flaky but fetching women, sitar music, artistic but teasing shots of nudity, silhouettes against the sunset, *ecstasy*."

Riley laughed uproariously, then nodded.

Michael again camped out on Riley's couch, but this time he worked. He wrote a treatment at an old rolltop oak desk. Together he and Riley worked out the budget. "You can write the script but you can't touch the camera," Riley warned. "Or else they'll still consider you a cameraman, a technician, not the producer and director. That's just the way they think in the front office."

Riley's star, as well as his ratings and sobriety, was already on the skids. Yet his knowledge of the chessboard moves of station politics and their relation to budgets was still keen. He still possessed strong contacts. With a phone call, he set up lunch with the head of advertising of a savings-and-loan company. The adman was an old friend of Riley and impressed that Michael had been a network field producer in Vietnam. That was how Riley had introduced him. The adman liked the treatment. It was not too controversial, yet it was "contemporary," something that would attract the young professionals and couples the finance company was interested in acquiring as new customers. The budget was in the ballpark. Underwriting the show would be good institutional advertising. It would give the company a "contemporary image." He used the word *contemporary* at least six times during lunch. Michael was a "contemporary" of his son at Stanford biz school.

The deal with the station had been a formality. If they had not taken the package, there were three other stations in town. Everyone loved the fact that Michael had been a cameraman with the station years before and had gone on to the network. It made great publicity copy. Of course, there was a new station manager, a new news director, and a new program director. Michael knew no one except a handful of cameramen, reporters, and film editors.

"If I had walked in the door, I would never have gotten past the receptionist," Michael celebrated with Riley over drinks.

"Sincere gratitude is a very attractive quality in a young man," Riley boomed back. "You should cultivate it assiduously." He was already drunk. He had had a few cards left to play in his hand and, for Michael's sake, he had played them out.

Now Riley was a corpse, one of the mutilated legion of the dead that stalked Michael in his nightmares—the heads, eyes open and staring, mouths agape, that terminated in bloody neck stumps, the festering decapitated bodies, the eyeless leering faces, the armless, legless, eviscerated torsos and charred limbs.

But tonight he could not hold them back with an ex-Saigon bar girl with a French name. Suzanna had made that kind of anodyne meaningless. He would have to ride out his nightmares.

It was going to be a very bad night.

11

SUZANNA BRAKED AS SHE DROVE PAST THE great black anchor at the main entrance to Mare Island. The stark iron anchor and its shattered wooden stock bore the bronze plaque of an official California historical site. It was all that remained of a Civil War sloop shipwrecked a century before. To Suzanna, the brooding monument was a sign that each time she passed through the Mare Island gates she was breaching some definite demarcation between present and past.

The marine sentry recognized her father's four-door Mercury sedan and saluted her through. The gate was actually on the mainland, and now she accelerated onto the narrow causeway across the strait to Mare Island. To the south of the causeway, toward San Francisco Bay, were the bustling piers, shops, and drydocks of the shipyard that now primarily built and overhauled nuclear submarines. The center of the causeway was a cantilever bridge, colossal enough to allow the passage of battleships and aircraft carriers, although they only made the passage now to the scrap pile. A half-mile north of the causeway the mothball fleet was moored, the towering masts and superstructures of the World War II derelicts forlorn and desolate against the darkening northern sky.

At the end of the causeway Suzanna turned south

onto Walnut Avenue, the street of the senior officers' residences. Walnut Avenue was actually lined with elm, locust, and catalpa trees that had been shipped around the Horn from Norfolk, Virginia, to biologically complement the transplanted Tidewater architecture.

The white pillars of Captain Blackwell's residence faced the street, and behind them the veranda was as cool and dusky as a cave, despite the glaring sun. Suzanna lingered there a moment, looking at the slumbering, dark wood of Alden Park across the street. The only evidence of the navy was the administration building that fronted the park at its north end. The two-story brick building was also an official historical site, constructed as Commander Farragut's headquarters in 1855, but the hip roof, gables, and framed arches were classic Colonial Williamsburg. The building would have been at home on the campus of William and Mary College.

Suzanna hesitated on the veranda, strangely reluctant to enter the house. She felt a chill, like a cold breath on her neck. Whatever this house harbored, was she sane enough, strong enough now to fight it?

Her father was working at a desk in the living room when Suzanna entered. He was wearing spectacles. Suzanna had never seen him wear glasses before, and when he peered up at her over the top of the frames, she had for the first time in her life the chilling perception that her father was now an old man.

"Did you have a good time?" he asked. "How was the play?"

"Oh, I'm glad you found my note."

"Ninety percent of my new job seems to be reading memoranda," Captain Blackwell grunted, and waved the sheaf of papers on which he was working. "Trying to stay on top of what the people who are supposed to be working for me are really doing." He was dressed in civilian clothes, a baggy gray wool cardigan, a white dress shirt without a tie, and dark slacks. Perhaps it was the nondescript civvies that made him look older. The tailored uniforms, with their gold braid of rank and candy-striped ribbons, cloaked his age with authority and dash.

"I'm glad you didn't try to drive home last night," he said. "I gather the visibility on some of the roads, especially the back one from San Francisco, was zero-zero."

Suzanna sat down in the easy chair opposite him. "Actually, I didn't go to the theatre last night," she said. "The producer who invited me to the station was gallant enough to take me to dinner. It was a wonderful opportunity to do San Francisco."

"Well, I'm glad it was fun for you."

"Not only that," Suzanna exclaimed. "But I have a job interview with the station art director next week."

"Oh, that's wonderful." There was something automatic in her father's response, as if he did not know quite how to answer.

"Incidentally, you've met this producer," Suzanna noted offhandedly. "Michael Lowenstein. He was here at the change-of-command ceremony."

"Lowenstein." Her father frowned and repeated the name. "Lowenstein. I don't remember anyone with that name. But then there were so many people."

"He was here with an anchorman named Ed Riley. They were filming a story."

She saw her father stiffen visibly as he suddenly recalled his brief encounter with Michael. "Oh, yes, that one." There was a sudden hardness in his voice and expression.

"Michael was the younger one, tall, dark, and interesting-looking." Suzanna laughed. "At least to women."

Her father stared at her for a moment, then said obliquely, "Oh, that reminds me, Bill Bingham called you."

"Who?"

"Bill Bingham. The marine captain of the guard. The one who escorted you home the other night after the O-club party."

"Oh, yes." Suzanna had almost forgotten him. A muscular young man with the broad, pleasant face of a good-natured jock.

Her father smiled at her, and there was a sunny beam of paternal pleasure in his expression. "I guess I have a new collateral duty as your social coordinator. In any case, he asked—with all due respect to the rank of the messenger—if you are interested in going water-skiing tomorrow afternoon. Apparently there's a ramp to launch pleasure boats at the north end of the base, and he skis up the Napa River. He said he mentioned something to you about it the other night."

Suzanna shook her head. "I was hoping you and I might do something together this weekend."

"Oh, I'm sorry. I've already made plans to play golf with Admiral Doyle."

Suzanna was suddenly furious, but she said nothing. The thought of spending this first Sunday together had never occurred to her father. She seethed with anger, irrational and deep, inflamed with the pain of un-healed childhood wounds. Her father had always been the absent but mythical figure, away sailing on the high China Seas off Korea when she had spoken her first word and taken her first step. He had been in the Mediterranean when she graduated from high school. Only when she married had he been there to "give her away" to the next generation of Annapolis men.

Her father was now perplexed by her hostile silence, and he offered uneasily, "Bill Bingham seems like a very nice young man. He's certainly a charger. He has a very promising career ahead of him."

"Oh, terrific," Suzanna spat bitterly. "That's just what I need right now. To get involved with another ambi-tious military man. There is certainly something about a uniform."

She glared at her father. But the puzzlement and hurt evident in his face made her feel ashamed and smothered her anger as quickly as it had flared.

"I thought you and Robert were perfect together," he said in a quiet voice. "I never knew what happened there."

Whenever Suzanna felt uneasy or embarrassed, she had the habit of looking away and nervously stroking her hair. She did this now, and only after many seconds turned back to face her father. "I was in love with the costume and the props. It's a little tricky to explain, I guess. The man playing the role was entirely different from the person I had created in my own mind."

"I'm sorry, I don't follow that." There was genuine concern in his face, as if he wanted very much to know.

Suzanna lowered her eyes. There was no need to hurt her father.

She raised her head and resumed, saying, "It's as if I were enchanted by a particular love story when I was a child. A fairy tale my mother told me. Then, when I was in college, no longer a girl and not yet a woman, I met a young man who I thought was exactly like the hero of this fairy tale, and the little girl in me fell in love with him.

"But after we were married and living together, I discovered he wasn't really Prince Charming. He spent a great deal of time away at sea. And I found I really didn't care, because when we were together we didn't have much to talk about. We didn't have the same interests, and we bored each other. My painting, my complaining about the hack work I was doing, and my wanting to go back to art school just got on his nerves. And I was climbing the walls playing the handmaiden to his career and ambitions. I mean, he was a capable, decent man, and he really deserved a more dedicated, loyal wife." She shook her head. "I guess I'm not talking about fairy tales anymore, I'm describing Robert

nd me." She took a deep breath. "Does that make any
ense to you?" In her own voice she heard a note of
leading.

Her father was silent, his eyes downcast. Finally he
aid, in a voice that broke Suzanna's heart, "I'm so
orry your mother died. She might have warned you.
'ou can't relive old fairy tales."

He stood, met her eyes for a moment, then averted
is gaze and walked from the room. In his eyes in that
ne moment of encounter, there had been deep pain.
uzanna realized that he had known about her mother.
Ie had always known.

Suzanna's father had retired almost an hour
arlier, leaving her in the parlor trying to read. She
ould not focus her mind on the book and soon gave
p. She made herself a bourbon and water and sat
uietly nursing the drink to sedate her jangled nerves,
nen carefully washed and put away the glass. In her
ather's house, she thought ruefully, she was fast be-
oming a secret drinker.

After a while she climbed the wide oak staircase to
er bedroom. At the middle landing of the stairwell,
he stopped and gazed out the stained-glass window.
'he geometric patterns of glass reflected back sepa-
ated segments of Suzanna, each a different color—a
rotesque cubist portrait in which she was shattered
nd reduced to multihued, distorted fragments that
ere only vaguely recognizable. The image frightened
er. She fled up the stairs to her bedroom.

On reaching the imagined safety of her room, she
tood inside the door and rubbed her arms for warmth.
'hey felt cold and prickly. Still feeling edgy and
reoccupied, she sat down at her dressing table and
eached for her hairbrush. It was not where she
emembered leaving it that morning. Then she noticed

that all her bottles of perfumes and cosmetics were als
missing.

Mystified, she stood up and looked about. She immedi
ately spotted all the missing items on her bed. A
unknown fear suddenly grew within her, like a thorne
bud about to open.

She walked slowly across the room to the bed with
mounting feeling of panic. She reached for the brush
but her hand froze, trembling over the handle. Sh
stared at the arrangement of the brush, jars, bottles
and boxes as if she were hypnotized, a bird transfixe
by a snake.

The missing toilet articles were neatly laid out in th
center of the bed in the pattern of a navy anchor.

She did not know what to make of it. Then her nos
literally twitched and she sniffed, as if unconsciousl
scenting danger. There was a faint but alien spicy odo
in the room. She could not at first identify it, but i
stirred a memory, half-forgotten, of the old-fashione
barber shops in which she had, on occasion, waited fo
her grandfather as a child. Then, with a cold stab o
fear, she remembered. It was the same scent that ha
been in the dining room two nights before, when sh
had discovered the ghostly love lyrics.

He—it—had been in her bedroom.

She ran out the door to her father's room, but the
stopped at the threshold of the master bedroom.

His door was partly open, and from inside, Suzann
could hear her father's troubled, grating snore. Hi
breath caught like an engine stalling, then started agai
with a wheezy blast.

If she woke him, what could she possibly tell him
Someone had moved the cosmetics from her toilet table
There was the smell of a strange after-shave lotion i
her bedroom. She felt at once terrified and stupid.

She retreated back to her own room and stood shiver
ing at the foot of her bed. The feeling that she wa

dreadfully exposed in some way became worse and worse.

She thought she might as well give vent to her fears. Feeling like a neurotic old maid, she got down on her hands and knees and peered warily under the bed, ready to bolt at any strange shadow.

There was nothing there but dust bunnies and her slippers.

As Suzanna stood up, she heard the sound of footsteps downstairs. She tiptoed to the door and listened.

The sound was now very definite. Someone was walking across the vestibule on the ground floor. Then there were the heavy footfalls of a man coming up the steps.

Hardly daring to breathe, Suzanna slid the bolt on her door as quietly as possible. The clunk of the thick metal rod locking into place was thunderous to her ears.

She backed away from the door, her legs trembling. The footsteps reached the second-floor landing and then started across the floorboards.

Suzanna suddenly realized that her father was in danger. She sprang for the door, slammed the bolt open, and violently flung back the door with both hands to confront whatever horror haunted this house.

She smothered a scream.

The hall was totally empty.

There was no one there.

There was nothing . . . except, hanging in the air like incense, the now familiar and frightening sharp smell of cloves.

12

MASTER CHIEF HULL TECHNICIAN ROGER SLADE could hear the owls from the line shack at the end of the pier. He sipped his coffee and stared through the greasy window at the black outlines of spidery masts and antennas.

In the high masts and crows' nests of the deserted old ships, black great horned owls staked out their territories. At night the owls swept down and fed on the pigeons that roosted in the tiers below them. Every morning Slade's crew came aboard the mothballed warships to paint, take humidity readings, check the machinery and electrodes. The first thing they saw each morning was the savaged remains of the previous night's massacre. Slade wondered if the pigeons ever knew what slashed into them each night while they slept.

No one ever saw the owls, because they only came out at night. You could not pay a man enough to work on these ships at night. The workers were civilians, often old navy men. They liked working around ships, even the old mothballed ones. But they never felt at ease going belowdecks. They always went in groups, constantly looking over their shoulders. It was not the owls that frightened them.

Slade drank his coffee. It tasted as corrosive as acid and burned the lining of his stomach. He put the coffee aside. The workmen could use it for paint and rust remover. He wondered if it was the coffee that made everything he ate burn through his guts like jalapeño peppers and made his shit look like black tar. Thirty years of sludge made with boiler water. Put a spoon in the cup, Chief Bendowski had ordered him: If it doesn't stand up, the coffee's not strong enough. If it doesn't kill you, it'll make a man out of you. That was the other thing Bendowski always said. It was not the coffee that killed Bendowski off Okinawa.

Slade rose, put on his jacket, and stepped outside. There was a damp chill in the air. The fog swirled about the ships in fleecy, luminous clouds. The ships, however, were always dry. The dehumidifiers kept the moisture down to thirty-five to forty percent.

He walked down the pier between the dark, massive hulks. How far would he go tonight? Why did he goad himself? He knew what waited for him at the far end.

There was a violent flapping of wings like a series of muffled explosions to his left, and then a strangled, brief squawk. He stared, but he could see nothing more than the dim outline of the ship's superstructure. In the morning there would be pigeon bones on the deck.

He kept walking. From somewhere downriver a fog-horn wailed. There was always electricity in the air about the ships. Each vessel was like a great storage battery. The navy had discovered that rust could be prevented by keeping a cathodic charge on the ships. It stopped the electrolytic action. But the air about the ships crackled and made the workmen nervous.

Slade was the only one who would regularly stay past nightfall. His usual excuse was to finish up some paperwork. He had been lingering down on the pier often since the death of his wife, Martha. There was nothing for him at home now except idiotic TV shows and newspapers with stories he no longer understood. He avoided the Chiefs' Club on base. They were all younger, blowhard whiz-kids in computers, electronics, and missiles. They were always bullshitting about the high-paying civilian jobs they were going to get when they got out. Slade did not even know what they did. Whatever it was, it had not even existed when he joined up. He was no longer sure what *he* did anymore. After thirty years with the rating of damage controlman, the navy had changed the name of his job to "hull technician."

He should have retired at twenty years, as Martha had wanted. Most of his cronies had done that. He would only have drawn half-pay, but he would still have been young enough to get into something else. But get into what? All he had ever known, or wanted, since he was a kid was the navy.

He was an overtimer. He should have been pensioned off after thirty years, but the navy had let him stay on active duty. He was still young—he had joined up at eighteen—and, they thought, still healthy. Who else wanted this job as the caretaker of a graveyard of ships?

A shriek and a demonic laugh were suddenly flung at him from the deck of the ship to his left. Slade spun to face the horror, the blood curdling in his veins. A pair of luminous yellow-green eyes flashed down from the rail above him. Slade could see nothing but the glowing, venomous eyes and a dark body, blacker than the surrounding night, encasing them. There was a sharp, catlike hiss, a fierce snapping of mandibles and the outraged ruffling of feathers.

Slade breathed again, but the ache in his stomach that never went away was a stabbing pain. He wondered if Captain Blackwell also had shit like black tar. He was only a year or two older than Slade, but he *looked* old: totally gray hair and a deeply creased, craggy face. Had what they had done eaten away at Blackwell all these years, as it had eaten away at Slade, until now it had acquired a malignant life of its own?

Hoo-hoo-hoo-hoo! Slade jumped. It was not an owl's resonant hoot, but a bone-chilling, sepulchral laugh. The great horned owl's variety of frightening cries and shrieks was unnerving. A half-century before, the old Irish workers who lived in a nearby hilly area of the island, called Dublin, had bolted their doors at this banshee cry.

Then, the pier on which Slade walked had been known as Rotten Row. Following World War I and the naval disarmament treaties, a fleet of four-stackers had collected barnacles and rusted away here, while the owls moaned and shrieked in the ruins.

Now the four-stackers and the Irishmen were gone, the shanties of Dublin were swept away, and even the hill itself had been leveled, but the owls remained. The maintenance crews left them alone. One of the younger men had spotted a nest and climbed up. It had taken thirty stitches to close the gashes on his face and head made by the talons.

The workmen also avoided the *Santa Cruz*. There had been other accidents. A wrench fell off an over-hang and struck a welder in the head. His partner, however, distinctly remembered placing the wrench down on the deck. In another incident, an electrician had tripped and fallen headlong down a steel ladder. In the hospital he insisted he had been pushed. It was as if the galvanic power that seethed through the ship generated . . . rage.

From directly above Slade, a banshee shrieked, the sound piercing him like an icicle. It was followed by a hideous cackle. Slade looked up from his brooding and saw with alarm that he was close to the end of the pier. He had never ventured this far at night before, and his stomach ached with fear and a strange excitement. The black wall that loomed up on his left was the *Santa Cruz*.

The *Santa Cruz* was the cruiser he and Blackwell had

served aboard in World War II. It was where it had all happened thirty years before.

Suddenly Slade heard a shrill, lonely whistle. He froze, his nerves tingling with fear. It was not an owl this time. He recognized the sound of a bosun's pipe.

Slade's head swung up, and he stared into the blackness at the top of the gangway. He thought he saw shadows flanking the quarterdeck.

The pipe held one long high-pitched tone and then stopped. Someone was piping Slade back aboard the *Santa Cruz*.

Master Chief Hull Technician Slade whirled and ran for his life back down the pier.

13

BILL BINGHAM WAS BRAWNY. THE TWIN SLABS of trapezius muscles made his neck look thicker than it really was, but radiated a palpable physical strength that flowed from his shoulders and back through his haunches to his powerful thighs. He was a few pounds overweight, but except for that he would have been a classic Renaissance art model, Suzanna speculated, one of the subjects Michelangelo had discovered sweating and straining in the marble quarries of Carrara. But the extra flesh refuted any narcissism.

Suzanna found herself automatically comparing Bingham's physique to Michael's leaner and wirier body. They were entirely different, but she felt a compelling attraction to both men. They each stirred something deep within her. It was not only sex; they represented opposites—the ambivalence of her affections and needs.

Bingham, clad only in a pair of slash-sided trunks, stood barefooted on the prow of his speedboat at the bottom of the loading ramp, unshackling the trailer. "Okay, we're floating free." He waved his arm. "Ease her up and out."

The car on the ramp moved slowly forward and the submerged steel frame surfaced like a submarine breaking water. The driver, another marine officer whom Suzanna remembered only as Jim, waved as he drove by to park the car and trailer. Suzanna and Jim's wife, a pale blonde named Alice, waited at the top of the ramp. Alice was a half-dozen years younger than Suzanna, chatty and eager to please, an officer's wife on her first station. Suzanna liked her and—from an embittered chamber of her heart—pitied the girl. They started down toward the boat.

Bingham waved them off. "The water here's a little dirty. No point in your getting wet before you have to. I'll drive around to the boat dock."

Adjacent to the loading ramp there was an L-shaped concrete pier. Its longer section paralleled the Mare Island Strait, and the flotilla of mothballed warships was moored along its far side, their sepulchral ranks thrusting into the turbid waters.

The short lower section of the ell bridged the long pier to shore. It formed a sheltered basin on the landward side—a marina in which were docked the dinghies and Rhodesclass coats belonging to the Mare Island Sailing Club. The pier was deserted at midafternoon. The active sailors were already on the water. The remaining cluster of jaunty recreational boats tugged listlessly on their lines, dwarfed by the massive pier and the gloomy giants chained to the seaward side.

The sun glared off the water and the air on the baking concrete quivered in rising waves. Despite the heat, Suzanna felt a chill as she and Alice walked down the pier. Ahead a lone, black-clad figure stared straight at her, and in the glare the figure seemed to shimmer, disintegrate, and re-form like a mirage. But as Suzanna drew near, she realized that the man's eyes never wavered from her.

He was a chief petty officer and his narrow, deeply lined face seemed remotely familiar.

"You're Captain Blackwell's daughter, ain't you, miss?"

"Why, yes, I am."

"I'm Chief Slade," he said, as if the announcement should have special significance for her.

Suzanna nodded, but she could not place the man.

"I've known your father for a long time. Over thirty years."

Suzanna smiled pleasantly. "That's longer than I've known him."

"You shouldn't be here, Miss Blackwell. It's very dangerous." He said it in a hushed voice, as if fearful of being overheard.

"Why is it dangerous?"

"There are a lot of old ships here."

"We're not going aboard the ships. We're going waterskiing." She pointed to the seventeen-foot outboard chugging up to the dock below them. "With Captain Bingham, there," she added pointedly.

"It's not good for you to be here," the chief insisted adamantly. He did not seem to recognize Alice in his warning at all. There was nothing threatening in his manner, yet his pinched, saturnine face and his voice radiated something frightening. He was a dark bolt of fear on the sunny quay.

Alice tugged at her sleeve, and Suzanna blurted, "Yes, well, thank you for telling me." They quickly moved down the gangway to the boat.

"Boy, that's pretty spooky," Alice commented. *"Beware!"* She giggled nervously. "Abandon hope, all ye who enter here."

Suzanna suddenly remembered that she had seen the chief at her father's change-of-command ceremony. They had apparently known each other well in the past. She glanced back over her shoulder. The pier was empty.

Alice turned about. "He must have gone aboard one of the old ships," she reasoned, then added in the theatrical tremolo of a Shakespearean soothsayer, *"Beware."*

When Jim trotted onto the dock, Alice gleefully narrated the encounter to her husband.

"I didn't see him anywhere around. Sounds like he's a little bonkers."

Bingham helped Suzanna aboard with a gentle grip on her arm. "Old chiefs like that always create their own little world on a base," he said. "They resent *anyone*, but *especially* young marine officers on their day off, disturbing them." He throttled the engine to a raucous purr, and the boat moved slowly out of the basin. The long, high pier blocked Suzanna's full view of the old warships moored on the far side. The masts, antennas, and gunbarrels overhead looked like the stark branches of a grotesque, metallic forest. "The older the chief, the more isolated the station, the more they've created their own strange little world."

The outboard rounded the end of the pier and puttered into a channel between the ranks of ships stacked side to side, their prows and sterns forming the jagged walls of a narrow canyon.

Suzanna trailed her hand in the water, relishing the cool tingle against her fingers and wrist as she had as a girl, boating on the Virginia Tidewater. The burbling wake of her hand set off refracting ripples in the water. The reflections of her boatmates, the superstructures of the warships, and the clouds overhead swirled, distorted, and transformed. In the water there were faces, the faces of men, masks twisted in agony, tortured, mutilated. Suzanna screamed and recoiled in horror.

"What's the matter?" Bingham cried out in alarm.

Suzanna stared up at the warship they were passing. The deck was empty. She peered back into the water. The reflections were gone.

"I . . . I thought I saw faces in the water," she stuttered, confused and not at all certain what exactly she had seen. "Horrible faces."

To her surprise, Bingham laughed easily. "If you

stare at the water long enough, you can see anything. I've seen mermaids, sea serpents, even ghost ships sailing through the mists at night. The reflections play tricks with your perception. It's like watching clouds."

"Boy, I believe you," Alice chimed in. "All these old ships are spooky."

"To hell with them!" Jim shouted exuberantly. "The sun's past the yardarm. It's time to break out the beer."

"I hear you," Bingham seconded.

Jim opened the ice chest and handed out cans of Budweiser all around. Bingham ceremoniously raised the first beer of the day. "Semper fidelis," he toasted.

"Semper fi," Alice and Jim echoed.

Suzanna drank gratefully. She was still unsettled by the illusion she had glimpsed in the water. They had seemed, if not as tangible as flesh and blood, at least no less corporeal than the images in a television tube. The churning water in their wake, the streaks of oil creating twisting, greasy rainbows, had combined to produce a hypnotic effect. One could probably imagine just about anything. It was a turbulent Rorschach test. Suzanna wondered what the hallucination presaged about her state of mind. The bright afternoon sun cast long, sinister shadows in which all manner of demons might hide.

The boat broke into the open channel of the strait. Bingham wheeled northward and slightly throttled up the engine.

Jim pointed back at the desolate ships. "Look at all those old buckets," he exclaimed. "Wouldn't I just love a piece of the scrap-metal concession on them."

"Hey, jarhead, have a little respect," Bingham chided him. "A ship is a proud, living being, not just a piece of machinery."

"That's a rather strange sentiment for a marine," Suzanna commented.

Bingham knelt on the driver's seat, steering the boat

one-handed. In the oblique lighting of the afternoon sun, all his muscles—pectorals, deltoids, biceps—were articulated. He looked strong, hard, and tan, as if he had spent a lifetime steering boats upriver. "I spent a tour with the fleet marines," he said, "in charge of the detachment aboard the *Midway*. Maybe because I came to it as a stranger in a strange land, I didn't take for granted the things a navy man never questions." He glanced at Suzanna to see if she was listening, and then his eyes went back to scanning the water ahead. "But a ship *is* a living creature, moving under its own power. It has a highly developed nervous system with electronic eyes and ears and a voice to talk to other ships. Elaborate systems to communicate commands and information to the different organs of itself, just as a body does."

"But men really do all that," Suzanna argued.

Bingham shook his head. "When you become part of a ship's crew, you give up your will, perhaps even part of your soul. You are there only to serve the ship. Your most fundamental functions—when and where you sleep, eat, work, what you wear—are all dictated by the ship's needs. That's your only context and purpose. Captains and crews come and go, but ships have continuing personalities, reputations of their own. The *Midway*'s a great ship, the *Ranger* is a terrible ship. Navy men say it so automatically they don't even think about it. And one ship *is* invariably sloppy, while another racks up navy E's for efficiency year after year. They are ceremoniously christened with proper names, serve proudly fight valiantly, and die in agony or retire. The fact is that any ship, but especially a United States Navy ship, is always talked about and treated as if it were alive. And you can't convince me that they aren't."

Suzanna laughed. "I don't think I'll even try."

Bingham smiled at her and shook his head. "I'll tell you, all the time I was aboard the *Midway*, I felt like

Jonah, swallowed up by the Leviathan. It would spit me out only when it was goddamn ready."

Suzanna did not comment. Bingham's comments had sirred up old resentments, disappointments that had cut Suzanna deeply first as a child, a daughter, then later, as a wife. It was not the navy to which her father and her husband had been vassals, but their ships. Long at sea, ship and shipmates had become their family, their community, their whole world, until their life ashore had become a fading dream. Her father in particular had always been like a space traveler, riven from wife and daughter, alighting only now and then as if from distant planets, a man who could never linger for long.

Bingham suddenly throttled up, and the boat reared ahead. The roar of the seventy-five-horsepower Johnson engine echoed off the steel hulls of the derelict fleet as if their ghostly cannons were thundering in the boat's wake. The outboard raced under the concrete span of the Napa River Bridge.

The Mare Island Strait was actually the debouchment of the Napa River. Just north of the island, the river made a dogleg to the east. The eastern bank was a solid, tree-lined earth levee, but the western shore was a marsh of shifting sloughs and tules that stretched for miles and isolated Mare Island on the north. Here the river was as wide and placid as a lake.

The bawling outboard motor disturbed a flock of gulls who launched themselves from the mud flats and circled overhead, squawking. Once again Suzanna was sharply reminded of Tidewater Virginia and the reaches of the Chesapeake.

Suzanna had not skied since college, and she was extremely nervous about getting into the water.

"It's like riding a bicycle," Bingham assured her. "You don't forget."

With that encouragement, Suzanna opted for the

single slalom ski rather than the easier double boards. But once in the water, struggling to keep the tip of her ski up and the snaking coils of tow rope from tangling about her, she panicked. The boat chugged ahead, pulling the line taut, then suddenly blasted to full power. The slam of the water against the ski buckled her knees. Fiercely she gripped the handles of the towline, but the strain on her shoulders was socket wrenching. Water gushed into her face, blinding and choking her. She struggled to pull herself up out of the water and suddenly felt both feet yanked right out of the ski by an irresistible force, the towline snatched from her hands. She crashed into the water, submerging, but the lifebelt immediately popped her back to the surface.

By the time she located the ski and struggled back into it, the boat had circled to her. "You almost had it," Alice shouted.

"You almost had it," Bingham repeated. "You were fighting too hard and came too far forward. Just lean back and let the boat do the work. You'll get it this time."

All this hollow encouragement from strangers was more humiliating to Suzanna than her actual failure. She was fiercely determined to get up the next time.

As the line drew taut, Suzanna leaned back in the water, holding her breath as the water crashed against her face, and a moment later she was on top, the ski planing with quickening speed. She was wobbly, but she was indeed up and skiing. She stayed to the outside of the boat, too timid to attempt to whip across the churning wake this first time up.

They all took turns skiing through the afternoon. Alice was a beginner and rode two skis, awkwardly bent forward at the waist as if wracked by stomach cramps, while her husband continuously bellowed instructions. Jim's noisy commands were so bellicose that Suzanna grew embarrassed for the girl, who was holding on for dear life.

"Jesus, give her a break," Suzanna said. It was a thought, really, but she voiced it loud enough to be heard. She had taken an active dislike to Jim.

Bingham glanced at the lower-ranking officer, then winked at Suzanna. "Jim here believes in equal rights. He treats his wife just like a platoon of grunts."

"Damn right." Jim nodded truculently. "There's the right way, the wrong way, and the marine way." But he quieted down.

Suzanna appreciated Bingham's good-natured, joshing correction of an unnerving situation. If, as she suspected, he deliberately chose waterskiing as a recreation to show off his physical prowess, he had also displayed flashes of humor, intelligence, and a certain courtliness that Suzanna rather liked. Stripped of the dashing dress uniform, he was still a strong, attractive man at ease with himself.

She had accepted Bingham's invitation on short notice primarily to please her father. She had planned to stay at home, working on her portfolio for her job interview the next day, but Captain Blackwell was uncomfortable with the idea of his daughter sitting at home by herself while he was off on a fairway with Admiral Doyle. She had considered calling Michael, but in spite of their intimacy she felt some trepidation. Had he been busy, it would have been humiliating for her. Her father, on the other hand, was extravagantly tickled to have acted as matchmaker with a young officer of whom he greatly approved. What stupefied Suzanna was to discover within herself, after all these years, a great desire to please her father.

After everyone else had skied, Bingham turned the wheel over to Jim. The latter sat down in the driver's seat with a determined frown and gripped the wheel. "I'll try not to cut the line this time."

"I'd appreciate that," Bingham said, and plunged over the side. He skied aggressively and very well, banking so sharply on turns that his shoulder almost touched the water. He jumped the wake so powerfully that Suzanna could see daylight under the ski. He was undoubtedly showing off, but judging from the beaming expression on his face, he obviously took great physical joy from the power, speed, and exultant soaring.

At one point they anchored the boat, lolled in the sun like lizards, and drank beer. Suzanna had felt edgy all afternoon. At first she had thought it was a vague sense of guilt about her date with Bingham—however innocent—so soon after her affair with Michael. Then she chalked it up to her anxiety about skiing.

Yet it had turned out to be a thoroughly pleasant afternoon, alternately lazy and physically exhilarating. The practice and Bingham's tactful coaching had improved her waterskiing to the level at which she had performed in college. But the tremulous feeling still remained, a nervous foreboding she could neither put her finger on nor shake.

"Want to ski all the way in?" Bingham offered. They were just above the Napa River Bridge, which demarked the northern end of Mare Island.

Suzanna hesitated. She finished her beer in a single swig. "Last beer, last run," she laughed. "Both will just about finish me.

"Go ahead," Bingham insisted. "It's a shame to waste the run in."

"What the hell," Suzanna exclaimed, and dove overboard.

The boat sped to mid-channel, and Suzanna, her wet hair streaming behind her like a black battle pennant, skied bravely. She was, she realized, a little high, but not enough to affect her coordination too seriously. It was a confident, pleasurable, relaxed feeling. She let go with one hand and gave Bingham the signal to speed up. The ski momentarily surged ahead, then flattened out, planing at the higher speed. She cut sharply into the wake, rode up the stern wave, and vaulted into the air. When she landed, there was a momentary sinking sensation that she was about to fall, but she settled back and regained her balance.

Ahead, the massive gray arch of the bridge loomed up. The center span was wide enough for several boats abreast, but the hulking concrete pillars rushing at Suzanna gave her a stab of fear. She concentrated on riding directly behind the boat, in the outboard's wake. The boat was still speeding up. The cold, dark shadow of the bridge passing overhead, the massive stone pilings now hurtling by on both sides of her, were unnerving.

On the other side of the bridge she suddenly burst into a blood-red sun, low and blinding. The great steel monoliths of the graveyard fleet were a threatening dark mass just to her right. The boat was still inexplicably going faster. Was this Bingham's idea of a sadistic joke? Suzanna was angry and badly frightened.

She signaled him to slow down, but the frantic gesture threw her off balance. Squinting into the stinging spray and glare, she had a glimpse of Alice and Jim wildly waving at her. Their shouts were obliterated in the accelerating howl of the engine.

The boat went faster, faster. She hung on desperately. The water was a slate blur. At such a high speed she was terrified to let go. Hitting the water would be like hitting concrete. Her ski clattered over the choppy water, pounding jackhammer blows that sent shocks through her aching ankles, knees, and thighs.

The ski suddenly caught something and ripped right off both feet. She was yanked forward by the towline and crashed headfirst into the water with pulverizing force. The lifebelt was torn from her. Stunned, knocked almost unconscious, she felt herself sink, too paralyzed to command her arms and legs to move. She drifted down languidly, as if in a dream, experiencing a dread that was as much curiosity as fear. Suddenly she felt cold hands clutching at her.

She willed her eyes to open. The mutilated, tortured horrors she had glimpsed in the water earlier swarmed all about her. A mute rage contorted their disfigured faces, and their hands clawed at her body as if they wanted to rip her apart. She screamed, only to swallow water, drowning in the brackish depths of the river. For a moment she blacked out.

Gradually she became aware of a strong arm about her chest and felt herself rising, the darkness brightening. She weakly moved her arms and legs. As they surfaced, she broke from her rescuer's grasp and twisted about. She stared into a handsome, unmarred face and blue eyes that gazed back with unquenchable longing.

Then she gagged and coughed up water.

"Suzanna! My God, Suzanna. Hang on. We've got you." From a great distance she heard Bingham's voice call to her over the idling sputter of an engine.

Her rescuer seemed familiar, the face in a vaguely remembered dream. She sensed rather than distinctly saw the khaki uniform and the silver collar bars.

"Suzanna! Hang on." Bingham's voice was nearer.

The young officer drifted away and sank into the water. She tried to cry out, but she was still retching. Through a daze, she had a vision of blond hair and tan cloth swirling in the water, then it all blurred and dissolved like dye in a fast current.

"Okay, we've got you." Bingham was suddenly in the water next to her, the boat alongside.

Jim and Alice hauled her aboard as if she were dead weight. "Are you all right?" they both said at once. Then Alice gave a cry of dismay and lunged forward to cover her with a towel. The top of Suzanna's bathing suit had been torn down, exposing her white breasts, pale and pathetically vulnerable in contrast to her red-dened and tanned shoulders.

Choking, Suzanna gestured weakly toward the water. "The . . . the . . ."

"The what, Suzanna?" Bingham asked. "Don't worry about the damned lifebelt. God, I'm sorry. The throttle just jammed wide open. I don't know what happened." He held up a lacerated, bleeding hand. "I had to hammer it until I was bloody to close it. You're sure you're all right?"

Suzanna nodded and managed to say yes. She was still dazed and confused, orienting herself as if she had just awoken from a too-vivid, terrifying nightmare.

"I'm inching back to the dock," Bingham announced. "I'm not taking any chances until I take this motor apart piece by piece and find out what happened." He studied Suzanna's face with concern, then shook his head. "I'll say one thing. It was the most horrendous fall I've ever seen. You really hit hard. The water quaked."

Suzanna managed a smile. "I'm still shook up."

Bingham patted her shoulder comfortingly. "You have a right to be."

Alice sat down next to her in the stern seat. "It was really spectacular," she said, as if Suzanna had performed an awesome stunt.

Suzanna peered into the murky depths of the water. The gruesome men and bodies, the young officer who had rescued her, they had all seemed so *real*. Then, in a flash of recall, she knew why that tragic, handsome face had seemed so tantalizingly familiar. And she knew it *must* have been a dream, as poignant and terrorizing as life, but only a dream.

The outboard chugged into the shadow of a large warship, the cantilevered stern hanging out almost over them. Suzanna glanced up. The black letters, dripping with rust stains that looked exactly like dried blood against the gray paint, read SANTA CRUZ.

A wave of nausea overwhelmed Suzanna. She heaved over the gunwales and vomited up a stinging bile of river mud, beer, and brine.

14

ED RILEY WAS ALIVE. HE STRODE ACROSS THE deck of a U.S. Navy cruiser, his step lithe and springy, charged with the remembered vitality of youth, his hawkish eyes narrowed against the glare off the water. The throbbing voice recounted a history that he had lived. "Off the Japanese stronghold and far from safe harbor, the ship was suddenly hit by an aerial torpedo." There was a slight pause, as though Riley felt the echo of that sickening quake still trembling in the frame and plates of the ship. "Twenty-three men were killed instantly." There was pain in the voice. He had seen the mangled bodies of seamen. The twenty-three men were not just a statistic to Riley.

Sylvia Fields, the videotape editor, turned to Michael. "I have zero interest in this sort of thing," she confided, "but his voice always gives me goosebumps."

"That's the idea."

Riley now descended a steel ladder into the Stygian fire room. "It's so dark," Michael complained. "Isn't there any more color there?"

Sylvia played with the gain on the editing machine. The picture at first brightened, then the color began to wash out. "That's it. You're not shooting on the sunlit deck here."

Michael grunted an acknowledgment and studied the

157

sequence, as Riley somberly recounted how the damage-control crews had battled to control the flooding and keep the crippled ship afloat.

Ed Riley now existed only as minute particles of magnetic energy along a strip of plastic tape. Yet his image and words still spoke movingly of the horrors of men sacrificed and the glory of the battle won. It was particularly poignant for Michael because it seemed that for this one last tape, Riley had again briefly become alive. He emanated the full strength of whatever power he had once possessed. Here was the personality before it had been eaten away by the booze, the anger, the slashing marriages and divorces, and the degrading hanger-on jobs. Here was the passion that once moved men and women to rage, tears, laughter, and action. Michael was determined to finish the documentary. It would be an eloquent memorial to the man.

This fragment of Ed Riley's life was forever frozen in time. It might be endlessly recreated, even transmitted across the Pacific to rematerialize there. Or it might be erased, totally obliterated, and the particles of magnetic energy rearranged into the sight and sound of a mass killer, an archbishop, a used-car salesman and his transportation specials, or the skyline of Oakland.

Michael suddenly felt a hand secretly stroking his behind, then a thumb hooking in his belt to tug him into a discreet hug. "Kim said you'd be here. She said it would be all right if I dropped in. Is it?"

"It's all right. It's terrific." Without taking his eyes from the video, Michael reached down and, with the backs of his fingers, stroked the thigh pressing against his own. "How'd the interview go?"

"I don't really know. Strangely," Suzanna mused in his ear. "I'll tell you about it later. Can I buy you dinner?"

Before Michael could answer, an apparition on the video display startled him. "What the hell is that?"

"We got ghosts," Sylvia announced.

"Oh, shit!" Michael spat it out. The video picture had panned away from Ed Riley standing on the pier, and up the gangway of a warship. On the deck, ghastly figures appeared, transparent, as elusive as mist, but discernible as men. The camera cut to a shot of a gun mount, but somewhere in front of the gun, as if another piece of film had been inserted, a spectral face loomed up, staring at them with features that seemed to be made of scorched and rent gauze rather than of flesh and blood. Michael cursed angrily as the phantom crew appeared in each successive shot.

"What . . . What is it?" Suzanna whispered in a quaking voice.

"Ghosts!" Michael declared with disgust. The picture cut to a sequence aboard an aircraft carrier, and the double exposures evaporated as suddenly as they had appeared. "Let's keep our fingers crossed that it stopped. We've lost those shots, but save the voice-over."

"I rather like the effect," Sylvia said. "They look like they're from some old horror film."

"We don't know whose material it is."

"What is it? What is happening?" There was a distressed note in Suzanna's voice that made both Michael and Sylvia turn to her.

"That's a tape of our microwave relay. Someone was apparently transmitting on a close frequency and we picked them up." In the dim, splotchy light, Suzanna looked pale and shaken. "Are you all right?"

"The interference could be anything," Sylvia volunteered. "A network satellite feed. Or one of the cable systems using a microwave feed. They bounce off the Bay and hills around here. You can never be sure."

"Oh," Suzanna said weakly. She looked faint, but it might have been the greenish lighting.

"You all right?" Michael repeated with concern.

Suzanna dismissed his question with an embarrassed flutter of her hand. "I thought I saw . . . I'm all right. I had a bad fall yesterday. I guess I'm still a little shaken up."

"What happened?" Michael was alarmed.

She touched his face. "I'm all right, really. It was only waterskiing." She smiled, her eyes still distraught. "I don't want to interfere with your work."

Michael studied her closely. He was, in fact, pressed for time. He had the editing room for only fifteen more minutes before the news department took it over. "You sure?" She reassured him a third time, and he turned back to the video screen.

*T*ell me a ghost story."

Suzanna, wrapped in Michael's terry robe, sat curled in the window seat, her chin on her knee, toying with a glass of wine. She watched him with shining turquoise eyes, amused and dreamy in their satisfaction. Twilight played in the green irises, revealing sparkles of aquamarine, copper, and cobalt.

"What?" Michael asked, confused.

"Tell me your ghost story." There was a languid and lazy drawl to her voice, the contented purr of a cat that had been fed and stroked. "You once mentioned a psychic experience you had that converted you to your present life of unredeemed hedonism."

He raised his glass to her. "Pleasure is its own redemption," he stated pontifically. There were soft, wheedling notes in Suzanna's voice that twisted Michael about her little finger. It was a voice that hinted of finer antebellum days and the secrets of hot, magnolia-scented nights. Her accent seemed to come and go arbitrarily, and that, for Michael at least, was its beguiling charm. Yet he remained wary that he was so easily captivated by her Dixie wiles.

Suzanna's sudden shifts in mood intrigued and excited him. When she had first come to the studio that day she had been very nervous and edgy. Her job interview had apparently not gone as she expected.

"Is Harvey gay?" she had asked Michael almost immediately afterward.

"Yeah."

She nodded, frowning, her suspicions confirmed. "I definitely got those vibes."

"Did he like your work?"

"Oh, he was very complimentary. But he seemed like he was—oh, I don't know—sort of *distant*," she said in a bemused tone.

Suzanna, a stunning woman with an impressive portfolio of work, was apparently used to making considerably more of an impression on personal interviews. The station art director had shown only an academic interest in her work.

"Maybe Harvey was in one of his bitchy, misogynistic moods. I gather he has them. Did he give you any hint on what your prospects are?"

"Not really. He said he was still looking at other people's work, but he was going to have to make a decision soon. And I'm definitely in the running." She cocked an inquiring eyebrow at Michael.

"He probably told you everything he knows at the moment. He won't tell me anything more than he just told you."

"Oh, I didn't mean for you to get involved."

"Yes, you did."

"Ah, me," she crooned. "What's a poor little old Southern girl to do in a wicked, perverse world?"

But Suzanna seemed fidgety, restless. She compulsively touched Michael in soft, intimate fingerings, as if she could not keep her hands off him. When Michael mentioned dinner, it was Suzanna who suggested they get a pizza to go and a good bottle of wine, and watch the sunset from his apartment. She gave every impression, Michael thought, of a girl who wants to get laid wham-bam. Yet there was a neurotic, almost frantic intensity that bothered Michael. It was like walking through an area that was mined, his nerves buzzing, waiting for the explosion.

When they got to the apartment, he put the pizza in the oven to stay warm, poured the wine, and lit a joint. They sat on the window cushion, sipping the cabernet, sharing the joint back and forth. Their fingers lingered as they touched, Suzanna holding Michael's hand to her mouth to take a drag, in a heightening foreplay.

Suzanna eyed him with the same expectancy she had held since coming into the apartment. The reddening sun tinted her skin and hair. Michael snubbed out the joint, cradled her face in both hands, and kissed her.

"You okay?" he asked softly.

She nodded. "Yes," she said, then took a quick, shallow breath and shook her head. "No. Everything seems to make me jumpy. Frightens me. I don't know what the hell I want or where I fit in anymore."

Suzanna looked up at him, searching his face as though silently asking him if this was where she belonged.

Then she abruptly shook her head again. "I'm sorry. I don't mean to be a drag."

"You're not."

A sudden shudder shook her, and Michael put his arms about her and hugged her to him.

After a while he kissed her again, and she responded with passion, thrusting her tongue into his mouth.

They stripped each other's clothes off, still sitting in the bay window with the sun warm and cozy on their skin. Michael lowered her to the rug and she immediately hooked her leg over his hip. He felt the tension in her body, the taut muscles in her back, the clutching of her hands, a desperation that made him uneasy.

It would not be good, he thought. He flashed on the

hero of Holden Caulfield's adolescent fantasies in *The Catcher in the Rye*, the literary character who played women like a violin. Inspired, Michael began fiddling around, a little pizzicato here, a gentle bowing there. He kissed her breasts and softly stroked her belly and thighs. To his consternation, she sighed impatiently as if she wanted him to get on with it. He kissed her stomach, and then his probing fingers lightly touched some secret enfolded nerve that caused her hips to tense and heave at him. He went down on her and flicked the tip of his tongue into that hidden recess.

She whimpered and thrust both hands into his hair and gripped it as if she needed to hold on to something. He brought her to a shuddering, violently convulsing climax before he finally plunged into her.

Afterward she said, "You know, Michael, you don't always have to *totally* satisfy me. It's okay just to hold me and make love." But she gazed at Michael with an expression of pleased astonishment, and he just nodded and gloated silently. They lay sprawled out on the floor, with every cushion in the room from the window seat, couch, and chairs piled thickly under and about them, forming an upholstered seraglio.

She ran her fingertips over his back and ass, gingerly pressing the scars there, as an exploring child might, to see if they hurt. "How did this happen?"

"A mortar."

"Was it very serious?"

He shook his head. "They took twenty pieces of shrapnel out of my tush. I was lucky. *Very* lucky. I had a backpack stuffed with cans of film, and it absorbed chunks that should have killed me. As it was, no organs or bones were hit. I was hunkered down shooting at the time, and I caught the effects of the blast on film. The network loved it."

"Is that what brought you home?"

He shook his head. "I spent a month in the hospital.

As soon as I could hump a camera, I was back making forays into the combat zone."

"Why on earth?"

Why indeed? Michael had the words to explain it, but he could never recapture the feeling. It had been burned out of him. "I felt lucky. I had been blooded and survived. I had originally given myself a year—that was a standard tour for Americans. But there were Australian cameramen, English photographers, a French girl, who had all been there for years. When my year was up, I was just getting to feel like a pro. I was on top of it. My best work was ahead of me, and the network would give me more of a free hand. That's pretty heady when you're twenty-four."

Suzanna eyed him silently, then exclaimed, "You liked the war."

He shrugged. "There's just no way to answer that. There were times when I *loved* it. It was a rush. It was the most monumental thing I'd ever been involved in, probably ever will be in. But there were other times I'd get so fucking angry, so outraged, I'd want to kill someone. Anyone. Either side. It didn't make a difference."

He shook his head and clenched and unclenched his hands. "And there were times when I was just quivering jelly. It's a goddamn cliché. But until you've been that frightened, you don't know how accurate it is." He stared at the floor. There were doors about to open that must remain shut. He took a deep breath and said, "The pizza must be cold. We'll have to reheat it."

Suzanna respected his silence and ceased her questions. But when the hot, spicy aroma of the pizza inundated the room and the wine was poured, they discovered they'd worked up powerful appetites and ate with gusto.

When they had eaten, Suzanna curled up in the window seat with feline laziness and gazed out the window. Michael followed the movement of her eyes across the gambrel and mansard rooftops to the Bay and then to the beaux-arts fantasy of the Palace of Fine Arts. The spotlights at the base of the rotunda and massive colonnades cast an unearthly glow in the misty twilight, as if the entire structure had just materialized eerily from another time and place.

It was then that Suzanna turned to him and asked to be told his ghost story. It was the last story in the world that Michael wanted to tell her. He wondered what had ever made him mention it. He had thrown it out rather flippantly, he now remembered, after drinking half a bottle of champagne with breakfast.

In vino veritas. In wine there is also bullshit. He held his glass up to the rose twilight and turned it in his fingers, watching the scarlet cabernet swirl like hellfire. " 'Drink, for this is my blood,' " Michael said, not drinking. "I was wounded in 1970, which was also the great year for Napa Valley cabernet. I bled into the earth and lo! fat, juicy grapes sprang forth." He sipped and stared back into the glass, not daring to look at Suzanna, evading her eyes.

"In Vietnam, every meal a peasant ate used to be like a Catholic communion. They had buried their families in the ricefields for generations. And they believed that the souls of their ancestors passed into the rice and were inherited by the present generation when they ate the rice, or whatever vegetables they grew. They even made a point of grazing their cows on the grass that grew on the graves.

"But during the war, with that wonderful relentless logic of the military mind, we resettled the peasants in relocation camps and burned the villages to create fire-free zones. Then, to win the hearts and minds of the peasants, we shipped in tons of American rice to feed the millions of refugees we'd created. But they wouldn't eat it. The American rice had no 'soul,' you see. Instead they sold the American rice for pig food to get money to buy whatever Vietnamese rice, or 'soul food,' there was on the black market.

"Of course, no one, not even those killed in battle, could be returned to his home for burial. And so now Vietnam is haunted by legions of *mas*, angry ghosts who wander through eternity, their souls never to be inherited by their descendants."

Michael finally looked up at Suzanna. "Is that the ghost story you were going to tell me?" she asked.

"You don't like it?"

She did not answer him. Her level eyes held his in a searching gaze. She knew he had not told her the real story and she was disappointed. The color of Suzanna's eyes seemed to change subtly with her moods, as if whatever passion that burned behind them had shifted slightly in its spectrum. Her eyes had been a smoky green and now there was a blue shift to turquoise, as if signaling harder, darker mysteries. She turned to gaze out the window.

"Once upon a time," she began in a soft voice, "after the death of my mother, I moved into my grandparents' home in Virginia." And she told Michael of her mother's visitations in that bedroom with its antique fretwork, Charleston chiffonier, and chiffon curtains, which overlooked the James River. It was a room in which she and her mother had, each in her time, passed through their dreamy, romantic, stirring adolescence. She narrated the story without explanations, either Freudian or metaphysical, but simply as it had happened to her. When she finished, she looked levelly at Michael once again, the turquoise eyes open and without guile.

"Do you think I was crazy?" she asked.

The question startled Michael. "Do *you*?"

She shook her head, but it was a gesture of confusion, not one of denial. "I don't know. I'm not sure of anything anymore. That's why I wanted you to talk to me, tell me your experience."

He nodded. It was his turn for trust. "There was a time when the war was over for me," he said. "I had been in An Hoa with a marine company, and it got very bad. My closest friend, my soundman Danny Van Dang, was killed. We had gone through the war together. Hell, he mothered me through it. I guess I was a little crazy. There was a lot of it going around. And the network called me back to Saigon. I caught a plane out of Da Nang and I remember no one would sit near me. I stank because I'd been in the field for days and I hadn't changed clothes. It was just as well. I didn't want to talk to anyone. I was totally burned out. Well, the first thing that happens to me at Tan Son Nhut, the airport outside Saigon, is that this gyppo taxi driver I told to take me to the hotel starts heading out in the opposite direction. So I yell at him that it's in the other direction and he says, 'No, no, I take shortcut.' And he barrels ahead. I think, hey, this fucker's going to roll me. He's heading off into the native sections, and I've got all this high-priced camera equipment with me. I'm also lugging Danny's gear and personal effects back with me. I'm strung out and all alone, and I figure this guy's got a couple of henchmen at the other end of the line.

"What he doesn't know is that for the first time in two years in Vietnam, I'm armed. The press aren't supposed to carry weapons. A few did. They thought they were John Wayne. I never did, on principle. But in An Hoa at one point we were in deep shit, cut off. And this marine captain yells at me, 'You got anything but that camera?' I said, 'Hell, no.' He threw me a forty-five and I took it. If they overran us, they weren't going to check my press credentials. Most of the North Vietnamese troops had never seen a movie camera with a zoom lens before. It looked like a bazooka to them, and I was number-one target. So I took the forty-five. *Gratefully.* So much for principles. And it was still in my pack when this character decided to take me for a ride.

"So I took out the gun and pushed it against his head and said again, 'Caravelle Hotel.' I don't think he understood what I was doing because he kept straight ahead. So I cocked the gun, put it next to his ear, and pulled the trigger. I blew out the right side of the windshield. He drove right off the road before he came to a screeching stop. Then I repeat again, 'Caravelle Hotel,' and he does a manic U-turn and heads to Saigon, his foot to the floor. And if he hadn't, I might have blown his head off right then and there. I really don't know."

Michael paused. Suzanna's eyes were fixed intently on him, her lips slightly parted, her face looking pale and wan. "This is all by way of preamble," he explained. "When I got back to the hotel, I was operating on autopilot and the first thing I did was phone the bureau. Did the film get there all right? 'The film is terrific,' they said, 'but wrap up your life, you're being transferred to Tokyo.' 'I don't want to go to Japan,' I said. 'It's Japan or nothing,' they said. My accreditation with the military had been yanked. The network would no longer be responsible for me. And that was it. It was all over.

"I guess I could have gotten a job with another outfit, but it really was over for me. Mostly it was Danny's death. I was responsible for his having been there. But it was *all* the shit. Images kept coming back to me. A kid in Cambodia. Here he's a kid in junior high school. There he's a combat soldier. He's standing there with a helmet two sizes too big over his eyes, grinning into the camera, holding up two heads by the hair like trophies. There were the bodies stacked for counting after an air strike. There's a big bureaucratic decision here. Do we count the women and children? Hell, yes, it's a Viet Cong village, ain't it?

"Once, up in Quang Nam, I drove into a rice paddy

to take cover. I stirred it all up and suddenly this body comes rising out of the water up at me. Black, decomposed, grinning at me. I won't even try to describe the smell. I almost jumped right out of the ditch. But it was either stay there or risk getting shot. I stayed. You can get used to almost anything. After a while I started talking to this crazy corpse bobbing in the water, laughing at me. 'Well, pal, you've had some experience in these matters. What do you think our chances are?'

"I just sat there on the bed, thinking about all that and about Danny bleeding to death all over me. And I kept bouncing the forty-five in my hand. I thought, who was I to be alive? What the hell was I going to do with the rest of my life, anyway? I never again wanted to hump another camera around.

"I was still in those filthy clothes, and I thought, not this way. I'll at least be Oriental and dignified about it. So I showered, shampooed, even shaved and splashed on some Old Spice. A regular rite of purification. And I dressed in these clean white Japanese pajamas I had. Then I sat on the bed and picked up the forty-five again. It was still cocked from when I had shot out the cab window. I was really going to blow my brains out, and it didn't matter because I was already dead. Totally dead. I didn't feel anything anymore. Not a thing.

"Suddenly I saw something out of the corner of my eye. I looked up and there was a woman standing by the foot of the bed. A lovely woman dressed in a long white robe or gown. I saw her as clearly as I see you now. She looked Vietnamese, or maybe Cambodian. I don't know. Not young or old, ageless, and quite lovely with long black hair. She just looked at me, as if she were waiting. And I had the notion that she was waiting for me to blow my brains out and that she would still be there. Then she would lead me somewhere.

"Out of the blue—I mean I hadn't thought about sex for weeks—I wanted to touch and smell her hair and I wanted to feel her skin. To open her robe. And with that I got a hard-on. I don't know whether she could read my mind or just see the bulge poking in my pajamas, but she gave me a small smile. And then she shook her head and just faded away. One moment she was definitely standing there, and the next she had totally evaporated.

"It wasn't a dream, because I was totally awake, up and out of bed. But it might have been a hallucination because, Christ, I was drained. I won't pretend I was sane. I hefted the forty-five and it suddenly felt *heavy* and *ugly*, another piece of brutal machinery. I thought, I don't want to blow my brains and skull over the room with that. What a mess that would be. It was almost morning by then. I could hear the street traffic outside. And suddenly I felt . . . *hungry*. Hungry as hell. I didn't remember having eaten anything for a long time. So I changed into my civvies and went down to breakfast. Steak and eggs and hard rolls and very cold beer."

"Did you go to Tokyo?"

Michael shook his head. "I bummed a ride back here, to Travis Air Force Base. A 707 full of guys so delirious to be going home that they got drunk on one beer. And a cargo of aluminum coffins that instantly sobered them up when they saw them unloaded. We really shouldn't fly the bodies home to be buried. We should plow them under in Idaho, the Texas grasslands, the Kansas wheatfields. Then maybe we could all absorb the souls of the war dead with our meat and potatoes and granola. And we wouldn't have to go through it every generation."

"Did you see the woman in white again?"

"No. But I remember looking for her in very strange places before I left Saigon."

"I don't think I want to hear that part of the story," Suzanna said softly.

"I was out of my mind. There was a lot of that going

around. It was the fear, all the freaking grass, the drugs, the whole fucked-up collective insanity of the war. People saw ghosts all over the goddamn place, especially on night patrols. A friend of mine, a correspondent for *Time,* swore to God he saw—actually *saw*—the Four Horsemen of the Apocalypse over Hue."

Suzanna stared at him. "Then you don't believe in ghosts," she said, as if surprised.

He shook his head.

"Then what did I see?"

"You saw your mother. Or a lonely, frightened little girl did. And she saw her for as long as she needed her mother with her in order to survive."

Suzanna said nothing. She neither nodded in agreement nor challenged him.

"I don't need ghosts," Michael said. "I have my nightmares for company. But I'll tell you, there were nights when I'd wake up in the middle of the night and I'd know, just know, that the hall outside was stacked with dead bodies. Not ghosts, you see, just the dead. They weren't bothering anybody. They were just heaped, waiting to be bagged and choppered out. I'd smoke a cigarette and think about it and then go back to sleep. And in the morning they'd be gone. I guess the chopper came and lifted them out of the hall."

Michael reached forward, shyly, tentatively, as if he expected that Suzanna too might suddenly evaporate into the twilight. He ran his fingers through the waves of her dark hair and down the soft, fragrant column of her neck, reaching into the robe to caress the hollows of her shoulder.

"I'm still here," she said in a lulling, honeyed voice. "I promise I won't fade away like the woman in white."

Suzanna did not stay the night, however. She left shortly thereafter to make the long drive back to Mare Island. Michael felt abandoned, more desolate than ever. He had ripped off the scabs and revealed the unhealed, still inflamed wounds beneath, and she had comforted him briefly and left. Now he had to confront the night, with all its newly aroused horrors, alone.

He walked back to the bedroom and directly to the nightstand beside his bed. From underneath the pile of underwear he withdrew the forty-five. Why did he still have it? To remind himself, perhaps, that he did not have to suffer his nightmares, when he might his quietus make with a forty-five. Lowenstein, the Union Street Hamlet and Berkeley English Lit minor, hefted the dead brute weight of the gun in the palm of his hand. But in that sleep of death he might never wake from his nightmares. Aye, there's the rub.

The comfort of warm, satiny flesh against his, breakfast of strawberries and champagne—those were his rewards for returning each dawn from the realm of the dead. He had never again seen the lady in white, but the others—the Cambodian kid with his heady souvenirs, his dreadful pal from the rice paddy, and Danny, bloodless and white as parchment—they all still visited him regularly.

He forced himself to imagine Suzanna, her dark hair tousled about flushed cheeks, her green eyes gazing at him from that smoky place behind the retina where desire lurks. That was a vision to hold up before him like a cross to ward off the ghouls of the night. Still, he had not told her everything.

The phone suddenly rang, jarring him. He carefully replaced the forty-five beneath his underwear and closed the drawer.

"Hello."

"Sam Tanaka here, Mike. What's happening? That's not a rhetorical 'What's happening?' It's a question. I got your note. This *is* the original tape of Riley in that graveyard of ships."

"It can't be. It's got transmission ghosts all over one section."

"I know. I ran it. But *remember,* you specifically said not to transmit it. It would only confuse the news department. They might use it and butcher it. That's what you said." Tanaka had been the cameraman on that story.

"I know what I said. But Salazar must have sent it by mistake," Michael insisted. Ben Salazar had been the sound engineer.

"No way. I checked with him. Believe me, Mike, this is the tape we brought back ourselves. I marked it."

"Then what the hell is it? The equipment?"

"We've been using the same camera and recorder all along. It hasn't happened before, or since. It might have been a bad piece of tape."

"But the tape is wiped clean before it re-records, isn't it?"

"It should be. What can I tell you? We're at the state of the art, and the art still has bugs. Hey, I kind of like the effect. It's spooky."

"It is that."

"The ghosts are only on that one ship. The old cruiser we couldn't get aboard."

"I didn't realize that."

"Yeah, that's why I had all zoom shots and high angles," Tanaka explained.

"How did you get the shots on the deck?"

"A zoom from the carrier. Riley wanted a lot of shots of the *Santa Cruz.* That was the ship he was on during the invasion of Iwo Jima. He was very nostalgic about it. A real pain in the ass. Finally I said to him, 'Hey, man, I don't really share all your enthusiasm for this. I mean, my mother and father and grandparents spent the war interned in fucking Manzinar.' "

Michael laughed. "What did he say to that?"

"Not much. In fact, I think it depressed the hell out of him."

"Where the hell was I when all this was going on?"

"On the radio to the station."

"I remember now."

"Mike." Sam held him.

"Yeah."

"Take another look at the tape." There was an odd note in Tanaka's voice.

"Sure. But why?"

"The perspectives and positioning of the ghosts. See if you notice anything strange about them."

"Okay. I'll take a look."

When he hung up, Michael stared out the bay window. The Palace of Fine Arts was already veiled in mist, the spotlights an eerie glow at the base of ethereal columns that might disappear into the clouds like Brigadoon. In the shrouded distance a foghorn cried out, an inconsolable sorrow at Lands End. Michael hoped Suzanna had beaten the fog home.

15

BLACK POINT ROAD CUT OFF FROM HIGHWAY 101 in Marin County, slashed across the moors at the north end of the Bay to Black Point, and then fled on levees across the desolate salt marshes to Mare Island. It was a forbidding road, and when smothered by fog it was as deadly as it was gloomy. At each of the rare crossroads along that bleak highway, Suzanna half expected to encounter a gallows with a blackened corpse dangling from the gibbet. She was, she admitted to herself, in a very bizarre and Gothic frame of mind.

She had the chilling presentiment that something ghastly and unreasoning was gathering about her. The demons that had clawed at her in the water the day before—dragging her down until her lungs nearly burst and she blacked out—she had almost rationalized away as an hallucination, creatures from the delirium of nearly drowning.

But she had seen them again today on a television tape. Michael and his film editor had had a "scientific" explanation, but she did not believe it. On the television screen in that darkened editing studio, one face in particular had suddenly loomed up, materializing out of the mists of her childhood. The day before, she had seen the same face. It was that of the young officer who had rescued her in the water. The recognition had shaken Suzanna badly. It was totally irrational, a crazier phantom than even her mother's ghost.

As soon as she left Michael's apartment, Suzanna had pulled into a gas station and called her father at home. She felt an enormous wave of relief to find him there. She had been terrorized at the prospect of being alone, or ostensibly alone, in that empty Colonial manor with its sinister creaky floors, clamorous plumbing, and echoes of tragedy.

"Well, did you have dinner in San Francisco?" Captain Blackwell asked immediately.

"Yes, with a friend at the station." Then she added rather quickly, "I think the job interview went well. But it'll be a while before I know anything definitely."

"Good. I hope it works out for you. If that's what you want."

There was a moment of awkward silence, as if her father did not know what else to say. "Now that I've got my feet wet, I'm going to try and set up some other interviews," she said in the breach. "Other TV stations, ad agencies. But it's a little intimidating."

"Why? You've done this sort of work before, haven't you?"

"Not quite. The work I did in Norfolk and San Diego is really bush league. San Francisco is the majors in commercial art. But the art director I saw today seemed impressed with the work I did in Rome. You've never seen it, have you?"

"I still have the drawings you sent me when you were a child," her father mused over the phone. "One of your mother in a yellow dress."

Jesus Christ, Suzanna thought, my childhood sketches and watercolors. She was at once both touched and angered. Touched that he still possessed and apparently cherished them, irritated that he equated them with her professional work as an adult. If she had been a son, perhaps following in her father's footsteps, would he have mentioned the toy boats the son had once sailed?

"I think I've improved on my technique since then," she said. "I'm in my more mature, blue period."

"Well, I'd certainly like to see your new drawings." There was a lack of energy in his voice, a listlessness that conveyed the lateness of the hour.

"I'll show them to you when I get home."

Now, driving back to Mare Island, Suzanna realized with a pang that she had been talking to a stranger about whose feelings she knew next to nothing. *I still have the drawings you sent me when you were a child. One of your mother in a yellow dress.*

Suzanna had pictured her mother as a regal dark swan, a wistful smile playing lightly on her lips. Her father, on the other hand, had always seemed to Suzanna a rougher-hewn presence. Yet there was something sad and enigmatic in his eyes, an inaccessible image that Suzanna had tried to sketch as a child but only captured in her memory.

Or was her memory playing tricks on her?

Her father was waiting up for her. There was a drink on the table next to his chair.

"Whom did you have dinner with?" he asked.

Suzanna rested her portfolio against the side of her own chair. "A friend at the station. A producer there."

"Oh, that Lowenthal fellow."

"Lowen*stein*," Suzanna corrected, surprised that he remembered at all.

Her father frowned. "I realize you have to make contacts in your work. But is it really necessary to play up to that sort of person?"

"I like him *personally*," Suzanna insisted. There was a silent moment while her father absorbed her vehement *personally*. Then she added, "But he seems to have a few psychological problems."

"What sort of problems?" There was an edge of alarmed interest.

"He spent a few years in Vietnam as a TV cameraman. His experiences there seem to have upset him. He was wounded and even then stayed another year."

"Really?" Her father's eyes narrowed with attention.

Suzanna knew she had thrown out this irrelevant biographical data because it might pique her father's curiosity, even his approval. Except that it had deeply scarred Michael, his history was of little more than academic concern to her. It was his brooding looks, the flashes of humor, intelligence, and vulnerability that animated his eyes and smile, that had hooked her.

"How has it upset him?" her father asked.

"I gather he still has terrible nightmares about it," she heard herself say. I found Michael torn and bleeding, she thought, crawling on the floor, his eyes glazed with a numbing terror, and that is how I casually mentioned it to my father.

Yet her father nodded, and there was a troubled depth to his gaze, a compassion, which hinted that Suzanna—even in her cowardice—had unwittingly struck a nerve.

Blackwell took a swallow from his drink, and his look suddenly hardened. "Most of those TV guys, they were really nothing more than glorified war profiteers." His voice sounded weary rather than angry.

The remark immediately reminded Suzanna of Michael's account of his confrontations with senior officers. Although they had never met in Vietnam, the enmity between Michael and her father had been sealed in blood there, and that thought spawned a terrible sense of hopelessness in Suzanna.

"Would you rather I confined my social life to navy circles? Do a tour as your hostess and then marry another promising officer?"

"Would that be so terrible?"

The question evoked too much pain and sadness to answer truthfully. But rather than hurt her father, Suzanna shook her head and said nothing.

Her eyes wandered about the room. Every piece was familiar, resonant with memories. The furniture, pictures, and bricabrac had been meticulously packaged and shipped from base to base, each time her mother had set up housekeeping. Many pieces, such as the Philadelphia Queen Anne chair on which her father now sprawled, and the Hepplewhite mahogany cardtable, were heirlooms passed from her grandmother to her mother. The oversized Venetian sofa was meant to decorate an antebellum ballroom rather than the cramped living quarters of a transient naval officer.

Grey Knolls had always had a surplus of furniture, entire unused rooms that had remained elegantly furnished from the prolonged, leisurely visits and soirées of a bygone age. Grace Blackwell had moved about with an overabundance of furnishings for their plasterboard-walled apartments and tract houses. Each new dwelling had been more a caravansary of goods in transit than a settled home. Suzanna's father had apparently acquired nothing of his own over the years. There was an intimidating timeless quality to Grace Blackwell's settings that allowed no new intrusions. Suzanna's mother had never set foot in this house in northern California, yet it could not have been furnished more to suit her tragic, romantic fantasy of life had she decorated it herself.

"How come you never remarried?" Suzanna asked suddenly.

"My God, where did that question come from?" her father exclaimed.

"It suddenly occurred to me. A handsome, dashing man like you just naturally raises the question."

"You sounded *exactly* like your mother just then. That same belle-of-the-South accent when you want to be charming."

"You're avoiding the question, Captain."

"Not really." Her father smiled at her, but there was

a wistfulness in his expression that was so deep it bordered on pain. "I guess I never really got over your mother."

"You loved her that much?"

He shook his head. "It wasn't only that," he said in a barely audible whisper. "It was because she *hurt* me that much."

He stopped and swallowed, his Adam's apple bobbing convulsively, as if the act of swallowing were an agony. "I'm sorry," he said in a constricted voice. "But this is very difficult for me. I can't talk about it."

"Please, oh, please," Suzanna begged, tears suddenly welling in her eyes, a few falling down her face. "I have to know. I've been through one goddamn lousy marriage. And it wasn't Robert's fault. He was just the victim. I was trying to live out my mother's life and it didn't work."

Her father studied her grief-wracked face. "Your mother was trying to live out her own shattered dreams, and that didn't work either," he said in a bitter, cutting voice.

"Why?" Suzanna pleaded desperately.

Her father looked away, silent, and Suzanna feared that he had totally withdrawn into his own grief. But then he began talking, his voice quieter, less strained, as if Suzanna's streaming tears had, for the moment at least, released him. "Your mother had been engaged to be married before—I mean before we were married. A classmate of mine at Annapolis. Doug Kennedy. I didn't know him very well at the Academy, but I'd see them together occasionally at hops or Doug escorting her on his arm about the Academy."

Suzanna had been to the same dances and on identical walks. In the intervening decades neither the place itself—the gardens, the granite monuments and buildings—nor the uniforms of the gallant young men had changed. She was immediately thrust by the nostalgia in her father's voice back to that timeless harbor on the Chesapeake.

"She was, of course, the sort of girl young men noticed. But I never met her until after graduation. Doug and I were assigned to the same ship, a cruiser in the Pacific. I remember we were both terrifically excited. The assignment had been what we both requested. Our first choice. It meant we were going to be in the center of the action in the greatest naval war in history." He shook his head in wonderment. "I was so very young. Just twenty. They pushed us through Annapolis in three years during the war.

"And since we were going to be shipmates, Doug and I immediately became thick buddies. We had to take a train to San Francisco and there get transportation to Hawaii, where we'd pick up the ship. The night before we left, he and I and your mother—and a girl I don't even remember—all went out together. That was the first time I actually met Grace."

"Did you fall in love with her then?" Suzanna asked, innocent, guileless, and as enraptured as a child hearing this romantic fable for the first time from her father's side.

Her father gave her a small sad smile and shook his head. "No. She was Doug's girl. They were officially engaged. At the ring dance they had walked through the giant class ring together. And thereafter duty, honor, and country forbade me to have any dishonorable intentions toward her. And I must admit they were a handsome couple. Right out of a movie. Not the sort of movies they make nowadays, but the kind they made then. Romantic dreams," her father added in a softened voice.

Suzanna envisioned her father then, an angular, sharp-featured youth, pining away for his best friend's girl. It was indeed a forlorn old movie. She had seen her father's graduation photograph. The war and time had hewn and matured that adolescent homeliness to a craggy handsomeness. She wondered if her mother had ever really noticed the transformation, or if, in a memory frozen by sorrow, she had always compared the gawky young man she eventually married to her lost dreamboat.

"What happened then?"

"Then?" her father echoed, his voice distant, consumed in some private reverie. "Then Doug was killed. Off Okinawa. On May 15, 1945. Three months to the day before the war ended. It was a terrible day. Three kamikazes hit us, one after another. It was a nightmare. Half the crew was killed or wounded. We barely managed to save the ship, but we had to be towed to Ulithi for emergency repairs. We spent all that night transferring the wounded to a hospital ship. Some of them were so horribly burned you knew they would never make it. Then at noon we began the funeral services. We buried the dead at sea, their bodies wrapped in white canvas. It took us until sunset. That night I wrote your mother how much I shared her grief. I didn't really. I was just too numb with the horror of it all. I don't think I ever really registered which of that endless line of white mummies dropping over the side was Doug Kennedy."

Her father's narrative paused, and Suzanna had a mental image, as if in a silent, slow-motion movie, of a white-shrouded figure falling falling falling through space, then plunging noiselessly into dark water and sinking into the blackness, the white body disappearing into oblivion like a receding ghost.

"The ship was still in the yard undergoing repairs when the war ended. And there was this tremendous release that we all felt. As though a new world were about to begin. I was waiting for orders and I took leave to go to Washington to see about my next assignment. I stopped by to visit Grace—a condolence call, I said. But I was the decorated returning hero. I had really come to woo her," her father said emphatically, his eyes flashing in remembrance. "And I did. Perhaps your mother immediately accepted me because I was such a tangible connection with Doug. I don't really know. At the time I didn't really question my good fortune, I just giddily accepted it. Your mother seemed eager to get married as soon as possible. I guess we all were. It was a national epidemic. And you, my dear, were one of the first firecrackers in the postwar baby boom." Despite his brief flash of humor, her father suddenly dropped into a moody silence.

"When did things start to go bad between you and Mom?"

Her father avoided her eyes and stared down at the rug. "The first night. The wedding night," he said at last. "Only at the time I didn't even realize it. I was so delighted and proud to discover that your mother was still a virgin, that I was the first. Things then were quite different than they are now. And after your mother and I made love for the first time, she cried. She cried as if her heart might break. I was tremendously touched by what I thought were her tears for her lost innocence. I admit I was a little slow. It didn't dawn on me for a long time that the reason she was crying her heart out was that it hadn't been *him*."

My God, Suzanna thought helplessly, what can I possibly say to this man? There was nothing of comfort she could offer that would not be a lie.

"You wanted to know, and you are certainly *entitled* to know," her father stated in a listless voice. "It seems to have affected your own life. Perhaps we should have gotten a divorce. Undoubtedly that would have been more honest and perhaps even less painful, ultimately. But we had you. We both loved you very much, and you were our bond. Perhaps our only bond, aside from my own hope. I kept hoping that your mother would one day come out of this grief of hers, that one day I would come home from the sea and it would be *me* that Grace would be in love with, not some schoolgirl fantasy, some memory of the past. But it didn't happen that way. I stayed at sea longer and she only seemed to get worse, more morose—never outwardly hostile, really, just cold, withdrawn. I even suggested that she see a psychiatrist, that perhaps we both go for counseling. That was really rather radical for an Annapolis man. But she wouldn't hear of it. She said that she did not care to entertain some weird little Jewish doctor with her sexual fantasies. Highborn Southern ladies, I suppose, consider it more romantic to nurse their shattered adolescent infatuations with drink. And occasional indiscretions." There was a hard, bitter bite to her father's voice that Suzanna had not heard before.

"In the end it killed her. And I came home from the sea one last time to bury her. I remember, after the funeral, putting my arms about you and crying," he said in a softer voice.

Suzanna nodded in remembrance, gazing at her father through a blur of tears.

"I was still in love with your mother, and I remember thinking at that moment that it was all over. She had never loved me. And now she never would. *Not ever.*"

At this confession, pronounced in a voice that quaked on the edge of breaking, Suzanna herself broke down, dropped to her knees, put her head in her father's lap, and wept.

*A*fter her bath, Suzanna sat before the mirror of her dressing table, brushing her luxuriant hair one hundred times, a nightly discipline instituted by Grace Blackwell when Suzanna was still a rambunctious child.

"You look so much like your mother, it breaks my

heart just to look at you sometimes," her father had revealed before he retired to his bedroom, looking haggard and emotionally spent. Suzanna had tenderly kissed him on the bristly gray cheek, and he had given her a wan smile and whispered, "You even smell like her."

That was the *L'Air du Temps*. Gazing into the dressing glass at her reflection, Suzanna wondered if she would have clung as tenaciously to her mother's scents and idiosyncrasies if her mother had lived and she herself had gone through a daughter's normal rebellion to establish her own identity. Probably not.

Suddenly the hair on the back of Suzanna's neck tingled with a seething electricity. A faint alien odor teased her nostrils. She sniffed and the smell grew noticeably stronger, sweet, spicy. The aroma of wild cloves permeated the air about her.

She glanced up into the toilet mirror and noticed that the reflection of the room behind her seemed blurred, as if there were a distortion in the glass. As she watched, the blur congealed to a mist floating behind her left shoulder. She turned about. There was nothing there.

She looked back into the mirror. The mist was now a thick opaque cloud hovering behind her. With a start, she whirled. *There was still nothing there*. The room appeared perfectly normal.

She stood up, now frightened, and turned back to the mirror with a fearful expectancy. The cloud had formed into the vague but recognizable and threatening shape of a man.

She cried out and for the third time spun about, falling back against the lowboy. But the room was still totally empty. The mirror was reflecting back an image that did not exist in the room.

She swallowed hard, her throat constricted with terror, and by a supreme act of will turned back to look into the mirror.

The blond young naval officer gazed back at her, the soft blue eyes beseeching, almost mournful. It was the same face she had seen in the water the day before, the young man who had saved her—in a delirium, she had thought then. But this afternoon she had seen him again, this time among the electronic ghosts on a videotape.

Once more she turned and searched about her. But the young man who stood beside her in the mirror's reflection of her bedroom was invisible on this side of the looking glass. Calmer now, she *felt* his presence as an electric buzz on the fine hairs of her arms and neck, a subtle pressure like a gentle breeze on her cheeks.

She turned back to gaze at the apparition in the glass, and the desperate passion in his eyes reached out to her. "Who are you? What do you want?" she whispered. And as soon as she had voiced the questions, she knew the answers.

Suzanna recognized the handsome face that now gazed at her with mute desire. Grace Blackwell, lonely, weepy and nostalgic with bourbon, had often indiscreetly shown her daughter the secretly cherished photograph. And Suzanna now also labeled the sweet, spicy masculine scent, the old-fashioned distillate of rum and bayberries. It loomed like a love potion in the same spellbinding romantic legend of her childhood. It was an expensive imported bay rum, a bottle of which her mother had given to her doomed fiancé before he sailed, so that he would remember her every morning when he shaved.

"What do you want?" Suzanna again begged the ghost of Doug Kennedy. And yet she knew intuitively that the phantom who stared at her with such longing somehow wanted *her*.

16

MICHAEL RAN THE VIDEO TAPE ON THE MONitor in his office. When he had played it completely through, he muttered aloud to himself, "What's Tanaka talking about? There's nothing wrong with their perspectives and positions, whatever the hell they are."

As soon as he had articulated the thought, its implication struck him. He immediately reran the tape, now carefully studying each segment, often reversing the tape, running it again, freeze-framing scenes and carefully examining them.

Then he sprawled back on the couch, perplexed at his discovery. There was nothing wrong with the perspectives and positions. That was what was mystifying. If the ghosts had been a random transmission or another recording superimposed on his own, then the images would have been all over the screen, oversized and undersized, having no coherent relationship to their background. One or two might, by coincidence, fit into their setting, but not *all* of them.

There had to be a rational scientific explanation for the tape. Michael lay back on the couch and closed his eyes. He *imagined* the tape—in the original meaning of that word—as he formed and re-created the mental pictures. In a minute he had the answer. Tanaka had used a telephoto zoom lens, which distorts and telescopes distances. In addition, the figures themselves were semitransparent. Confronted with these two ambiguities, the mind automatically registered the images where they rationally should have been. But their apparent position was only an optical illusion.

For a third time, Michael ran the tape, again reversing it often, freeze-framing and analyzing the pictures in detail. His amazement leaped, scene by scene. When he finally sank back on the couch he was utterly dumbfounded. He sat entranced, staggered by the mystery of what he had discovered. He was oblivious to the calls and busy comings and goings in the adjoining office.

Suddenly there was a massive figure hovering over him, the bulk ominously blocking the light and casting a dark shadow on him. *"What the hell!"* Startled, Michael bolted up off the couch.

"Ha! You must have some guilty conscience. What have you been doing?" Morrison laughed.

Michael was almost as surprised to find the beefy sheriff's deputy from Contra Costa County in his office as he would have been if one of the taped apparitions had materialized. "I didn't hear you come in."

"Hell, you were in another world. I guess that's what they pay you to do. Dream up ideas for new programs. This one must be a lulu."

Michael nodded, still disturbed by Morrison's visit. "What brings you here? I thought you guys from the East Bay go into culture shock when you cross the bridge."

Morrison shook his head. "Naw. You just have to keep San Francisco in perspective, understand it's not for real. It's like Disneyland. Then you can handle it." He patted his thick gut. "Except the food. That's for real. Do you eat lunch?"

Michael checked his watch. It was past noon. He had spent the entire morning mesmerized by that tape. "Sure," Michael said. "What do you like?"

"Italian. But it likes me too much. I always get the sauce on me. And I got my *good* summer suit on."

Morrison was dressed in a light blue seersucker with a clean white shirt and a rep tie. With his bulk and florid face, he looked like a prosperous Southern lawyer. Whatever business had prompted his visit to San Francisco, it was not with Michael. It was probably to testify in federal court on a case. Morrison was just hitting him for a fancy lunch. If he were pounding a beat, he would be cadging apples.

"We'll get you the linguine and clams at Vanessi's," Michael said. "The white sauce won't show."

"Sounds good," Morrison agreed heartily.

On the drive to the restaurant, Morrison commented, "Couldn't help but notice you've got a lot of good-looking stuff at that station. I'm in the wrong business."

"That's TV. That's what we're selling. It's a visual medium. All good looks and flash."

"How'd *you* get the job?"

"Like you said, they still need one or two people to think it all out for them. It's a dirty, unglamorous job, but someone has to do it." Then, almost in the same breath, Michael shot, "What's new on Riley's death?"

"It's complicated," the cop said mysteriously. "I'll tell you about it at the restaurant. It takes some telling."

*V*anessi's was an old, comfortable North Beach restaurant, one in which even an Oakland cop would feel at ease. Morrison ordered a Coors and Michael did too. In the lull before the beer was served, Morrison started talking. "The black guy we picked up has changed his story, and this one's checking out. He still claims he never saw or heard of Riley."

"Then where'd he get the car?"

"Well, this is the story. He says he just found it open, with the keys in it, on Mare Island. Actually the keys were in the glove compartment lock. Maybe the last thing Riley did was take a hit off of that fancy flask. In any case, our alleged car thief had his own car, an old wreck, in the service garage, which is at that end of the base. But there was nothing they could do to get it running. Short of putting a new engine in it, that is. Which he couldn't pay for. So he claims he was just walking around down by the pier feeling very sorry for himself, when he spots this big, shiny Cadillac just sitting there wide open, the keys in it, a visitor's pass in the window, and no one in sight.

"Like I once said, this guy's no great long-range thinker, so he just jumped in and drove off the base. The thing is, we checked it out and we got lucky. The marine guard at the gate remembered this dude. The guard is also a blood, but one of these sharp guys that misses very little. And a brother, especially a bug-eyed, flaky one about his own age, driving a fancy land yacht, just naturally caught his attention. And he said something to the guy like, 'That's a *baaad* car, man,' or whatever they say to one another these days. But the guy doesn't say anything back. He just drives on through. The guard has got no reason to stop him. The guy had a regular visitor's pass. But"—and with this, Morrison tapped his temple and got a shrewd glint in his eye—"he definitely remembered the car and the dude with bug eyes."

The white-coated waiter brought the beer, and the conversation came to a halt while he poured. Morrison thirstily drained three-fourths of his glass and then let out a long appreciative sigh. "And that's why I'm here," he concluded.

"You got dressed up to tell me this?"

Morrison laughed. "Shit, no, not you. The FBI."

"The FBI?"

"Yep, a crime committed on a military installation is

their jurisdiction. It's out of my hands. It's their problem now."

"What about Riley?"

Morrison swirled the glass in his hand and stared down into the vortex of foam. "Yeah, that too," he said glumly. Michael had the impression that the cop was struggling to formulate a tactful withdrawal. "There's a new operative theory about that."

"For instance?" Michael said sharply.

"It was probably an accident of some sort." Morrison did not take his eyes off the beer glass.

"Of what sort?" Michael interrogated him angrily. "Your last goddamn 'operative theory' was that Riley was boiled to death after an orgy at the Sodom and Gomorrah Bathhouse."

Morrison held up his hands in surrender. "Okay, okay," he said sheepishly. "You want to hear what we've got or not?"

"Yeah sure."

"The pop-eyed queen didn't drive Riley's car off base until about six that evening."

"*What?* That doesn't make any sense."

"It checks out. That's when the guard saw him. And he didn't even leave his ship until four. That's when liberty went down. Now you left Riley on the dock about noon, right?"

"A little before." Michael had a painful memory of Riley, his pride wounded, a forlorn figure sulking on the pier as they drove off in the van.

"What happened to him?" Michael asked at last.

Morrison shrugged as if to plead ignorance.

"I mean the new operative theory."

"Let me ask you something first. There's nothing but old, mothballed World War II ships on that pier. The Pacific Reserve Fleet, that's what they call it officially. Your friend Riley, did he have any reason to ramble about by himself? Maybe hop aboard one of the ships?"

Riley, the once war correspondent and late middle-aged melancholy bard. Michael had an image of Riley wandering through the cocooned turrets and sealed ships' bridges, as desolate and silent as mausoleums. "Yeah," Michael said, nodding. "He was afflicted with terminal nostalgia. What happened to him?"

"This is only my guess. It's not official. The FBI guys, they get paid a lot more money because they have law degrees. But they don't have my experience cleaning up after freak industrial accidents. The Shell Oil refinery, Port Chicago, chemical plants, you name it."

"What happened?" Michael insisted a third time.

"With all due respect, I think your friend Riley blew himself up. There's a lot of volatile crap around these old ships. Any ammunition still around would be unstable as hell. But my guess would be a concentration of fumes, say in a closed compartment. He probably wouldn't have smelled anything, because gasoline kills your sense of smell. Riley might have lit a cigarette and *pow!* got blown right off the ship. Or he might have deliberately dove in, because he was on fire. That would explain the flash burns. The pain and shock would have been enough to stop his heart."

"But how the hell did his body get to Richmond?"

"Off Richmond," Morrison corrected. "The same way men traveled for millions of years before the wheel was invented. Just float on down the river. When the Bay's at ebb tide, the current at the end of that pier is fierce. It would carry him right into the Carquinez Strait at the south end of the island. And that current would sweep him right into the Bay near Richmond, which is exactly where the fishermen found him."

The waiter suddenly slapped two steaming, reeking plates of linguine and clams on the table. The long, narrow tongues of white pasta and the gray slugs of meat looked like a disembowelment. Michael's stomach heaved.

With great appetite, Morrison sprinkled cheese all over his plate. "You know, we got pretty good Italian restaurants in Oakland and Berkeley," he chortled hungrily. "But the food doesn't smell and taste the way it does here. I'll give you that." He forked greedily into the linguine. "It must be something in the air."

Michael nodded, agreeing, but he just felt queasy.

Michael did not go back to the office. He was too upset. Morrison's revelations had spawned a damning suspicion. If Riley had "accidentally" killed himself, as the police believed, then it was also possible he may have intentionally ended his own life. Had Riley committed suicide?

Michael had to think things out. He drove out to Aquatic Park and walked along the beach. The afternoon haze, shimmering with oblique sunlight, covered the Bay. Beyond Michael's sight, where the great Pacific tide through the Golden Gate finally faltered, was Mare Island.

He stared into the shining mist and visualized the row upon row of forsaken warships there, the wind making deep, amphoric sounds in their stacks. That last morning of Riley's life, the camera crew had driven directly from the change-of-command ceremony down to the desolate pier.

Riley had stood staring up at the cruiser moored alongside. He had then gazed down the long length of the pier, studying the formidable fleet fanning out into the brown waters of the channel behind it.

"Jesus Christ, look at them all," Ben Salazar, the soundman, swore softly. "I'll tell you, man, this place is bad karma." He and Sam Tanaka stood close by the news van, as if intimidated.

Michael stood nervously chewing on a fingernail. It was the first time he had been on a military base since his return from Vietnam. The pain, which he thought he had finally submerged, he now felt again, roiling in his guts. The sound of the wind was faint cries, whispers, murmurings through the bridges and guy wires. The sounds were as stirring as Michael's tortured memories, as elusive as the wind itself.

"This is hallowed ground, Michael," Riley said, staring at the great dark bastions about them.

Michael sensed it also in the windswept, lonely ruins, and it both drew him in and terrified him. "I've seen enough of blood-soaked hallowed grounds to last me to kingdom come," Michael responded.

"What the hell are they going to do with them all?" Salazar asked.

"Sell them for scrap."

"What a waste."

"There's no other use for them now."

It was evident that a great many ships had already been towed away and scrapped. From Michael's angle, the cruiser at the end of the pier, the *Santa Cruz*, looked like the point ship leading a great phalanx into battle. Large gaps had already been blasted in their ranks, but the *Santa Cruz* steamed ahead, separated from the aircraft carrier *Hancock*, the sleek cruisers *Providence* and *Canberra*, and the decimated lines of escorting destroyers.

"Where do you want to start?" Michael asked Riley.

The older man stood in the cold shadows of the cruiser and stared up at the dark, empty decks above him. They had been instructed not to go aboard the *Santa Cruz*. She was in a state of dangerous disrepair. From where he stood, Michael could see jagged tears in the ship's hull, gaping wounds in the superstructure that had been only superficially patched with sheet metal.

From the rapt expression on Riley's face, he had not heard a word of Michael's question.

"Ed . . . Ed. This is Mike. Do you read me? Over."

"What?" Riley blinked and stared at him, his eyes distant and confused.

"Where the hell were you?"

Riley shook his head. "I don't know. Okinawa. Iwo Jima. What? Thirty years ago." He said it with wonder, with regret, the memory more vivid, more exciting than his immediate life. He pointed over Michael's shoulder. "That's one of the Murderers."

"What?"

"The *Hancock* there. Before the invasion of Iwo Jima, literally hundreds of ships gathered in the lagoon at Ulithi. And in the center were the great carriers, almost a dozen of them, the *Wasp*, the *Hornet*, the *Yorktown*, the *Hancock* there." He rolled the names off, resonant and reverent with history, as if narrating a documentary unreeling somewhere in his mind's eye. "All lined up, one after another. We called it Murderer's Row."

Michael grunted. "That's the sort of lurid copy you get when you send sportscasters off to cover a war."

Riley did not hear him. "I flew combat missions from the deck of the *Hancock* there. In torpedo planes, blasting the Japanese fleet off Luzon. Dive-bombers smashing the guns on Okinawa." He was off again, back aboard a fast carrier task force, sweeping across the Pacific, hopping from island to island.

He turned slowly and gazed up at the *Santa Cruz*. "From that bridge, I watched the first marines crawl ashore on the black sand of Iwo Jima. The volcano Suribachi looming above us, etched in shellfire." Riley sounded as though he could see the glowering cone, sharply outlined against the bursts, and smell the choking billows of smoke.

"That's great stuff. Is it all in your story?"

Michael again came slowly into focus. Riley nodded. "That's what it's all about." He made a grandiose sweeping gesture with his hand. "These are the vessels of my history, Michael my boy. They are an augury, a portent that no matter how valiantly we beat on, like boats against the current, we are borne back ceaselessly into the past."

Michael arched an eyebrow. "Yeah, you and F. Scott Fitzgerald."

"Another bard of brooding Gaelic persuasion."

"From whom you borrow copy on occasion."

"I never borrow another man's work," Riley boomed in his most theatrical basso profundo. "I *steal* it. Remember this lesson, Michael. That which you borrow you must acknowledge and give back. But that which you steal you keep and make your own. All great men, whether artists or oil tycoons, are first of all great thieves."

Michael eyed him suspiciously and thought, Christ Almighty, it's not even noon and he's already half bagged. "Your purloined letters will hopefully inspire Sam here."

The lanky, adolescent-looking Japanese cameraman readjusted his battery belt and hoisted the minicamera back up onto his shoulder.

Riley regarded Tanaka with fishy eyes. A tall Sansei in Levi's jeans, swinging with miniaturized invented-in-America and made-in-Japan electronics, would record Edward Riley's *Götterdämmerung* for posterity. There was irony in that, laughter of the gods that mocked Riley, and Michael saw in his eyes, which had suddenly gone flat, that Riley felt it sharply.

Michael turned to Tanaka. "Get the pictures. Dramatic silhouettes of the guns, the ships, radar and superstructure against the sky. After the establishing shots, I don't want to see the shipyard or those hills in the background. Just water or sky. Play with the exposures. Use the ships to eclipse the sun, then pan to get a lens flare."

The cameraman stood nodding, eyes narrowed to

slits in concentration. He was Michael's protégé, as Michael had once been Riley's discovery. The young cameraman totally absorbed what his mentor was now explaining. Whenever he worked with Michael, he adopted the posture of an obedient student.

Tanaka was, by nature, not as aggressive as Michael, nor did he have his instinctive sense of story and drama. But Michael had recognized that Tanaka had an innate sensitivity for color and detail, an attention to composition so automatic it was unconscious. Frame for frame, he was a better cameraman than Michael had ever been.

"Ed got hold of great combat footage from the navy of the actual battles these ships have been in," Michael explained. "We plan to intercut the old film with your footage, sometimes superimpose it. Create the effect that these old ships are haunted with the sights, sounds, and crews of World War II. So we'll need long traveling shots down the empty decks, slow pans about the interiors." It would be an interesting film, but Michael could not work up any enthusiasm for it.

"What about the ships we're not allowed aboard?" Tanaka asked.

"In those cases, use your zoom." Michael pointed up at the *Santa Cruz*. "Slow zoom to the bridge. Closeups on the portholes. If we can find the right stock footage, we can create reverse points of view from the bridge and out of the portholes, so we look out of them into the battles of 1944 and '45."

Salazar heaved up to them, lugging the weight of the recorder as if it were a cement sack. Michael fixed his attention on him. "See if you can pick up some good eerie sounds. The wind, creaking moorings, water lapping against mournful derelicts."

"The sound of 'mournful derelicts.' You're kidding me." Salazar shook his head. "Jesus. That's what you get when you make a news cameraman into a director. You get a roadshow Bergman."

Michael laughed, but even in his own ears the laugh had a hollow, perfunctory sound. This graveyard of ships gave him the creeps.

He turned back to Riley. "Where do you want to start?"

"The *Canberra* there." He indicated a large warship some distance down the pier. "She fought at Eniwetok, Palau, Wake Island, the Marianas, the Battle of the Philippine Sea." His rich, vibrant voice rang off the names like bell tolls of history. He knew the copy by heart although he had not memorized it, because it was the most vivid drama of his own life.

The shooting went very quickly. Michael spotted immediately what shots he wanted, as if he too were working from a rehearsed scenario. Riley strode across the forward deck of the attack cruiser. Behind him a triad of long, slender naval guns sighted on a distant enemy. "Off the Japanese stronghold and far from safe harbor, the ship was suddenly hit by an aerial torpedo. Hit below her armor belt. A great, jagged hole was blown in the *Canberra*'s side. Twenty-three men were killed instantly." Riley turned and entered a hatch leading down into the ship's interior.

He descended a steel ladder, his steps clanging loudly, reverberating in the great steel cave of the fire room. "Forty-five thousand tons of water poured into this fire room and both engine rooms, completely flooding them. The *Canberra* stopped dead in the water, helpless."

Tanaka shot a sequence of dark, strongly shadowed cuts of abandoned engineering stations—a half-closed throttle, a broken steam-pressure gauge, an engine-order telegraph frozen in mid-signal.

On the bridge, Michael directed the cameraman to take a similar closeup of the engine-order telegraph there. The camera then pulled back to reveal Riley in a commanding stance, peering out through the weather screen. He turned to the camera. "The ship fought off one devastating air attack after another. A second American cruiser was gutted by a torpedo. Admiral Halsey, the task force commander, then ordered his other ships to withdraw, desert the two crippled cruisers. But Halsey was using them as bait. He wanted to lure the Japanese fleet out into the open, right into his mousetrap. The Japanese nibbled the cheese. Then their fleet sortied out from the Inland Sea to sink the *Canberra*."

The pager on Michael's belt suddenly buzzed. He cursed and hurried back to the news van to radio the station, rattling off instructions for the pickup shots as he exited.

When the news crew returned to the van, Michael was at the end of the dock, peering down the channel to the south. "Hiding somewhere out there in that mist and smog is Mount Diabolo. I think we have a clear shot to our microwave relay there," he said to Salazar. "They want to try a live pickup for the noon news. Let's see what kind of picture they get."

"Gotcha." Salazar hustled off to the van.

"What the hell do they want a live shot for?" Riley snapped. "We've already transmitted the story on the change-of-command to them."

"And they love it," Michael said. "They like it so much, they want you to do a live intro and tag since we're still here. It'll give the story more immediacy and importance."

"They just want to play with their electronic gimmicks," Riley said angrily.

"Hey, we need all the practice we can get."

All the new and unfamiliar electronic gadgetry made Riley very nervous. The two-pronged antenna on the news van's roof, looking like a raygun in a science-fiction B-movie, rose straight up out of the truck on a shining, stainless-steel piston. The raygun tilted up, then down slightly, pivoted to the left, then back to the right, zeroing in on its target.

Salazar came out of the van at a trot. "They got a good picture. They want a voice check." He handed Riley the microphone and adjusted the miniature earphone that was patched into the circuit in the studio. He then set up a small portable TV set, from which Riley could monitor what the station was transmitting. They were now in a commercial break. An Olympic champion was touting the virtues of a deodorant tampon.

"Any ideas for the live shot?" the cameraman asked.

Michael gestured impatiently. "How about Ed over here, so we get the ship and big guns in the background? He'll punditize on the navy and Mare Island's historic role for twenty seconds. After the establishing shot, a slight pan to the right picks up the other ships." Michael demonstrated, turning on his toes, his hands cupped to frame the shot.

"Continue the pan to pick up the shipyard activity farther down the waterfront, then start a slow zoom to that crest of trees behind the shipyard area. That's about where the park is. That way, when the station cuts to the footage in the park, the viewer will know exactly where he is and have a sense of the scope of the place. Unless, of course, you have a better idea."

Tanaka shook his head. "I'm very sorry I asked." He adjusted the camera on his shoulder and immediately began practicing the tricky shot.

"And don't linger on the ships," Michael snapped. "I don't want anyone to see that this is a mothballed fleet. That's another story entirely."

He sensed Tanaka's irritation, but the cameraman said nothing. He was pushing too hard. The currents of energy that flowed through their cameras and mikes to the microwave antenna to the station and then were transmitted back to them, amplified to one hundred thousand watts, seemed to charge Michael. It made his nerves buzz, crackle, and pop.

He studied the massive hulks of the old ships looming about him. Sunlight shifted in the shadows on the bulkheads, and in Michael's reverie the flashes became reflections of the muzzle flares of the big guns, shellfire on the beach.

It was not the remote broadcast that was making him jittery. It was these warships. The wind sighing and creaking in the masts and wires sounded like an angry whispering, murmurs of the rage that stirred in Michael's own uneasy heart.

He looked over at Riley. The man looked haggard, as if he had suddenly aged. Despite the breeze off the water, his face shone in the sunlight from an unhealthy, oily sweat. He nervously fingered a sheaf of notes and gazed with longing at his Cadillac, which stood parked on an asphalt pad at the water's edge.

From the way Riley smacked his lips with the dry, cottony taste in his mouth, Michael was certain the man was thinking about the flask in the glove compartment. It was a handsome flask, bound in leather etched with figures of pointing English setters and winging pheasants, the flask of a gentleman sportsman, one with which to ward off the chilling wet wind that blew off the Bay at night games in Candlestick Park, to nip the December frost in the stands at Kezar Stadium. But it was now high noon in July, and Ed Riley's need for a drink was no longer sporting. It had become like a great, gnawing toothache that permeated the man's entire mind and body.

"We're on five minutes in," Michael reminded him.

Riley was jarred from his alcoholic lusting. He nodded, said nothing, and concentrated on the chatter between the director and studio floormen coming over the receiver in his left ear. Everything today seemed to overload and confuse Riley, Michael noted.

Michael leaned into the news van to watch the TV monitor over Salazar's shoulder. The intro for "The News at Noon" was an urgent razzle-dazzle of whirling helicopters, jet-hopping politicians, Mideast tank battles, African famines, floods, fires, freeway carnage, and parades of gay libbers, images that flashed on the small screen and then dissolved to a closeup of bright, beaming Colleen Whitely, anchorpersonality of "The News at Noon."

On a second TV screen in the van—one that monitored Tanaka's camera—Michael watched Riley's eyes focus on the pretty, perky face. For Riley, Colleen was representative of the whole casting call of TV models, one-role actors, and cosmetic salesmen now posing as newsmen, the glossy wrapping on the TV news packages. Their faces and personalities were as interchangeable as department-store mannequins, but they furnished Riley with names and images to hate, a target for the confused frustration and anger churning in his guts. It was one of the few passions he could still get up.

There was a cue from the studio director, and simultaneously an image of Riley materialized over Colleen Whitely's left shoulder, an electronic mirror leagues away that reflected his slightly startled expression, his worried, averted eyes as he tried to decipher the garble of Colleen's chatty, unexpected question.

Then Riley looked up and stared into the black Cyclopean eye of the camera, his deadpan face hiding the thoughts nervously racing to frame an answer. "Yes, Colleen, the military budget cuts in Washington have caused more than a little concern here at Mare Island. It's not a political choice of guns or butter for the more than ten thousand civilian workers here, and the twenty-five hundred navy men and marines. For them and their families, the navy's big guns are their bread and butter."

The camera panned away from him, sweeping over

the fleet and shipyard beyond. Michael leaned out of the van. Riley was peering down at the clipboard the field in his right hand just below camera level, desperately scanning his scribbled notes to pick up his original storyline. "Since 1854, Mare Island has been building, repairing, and sending out the United States' big stick, our ships of war. This base was founded by David Farragut, one of the navy's greatest heroes and the nation's first admiral." Riley could hear the director's urgent countdown ticking in his ear, and he sped up. "Today another navy hero took his place in that long, historic line."

Michael glanced back at the monitor in time to note the almost imperceptible cut from the live shot to the videotape of the change-of-command ceremony taken two hours earlier. The navy band music swelled up into a rousing Sousa march, stirring jingoistic hearts for a few bars before fading under Riley's previously recorded narration, thus creating a seamless transition of time and place.

ENG—electronic news gathering. The speed of it always disoriented Riley. Pushbutton editing and instant replay merged with direct live transmissions from the field. There were no clear boundaries between the here and now and the then and there. With the old newsreel there had always been a clear line. Film was physical. It took time to be motorcycled, shipped, or airmailed, then chemically developed and mechanically cut. Riley could grasp it in his hand, hold it up to the light and look at it like a snapshot. It was always a tangible artifact of the past. A past, however recent, that he had always had time to absorb and integrate.

But TV news had leaped from the mechanical age of film to the electronic age, an eerie, timeless limbo of fleeting images on which Riley was never able to get a handle.

Michael now watched Riley interviewing Admiral Doyle

on the parade ground. Then there was a wider view of the park, and the camera panned to show the shipyard. Suddenly Riley, clutching his mike listlessly as if it were a dead drink, was on the screen to tag the story. He didn't speak, but kept staring somewhere off camera, and Michael realized with a sickening stab of panic that Riley did not know he was now on the air, *live*. Riley glanced up into the camera's omnivorous eye, and somewhere behind it he apparently glimpsed Tanaka gesturing wildly at him. He stared down frantically at his monitor to see himself staring down.

Then he looked back into the camera and ad-libbed something utterly banal, the pontificating timbre of Riley's voice disguising his panic and confusion. He glanced at his copy, extracted the last two lines, and then blew it all with a stentorian flourish: "This is Edward Riley at Mare Island. For the KSF Evening Edition."

Evening Edition. Oh, Jesus Christ. Riley stared into the fathomless, unforgiving lens.

"We're clear," Tanaka announced in a flat, expressionless voice.

"I didn't hear the director's cue coming out," Riley pleaded as Michael jumped out of the van. "Did he give one?"

"Loud and clear."

"There wasn't too much dead air, was there?"

"It seemed like hours. Where the hell were you?"

"Don't you dare talk to me in that tone of voice. I was doing the big stories when you were still shitting in your diapers."

"Before any of us were born," Michael bit off angrily. He felt betrayed. "I didn't want to do this goddamn gig in the first place. You talked me into it. Couldn't you at least have stayed sober for it?"

Michael regretted every word as soon as he had spoken. He saw the humiliation that engulfed Riley like a wave of nausea. Riley just stood there, the rheumy eyes blinking, as if he had been slapped.

There was nothing Michael could say, no apology he could make. What he had said was true, and he sharply felt the shame of it, both for Riley and himself. It had come to this.

"Let's wrap it," he ordered Tanaka and Salazar.

As the van drove off the pier and accelerated onto the road toward the causeway, Michael looked back. Riley had not moved. He stood at the foot of the gangway of one of the warships, as if defeat had settled on him like a black leaden cloak and he was too weary to take a step.

Michael would never forget that last sight of Ed Riley alive. The memory of it wrenched his heart.

The police now claimed that Riley had died there. A defeated old man had "accidentally" died on a deck of a ship on which he had stood in the full flood of his youth, every nerve end buzzing in the exhilaration and terror of those bygone battles. For Michael, that coincidence defied all probabilities.

No, Riley's death had to have been self-destruction, some strange, insane immolation. That thought pierced Michael with pain he thought he could not bear. Because, in part, he was responsible for Ed Riley' death.

The huge granite boulder thrust into the Pacific at Lands End, and Michael squatted crosslegged at its edge, staring out to sea. The sun was just breaking the hills to the east. It was too early for anyone but the most fanatic joggers on the shoreline trail. The infrequent runners who noted Michael on his perch above the waves would have assumed he was a meditator practicing his own morning discipline.

Michael was, in fact, casting Edward Riley's ashes into the sea. That had been specified in Riley's last will and testament. The will had been notably recent and detailed, as if he had had a premonition of death. Riley had left his house in Sausalito—acquired when he was in the chips, and real estate there was merely unreasonable rather than insane—to his estranged daughter, along with whatever was left of his money.

To Michael's surprise, Riley had willed "my young colleague his choice of any and all furniture, books, and artifacts in my house." Michael's first impulse was to defer to the daughter. It was not gallantry. He instinctively wanted to slough off Riley's memorabilia as a snake does an old skin. But when Michael met Kathleen Riley Smith, he changed his mind.

The daughter of Riley's first marriage had also inherited her father's defined patrician brow and nose, the strong jaw, but she had not lived happily in that handsome façade. Now in her mid-thirties, she looked embittered, shrewish. More than grieved, she seemed enraged by her father's death. Her hatred of him was barely contained. Michael felt that to turn over everything to her would be an offense to his friend's spirit.

Michael had inspected the house in Sausalito while the woman trailed him, her mouth pressed in a tight, cruel line. He selected the old oak rolltop desk, its chair and brass lamp. He and Riley had worked together at that desk, creating the first show after Michael's chaotic homecoming from Vietnam.

"It's a very good desk," the daughter said. She made it sound like an accusation rather than an evaluation.

"Yes, it is."

"I shouldn't let you have my father's things."

Michael said nothing, but he stared at her and thought, I'll get a court order and take everything if you don't back off. She must have read the thought in his face. She turned on her heel and walked away. She stood silently fuming while Michael went through Riley's library, book by book, and selected half of them.

He had then volunteered for this last rite. There was a commercial burial-at-sea service that sailed regularly from San Francisco to cast ashes upon the water for bread. But Michael felt compelled to carry out Riley's last request with his own hands.

"Were you and my father very close?" For the moment, Kathleen Riley Smith's curiosity overrode her spleen.

Michael explained briefly how Riley had given him his first job and interceded with the draft board when he ran off to Vietnam. He pointed to the couch in the living room. "I crashed here when I came back. I wasn't in very good shape."

"It sounds like he was a better father to you than he was to me." Bitterness twisted Kathleen's features, that handsome stencil of her father's, into something ugly.

Michael said nothing. Kathleen was married, and from her distraught looks and comments in his brief conversations with her, Michael had the definite impression that it was not a happy marriage. He pitied the poor husband she now flagellated for her father's sins of omission.

But she was right. In his way, Riley had loved Michael more than his own kith and kin. And in the end it was Michael who had delivered the unkindest cut of all. That guilt hung over him like a black, chilling cloud.

Now all that was left of Edward Riley were the ashes in the urn between Michael's feet at Lands End. He stood and removed the lid. It was illegal to dispose of the remains of the dead this close to shore. But Michael felt strongly that this promontory between San Francisco and the sea was the dramatic setting that Riley's theatrical spirit required.

The morning sun had risen by then. The Monterey cypresses, twisted and bent by the strong, shifting winds so that they resembled giant bonsai, threw long, grotesque shadows down the slope. Michael stood at the dizzying edge of the rock and slowly poured the ashes into the sea below. At this hour there was a strong offshore breeze at his back. It swept the ashes off into a silvery cloud that dispersed before reaching the water.

" 'Glorified and sanctified be God's great name throughout the world which He has created according to His will,' " Michael recited aloud. He sang the *Kaddish*, the mourner's prayer he had sung for his own father.

" 'May His great name be blessed forever and to all eternity. Blessed and praised, glorified and exalted, extolled and honored. . . .' " When the last of the remains swirled off into the air, Michael smashed the urn on the rock and flung the shards into the sea. There was now nothing left of Riley. Not a mote. He had disappeared somewhere on the wind.

There was a sudden gust, and the wind shifted. It blew a thick gray cloud back into Michael's face, coating him with the ashes. He was horrified. He gasped and frantically beat the ashes off him.

Then it struck him that it was, after all, Riley, a final embrace staged as a ghastly joke. Anything more maudlin would have been out of character.

Michael laughed uproariously, slapped his clothes, and vigorously rubbed and shook his hair. The stiff wind washed the light ash completely off him. But a passerby on the winding trails at the top of the headland, seeing Michael rollicking on that precipice below, would have thought he was absolutely, dangerously mad.

17

I'll be seeing you
In all the old familiar places
That this heart of mine embraces,
All day through."

The voice was knowing, almost mocking. There was a slur and insinuation to it that had not been there twenty years earlier. The brass blared out, jazzy and discordant, and the beat had a heavy erotic throb.

"In that small cafe,
The park across the way,
The . . . the children's carousel,
The chestnut tree, the wishing well."

Frank Sinatra's voice trickled and bounced over the lyrics, juiced up a phrase here, crooned a word there, leading the band with total confidence, even as it sliced through rhythms and stretched out phrases long past the beat.

The ghost of Doug Kennedy had once written out the lyrics for Suzanna. She still had that handwritten note, a love letter that transcended the barriers of time and space between them. It was his only physical manifestation. Two nights before, he had appeared to her fleetingly, a silent, poignant image reflected in her bedroom mirror.

Had she hallucinated that?

Was she going insane?

Suzanna had tried to tell Michael about the ghost. But he would not believe it. He did not believe Suzanna had had the power to materialize her mother as a child. Michael was convinced of his own craziness when he had seen a ghost, and that still frightened him.

But if Suzanna had not imagined Doug Kennedy's ghost, if he really existed, then her mother's spirit had also been real. She had not created it in some neurotic childhood fantasy. Her mother's love had been strong enough to transcend death and nurture her. If Suzanna knew that with certainty, then she would be whole, complete, freed from the doubts and obsessions that plagued her.

For Suzanna, it was a choice between insanity and finally being released from the past to live her own life.

She had to know.

She had to communicate with the spirit that haunted the house on Mare Island. But Suzanna needed something to bridge the years, a charm that resonated physically with Doug Kennedy's tragic heart and tugged at him. She felt intuitively that the old song to which he and her mother had danced, and that was on their lips as a vow, might have that power.

Suzanna combed record stores all over San Francisco, searching for a recording of "I'll Be Seeing You." It had been her mother's threnody for her lost sweetheart, the waxed lamentation she had spun over and over and over at seventy-eight revolutions per minute on the empty, bourbon-stoked nights. It had been "their song," with all the romantic, pubescent magic and heart-tugging that cornball phrase evokes.

Suzanna was terrifically excited when the shop owner

in a store that specialized in out-of-date collector items, an enormously fat man, waddled back from the dusty racks in the rear of the shop proudly bearing the album *I Remember Tommy*. . . . It was a tribute to Tommy Dorsey that Sinatra had recorded in 1961.

But from the opening blare of brass, Suzanna's excitement steadily ebbed. This was not the sentimental ballad of lovers separated by the World War. It was not the voice of an innocent young man mooning for his betrothed. On her mother's recording, the young Sinatra's voice had been manly and sincere, a voice without guile or sophistication that had only recently breached adolescence. Behind it, Dorsey's dance band, with its romantic trombone and swinging woodwinds, called up the young couples smoothly swaying on a moonlit terrace.

But the newer recording was a hip, belting version by an older, wiser Sinatra sexually teasing a casino showroom. It was as sentimental as a one-night stand in Las Vegas.

> *"Yes, I will dig you in the early bright,*
> *And when the night is new . . ."*

The punched-up intonations and phrasing would be as alien to the spirit of Doug Kennedy as the modern, dissonant riffs.

> *". . . I'll be looking at the moon,*
> *I'll be looking but I'll be seeing you."*

There was a concluding blast of brass, and it cut off abruptly. Suzanna knew that this arrangement would never work. She needed the original recording, the transported ghost of the music of that bygone time.

But if she did recreate the old music, the song

indelibly transcending the years, what would happen then?

The question both frightened and thrilled her.

       Please have lunch with my father and me next Wednesday."

"Your father hates me."

"My father doesn't hate you. He doesn't *know* you."

"He knows I'm making love to his daughter."

"He doesn't know that."

"Oh, yes, he does. Believe me, fathers have special Freudian antennas for that sort of thing where their daughters are concerned."

"Oh, really."

Suzanna sat ensconced in the bay-window seat of Michael's apartment, toying with a glass of wine. She stalked Michael with her eyes.

There was something essentially alien and attractive about Michael. He did not remind her at all of her ex-husband, or her father, and without those built-in inhibitions she felt comfortable and somehow more free in his company.

And she loved Michael's apartment, especially the window seat with its teasing view of the Bay, the Greco-Roman rotunda and columns of the Palace of Fine Arts, the Golden Gate Bridge and the Pacific sunset, each framed by the adjacent roofs, gables, and Victorian peaks. The thought of moving in with Michael occurred to her, and with it, like a dark wingmate, immediately flew another, more disturbing thought.

"Do you have a girlfriend?"

"What?" Michael was startled by the question.

"Do you have a girlfriend?" Suzanna repeated. "I mean, you're an attractive man. You're successful in a glamorous job. There's lots of good-looking women available. You should have a girlfriend. Someone relatively steady. I'm curious. Hell, I'm more than curious. Are you juggling two or three of us?" Suzanna had meant the question to be humorous, bantering, but she heard the sharp edge in her own voice.

"Well, for Chrissakes, this . . . this has been just like having an affair with a married woman. I mean, you pop into town for an interview, or to go shopping. We come here for a brief romantic tryst, and then you have to hurry home. Do *you* have someone you haven't told me about? Or someone you're living with?"

It was Suzanna's turn to be startled. "No, of course not. You know I'm living with my father. It's just that he—" She did not finish the thought. It struck her that Michael was right. There was always something rushed and clandestine about their rendezvous, as if Michael were to be kept secret from her father and whatever ghosts hovered about her on Mare Island. It was perhaps that atmosphere of assignation that gave her lovemaking with Michael its delicious quality.

"You're rather old to be living with Daddy, still answering to him."

"I don't have to answer to my father. *Or to you.*" Suzanna was defensive, angry.

She took a deep breath to calm down, then shook her head. "There's no one else . . . like that." Even she heard the hesitation in her voice and wondered about it.

"Then stay the night."

"I can't. I just can't."

Michael said nothing, and there was a heavy, hurt silence.

She smiled at him. "You're evading my question. Do you have a girl?" Again there was an involuntary bite to the question, where Suzanna had intended to be teasing.

There was a meanness in Michael's grin that Suzanna did not like. "I have lots of girls," he said nastily.

Suzanna's anger flared. "You can really be an asshole sometimes," she snapped. "Did any of them ever tell you that?"

"Oh, yes," Michael nodded. "Usually on the third date. Or after we've slept together. Whichever comes first."

"You son of a bitch." She flung the glass of red wine right in Michael's face.

She had been so swift that Michael had had no time to react, and he sat stock-still, shocked, the red wine dripping down his face and onto his neck and shirt in bloody rivulets, looking like the victim of a ghastly head wound. Suzanna felt immediately contrite.

He started to rise, but Suzanna immediately leaned forward and kissed him. "I'm sorry," she murmured. "There's no one else, believe me." She kissed him again, then licked the corner of his mouth. "You've just been bloodied in our first lovers' quarrel."

He kissed her back. "You're getting wine on me," she protested.

"Serves you right."

She licked the wine off his chin and cheeks.

"There's no girl," he offered. "I haven't been very good at long-term relationships. I don't age very well."

"You taste just fine to me." She flicked her tongue at the scarlet beads dripping off the tip of his nose. "A little young, impudent perhaps."

"But I'm getting better," Michael whispered. "Stabilizing. Getting mellower. God, how I'd like to be mellower."

Suzanna licked the bridge of his nose, then tasted rather than kissed his forehead.

"Hearty, robust, and mellow. That's what I'd like to be when I finally mature," Michael muttered. "With a tantalizing aftertaste that lingers on the palate."

She licked the wine from his ear. "You sound delicious. I can hardly wait."

Michael took her face in both his hands and studied

her solemnly. "Most girls would have been totally spooked by that first night. The nightmares. Wondered what kind of psycho they were involved with."

"I'm not a *girl*." Suzanna put her lips lightly against his. "I don't spook that easily." She kissed him on the throat. On the contrary, she felt free with Michael, she realized, because from the very first night he had been so totally naked and vulnerable in front of her.

She unbuttoned his shirt, planting a kiss on his chest at each undone button. At his stomach she felt the quick intake of breath, and his abdomen quivered under her lips.

She looked up at Michael, eyeing him like a mischievous, experimenting child who is intent on being wicked. She unbuckled his belt and tugged his pants and underpants down over his ankles. Then she removed her own blouse.

She bent over his ankles and made several quick skipping, playful kisses up his hairy calf to the crook of his knee, then ran her mouth up his inner thigh, nibbling at the soft white flesh. She could palpably sense his mounting excitement, the rock-hard tension in his thigh muscles, as her succulent mouth approached his cock. But she angled off to the left, teasing him, her mouth a curious puppy moving up his loins. She bypassed his inflamed penis, red and painful in its engorgement.

Again she gazed up at Michael, her shining wet mouth twisting into a provocative smile, and nonchalantly tossed her head. Her long dark hair swept across his belly, gently enveloping and swirling about his distended prick, her tresses flowing and seething like a fall of black water in slow motion. The caress of it had a galvanizing effect on Michael. He lay back with his eyes closed, the delicate lids fluttering, his mouth agape, in an ecstatic torment.

Suzanna moved her head in that slow, sweeping circle several times, each time glancing up to watch his face. It was a strange pleasure to tease and intimately explore Michael's body, testing his reaction, how he writhed or relaxed at different touches. Her lips now moved from left to right across the white flesh of his belly, peppered with black curling hairs. The transit brought her breasts against his cock, first one, then the other, the soft globes cushioning against it, cradling and squeezing the hard, insistent, feverish rod between them. At each touch she felt Michael quiver as if he might explode under her.

She moved down his right loin until her lips were at his scrotum. The hairy, wrinkled sack that was so sensitive, so vulnerable—that Achilles' heel of all men—elicited her tenderness, provoked amusement. She took one ball gently in her mouth, softly sucking it, then the other. She fixed her teeth on it, holding it between them for a moment, and felt Michael tremble. She gave it a slight playful nip, and a bolt of pain momentarily stiffened his body. "Jesus," he whimpered. She immediately released his balls, but she sensed that the stab of pain had, for a moment, been no less tantalizing than her strokes of pleasure.

She tilted her head and now took the root of his joint between her lips, sliding her mouth back and forth along it, still playing the wicked little girl. She drew back to study the head of his penis, the glans swelling from the taut shaft like an angry red bud about to burst into some extraordinary lush flower. She flicked her tongue at it like a serpent sensing its textures.

Then she took it in her mouth, fully tasting it for the first time. She fingered his balls in one hand, grasped the root in the other, and sucked at him with a voracious insistence that almost immediately made him come in an exploding hot rush.

He moaned and his hips thrust and heaved under her, and then he melted back, panting. She still held on to him with both hands, sucking and licking away the sticky white roe, tasting its bland, buttery flavor, licking at the milky strings that stretched at the corner of her mouth and from her lips to Michael's penis. She suddenly started giggling.

They then rested on the floor, cuddling on the cozy heaping of pillows. She ran her fingers through the curly, soft black hairs of his chest, fascinated by the way the hair thickened there but the muscles on his shoulders, upper arms, and back were perfectly clear. Of all the parts of him, she particularly loved Michael's chest. It demanded nothing of her, but was there, solid and comforting, for her. "Do you think it's all just sex between us?" she mused.

"I certainly hope so. I'd hate to think we were getting emotionally involved."

Suzanna raised herself up to look at Michael. There was a playfulness in his eyes that caught and held her glance. Its very teasing quality acknowledged that they were, in truth, involved, deeply and intimately.

After a moment Michael asked in a soft voice, "What the hell were you laughing at before?"

"I wasn't laughing. I was *giggling*."

"Okay, giggling then."

"I just had a thought." She wiggled up his chest to play with his earlobe. "I remembered what you said once about the Vietnamese concept of absorbing their ancestors' souls with their food. And I wondered what sort of holy—or unholy—communion we just had."

"You swallowed my soul," Michael laughed softly. "My primal fluid, my seed is passing from your stomach into your blood right now. It's flowing through every cell of you. I'm a part of you. Does that frighten you?"

"I told you I don't frighten easily. Actually it's an exciting thought."

"Great. Let's do it again."

"Oh, no. Turnabout is fair play. Unless you're up to something else."

At that moment the phone rang, sending a start through Suzanna. She and Michael looked at each other warily. The phone jarred them a second time. Michael moaned and struggled to his feet. Suzanna was very apprehensive. To her, the jangling bell announced a rival. It smashed the intimacy of the moment, shattering it forever.

"Hello." Michael answered the phone rather than let his answering machine take the message. Suzanna wondered if he expected a call or was simply taking a chance that it was not some other liaison calling. Her jealousy ebbed for the moment or two it took Michael to listen to the party on the other end of the line and then comment softly, "Now that's not true. We had dinner together last week." There was something in his tone, at once defensive and charming, that indicated to Suzanna that he was talking to another woman. She got a hollow fluttering feeling in her stomach, and her cheeks flushed hotly.

"No, I'm fine. Working hard." Suzanna could hear nothing of the other end of the conversation.

"I'm still working on that. And I'm trying to put together 'The New Frontiers,' that pilot for syndication I told you about." Pause. "That's a bizarre question." There was another pause. "A woman here with me?" Michael seemed very disturbed by the question.

"Yes, as a matter of fact, there's a beautiful woman lying sprawled nude on the floor at this very moment, waiting for me to take my pleasure on her body."

Suzanna seized one of the huge pillows and hugged it to her to cover her nakedness. She was infuriated. The mocking manner of Michael's tone was meant to indicate to his caller that he was not to be taken seriously. The truth, by inflection, had become a denial.

"You saw me with a mysterious dark-haired lady," Michael bantered in the same satiric tone. "What were we doing?" He gave Suzanna a quizzical look.

Suzanna's suspicions as to why Michael had not answered his phone call on her previous visit were confirmed. She wished to hell he had not answered this one either. "Okay, dinner Sunday . . . I don't know . . . I have to find out. I have some explaining to do. . . . Okay. Love. Good-bye now."

Michael hung up and stood with his hands on his hips, both hands were framing the limp, pink penis dangling prominently against its dark foliage. He was stark naked, and with his consternated expression he looked totally ridiculous. In her own nudity and compromised position, Suzanna herself felt acutely embarrassed, as if the caller had actually walked in on them.

"Well," Michael exclaimed.

Suzanna instinctively shielded herself with the pillow as if to soften the blow. "And who was that?" She heard the cloying sweetness of her own voice.

"My Aunt Rita. My mother's sister. But she's always been more of an older sister to me than an aunt. I mentioned her to you. She has the boutique in North Beach."

"*Oh!*" The immediate wash of relief swept away Suzanna's roiling jealousy.

"She has invited us to dinner."

"Me too?"

"*Especially* you."

"Just what have you been telling her about me?" Suzanna was touched and pleased that Michael had been discussing her with a confidante in his own family.

"Well, that's just it. I haven't seen or talked to Rita since you and I have become . . . an *item*."

Suzanna smiled at the term, with its connotations of celebrity and whirlwind romance. "Then how does she know about me . . . us?"

Michael sprawled down among the piles of pillows beside her. He fingered and nuzzled her breast in an absent, distracted way. "Well, that takes some explaining about Rita."

18

RITA COHEN-DELANEY WATCHED HER DAUGHter Bridget circle Michael warily, then settle on the arm of his chair. "When's your girlfriend gonna get here?"

Michael shrugged. "I don't know. It's a long drive in from where she lives."

"Why is she coming to dinner here?" Rita sensed the thirteen-year-old's confusion of emotions, the quickly changing colors of her aura.

"Your mother the *yenta* wants to check her out. See what kind of wild women your cousin's been running around with." Michael glanced at Rita and winked. "What's happening in *your* love life?" he asked Bridget.

"Ask me no questions, I'll tell you no lies," Bridget recited cryptically. "Wanna see our new cheerleading routine?" she asked, immediately changing the subject.

"I'd love to."

Bridget jumped to a stance with her hands on her knees, then undulated into a dance step.

> *"One potato, two potato,*
> *Three potato, four.*
> *Hit 'em again, Hit 'em again.*
> *We want more."*

Michael's eyebrows arched in surprise at the suggestive-
ness of the movement. "That's terrific. Where'd you
learn to move like that?"

"My friend Vivian. She's black. It's called soul."

"It's called sex," Michael said. "You stay away from
Vivian. She's too old for you."

"She's the same age as me."

"I think Vivian skipped thirteen. Probably fourteen,
fifteen, and sixteen too."

Bridget settled back on the arm of Michael's chair.
"You know first cousins aren't supposed to get married."

"I know," Michael sighed glumly. "Your mother told
me all about Mendel's peas. First cousins make too
many black peas, or something like that. I was shattered.
There's no hope for us."

Bridget stared at him, her eyes narrowing to slits,
then suddenly she lashed out and punched him in the
arm.

"Ow. That really hurt. Where'd you learn to punch
like that?"

Bridget smiled slyly and threw another punch at
Michael. "P.E. They make us do pushups now too."

"Is nothing sacred? Whatever happened to home
economics for girls?"

To Rita's astonishment, her daughter feint a kick to
his groin. "It's self-defense. In case you get raped or
something."

"Raped! For Chrissakes, you're only thirteen. What
are they teaching you?"

"One of the girls at school was raped. She was dragged
into a car on the way home." The mischievousness
evaporated from Bridget's face, and it was now solemn.
There was a hint of fear in the bright blue eyes that
acknowledged that there were terrible things lurking
in the world, even for a cheerleader.

But Bridget was relatively safe. It was Michael for
whom Rita was frightened. Her vision, a nightmare

really, had been too vivid. She knew from painful experience that it had not been some mishmash of Freudian lusts, but a premonition.

"Your girlfriend, is she very pretty?" Bridget asked shyly.

"You'll see," Michael teased. Then he lovingly stroked the girl's hair and said with great sincerity, "But I'll tell you. She's very pretty, but she's not as beautiful as you."

Rita watched the child literally glow, and she was touched by the emanation. When she looked at her own child, Rita forgave her ex-husband all things. Peter Delaney's heady boast, proclaimed during their Greenwich Village courtship, that he was the next John O'Hara had dissipated into unfinished novels, booze, abuse, and affairs with skinny secretaries from ad agencies. But he had made good his promise of beautiful children.

In part, Rita had moved to San Francisco to get away from his periodic drunken harassments. But also she had come here to be near Michael. He had come back from Vietnam the confirmation of all her nightmares: a gaunt, haggard man looking years older than his age, enveloped in a black cloud and fighting for his life and sanity.

Rita studied him now talking quietly to Bridget about school. There was a steady blue aura about him. He was healing and healthy.

"Talk to your mother recently?" Rita asked.

"She's well. She sounds happy."

"Steve's a nice man. He makes her happy."

"I'm happy she's happy."

"Your father was not the easiest man in the world to live with, you know. She's entitled."

"Look, I'm happy she's happy. But I don't have to love the guy too. I get the feeling everyone thinks I should love him. Actually I have enough trouble *liking* him. Whenever I meet him, or talk to him on the phone, I get the feeling he's hustling me, trying to sell me the new fall line."

"He wants you to like him. He's a salesman. That's his way."

Michael said nothing.

"He's been a tremendous help to me, Michael."

"Mazel tov," Michael said caustically, closing the subject.

At that moment Rita turned toward the door. *She's here.* A few seconds later the doorbell rang. Michael started to get up, but Rita motioned him down. "Thank you, I'm the hostess."

She hesitated at the door, then opened it and her heart lurched. It was the girl in her nightmare.

"Hello. You must be Rita. I think I'd recognize you in a crowd from Michael's description." She was a little breathless, excited, expectant, enveloped in a shimmering orange-pink aura. Despite her deep fear of this woman, Rita had an urge to embrace her. Instead she held out her hand and said, smiling, "Did you have trouble finding the place?"

"No, I had to make a stop to buy an old record, a collector's item. It took a little longer than I expected," she apologized, then added, "It's a present for my father." She averted her eyes momentarily, and her aura fluxed to a dirty green.

Why is she lying about a thing like that? Rita thought. The present was maybe for another lover? Disturbed, Rita turned and led the way into the living room.

"Your apartment is lovely," Suzanna exclaimed. Then she spotted Michael. Rita watched as both Michael's and Suzanna's auras deepened to orange and flowed out to one another.

"Find a place to park?" Michael asked.

Suzanna smiled and nodded. "I got lucky." There was a throatiness to her voice, and both auras reddened. These two are some hot number, Rita observed.

On being introduced, Suzanna immediately captivated Bridget. "You're every bit as beautiful as Michael said you were." She knew instinctively that the pubescent junior-high-schooler had a crush on her dashing older cousin. It was Michael's opinion of her that was important to Bridget, not that of her imagined rival.

Rita was troubled by inklings of a black nimbus that surrounded Suzanna, but every time she focused on the girl it disappeared, like something seen out of the corner of your eye, which vanishes when you turn to look directly at it. What she definitely saw was the almost palpable rosy-orange lovers' aura that enveloped both Suzanna and Michael, shooting out intertwining rays whenever they looked at, spoke to, or touched one another.

The dinner went well. Rita had prepared the Oriental Israeli dishes—lentil soup, grape leaves, *kibe*—she had experimented with on Michael a week before. The *kibe* was still a little dry for Rita's taste. The recipe called for too much cracked wheat.

"Michael took me window-shopping by your boutique," Suzanna said to her. "Your things looked lovely."

"Please come by. Michael will treat you to a present," she volunteered, not bothering to check with the surprised giver.

She studied Suzanna. "I have some lovely new silk things from Milan that will look stunning on you."

Suzanna self-consciously fingered her Italian blouse. "I'm not sure of my size anymore."

"You're unsettled now. One day you're bingeing on food and the next you're fasting. Also, you're burning up with a lot of nervous energy. But when you settle down, you're a lovely size eight."

"My God," Suzanna laughed delightedly, "Michael warned me you were practically psychic. Do you tell fortunes too?"

"I'm terrific at fortunes."

"Really?" Suzanna exclaimed. "What do you use?"

"Sometimes I play with tarot cards." Rita caught a look from Michael, but she ignored it. She needed a firm reading on this girl. There was something terribly frightening hovering about her.

"The tarot designs are originally Italian, aren't they?"

Rita shrugged. "They became popular there. Actually the Crusaders brought them back from the Middle East. They're Hebrew and Egyptian in origin. I use a school of interpretation based on the Kabala."

"That's fascinating. I'd love to try it."

"Maybe after dinner, we'll do a reading for fun."

Suzanna turned to Michael. "Does Rita ever tell your fortune?"

He glanced at Rita, then shook his head. "No."

"Michael believes in making his own fortune," Rita said.

"It's not that," Michael insisted. "I'll give you an example of Rita's prophetic powers. Once, when I was in high school, she telephoned our house very upset. She said she had a vision, or a dream, I don't remember which. She saw me being carried off the basketball court in great pain. But she spoke to my father, not me. And he, as they say, took it under advisement."

"I'll tell you what he said," Rita interrupted. "He asked me, 'Is Michael alive?' And I said, 'Yes, but he's hurt.' And he said, 'Don't say anything to him. I'll take care of it.'"

"What happened?" Suzanna asked.

"I had a game that night, and my father didn't say anything to me. It was a very close game. In the last quarter, things got rough under the boards and, as advertised, I broke my ankle and was carried off writhing in agony."

"That's awful," Suzanna exclaimed, looking from Michael to Rita and back again.

"Not really," Michael said. "My father didn't really

believe Rita's prophecies. But even if he did, he would probably have done the same thing."

"How could he?"

"Because he knew me. He knew that I'd believe Rita and I'd be upset and frightened. But I would still have insisted on playing, because it was a big game. And all the while I was playing, I'd be worrying about getting hurt, which is a very good way of insuring that I *would* get hurt. I'd have tensed up."

"But you did get hurt."

"It could have been much worse. I might have ripped out ligaments and tendons and been injured permanently. This was a clean break that healed quickly. And I had a terrific game, one of my best up until that point. And we won."

"So Michael was a big hero," Rita chimed in. "Everyone in his class signed his cast. Every morning a girlfriend drove him to school. But his father"—she sighed tragically—"his father carried around the pain, the guilt for months."

"I didn't know that," Michael said quietly.

"There's a lot you don't know about what your father carried around with him."

After dinner, Suzanna helped Rita clear the table. "Does Michael take after his father?" she asked.

"Yes and no. He looks a lot like him. His father was the spitting image of John Garfield, you know, the movie star. In the forties. Always played the tough guy. David, Michael's father, not only looked like John Garfield, he acted like him half the time, even though he was a well-educated lawyer. They came from the same neighborhood."

"John Garfield." Suzanna smiled. "Yes, I definitely see that in Michael. The dark, good-looking tough guy."

"Oh, Jesus, John Garfield. I haven't heard that since I was a kid." Michael shook his head in wonder.

"Of course, he was before my time," Rita said. She

caught a glint of amusement in Michael's eyes. "Well, he was," she insisted, her vanity piqued. "Remember, I'm much younger than your mother."

"I know, I know," Michael said, holding up his hands in surrender. "That's not what I'm laughing at. John Garfield's not before anyone's time. He's in eternal television reruns. Look in *TV Guide*. I'll bet *Body and Soul* is on the late show sometime this week."

"Don't get smart. You know what I mean."

"I know *exactly* what you mean. Don't worry, Rita, you'll always be younger than springtime. That's your magic."

Rita smiled and held out her hand as if introducing Michael. "My nephew, the con artist."

"And how does Michael take after his mother?" Suzanna asked.

Something in the inflection alerted Rita. It was not an idle question. The girl was subconsciously sizing Michael up as a potential husband. Rita did not know whether to be pleased or panicked. Once again the black nimbus flitted in and out of perception, like the shadow of an assassin. "The artistic and creative talent, that comes from my sister Selma. She was studying to be a designer when she married Michael's father. Also, Michael's taller, more graceful. That's from our side of the family."

Suzanna laughed, tickled with Rita's familial conceit, and her eyes shone with delight. Rita thought she was really a very lovely girl.

"So come," Rita exclaimed, taking her hand. "I'll perform my soothsaying act for the company."

Suzanna shuffled the tarot cards, cut the deck three times, and placed it face down in front of Rita.

Rita hesitated. She had not yet decided on a pattern.

She might build a pyramid, reading Suzanna layer by layer—the physical face she showed the world, her subconscious mind and buried emotions, the spiritual forces at work. But that pattern used twenty-one cards and might take hours. She must keep up the pretense of a parlor game.

"I'm going to use an ancient pattern, one called 'the magic seven,'" she explained, studying the girl. "It's very powerful."

"That sounds exciting," Suzanna said, and indeed there was a flush to her cheeks.

The pattern was actually the six-pointed Star of David, constructed of two interlocking triangles. The seventh and last card, representing the final outcome, was placed in the center of the star.

Rita picked up the first card. She placed the card to form the apex of the star, then flipped it over.

Oy! It was the gowned and cloaked figure of the High Priestess. In itself the card was not malignant. But in shuffling and cutting the cards, Suzanna had turned it *upside down.* There were dangerous spirits all about this girl, invading the deepest pools of her unconsciousness. Suzanna was very close to insanity.

Rita suffered. How much should she tell the girl? That was always the dilemma in a reading. The reader must never lie, but there was only so much of the truth that she could share. "This first card symbolizes your past, the influences that are the cause of your present situation," Rita explained, forcing her voice to be calm, reassuring. "The Priestess is someone in your family very close to you, strongly influencing you subconsciously. It's a woman, of course, probably your mother."

From the girl's nodding, Rita knew she was right on target. "The Priestess is a uniting intelligence, and you are uniting with your mother in some way." Rita glanced up just as a darkness fell across Suzanna's face, as if a cloud were passing between her and the light. "Your mother is dead," Rita said suddenly.

"Yes," Suzanna whispered.

"Perhaps you're uniting with her in your dreams," Rita said hesitantly, trying to tease out images and impressions. "But . . . but your nights are not peaceful, your dreams are very disturbed. There's mystery about you, too many secrets. There's a relationship. Somehow it's connected with your mother, and you're about to be involved. You should be cautious, very cautious."

The girl's eyes were wide, taking it all in, casting her own figures into the plot, but Rita could not see them. They were only threatening shadows.

She reached for the second card and formed the right corner of the upper triangle. "This card is the present, that which flows from the past." She turned the card over with a snap. The horned, goat-faced, bat-winged Devil stared up at her.

Rita's fingers touched the two nude figures, a young man and woman, chained to the block on which the Devil sat. "You're shackled to an illusion of some sort. You feel as if you have no control in this matter, as if you were out of control. This is a card of obsession," she explained to Suzanna. "You are obsessed with the past. You really have to start living in this world," she advised solemnly.

Again the girl nodded mutely, the flush now gone, her face pale. Someone from the past had control of her mind, and that someone—was in Hell.

With a heavy, reluctant hand, Rita picked up the third card and positioned it to complete the base of the triangle. "This is the immediate future," she pronounced, and turned it over with a theatrical flourish. The Lovers.

"Well, that looks promising," Michael kibbitzed, and Suzanna turned and smiled at him.

Maybe yes, maybe no, Rita mused. Was Michael the male figure? He had to flow from the past to the present to the immediate future. The pattern had to be complete. Michael was certainly of the present, but was he also of the past? He was, if their relationship was based on an old neurotic obsession. In that case, this hot romance might come to no good. She glanced back at the first two cards. The pattern looked ominous, evil.

And if there was a rival, he was going to undo Michael very soon. In either case, her nephew, the born sucker for a pretty face, had no cause to gloat.

"You have a lot of decisions here," she advised Suzanna. "You have to be very careful in your choices. Very careful to avoid obsessive relationships, ones that are not healthy or healing for you."

On the card, Raphael, the Archangel of the East, hovered above the two lovers. "Your relationship is almost a mystical one." For Rita that was a question, not an answer.

Suzanna appeared entranced by the card. The male nude stood in front of the Tree of Life and the female before the Tree of Knowledge of Good and Evil. "It's the Adam and Eve card. It could indicate a very healing relationship on the physical plane of this world," Rita said hopefully. There was always that dichotomy in the cards.

She impatiently placed the fourth card at the bottom point of the star, the apex of the inverted second triangle. "And this is what you must learn in order to handle this . . . this situation in which you find yourself."

She flipped the card, and there was the bony knight in armor riding a white charger. Death.

"My God, that's ominous," Suzanna gasped.

"No, not really," Rita insisted. "It symbolizes rebirth. It means that you have to give up the past. And walk through that new door that's bringing life." Perhaps there was hope for these two, after all. She stared at the card, watching the white horse prance and strut, its muscles undulating. "There's a tremendous amount of sexual energy here. This card follows the Lovers, so we're talking about a very strong physical relationship."

She tapped the black banner that Death carried. "But the flag is also strong, and that means this hot relationship is being resisted by something in the past." Rita could sense the tensions, the tuggings.

Her fingers moved down to the bottom of the card, where a little girl and an older girl or young woman knelt, mourning by a fallen figure, an overturned crown by his head. "There's a death going on somewhere in your consciousness," Rita said vaguely, "and you have to let it go." If you don't, she thought, it will drive you mad.

"So now let's see what effect your present surroundings have on all this." She reached for the fifth card and slapped it down at the left upper point of the imaginary star. The card was the Tower, one of the most ominous of the major arcana.

Two figures, a man in a cloak and boots and a gowned woman, plunged headlong out of a burning tower. For the first time during the reading, Rita was terrified for Michael. He was caught up in this young woman's obsession with the past. Something terrible was going to happen to them both. It would happen suddenly. Rita was powerless to stop it. A lightning bolt blasted the top of the tower, and there was the Hand of God in that bolt.

Rita's mind was in turmoil, her heart ached within her, but she gave the most optimistic interpretation she could read in that tarot of disaster. "This is a breaking away from your environment," she said almost in a whisper. "But I must tell you this is a painful break." This card, above all, was great pain.

With a leaden hand, she picked up the next-to-last card and formed the sixth point of the star. "The opposing forces," she announced, and revealed the face of the card. The Moon.

"*So*. Whatever is going to happen will happen this month," she thought aloud. She looked up and stared into Suzanna's fathomless blue-green eyes and felt the powerful whirlpools raging just beneath the surface, sucking the girl down into a terrifying abyss. The girl's expression was expectant, fearful. Suzanna knew this was not a parlor game. "You're going to have to believe in yourself, trust only yourself," Rita counseled. She heard the singsong quality of her own voice, and it sounded as vague and phony as that of a charlatan.

Rita bent her head and meditated on the tarot images of the two dogs baying at the moon. "Your sleep is extremely disturbed." She pointed to the female face of the moon. "It all has to do with your mother again." Somewhere in her dreams, this girl might be lost and never return again.

Rita reviewed the cards configured before her. She had never seen a more frightening constellation, with its currents of obsession, insanity, and death. What made it devastating was that out of seventy-eight possible cards, all of these were the powerful Major Arcana. None of the fifty-six Lesser Arcana had turned up. It defied the odds. But more ominously, it meant that whatever terrible thing was going to happen was inevitable. Unless . . .

With a trembling hand, Rita reached for the seventh card. She placed it carefully in the center of the star. "The final outcome," she announced. She turned up the Sun.

"Well, that's a cheerful-looking card," Suzanna said with a noticeable sigh of relief. Under a beaming sun and surrounded by sunflowers, a naked little girl romped on the back of a gray horse. She held in her hand the staff of a long, shimmering pennant that unfurled about her like a path up to the sun itself.

Rita smiled at Suzanna. "The child in you will awaken and come alive again. You are going to be very spiritual and find great faith in yourself to get through all of this. And in the end you will finally be free."

Rita's heart was absolute ice. In the Kabalist system, with its emphasis on transcendence, the card had one overpowering interpretation. *Death!*

19

"*I*T'S A TOTAL GODDAMN MYSTERY TO ME," MI-
chael exclaimed. He froze the frame on the videotape
player. "My first thought was that the perspective was
an optical illusion created by your telephoto and the
transparency of the image."

Michael pointed to the ghostly figure on the screen.
"But if you trace a horizontal line from where his feet
are supposed to be on the deck, it intersects the bulkhead *here* on the left. The hatch right here is about the
same height he is. That's what it should be."

Sam Tanaka nodded. "So it's all in scale."

"I went through this tape last week three, four times.
Every setup. And they all checked out. You have any
other ideas?"

Tanaka shook his head. "No. I wasn't that scientific
about it, but that was the intuitive feeling I had too."

"The thought occurred to me that it might be a gag.
Something you cooked up with your perverse sense of
humor. But when I tried to figure out how you did it
technically, it was just too complicated. It takes an electronic board and switcher more sophisticated than the
one we've got here."

"Well, so far you've told me all the things it's *not*,"
Tanaka said. "Then what is it?"

"You tell me. You shot the tape." Tanaka sat silent, his eyes hooded and impassive.

"Sam, please don't get inscrutable on me. If you have any ideas, I'd like to know them. If there's any way I can salvage this tape or use it, I want to. It's the last stuff we have of Ed Riley."

Tanaka nodded, looked directly at Michael, then gazed away, visibly collecting his thoughts. "In downtown Tokyo, in the business district of Otemachi, there's a tiny Japanese garden in the midst of the towering glass-and-steel office buildings. According to legend, it's the spot where a great warlord, Masakado Taira, was beheaded a thousand years ago."

Tanaka glanced at him to see if Michael was paying attention. Michael fidgeted. Tanaka did not have an answer for him, he had a goddamn parable. Sometimes, he swore to God, Tanaka was worse than a Hasidic rabbi.

"There's a stone plaque where his head fell," Tanaka went on. "The garden drives real-estate developers crazy because the ground alone is worth about ten million dollars. But no one will touch it. Too many people believe the ghost of the old warrior would wreak his fury on them if he was to be disturbed. Actually there are hundreds of very well kept shrines like that all over Tokyo. Not monuments in the Western sense, but places where people really believe that ghosts hang out.

"The people pray to them, offer sake and rice, but mainly they just want the ghosts to stay where they should. My grandfather once told me that the spirit world is only a very small step from our world. And you have to treat them with respect and appease the spirits. If they wander back and forth between their world and the here and now, it's usually for vengeance." Tanaka fell silent.

"Ghosts! *Real* ghosts! The avenging spirits of the dead. Is that what you're suggesting we've got on tape?" Michael asked angrily.

"I'm not suggesting anything, Mike. You know as much as I do."

"But did you *see* anything there?"

"No. But then I don't see X-rays. I don't see infrared or ultraviolet images either. But I can record them on film. The film is sensitive to their energy, and abracadabra! there they are in the picture. Perhaps the videotape did the same thing."

"You think it recorded a wavelength we can't see, and plays it back in the visible spectrum?"

Tanaka shrugged noncommittally. "It's a theory. Physically, maybe they're really there. But on another wavelength. Just as my grandfather said. They're just a small step from our world."

Tanaka cocked his head. "Why don't we go shoot some more tape?"

"*No!*" Michael snapped it out so vehemently that Tanaka visibly recoiled.

"Ed Riley," Michael explained in a hushed voice. "The police think he was killed *right there*." He pointed to the threaded tape. "They think it was a freak accident and his body was washed down the straits to Richmond. The FBI's in on it now."

"What kind of freak accident?"

"That's the sixty-four-thousand-dollar question."

"Do you think we should show the tape to the FBI?"

"What are we going to tell them?" Michael asked with bitter sarcasm. "Do you have a picture of two flaky media types waltzing into the offices of those WASP federal cops, who have ramrods up their asses, and saying, 'Hey, fellows, we have a tape of some spooks we shot on a high-security military base. We think it might have something to do with Riley's death.' "

"You don't trust the system, Mike."

"Oh, I trust the system, all right," Michael said nervously. "Over a ten-year span. But on a day-to-day confrontation, it can kill you. And I've got the scars to prove it."

But he saw that Tanaka was disappointed in him. Tanaka was a Sansei, a third-generation Japanese-American. He expected Michael to do something. Oh, brave new world, that has such trusting people in it.

"Look," Michael insisted vehemently. "There's an explanation for this, and it's electronic, not supernatural. Believe me. There's more horror and insanity in *this* world than I can cope with. I don't have to look for it in other worlds."

Michael was frightened. In the pit of his guts he felt that Ed Riley's death did not make sense. He just could not let it be.

After Kim had left for the day, Michael sprawled out on the couch in his office with a thick manila folder, Riley's research on Mare Island. At the end, Riley had had no office of his own and had used a filing cabinet in Michael's.

The folder was crammed with a ream of mimeographed papers, all official U.S. Navy handouts. There was a thick history of Mare Island, histories of individual ships, and a *Biography of Captain John T. Blackwell.*

Michael had hastily scanned the material before his and Riley's visit to the base, but now he avidly studied it. He was having lunch with Suzanna and her father the next day.

The biography barely covered a page and a half. Apparently the navy did not find its men as fascinating as its ships, each of which had a history at least ten times as thick.

"Captain John T. BLACKWELL, a native of Philadelphia and son of Mr. and Mrs. Thomas Blackwell, was born April 18, 1922. He was commissioned an Ensign upon graduation from the United States Navy Academy in June 1943, and reported to the U.S.S. *Santa Cruz,* in which he served during World War II."

The *Santa Cruz*. Every hair on Michael's body tingled. It could not be just a coincidence. He excitedly read the rest of the bio. The next three paragraphs were a compilation of assignments: a destroyer in the Mediterranean, a battleship in the Korean War, navy schools, gunnery officer aboard an aircraft carrier, a destroyer squadron in the Far East, Deputy Chief of Staff, Cinc Pac, Surface, Pearl Harbor.

Nothing rang a bell until Michael read, "Captain Blackwell assumed his present assignment at Mare Island, Vallejo, California, on July 13." It was the day Riley was killed. Another coincidence? The pageantry of the change-of-command ceremony was one of the reasons they were there. The bio was a press release sent out before that date.

Blackwell's private life comprised a sentence: "A widower, he was married to the former Grace Hall, and they have a daughter, Suzanna, an art student in Rome."

Michael could write sonnets about his dark lady, an awkward first novel at least, and this bureaucratic *putz* was knocking her off in a single phrase.

The concluding two paragraphs listed Blackwell's decorations and commendations. Michael impatiently skipped over them. Michael also had faced danger and death. All he had to commend him were his scars, his nightmares, and a dusty stack of outtakes too horrible to be shown on TV, now buried in a network bin in New York. Blackwell's display of ribbons and tinsel only angered him.

He stared at the double-spaced lines of type as though trying to read some secret message hidden between them. The *Santa Cruz* was the ship Riley had been on as a correspondent during the invasion of Iwo Jima. It was the only ship on which the electronic ghosts had popped up, ruining the tape. What the hell was going on? Rather than answers, Michael was coming up with more mysteries.

He shuffled quickly through Riley's pack of research, throwing the irrelevant papers all over the floor. *History of U.S.S. Santa Cruz.* It was a packet of single-spaced mimeo paper printed by the Office of Naval Records and History, Ships' Histories Section.

Santa Cruz, Michael read, had been launched December 14, 1941, one week after the attack on Pearl Harbor, by the Newport News Shipbuilding and Dry Dock Company in Virginia. A Miss Mary Caroline had been the sponsor. Michael suspected she was a beauty queen who broke the magnum of champagne over the Cleveland-class cruiser's bow. The ship was commissioned July 26, 1942, with Captain James L. Warren in command, and thereafter in the ship's lengthy official history—Michael was to recall later—not another human was mentioned by name. Only the ship had an identity. Those who served aboard were recorded only by function or as casualty statistics.

As if anxious to get to war, *Santa Cruz* (the navy did not use article adjectives in referring to ships) sailed from Norfolk a few months later, arriving at Espiritu Santo in time to plunge immediately into the battle for Guadalcanal. On January 29, 1942, while protecting troop transports, the ship slugged its way through a heavy air attack and made its first kills, three Japanese planes.

Like some truculent buccaneer, *Santa Cruz* sailed the Solomons, bombarding New Georgia, Munda, and Bougainville as the marines stormed ashore. Michael suddenly envisioned his father, rifle held high to keep it out of the water, wading through the surf as the cruiser's big guns roared overhead, and the mimeographed facts were transformed in his mind into an old newsreel, one that was vivid with his own personal history. He saw again his father's photos of the Japanese troops ashore that those shells had blown to pieces. How many men had those distant, impersonal guns killed? Michael read on.

Santa Cruz then joined the fast carrier task forces roaming the Pacific, raiding the Japanese-held islands. Cross-checking the chronology, Michael figured that it was during one of the stopovers in Pearl Harbor that the freshly minted Ensign Blackwell came aboard. He was in time for the campaign up the chain of Solomon Islands.

Covering the landings at Bougainville, *Santa Cruz* was hit by a torpedo during an air raid. Like an instinctive counterpuncher, she shot down the Japanese plane, but she was briefly out of the war for quick repairs.

Santa Cruz steamed back into action in time to take part in the invasion of Saipan, the Battle of the Philippine Sea, the invasions of Tinian and Guam. Then the invasion of the Philippine Islands began.

On the night of October 24, 1944, the great Japanese fleet sailed in single file through the Surigao Strait into Leyte Gulf for a showdown. Gallant American PT boats and destroyers pecked at them like sparrows. But the main American force, the sleek new cruisers including *Santa Cruz* and the few old battleships that had survived Pearl Harbor, lay waiting in a line across the mouth of the strait. As the Japanese column came out, one by one, every gun in the American line hit them. The tactic was called "capping the T" and it was the most classic maneuver in naval warfare. The battleship *Yamashiro* sank and the remainder of the Japanese fleet, heavily damaged and devastated, retreated back through the strait.

Michael could imagine the delirium in the wardroom aboard *Santa Cruz,* where Blackwell and the other officers celebrated. They knew they had literally written history.

The jubilation lasted exactly one day. On October 25, Vice-Admiral Takijiro Onishi made obsolete all the books on naval tactics that Blackwell and his classmates had studied at Annapolis. He unleashed the kamikazes. The

first wave sank the escort carrier *St. Lo* and damaged
four other American ships.

Santa Cruz was assigned to protect the convoys invading Mindoro. On December 13, the kamikazes came in
swarms. One, flying low over the water, crashed alongside *Santa Cruz*. Moments later a second suicide attack
roared out of the sun. Antiaircraft fire exploded the
plane above the ship and a section of its fuselage hit the
forward deck and burst into flames.

In Japanese, *kamikaze* means "divine wind." Michael
could only imagine the terror and awe of the American
sailors aboard *Santa Cruz* toward the fanatical fliers
committed to dying just to massacre them.

But a few days later an even more awesome wrath of
heaven struck the ship. On December 18, *Santa Cruz*
ran head-on into an unpredicted killer typhoon. Waves
fifty-five feet high broke over the deck and bridge, and
110-knot winds tossed the ship about as if it were flotsam.
In Admiral Halsey's fleet, three destroyers sank and
twenty-one other ships were damaged, nine so badly
they were out of the war. *Santa Cruz* rode out the storm
with minor damage. Ship and crew had again survived
with a tenacity that defied "divine winds" and the wrath
of heaven.

In mid-February, *Santa Cruz* sailed north toward
Tokyo, part of the horizon-to-horizon Task Force 48
making the first air attack against the Japanese home-
land since Jimmy Doolittle's daring raid from *Shangri-la*
two years earlier. Then the entire task force raced
southward to Iwo Jima.

At this point the stilted official narrative suddenly
purpled in prose, as the anonymous scribe in the Ships'
History Section became inflamed with the thunder and
blood of battle. *Santa Cruz* was detached from the carriers and navigated close to shore, near sharp rocks
and jutting ledges. The cruiser's six-inch guns silenced
gun batteries on the glowering volcano of Mt. Suribachi.

Thousands of small craft darting back and forth between the beach and transports made collision imminent.

Santa Cruz launched her own Kingfisher spotting planes to direct gunfire. She smashed pillboxes, ammunition dumps, fortified caves. The pinpoint bombardment turned back a strong Japanese counterattack at midnight.

Michael was irritated by the detached, vainglorious account probably rewritten from the ship's log. A few hundred yards away, marines were burning the Japanese out of caves with flamethrowers. Yet he recalled that Riley had witnessed the assault from the deck of this ship and had had a similarly bombastic perception of it. That volcano, etched in flames, hovering over the marines bleeding on black sand beaches, must have made it seem the Twilight of the Gods.

Michael impatiently skimmed pages of the bloodless chronicle of bloody battles. There were warships with similar histories. What was extraordinary about the *Santa Cruz*? In his haste he almost missed the answer.

On Easter Sunday, 1945, began the largest amphibious assault of the Pacific war, the invasion of Okinawa. The home islands of Japan were now under attack. Wave after wave of desperate kamikazes struck in a massed suicidal fury, which the American fleet had never experienced before. The offensive was named *ten go*—the translation: "heavenly operation"—to reflect the spiritual purity of the kamikazes. Their divine purpose was to annihilate the American fleet so that it could never invade Japan. The assault vessels and fast carrier task forces were boxed in the narrow seas around Okinawa, where the kamikazes knew exactly where to find them. They found *Santa Cruz* on May 15.

Here, curiously, the history became terse, almost cryptic. The first kamikaze crashed into the port five-inch gun mount, the suicide plane's two bombs exploding about ten feet off the deck. Gasoline fires and exploding ammunition made *Santa Cruz*'s midsection an inferno. One hundred and thirty-three men were killed and 190 wounded.

The ship's remaining five-inch guns continued antiaircraft fire, but a second kamikaze crashed into *Santa Cruz* on her port quarter. This plane and its bombs penetrated several decks before exploding, blowing a huge, jagged hole in her side. Thirty men were killed and forty-four wounded. Before damage control could isolate the compartments, tons of water flooded the after fire room and engine room. The ship was again set afire. Explosions blew the after turrets out of action. Deliberate flooding of two magazines stopped further explosions, and impressive damage control enabled *Santa Cruz* to continue her shore bombardment with her two forward turrets.

The cruiser was then hit by a third kamikaze, knocking out six gun directors and gun mounts. A total of 187 of the crew were dead and 331 wounded. Yet, drastically shorthanded as she was, *Santa Cruz* again put out the fires, isolated her damage, and kept firing.

To Michael, reading the brief account thirty years later, it seemed that the fanaticism of the Japanese had infected the crew of *Santa Cruz*. Perhaps it was the only way to survive the slaughter.

In the waters immediately about *Santa Cruz*, the sacrifices of 1,465 Japanese pilots had killed 3,048 American sailors, wounded another six thousand, sunk twenty-nine ships, and severely damaged a hundred more.

It took *Santa Cruz* and her decimated crew a month to limp across the Pacific to Mare Island for repairs. The ship was still there when atom bombs were dropped on Hiroshima and Nagasaki. On August 15, the order "cease offensive operations" was radioed to the fleet. The ship was awarded the Navy Unit Commendation for her crew's accomplishment in saving their ship and carrying out their mission on Okinawa. She received a total of thirteen battle stars for her World War II service, and on October 9, 1945, *Santa Cruz* was decommissioned and attached to the U.S. Pacific Reserve Fleet.

Once again, Michael was struck by the feeling he was not reading about a piece of machinery, but a person. But it was a macabre note in the next-to-last paragraph that seized him with a queasy horror: "When *Santa Cruz* arrived at Mare Island, several of her sealed compartments still contained dead bodies. One of the shipyard's problems was to remove the remains."

Michael reread the last few paragraphs. A phrase here and there teased him. He again seized Blackwell's brief biography. In his irritation, he had skipped over Blackwell's decorations. There it was—a Bronze Star and a brief phrase of commendation for his actions off Okinawa. But it was just another piece of the puzzle. He still could not picture what it all meant.

He closed his eyes and leaned back on the couch. For the first time he forced himself willingly to recreate the horror he had suppressed all these years, images of men dead and dying. He relocated his own nightmares in the bowels of a U.S. Navy ship, and among them he visualized Blackwell, the young Annapolis man the same age Michael had been in Vietnam. The images he conjured up were so charged with agony and terror that he sat sweating and trembling. He played out the scenario in his mind, the only one that was possible from the facts.

"My God, how does he live with it?" Michael whispered aloud, when he finally saw what Blackwell had done. He stared with unfocused eyes at the ceiling, his mind's eye still unreeling the vision of hell he could not stop.

20

FLIES SWARMED ABOUT THE TARPAULIN, AT-
tacking it. The buzzing had a ferocious sound to it, like
a growl, as if the flies were trying to bite and claw
through the black cloth to get at the body beneath.

The body lay at the bottom of the gangway of the
Santa Cruz. The maintenance crew who had discovered
it the first thing that morning now hung back, halfway
down the roped-off pier. Their faces were pale and
stricken as they watched Captain Blackwell approach.
The yard police and marines milling around the tarpaulin looked just as ashen.

"It's Chief Slade?" Blackwell asked.

The yard police chief nodded and indicated the maintenance crew. "Yes, sir, they identified him."

One of the yard policemen bent to uncover the body.

"I don't think you should, sir," someone said. Blackwell
glanced up. It was Bingham, the marine captain of the
guard.

Blackwell glared at him and then nodded to the yard
policeman. He lifted the covering cloth, and the flies
swarmed in to feed.

Slade still had his hat on. His face, resting on its right
cheek, looked, in profile, oddly at peace.

"It's the owls around here, sir. They've been known
to strip a dog clean."

"Owls?" Blackwell asked, confused.

There was a movement of the tarp, and Slade's head rolled to face Blackwell.

Blackwell's knees threatened to buckle, and the bile in his stomach surged to his throat. He had to clench his teeth to keep from throwing up. He swallowed the bitter gorge with great difficulty. Sweat broke out all over his body, and he felt it stream from his face.

One-half of Slade's face was stripped to the skull. Under the immaculate chief's cap, a face that was one-half Slade's and half a death's head, a few bloody strings of flesh still clinging to the skull, stared up at Blackwell with an accusing eye and a gouged socket.

Blackwell reeled away from the sight.

21

MICHAEL STOOD ON A STONE AND SAND SPIT at the southern tip of Mare Island. The upper bay of San Francisco Bay spread out before him like a great inland lake, its surface whitecapped by the wind. To the south, directly across the water from Michael, steep hills and palisades curved away toward the refineries and wharves of Richmond. Off there, Riley's body had been hooked through the neck by a fisherman casting for striped bass.

Michael's eyes carefully backtracked the course the body was supposed to have taken to get to that point. To the east, the stark iron framework of the Carquinez Strait Bridge landmarked the fierce debouchment where a half-dozen Northern California rivers poured into the Bay. Just above the bridge was the mouth of the Mare Island Strait.

Michael had had to see it for himself to be convinced that Riley's body, like a reeking piece of wreckage, had really washed down the strait from the *Santa Cruz* and halfway across the Bay. By automobile it was a long, convoluted ride across several bridges and through three cities, but at ebb tide it was a straight shot.

"Once upon a time there was a lighthouse on this spot," Suzanna informed him. Her voice startled him. For the few painful moments during which he traced

Riley's passage, he had forgotten Suzanna was beside him. He turned to her.

The wind whipping up the Bay swept Suzanna's hair back from her cheeks and elegant neck, as if the movement had been deliberately contrived to dazzle Michael. Her voice was breathless and her eyes now sparkled in a way that signaled that what she had just said was not irrelevant data but the beginning of a tale.

"For thirty-five years the keeper of the lighthouse here was the widow of a young naval officer. He had been killed at sea off the coast here. Her husband had been the son of a former commandant of Mare Island, so she was allowed to live in the lighthouse until the day she died. Can you imagine her in that lighthouse, alone, for thirty-five years?" Suzanna's eyes were as wide as those of a child with an awesome secret.

"Why do you think she stayed here?" she asked.

"I have a strong feeling you're about to tell me."

Suzanna's mouth pursed in a half-smile. "I think there were nights, nights when the fog came in from the sea and enveloped the lighthouse and the full moon pulled the tide so that it lapped against the house. On those nights she met and consorted with the ghost of her dead husband."

Michael was vaguely disturbed that Suzanna was so enraptured with the story.

"That's a terrific story," Michael said. "I think you should immediately give up art and start writing gothic novels."

Suzanna nodded. "You're talking to a passionate Brontë buff. Read everything they wrote when I was a moonstruck teenager. And then reread them all in college for a term paper. I lost count of how many times I've seen the movie of *Wuthering Heights*." She suddenly pulled close to Michael. "See how you've benefited?"

"*Me?*"

She nipped at his earlobe. "Aren't you my Heathcliff? The wild, dark gypsy boy my father brought home?"

Suzanna kissed him, then immediately broke away. She glanced at her watch, then reached up and straightened his collar and tie, looking up at him with an unsure, seeking look.

"Are you nervous about this lunch with your father?"

"I don't want to be late. He's uptight enough about you."

"Why, what did you tell him?"

"I really haven't had a chance to say much of anything. When I stayed overnight at your place, I just didn't lie and say I'd stayed at a hotel. For Chrissakes, I'm a divorcée and I'm pushing thirty."

"What'd he say?"

"Not much. He just sort of seethed. I think it'll help if he just gets to know you better. You don't mind, do you?"

There was a look of pleading in Suzanna's eyes, as if imploring him to be charming and tactful with her father. Michael lightly stroked her cheek to reassure her. In spite of every difference, he was in love with this woman.

"No, of course not," he said persuasively. "I'm looking forward to it."

But Michael had great trepidation about his confrontation with Blackwell. In his bones he felt he was engaged in a struggle with the man over Suzanna herself.

What Blackwell had done aboard the *Santa Cruz* thirty years before had been inhuman. It was beyond Michael's compassion. He loathed and feared the man. But he had to tread very carefully. Suzanna loved her father and was fiercely loyal to him. It was evident to Michael in the way her eyes flashed and her back stiffened whenever Michael mentioned Blackwell with any hint of hostility.

Michael still did not have any idea how Riley's death

tied in with Blackwell and the *Santa Cruz*, or—and this was more important to him now—how it might affect Suzanna.

Michael searched for some seed of Suzanna in the face of the man seated across the table from him in the officers' club. He recognized nothing. The face was narrow, hawkish, arresting in a stern, chisel-featured way, with deep lines etching the mouth and eyes. Blackwell's hair and brows were steel-wool gray. He looked older than the early fifties that Michael knew his age to be. The eyes that closely examined Michael were brown, but without warmth. Whatever cordiality he directed toward Michael was out of politeness only.

Suzanna sat beside Michael, smiling expectantly from one man to the other.

"Did you know Ed Riley?" Michael asked.

"I believe I met him at the same ceremony at which I met you."

"No, I mean during World War II. Aboard the *Santa Cruz*."

Blackwell's eyes narrowed. "Oh, was your friend aboard the ship?" There was an edge of tension in his voice, and he glanced at Suzanna. Blackwell had secrets to hide from his daughter.

"He was a war correspondent. He was aboard the *Santa Cruz* as an observer during the invasion of Iwo Jima."

"God, that was a lifetime ago. I don't remember meeting any of the correspondents. But then I was pretty busy with my own job at the time."

"In damage control?" Michael asked casually.

For an instant Blackwell's face turned to stone, but then he blinked. "How the hell did you know that?"

Michael's shrug conveyed that it was general knowledge. "Your official bio. It mentioned it in your citation for the Bronze Star." Michael was getting dangerously close. He could see it in the hardness in Blackwell's eyes. He did not like baiting the man, but he had to know.

Blackwell's bloodless lips twisted into a tight, ironic smile. "You really do your homework."

"Isn't that an incredible coincidence?" Suzanna said.

"What, dear?"

"That Michael's friend and you should have been together at that time and place."

"Not really," Michael said. "Riley was a hustling correspondent, your father an ambitious military man. They both gravitated to where the action was."

To Michael's surprise, Blackwell favored both him and Suzanna with a charming smile. "I don't know if I appreciate being compared to a reporter on the hustle," he said in a droll voice. "There is, after all, a sense of duty in my case."

"You don't think reporters operate from a sense of duty?"

"Was that your motivation in Vietnam?" Blackwell was now baiting *him,* leading him away from the *Santa Cruz.*

"Not entirely," Michael admitted. "But I also operated under the rationale that the public ought to see what was happening."

"That was a prime example of too much information confusing the public. Disastrously. There are those of us who believe that General Westmoreland lost the war right at the beginning when he didn't clamp down on the press."

"You prefer World War II, when everything was tightly censored?"

"There was a sense of *total* commitment then. The press was not allowed to eat away at it with sensationalized reporting." Blackwell stared straight at him, and in the black regions behind the irises of the eyes, Michael saw the hatred flash out at him.

"Bill! How are you?" Suzanna suddenly exclaimed.

"I'm sorry. I didn't mean to interrupt you," a strange masculine voice apologized.

Blackwell broke off his stare and looked up, and his face broke into a beaming smile. "Not at all, Bill. Glad to see you."

A tall, ruggedly built marine captain stood at the table. "I saw familiar faces across the room, and I just wanted to say hello." He looked at Michael with interest, then back at Suzanna.

"Bill, I'd like you to meet a friend of mine, Michael Lowenstein. Bill Bingham."

Bingham reached out a suntanned paw, and there was a glint of recognition in his smile. "I see, Major, you're wearing your hair a little shorter."

Michael frowned. He could not place this guy at all.

"Major?" Blackwell questioned.

"An Hoa," the marine reminded him.

Yes, of course, it would have to be An Hoa.

"It was quite an introduction," the marine said, addressing Blackwell and Suzanna. "I saw what I thought was a marine with long, shaggy hair and I commented on it. He promptly informed me that he was a network cameraman entitled to the respects and privileges of a major. And he offered several salty suggestions about what I could do with my opinions on his grooming."

Michael could still not place the marine, but the story was familiar.

He addressed Michael again. "We use your film for training. Show them what it was like."

"What film is that?" Blackwell inquired.

"*Able Company's War*. A network documentary. He shot three-fourths of it. All the heavy combat footage. The producer and camera crew were lifted out when the mortars started falling."

He looked back at Michael. "You heard about Vincent?"

Michael nodded. "Someone wrote me." Vincent had been company commander, or he had become company commander when the first one was hit. He had brought them out of it and had thrown Michael on a helicopter.

"You doing okay?" It was not a casual question. Blackwell caught the inflection and his narrowed eyes darted between Michael and the marine.

Michael nodded. "I'm doing very well. Better than most."

"Good. Well, you're in terrific company." Bingham smiled at Suzanna and her father. "I just wanted to say hello."

Politely he took his leave, and Blackwell's eyes followed him with curious interest, then came back to Michael.

"Undoubtedly another case of an ambitious officer and an ambitious correspondent meeting where the action is."

"Just two soldiers of fortune," Michael agreed.

When they had finished lunch, Suzanna excused herself to the ladies' room. Michael and Blackwell were left at the table, staring at one another.

"You know, Suzanna believes we're getting along just fine. We find each other 'interesting,' " Michael said.

"Suzanna takes after her mother a great deal. She lives in a romantic haze."

"May I ask you a very direct question?"

"You may certainly ask."

"There are a few people with whom I work that know me fairly well, and dislike me. It's rare, but not unknown, that I run into someone who hates my guts on first sight. It's usually because they're wary of anyone with the media. Or because they just hate any Jew automatically. Which is it with you?"

Blackwell nodded, a half-smile on his face. "A fair question. I certainly view your 'hustling' profession with great misgivings. As for your ethnic background, I find the question itself personally insulting. At this base we're essentially working for Admiral Hyman Rickover, one of the toughest, most brilliant sons of bitches in the navy, and an officer for whom I have nothing but admiration. So you're way off base there. Under other circumstances, I probably would find you an 'interesting' character. I might enjoy having a drink with you. But this is not other circumstances. This is a very personal matter. And the fact that my daughter is sleeping with a . . . a joker like you makes me sick to my stomach. Now if you'll excuse me."

Blackwell rose and left. As he exited from the dining room, Michael saw him stop at the table where Bingham was lunching with two other marine officers.

"Well, did you and Daddy get along?" Suzanna asked when she returned.

Michael smiled. "We're in perfect understanding."

22

LUMINOUS FIGURES OF SAINTS, MADONNAS, ARCH-
angels, prophets, apostles, and knights, thirteen on each
side, flanked Suzanna. At the end of this aisle, above
her head, the ascendant Christ floated in a glowing
cloud. He was vibrant, powerful, not at all the twisted,
agonized figure on the Cross with which Suzanna was
uncomfortable. This was the Old Testament Deliverer,
and cloaked in a full white robe, He held out strong
hands, unmutilated by stigmata, with which to raise the
dead.

"I just discovered the chapel a few days ago," Suzanna
whispered in a hushed, excited voice. "I wanted to
show it to you. Isn't it beautiful?" She took Michael's
hand.

"I love to stand here in the dark, with the only light
coming through the stained-glass windows. It's breathtaking. As if you've just died and are being welcomed
to heaven." Somewhere, undoubtedly in a dream,
Suzanna felt she had been here before.

"It's the oldest chapel in the navy," she informed
him. "Tiffany did the windows before the turn of the
century, and there's not another collection quite like
this."

"Yes, I can believe that."

She moved away from the entrance and switched on

the light. The chapel was the size of a small church, but the two-story-high, steeply peaked ceiling gave it a feeling of great spaciousness. The slanted ceiling was paneled with boards that ran fore and aft, and a bridgework of heavy, crisscrossing beams supported the exposed rafters and framing of the roof. The construction of the roof resembled the hull of an old wooden sailing ship, inverted and set on the upright rectangular walls of the chapel.

The light from the suspended ceiling lamps was swallowed by the dark polished wood, but as Suzanna's eyes adjusted, she saw that the lower panels were hung with handcarved tablets: *Fleet Admiral Chester W. Nimitz, USN, 1885–1966 . . . In Memoriam* U.S.S. Thresher *10 April 1963 . . . 1st Marine Division Guadalcanal Korea . . . Stephen Decatur. . . .* She had not noticed them on her previous visit, when she had been completely enraptured by the effect of the Tiffany glass windows in the dark chapel.

Other plaques, predominantly of bronze, lined the walls. One that remembered the *Maine* was cast from metal recovered from that sunken battleship in Havana harbor. The entire chapel was a memorial to the navy dead, both men and ships, as if they had inseparable identities in death.

Life outside the navy was simply not recognized. A birch and mahogany plaque read: *John Fitzgerald Kennedy, USNR, 1941–1945; Commander-in-Chief, 1961–1963.*

Michael sat down in one of the carved wooden pews and patted the seat next to him. "Come, hear my confession," he invited Suzanna.

"Oh, God, there *is* another woman," she exclaimed, sitting down next to him.

"Nothing that exciting." He indicated the tablets on the wall with a nod. "I used to have my own swashbuckling hero, my role model. A swarthy Jew who was the All-Time—All-American combat photographer."

"I can't imagine why you identified with him."

"Robert Capa. His creed was, 'If your pictures are no good, you aren't close enough.' In World War II he landed in the first wave on Omaha Beach. He was in the first parachute drop in Germany. And he was the first American correspondent killed in Vietnam. Back in 1954, after the French lost Dien Bien Phu.

"But the most famous picture he ever took, the one that made him a celebrity, he took during the Spanish Civil War. His first war, when he was twenty-three. He caught a Loyalist soldier at the instant of death, when he was shot in the head during a charge."

Suzanna regarded him with her cool aquamarine eyes, waiting for him to get to the point.

"There's a Capa Memorial Award. When I got to Vietnam, one of the first people I met was a photographer who had won it there. The walls of his office were papered with photos the news service had refused to run: a grinning eighteen-year-old infantryman posing like a big-game hunter with his foot on the chest of a peasant; lopped-off hands and ears strung up like trophies; floating heads with their eyes out; men being tortured. The photos had comic-strip balloons that said things like, 'That'll teach you to talk to the press.' "

Suzanna shook her head, as if trying to throw off the pictures Michael had drawn. "Why are you telling me this?"

"Because I want you to know how it was. You go in having the noblest of intentions. Or at least I kidded myself that I did. And then, without realizing it, you become a ghoul, living off the dead. When I got wounded, I was trying to get my . . . my 'Capa shot' for TV. I was following twenty yards behind a line of advancing marines. I had the camera focused on the men in the point. In the corner of my eye I could see the approaching mortar bursts. But I was so intent on the shot that it never registered that the mortar shells were 'walking' toward the camera, not the subject. Poetic irony there. I almost made a film of my own instant of death, not a marine's."

Once again—in a characteristic way that Suzanna had noted before—Michael's voice had a sardonic, almost flippant tone, but the pain in his eyes testified that every roll of film he had shot had recorded the step-by-step withering of his own soul.

Suzanna put her fingers softly on his lips. "Michael, all that's past. It doesn't matter anymore."

"Yes, it does matter. That marine who came to the table at lunch."

"Bill Bingham?"

"He remembers me from An Hoa. I don't remember him. But he remembers me."

"What does it matter?"

"That's where all the shit came down on me. I cracked up. My soundman was killed there."

"You've told me that, Michael."

"Danny was Vietnamese, and for two years he took care of me," Michael rushed on, as if compelled to explain it. "He practically adopted me. He said we were soul brothers, because he'd become a newsman to avoid the draft too. Actually it was common among the Vietnamese cameramen and soundmen. It wasn't a matter of principle with them. They could make more money than they could in the army, but mainly they were afraid that the corruption and incompetence of their own officers would get them killed. Danny was wrong. I was the one who got him killed."

Suzanna shook her head. "I don't want to hear about it. It doesn't matter," she said for the third time, and kissed him on the lips, a soft, tender, comforting kiss.

"I'm sorry the chapel brought back bad memories," Suzanna said. "I thought it was lovely and you should see it."

She clicked off the lights. The wooden and metal tablets memorializing the war dead disappeared into the shadows. The two flanking rows of saints, shepherds, knights, and prophets appeared to step forward, surging with light, once again forming a radiant corridor to the ascendant figure of the Son of Man shining in the western sky above them.

"It is beautiful," Michael said. "I wish it were the way death really is. But it isn't. I know it isn't."

From the damned expression on his face, Suzanna was grateful at that moment that she did not share his terrible knowledge. She never wanted to know it.

23

OUTSIDE, MICHAEL STUDIED ST. PETER'S CHAPEL. The vestibule was crowned by a skirted tower that looked like a witch's hat. The tower, vestry, steeply gabled roof, and walls of the chapel were all covered with mahogany-stained wooden shingles, giving it a somber Gothic appearance.

In the nave of the chapel, Michael had tried to tell Suzanna the worst about himself, but she did not want to hear it. To Suzanna, it was not a place of the wasted dead, but one of beauty and resurrection.

There had been the same thrill in her voice as when she had narrated the fantasy of the widow in the lighthouse. Her father was right on one score: Suzanna often existed in a romantic haze.

For Michael, Mare Island was a forbidding place for romantic fantasies. Just a few yards away, screened by a stand of pines, a steel fence topped by barbed wire was posted with bright yellow signs reading *Restricted Area— Keep Out.* Beyond it, nuclear submarines that launched ballistic missiles were being constructed and serviced.

And in the rolling hills just above the chapel sprawled a quiet campus—the Combat Systems Technical School— where the high tech of computers and guided missiles was taught. All about St. Peter's, the preparations for Armageddon went on.

The chapel sat isolated in a grove of eucalyptus at the end of Walnut Avenue, the row of white-pillared manors that housed the senior officers. Michael and Suzanna strolled back to her home through the cool woods of Alden Park. The park itself was an arboretum, with plaques identifying incense cedars, blue gums, beefwoods, and trees of heaven that had been transported there by ship in another century.

After lunch, Suzanna and Michael had spent the afternoon touring the island. Michael's excuse to take off from work was that he was researching a documentary. Certainly there was more than material enough. Mare Island was populated and furnished by the revenants of its history. They could not turn a corner without banging into an ancient graveyard, brick stable, or naval cannon with a bronze plaque recognizing it as a National Historical Landmark or California Historical Marker.

But Michael's interest was a ruse. He was really searching for any clue to Riley's death.

Suzanna, on the other hand, revealed a studious passion for the past. At each site she disclosed details of the island's history in a voice that held uncanny echoes of crinolined forebears who had ordered slaves about and devastated Confederate gallants with the flutter of a fan.

Suzanna's accent was an instrument of her mood. At times it disappeared completely, and her voice became as low-pitched and nonregional as a TV anchor lady. On occasion, for comic effect, she laid it on as thick and sticky as blackstrap molasses, an outrageous parody of itself. But now there were natural honeyed inflections in her voice, a lazy, sensual Tidewater flow that caressed Michael's ear.

"Poetry," Fitzgerald had written somewhere, "is a Northern man's dream of the South." For Michael, Suzanna had become that poetry.

At the north end of the park, across the tree-lined street from Suzanna's antebellum home, was the ceremonial area where he had first seen her. In the fragrant twilight, with a hot scent wafting from unseen white blossoms, it seemed very much the square of a small Southern city, with its empty white bandstand and black Civil War cannons. It belonged to another time and space, one created by past generations of navy officers. More than ever, Michael felt himself the outsider, the alien.

He suddenly grabbed Suzanna and kissed her, smothering her mouth with his own. She was surprised, yielded uneasily, then pushed him away. "Well, what was that about?"

"I felt a little strange. As if you weren't quite real."

"I'm totally real, sugar. You, of all people, should know that."

Michael glanced over her shoulder and, with a start, noticed Captain Blackwell on the veranda of his house, glaring at them. Even at a distance, something in his stance conveyed his anger.

"Oops."

"What's the matter?"

"Your daddy, the captain."

Without looking about, Suzanna fussed nervously with her hair and dress, straightening them. Then she turned, took Michael by the arm, and led him up to the veranda, dusky with its hanging and weaving vines.

As they approached, Blackwell turned and stepped inside. They followed him into the living room. Surrounded by the antique furnishings, Michael once again had a feeling of being misplaced in time.

"You're home early," Suzanna greeted her father.

"I had to get a few things together. I have to fly down to San Diego again tomorrow morning. I'll just be gone overnight and be back Friday." His glance at

Michael conveyed his sharp displeasure at leaving his daughter with the likes of him.

Then, unexpectedly, with a sardonic, almost cheerful note of contrition, Blackwell said to Michael, "Well, it seems I owe you an apology."

"Oh, why is that?"

"For doubting your dedication to covering a war." Michael said nothing, but a chill ran through him. "You enjoy quite a reputation even among combat-hardened marines."

"What are you talking about?" Suzanna asked in an uneasy voice.

Michael broke out in a cold sweat. He no longer heard Blackwell's voice. He was suddenly back on patrol south of An Hoa. The gunfire was deafening and the stench of cordite choking. He could not see any of the North Vietnamese. The fire was all from the right flank. After two years, Michael instinctively homed in on the place from which the fire came. In the bush it was confusing. It had taken him a few firefights to learn to spot it immediately and put a rise of earth, a furrow, a tree, or brush between him and the fire. It was one way to stay alive.

Another was carefully picking the company in which he traveled. He and his soundman, Danny Van Dang, always chose very carefully. Danny had survived the war for five years. Michael would not have felt safe without him. Marines, Michael felt, were good. They covered a TV cameraman as they would a medic. But Danny had wanted to take the chopper out with the rest of the film crew.

Like many correspondents in Vietnam, Danny did not share Michael's romanticism about the marines. They took too many casualties. What was worse, they took pride in it. "Marines, all I got to say, Mike, is *fuck that*."

"If we aren't close enough, the film's no good," Michael insisted. Danny loyally stayed with him. This time Michael was too close.

He kept his eye pressed to the viewfinder. The action was motivated by fear, not by professionalism. He sought protection, distance, behind the camera. The zoom lens disassociated him from the danger about him. Nothing was quite real. It was distorted, bigger than life, very much like being stoned. Michael was there but somehow not there, a detached, spaced-out viewer.

The company commander, Vincent, was crouched behind a tree. He shouted to the point squad to fall back and cover the flank. The sudden *pop-pop* of an AK burst from that direction. Michael heard the bullets shred the bushes behind him. He panned the camera about in that direction, and then he saw Danny. There was a piece out of his neck, and he was spouting blood.

Framed in the viewfinder, there was something artful in the twisted, blood-gushing body on the ground. Danny's eyes sought his through the zoom lens, and the horror and betrayal there suddenly slammed into focus. Danny's outrage was not at dying but at the comrade he had protected and loved now coldly photographing, *using* his death.

Michael dropped his camera and crawled back to Danny. He sat in the puddled blood and held Danny's head in his lap, trying to stop the now trickling flow from his neck until it ceased altogether. Danny was literally drained. He had bled to death, that look of having been betrayed now frozen into the glazed eyes that stared up at Michael.

Numb, Michael crawled back and picked up his camera. He moved out to the right, toward the fire. There was one last, *ultimate* shot to take: the North Vietnamese who had killed Danny and would kill him.

Vincent jumped him and sat on him until the other companies finally came up to reinforce them and the

North Vietnamese disappeared into the bush as if they had never been there.

"Michael!" Suzanna stared at him, and in her eyes he saw something of the horror he had seen in Danny's eyes. He glanced down and saw that he was wearing a tweed sport jacket and flannel slacks, not the blood-soaked, reeking fatigues he had, in his craziness, refused to take off back in the assembly area or at Da Nang or aboard the plane evacuating him to Saigon.

He was in the Blackwells' living room. For several moments he was disoriented, as if he had awakened from an old and too-vivid nightmare. He had not heard a word Blackwell had said. He had flashed back. It had been a year since he had had his last flashback. He had thought they were over.

"What?" he said in confusion.

Blackwell glanced at his daughter and then back at Michael. "Apparently you displayed the same contempt for your own life as you do for others. Your recklessness endangered the men who were trying to protect you."

"Why? Why are you going into all this?" Michael asked, feeling somewhat dazed.

"I'm very worried about my daughter." His voice was quiet, heavy with concern. There was no rancor in it. "The stability of the man, his character, that she's . . ." He faltered over the thought. "That she's involved with."

Blackwell looked at Suzanna again. "I didn't think it fair to bring this up without giving you an opportunity to explain your side of things."

"To explain what?"

"Your actions. If you had been a marine or navy officer, they would have shipped you out as a case of battle fatigue. Or court-martialed you. I'm not sure which."

Michael stared at the fruit salad of ribbons on

Blackwell's tunic. "They might have given me a Bronze Star."

He forced himself to look at Suzanna. Her face was distraught, her eyes tearful and despairing.

Blackwell had deliberately humiliated Michael in front of his daughter in order to break them up. For that reason alone, Michael felt he owed the man no quarter. But the self-righteousness of Blackwell's attack enraged him beyond any thought of restraint.

Michael stood up and wandered to the front window and stared out. Across the street was a three-story-high Polaris missile, one of the park's historical exhibits. The thick gleaming white trunk seemed somehow sinister amid the slender evergreen trees.

"May I ask you a question out of left field, Captain?"

"Yes, of course," Blackwell's voice was wary.

"When the *Santa Cruz* sailed back from Okinawa here to Mare Island for repairs, did you go down into the holds to supervise the removal of the bodies?"

Michael turned back. The blood had drained from Blackwell's face. "What the hell does that have to do with anything?"

"Your great concern about the character and stability of men, particularly the men with whom your daughter is involved. It might give Suzanna perspective on the standards by which you've judged *me*. I mean, weren't you even curious?

"About what?"

"What the bodies looked like." Michael's voice was low, menacing. "How many had really died from the explosions or the fire, or had been scalded to death when the steam lines burst? How many were just wounded and might have been saved? Or how many of the dead had no mark on them except, perhaps, that their fingernails were ripped out and their hands beaten to pulp from trying to claw and pound their way through the steel doors, the doors you had shut and locked on them? How many were trapped and drowned like the proverbial rats when you sealed off the flooding engine room? The boiler room? When you deliberately flooded the magazines while they were still manned?"

"Those men died in combat," Blackwell practically shouted. His voice was thick with his hatred of Michael. "We brought the ship half-flooded across the Pacific. After weeks in warm salt water, I imagine it would have been difficult to determine anything from the bodies."

"I don't have to imagine anything, Captain. I've been up to my ass in rice paddies with month-old corpses. They still haunt me. And I didn't kill them."

"Goddamn you!" For a moment Michael thought Blackwell was going to lash out and hit him. "We had to do it to save the ship. And we did save the ship."

"Yeah, I know. They gave you a medal for it. I read the citation."

"Your friend Riley must have told you one hell of a story."

"No, Riley wasn't aboard in Okinawa."

"Who, then? Someone around here with great moral twenty-twenty hindsight must have told you the story."

"You just did."

"Somebody put you on to this."

"The dead," Michael said. Blackwell stared at him with a strange expression.

"There were too many of them. The ratio of the dead to the wounded in the ship's official history. It was all out of proportion in my combat experience. There was a note that your wounded were transferred to a hospital ship that afternoon. More should have been saved."

"How did you connect that with me?" Blackwell's voice was a whisper.

"I wondered how you go about saving a ship when all hell has broken loose. The first time I'd been aboard one of these ships was when I shot the story here. But the watertight steel doors and hatches made a great impression on me. The big screw wheels to lock them down shut."

"And you just put two and two together. That was very creative of you. But then, that's what you do now, isn't it? You're creative." There was no malice in his voice now, only great sadness and weariness.

"Was Mother's fiancé one of the men who were trapped?" Suzanna's voice came as a jar to Michael. He had, for a few moments, forgotten she was witness to this confrontation.

Blackwell turned to his daughter, and there was deep pain in his eyes.

"Was he?" she demanded.

"No. I told you, he was a gunnery officer on deck when we took a direct hit. That was the truth," he said softly. "What in God's name are you thinking?"

"I'm sorry," she said. She turned to Michael. "I think you had better leave."

At the door she asked, "How could you do that to my father?"

"What the hell did he do to me?"

"I told you before, it didn't matter to me. It was all past."

"Dammit, it mattered to me. He cut me to pieces."

"No, he didn't. He didn't say anything you hadn't already told me in one way or another. He was just trying to protect me. But you, you were vicious. You went out of your way to try to destroy him. His reputation. Everything I feel for him. There was no justification for it."

Her eyes were red-rimmed, as though she had been crying slowly and painfully for hours. "I don't want to see you ever again," she said brokenly, and shut the door.

*M*ichael, his thoughts tumultuous, drove off base and turned north on the shoreline road. He rode slowly, paralleling the strait, reluctant to leave the area of Mare Island, as if in leaving he would be losing Suzanna forever.

Just before the Napa River Bridge there was a turnoff, a paved parking area overlooking the strait and the ghost fleet directly opposite. The sun was setting in the hills beyond, and the ships were a jumble of forlorn silhouettes.

Michael noticed a handful of cars parked facing the water. On his right there was an old pickup truck with its door open to catch the breeze off the river. The driver, a middle-aged, barrel-gutted man, sat staring at the ships, sipping a can of beer from the sixpack on the seat next to him. On Michael's left, a younger man with long, scraggly blond hair sat smoking. In both men's postures and averted faces Michael sensed the same lost and yearning loneliness. Both looked like regulars who parked here often, isolated in their cars. What fantasies, or wistful memories, did those dark abandoned vessels stir in these men?

Michael located the *Santa Cruz* by its isolated position at the end of the pier, a little apart from the nests of destroyers and assault vessels. That brooding shape was Blackwell's justification. *He had saved the ship.* And perhaps he had even saved scores of lives—the wounded, the sailors in shock or trapped in gun turrets and belowdecks who might never have survived if the *Santa Cruz* had gone down.

How could Michael compute the lives saved against those that Blackwell had willfully sacrificed? The insanity of war demanded insane calculations. What Blackwell had done was standard procedure in the navy. But with compartments flooding, fuel lines erupting flames, men dying all about him, it had demanded a terrible sense of duty. The navy had honored Blackwell for it. And Blackwell was an honorable man.

Staring at the derelict hulk across the river, with its masts and antennas spiking the sky, Michael could almost believe Tanaka's theory that the vengeful spirits of its dead haunted the decks and catacombs of the *Santa Cruz.*

If they did, Michael would readily abandon Blackwell to them. They would not do any more to him than the horror to which he had condemned them. *But was Suzanna in danger?*

The question itself frightened Michael. He violently rejected the idea of ghosts, because once Michael had opened his mind to that possibility, there was no end to the murdered phantoms from his own past that might haunt him.

But if Suzanna was in peril, Michael had to know the truth.

He backed out of the parking area and regained the road, turning onto the bridge and across the dreary salt flats toward San Francisco. He had to seek the scientific advice and counsel of the brightest—and weirdest—person he knew.

24

SUZANNA FELT WOUNDED, AS IF PIECES OF HER had been ripped out and her life was bleeding away. She languished in bed all morning in a fitful depression that was neither sleep nor rest. When she finally rose she was nervous, fidgety. She did not know what to do with herself.

Her father had hardly spoken to her the previous night after Michael left. The despair hovering about her father seemed almost touchable, a dark cloud that was chilling and damp to her fingers. She tried to reach out to him, but he withdrew from her as though even her presence was painful to him.

Old wounds that had never really healed had been ripped open again. It was the lover she had brought into her father's house who had done it.

The phone rang and Suzanna's nerves were jolted.

"Suzanna Blackwell, please." The voice was vaguely familiar.

"Yes."

"Oh, hi. This is Harvey Alexander." The art director at Michael's TV station. Suzanna had a queasy feeling of apprehension. "We've finally made a decision on that position in the art department. We were all very impressed with your work." Suzanna heard the condolence in his voice and she felt as if someone had walloped her in the stomach.

"But we've decided on another artist. He's a young man from Los Angeles who worked for several years for one of the stations there," Alexander continued in an unctuous voice. "He's had a great deal of experience specifically in this field. At this point we really need someone who can jump right into the shop and hit the ground running, rather than go through a training period."

"I understand. I appreciate your calling."

"Well, I felt I owed you the courtesy. You're very talented and I wanted to stay in touch. I'm sure you'll find something. Good luck."

Suzanna hung up. She felt defeated, humiliated in a vague, pointless way. Her first thought was to call Michael, to seek his commiseration. But now that was unthinkable. With a deep sense of loss she realized she had bounced not only her lover but her only close friend in the area.

Distracted and lost, she wandered through the dusky rooms of the house, feeling disenfranchised both as a woman and as an artist. Her dreams of a new life had simply blown away like smoke. Even this hulking building she had once thought of as home had proven to be a frightening illusion. She wanted to crawl into its woodwork and disappear.

Oh, God, she thought, I need a drink.

Her father was in San Diego, and this evening she might as well sit alone and get quietly, genteelly drunk, as her mother had before her.

She made herself a very tall drink. Suzanna had not eaten anything all day. The coolness and the alcohol of the first drink somewhat eased her depression.

She ambled back into the darkened front parlor. She would not be alone, she realized. The ghost of Doug

Kennedy haunted this house, and with each visit he was more insistent, more manifest.

The window was open and the summer breeze stirred the lacy white curtains. She studied them. Only a delicate curtain, a fragile scrim of time, now separated her and Doug Kennedy. It would be so easy to rip it apart.

Suzanna gazed dreamily at the clouds of perfumed steam rising from the blue bathwater. She felt confused, disoriented. She was slightly giddy with the heat and alcohol.

She bathed and sipped her drink, humming sotto voce to herself. I am, she thought, as transient as any ghost. I am suspended in limbo between the past and the future. The present is merely warm mists and perfume.

She stared at the heavy paneled door leading to her bedroom and then at the medicine cabinet, half expecting them to explode open at the blow of some invisible presence. They remained still, inanimate.

Well, if there was a ghost creeping about the old family mansion, it was definitely not her mother this time. Suzanna was being haunted by another spook from her personal history, the woeful spirit of her mother's star-crossed betrothed. Either that or she had gone totally wacko. *Looney tunes.*

Was she amnesically forging love lyrics to herself in a man's handwriting?

Was she hallucinating smells and a face in the mirror?

Was she projecting her nightmares into the electronic "ghosts" on a videotape?

Aha! Did the fact that she could frame the questions prove that she was sane? Or insane?

She took another sip from her drink, leaned back in the bath, and closed her eyes. Then she opened them sleepily, and in the mists that rose from the fragrant and oily water she conjured up images. There was this present place, the events and people in the past, and ghostly spirits that winged between now and then. The images arranged themselves like a nightmarish, mystical Chagall mural. *Time Is a River Without Banks.*

Suzanna envisioned the spirit of Doug Kennedy, the frustrated bridegroom, still fettered to the earth by the passion of his unsatisfied love. She saw him surrounded by a crew of other tragic young men, each mortally wounded in a horrible way, shipmates bound to each other in death as they had been in life. Suzanna somehow had the power to bring him ashore, release him, at least temporarily, from his demonic bondage. In her mind she pictured all this, as she had once sketched and painted tableaux of her mother's ghost.

After a while she rose from her bath, toweled her body dry, perfumed herself, and brushed her hair, full and shining. She put on a floral silk robe and stepped into the bedroom.

The evening was warm, with the crackle of summer lightning hovering in the air. She paused on the threshold, and the wild-clove aroma of bay rum immediately came to her.

Suzanna pulled her robe tightly about her and stood very still, her heart pounding. Doug Kennedy's spirit was at that moment somewhere in the room. He was invisible, as incorporeal as vapor before it condenses to water, but he was there. She could *sense* his presence.

Suzanna felt the surge of electricity, and the air about her seemed to seethe. She stood still for several minutes but nothing further happened.

Once again she questioned her own sanity. Was this just a flight into a childhood fantasy? She had to know.

Feeling extremely self-conscious, *knowing* she was being watched, she crossed the room. The stereo was by her bed. She turned it on and carefully placed the old record she had found in San Francisco on the turntable.

There was an easy, trickling piano intro, a melancholy riff of muted brass, and then the honeyed voice:

> *"I'll be seeing you*
> *In all the old familiar places*
> *That this heart of mine embraces,*
> *All day through."*

It was a siren's voice, one that breathed in familiar loveliness with the night.

According to the liner notes, Billie Holiday had recorded the song in April 1944. It had originally been recorded in monaural, but the reissue Suzanna had discovered was stereophonic. It was more than an old record of the forties; it was practically the original sound.

> *"In that small cafe,*
> *The park across the way . . ."*

There was a yearning in the voice for joys never fully realized, the sweetness that had been savored all too briefly. The trumpets and trombone riffs in the background stirred poignant, incomplete memories.

> *". . . The children's carousel . . ."*

The words ached with the marriage and romances that had left Suzanna with ashes, not children.

> *". . . The chestnut tree, the wish-ing well."*

The phrasing was deep, vibrant, and it raised goosebumps on Suzanna's flesh. The song no longer concerned her mother. Nor was Suzanna conscious that a long-dead black woman was singing. It was Suzanna's own song, and it sprang from the deepest longings of her own heart.

> "I'll be seeing you
> In every love-ly summer's day . . ."

The voice that resonated within Suzanna stretched syllables over two and three notes, riding on the waves of the tune, speaking the lyrics as an affirmation to a lover.

> ". . . In everything that's light and gay.
> I'll always think of you that way."

Suzanna felt weak, almost paralyzed. The light in the room appeared brighter, more intense. The light seemed, somehow, to draw its energy from her and the timeless song that flowed through her, reverberating in secret warrens of her memory, stirring her.

> "I'll find you in the morning sun,
> And when the night is new . . ."

The light coalesced into a mist, and as Suzanna watched, her breath frozen, it became a glowing ball that quickly transformed into a transparent body.

> ". . . I'll be looking at the moon
> But I'll be seeing you."

As the song ended, the anguished word *you* dissolving into a hushed breath of brass, Doug Kennedy materialized before her.

He wore a white formal officer's uniform, exactly as he had been dressed in the photographs over which her mother had wept, and he smiled at her as sweetly and shyly as a bridegroom.

Before the next song on the record started and broke
the magic spell, Suzanna quickly reset the needle. The
old song began again with that same dreamy riff of
piano.

Doug Kennedy smiled at her and held out his arms
in an invitation to dance. As if she were a magnet
drawn irresistibly to its opposite pole, she moved into
his arms, at first slowly, and then in a rush. They
embraced, then slowly danced. *He was not a hallucination,
not a dream.*

He kissed her, and where his arms and hands held
her, where their breasts, bellies, and thighs pressed
together, there was a warm electric charge, as if Suzanna's
nerve ends had been stripped. All her senses were
sharply magnified, each sensation striking a mirror that
reflected it back on itself until a kiss or a touch was
almost unendurable.

Suzanna's robe dropped to the floor at her feet.
Doug Kennedy's radiant white uniform simply seemed
to melt away, as if it were snow.

Her desire was a craving that consumed all other
thoughts. She fell back on the bed and he flowed with
her, his body weightless, magnetized to hers. She raised
her legs and enveloped him. He entered her as an
electric shock, a giddy ecstatic bolt that discharged
throughout her entire body.

Suzanna felt as if she were disintegrating, breaking
down into atoms and electrons that interflowed with
his, the two bodies dissolving together in a flux that
pulsed back and forth. The pulsating was beyond the
sensuality of the flesh. It was as though their bodies
glowed, radiating energy like a star.

Gentle waves of electricity passed between her and
the spirit of Doug Kennedy, a slow, unvarying vibra-
tion that ran from her toes to her crown. With her eyes
closed she could see a ring of light encircling their
coupled bodies like a hoop, sweeping up and down

about them. As it oscillated over each part of her body, Suzanna experienced a warm buzz there. As it passed over her head, a great roar surged through her brain.

After a while she felt herself floating upward as though she were a cloud. In the same movement she and her lover drifted apart, their separation natural and serene. Each was now satisfied, tranquil, complete.

Suzanna looked down, and six feet below her she saw her own nude body lying sprawled on the bed, her eyes shut, her mouth open in a silent cry, as if she had fainted in the midst of ecstasy. She felt strangely detached and calm, yet she knew she was not dreaming. She was alert, pleasantly aware of all the details of the room. Rather than being frightened, she felt buoyant, joyful.

She and Doug Kennedy both drifted into upright positions, now moving upward with increasing speed. He held out his hand to her and Suzanna reached for it, following him upward. His fingertips touched hers, and he took her hand.

She glanced down and saw that she was now above her house, perhaps two hundred feet above the homes along Walnut Avenue, traveling up and away toward the southwest at a greater speed.

She turned back toward Doug Kennedy. They both had bodies of light, like the clouds of a magnificent, constantly changing sunset, the hues of the spectrum endlessly shifting.

They were very high now, rushing toward the open sea. Ahead of them was a vast dome of eternal starfire. Still they soared, as their speed accelerated.

For the first time, Suzanna became terrified. She would be lost forever, unable to find her way back. She yanked back her hand.

She sensed herself suddenly slow down. Doug Kennedy reached out for Suzanna, but he was too far away, the distance between them widening.

She watched with a panicking heart as his body of light became more and more distant, until it became a fading beacon and then, finally, Doug Kennedy was lost among the stars.

She now felt herself being drawn back, falling slowly back down the astral path along which she had soared moments before. She shut her eyes and cried out. Still she fell.

There was no pain, no shock, only an increasing awareness of weight. The heaviness permeated not only her body but her soul. She did not have to open her eyes to know she was back in her flesh, in her bed. The desolation she felt broke from her in great, wracking sobs. She wept bitterly, the tears gushing from eyes in a confused outpouring of relief and grief for an irretrievable loss.

25

WITH HIS CATERPILLAR EYEBROWS, HORN-rimmed glasses, beak, and bandit mustache, Seymour Halberstam looked like a young Groucho Marx. On one wall of his cramped, littered office at the University Research Institute in Palo Alto, there was a poster of Albert Einstein with a goofy grin, balancing precariously on a bicycle. Behind his desk was an eye-level, hand-lettered placard that read:

> "All rational approaches to reality are limited."
> —*Fritjof Capra*

"We're very paranoid about the media around here," Halberstam said as soon as Michael sat down.

"Is that an institutional 'we' or a personalized, academic 'we'?"

"Both. Most of our research is for private clients who don't want their competitors to know what they're up to."

Halberstam had been a high-energy physicist, but he had resigned his job at the Lawrence Berkeley Laboratory when he came to the personal conclusion that he had moral objections to every current use of nuclear energy. As far as Michael fathomed, his research now concerned extrasensory perception. Interestingly, its sponsor was the same as it had been at Lawrence—the Defense Department.

"Why are *you* paranoid?"

"The research we're doing is considered academically flaky. It's got no future that I can see. I may be lousing up my career terminally. But the powers that be wanted physicists, not psychologists, on it. Everyone knows physicists are the *real* scientists, right? The irony is that when I sit down with some behaviorist or Freudian whose scientific paradigms are from the nineteenth century, and I lay basic twentieth-century quantum theory or relativity on them, they think *I'm* some kind of fucking mystic."

He took a quick series of puffs from the cigarette that dangled from the corner of his mouth. "But enough of my midlife crisis. Let's see your movie."

Michael had set up a portable video cassette player on the desk. He now ran through the tape, simultaneously briefing Halberstam on all he knew about the *Santa Cruz*. Halberstam remained silent, his eyes fixed on the screen, all the while puffing on a cigarette like a nervous locomotive trying to get up a head of steam.

When it was over, he pointed histrionically to the screen. " 'Be thou a spirit of health or goblin damn'd?' " Halberstam intoned. "That is the question. That's how Hamlet challenged the spook that stalked the ramparts of Elsinore. And that's the question here. It's fucking fascinating."

He glanced nervously over Michael's shoulder at the door. "If one of my colleagues pops in with a burning intellectual question, don't say you're a TV whatever. Tell them you're an old classmate of mine from Berkeley."

"I *am* an old classmate from Berkeley."

"I'm a high-powered scientist. Would I lie?"

"Actually, I remember you were a year or two ahead of me in Berkeley."

"No kidding." The furry eyebrows arched in consternation. "You must have been old for your age."

"My beard was much thicker than yours. That used to bother you a lot, as I remember." Michael pointed at the video cassette player. "What the hell is that?"

"A classic contemporary example of spirit photography. Psychic societies the world over will go out of their gourds studying it frame by frame. Then someone will write a detailed paper jerking off on how you faked it. But I'd love to have a copy for my collection."

"You have a collection?" Michael was astonished.

"Spirit photography is as old as cameras. There are old daguerreotypes of spooks." He ambled to his teeming bookshelves and pulled out a large volume with a cracking red binding. He leafed through the pages. "Here," he pointed. "The distinguished-looking chap with the beard is Sir William Crookes, discoverer of the cathode ray and the element thallium, inventor of the radiometer, a preeminent scientist of his day and president of the Royal Society. The exotic-looking lady in white was named Katie King. She was a materialized spirit. During his research, Crookes took some forty photographs, set up elaborate precautions and controls, even took galvanometer readings. But in the end his scientific brethren shat upon it all. Some even accused him of using the seances and elaborate tests to cover up a torrid affair with the medium."

Halberstam shrugged diffidently. "Need you wonder why I'm paranoid? I'm just a vagabond academic in search of my next research grant."

He turned the page. "This one. It's a double exposure of a lady in a white sheet going up the staircase of Raynham Castle. Right? Except that the picture was taken under reasonably controlled conditions, and several reputable people swore that they saw the apparition. However . . ."

He flipped the page. "Nobody saw the old lady in

this snapshot until the picture was developed. The fellow grinning into the camera next to her was her son. The thing is that she had been dead and buried for five years when the picture was taken. And that's the most common situation in these spook pictures. The ghost shows up in the picture, but no one saw it at the time it was taken." He elaborately tapped ashes from his cigarette and pointed at the video cassette. "*Quod erat demonstrandum.*

"Look," Halberstam went on, "forget the crap about ghosts being unscientific. That's nineteenth-century science. Newtonian physics. A static, three-dimensional, mechanical, Cartesian universe. Modern physics at the subatomic level and in the space-time continuum gets *very* spooky."

Halberstam puffed on his cigarette reflectively. "Hey, I just flashed on something. Tell me again how they preserve these old ships."

"With lots of paint."

"No, the electricity."

"It keeps them from rusting. They keep a charge on all the ships. It's low voltage, but it stops the electrolytic action."

"It's still a hell of a lot of juice. Each of those ships is a big steel mother."

"What are you getting at?"

"I don't know. I'm just brainstorming. In the literature there's some correlation between ghosts and electromagnetic energy. They excite sensors. They are most active before electrical storms. That sort of thing. And now you're telling me each of these ships is like a huge capacitor storing energy."

Halberstam seemed to be excited by the idea and nervously paced his office. "I mean, think about it. A modern ship is a terrific complex of machines all wired and linked together to transform one form of energy to another. It starts with your basic organic fuel. Then the fire rooms, boilers, steam turbines, and generators turn that into electricity. The electricity is stepped up, or down, by transformers and zapped into the radar and radio transmitters. That energy is broadcast out through antennas and dishes, which are also designed to pull in electromagnetic waves and feed them back through the system."

"Sy, what the hell are you babbling about? You've lost me."

"I mean if a couple of Tibetan monks with engineering degrees were to design a gigantic ghost catcher, they'd probably come up with something like that ship there."

"What about the constant charge of electricity?"

"My hunch is that it would work like an electrical storm. A source of energy that would make them more active, more manifest, stronger."

"Jesus," Michael swore softly. "Crazy Halberstam's Unified Field Theory of Spooks. What the hell are you smoking?"

He watched Sy light another cigarette from the butt of his current one. He had apparently recently become a chain smoker. The two fingers that held the cigarette were stained umber.

"Just your basic Carolina carcinogens. I have a profound death wish. At least that's what Gwen said."

Michael caught the past tense. "How is Gwen?"

"Okay, I guess. I don't really know. She's back in Cambridge."

"What's that all about?"

"She's left again."

" 'Left' as in 'left for a visit'? Or 'left' as in divorce?"

"Divorce."

"I'm sorry." Michael was not surprised.

Halberstam fluttered his eyebrows in his Groucho Marx imitation. "Well, time wounds all heels." Then his animation suddenly deserted him, and Michael saw the pain in his eyes, the hurt there intensified and magnified by the lenses of his glasses.

"She says I'm crazy."

"You are crazy. But she knew that going in. It's your charm. Your genius. Your stock in trade."

"Thanks, I needed that."

"What else can I do for you?"

"Bring me your problems. Problem-solving is what we do here."

"I'm serious."

"I know you are. I appreciate it. But I don't want to cry anymore. Really. At least not today. What were we talking about?" Halberstam insisted.

"Tibetan ghost catchers."

"Oh, yeah."

"Do you really believe all this psychic theory?"

"Who am I to refute all the world's major religions? The Jewish Kabalists. The Catholics. The Moslem Sufis. Buddhists. Taoists. They all have elaborate eschatologies of ghosts."

"You're talking about old superstitions."

"No, dammit, I'm talking about advanced mysticism," Halberstam practically shouted. "And today's mysticism is tomorrow's science."

"Christ, now you're quoting Marshall McLuhan to me."

"Well, in this case, the medium is the message." He hopped to the center of his office and held up his hands as if holding up a basketball. "Totally empty space, right? There's nothing the fuck there. Just air, right? Wrong! I happen to know for a definite fact that at least a half-dozen very violent, passionate worlds exist side by side in that seemingly empty space. There are wars, murders, intrigues, adulteries, love affairs that would wring your cynical heart going on, *right now*, all in this space. And I can prove it to you."

He paused for dramatic effect, but Michael said

nothing. Halberstam was so wound up he did not want to interrupt his spiel.

"All I have to do is move the TV set to this spot." He checked his watch. "It's just about time for 'General Hospital.' Or an old war movie on channel two. I'm being cute, of course. It's my graduate teaching assistant *shtick* for making a point. But that's what a medium— one of those dotty ladies in flowing gowns—does. She has an uncanny natural ability to bring in the channels that are out there but that we can't see. There are good mediums, bad mediums, and phonies, just as there are good doctors, bad doctors, and quacks. Here, speaking of doctors." Halberstam whirled back to the bookcase.

He searched for a few moments, then plucked out a normal-sized yellow volume. "*History of Spiritulalism,* Volumes One and Two," he announced, "by Sir Arthur Conan Doyle."

"Sherlock Holmes?"

Halberstam searched for a particular page. "Writing fiction was a sideline. He was a doctor, a brilliant guy knighted for his medical work in the Boer War. Actually, Holmes was based on a medical teacher at the University of Edinburgh, the diagnostic technique applied to criminal investigation. But *this* became his real life's work. He apparently had boundless energy. This is a solid work. A review of the literature, evaluations of the various psychic review boards in Europe and the United States, analyses of individual mediums, detailed accounts of his own psychic experiences."

"Is *that* what you're working on here?" Michael suddenly asked.

"No. It does have to do with *psi* phenomena." He gave a short, nervous laugh. "*Psi* is the twenty-third letter of the Greek alphabet. In scientific formulas its defined meaning is, quote, we don't know what the fuck we've got here, unquote. What we suspect is that there is not one *psi* but a continuum of interconnected weirdnesses. That's why my reading has spilled over somewhat into the wonderful world of spooks. And this is mind-boggling shit. *Here!*"

He apparently found the information for which he had been searching. "Circa World War I, a professor of mechanical engineering at Queen's University in Belfast, one Dr. W. J. Crawford, took continuous weights of everyone at a high-powered seance, one in which the ghosts materialized and did tricks. Crawford found that everyone—the live ones, that is—lost weight during the seance. In one recorded case, the medium lost a whopping fifty-two pounds. All of the weight came back as soon as the ghosts dematerialized. The medium wasn't in a trance. She was comatose. The spooks drained her in some way to create their own temporary bodies."

"But are they dangerous?" Michael insisted. "Could they, for instance, have killed Riley?"

Halberstam shook his head. "I don't know. There are documented cases of poltergeists, which simply means 'noisy ghosts' in German. But they knock people down, break things, start fires. Certainly there are cases of people dying under very bizarre circumstances. The working theory is that ghosts are neurotic, even psychotic personalities. They are obsessively hung up on something that happened to them in this life. Or on someone. Love, lust, hate, revenge. These are terrifically powerful emotions, and they can become all-consuming and destructive even if you're alive. The motivation doesn't necessarily have to be evil. There are reportedly ghosts of monks haunting an old chapel at Glastonbury out of pure devotion. Of course, the spooks aboard that floating crypt of yours might be there out of devout patriotism, but from what you told me I wouldn't count on it."

Michael was silent.

"My advice would be to stay the hell away from that ship. According to theory, ghosts aren't very mobile.

They never pop up a quarter of a mile away from the scene of the crime. Unless, of course, there's a good medium around. He, or she, might be able to materialize them anywhere."

The expression on Michael's face caught Halberstam.

"What's the matter?"

"Suzanna. She once told me when she was a girl, her mother used to come to her at night, talk to her, hold her. It continued until she left home for college."

"So? She had a terrific mother."

"Her mother died when she was eleven."

"Ho boy. She's a natural medium and probably doesn't even know it."

"But is she in danger?"

Halberstam puffed on his cigarette deep in thought. Then, unexpectedly, he ogled Michael, wiggled his eyebrow, and tapped his cigarette in that Groucho Marx imitation which came so naturally to him. "So tell me, Michael," he asked in a raffish voice, "is she a very sexy lady?"

"What the hell kind of question is that?"

"A serious, scientific one. Really. Give me a serious, scientific answer."

"She's a fucking mink."

"That's bad."

"Why, for Chrissakes?"

Halberstam shook his head. "I don't really have any hard data." He waved at his bookshelf. "All those very proper gentlemen who did terrific studies were Victorian in every sense of the word. They never mentioned sex, sex appeal, sensuality. But they always used gentlemanly words like *attractive, handsome, dynamic, arresting* when they described the mediums. The operative pop phrase is *charisma*. We've forgotten that originally the word meant having a special spiritual power or gift.

"Rumors, innuendos have always whirled about psychics and mediums that they were very sexy characters.

There's an electrical engineer in Virginia who has been documenting out-of-body experiences for the past twenty-five years. He maintains that the physical sex drive is the most vital factor."

"Sigmund Freud meets E equals MC squared," Michael commented.

Halberstam applauded. "That's very good for a liberal-arts major. But that's probably it. The unconscious screwing around with mass-to-energy conversions and time-space continua. That's why it's so damn hard to get a handle on. Let's go for a walk," he said abruptly. "I'm getting claustrophobic."

They strolled between the modern glass and white concrete buildings sprawled in pleasant, landscaped quadrangles. The University Research Institute had sprouted in a corner of the Stanford physics department right after World War II. Now, a generation later, it was independent of its alma mater, an athenaeum of high technology on a separate seventy-acre complex a few miles down the road.

"You came to the mad scientist for advice, right?" Halberstam asked.

"Yeah."

"Then forget it. Erase your tape. Better yet, give it to me. I'll hold on to it for some time in the future when we know more about what we're dealing with. Right now, you can only louse up your career and life. People will call you a faker and a liar, and they'll prove it. At least to their satisfaction. This isn't a scientific problem, it's an emotional one. It stirs up religious passions and a lot of craziness. It attracts all the weirdos, hallucinating druggies, cultists, charlatans, devil worshippers, neurotics, and bereaved widows. Even top scientists coming up with hard data get smeared with shit. In comparison, alchemy is a respectable science."

"Would you go to Mare Island with me?"

Halberstam shook his head vehemently. "Not me. I'm chicken. Right now even my divorce terrifies me."

"Are you going to be all right?"

"I don't know. It's rough."

"You have friends here?"

Halberstam's eyebrows arched and he made a vague gesture toward the mirrored panels and concrete slabs of the physical-science building. "Colleagues," he said.

"You want to come up and stay with me awhile?"

Halberstam hesitated and bit his mustache. "Maybe. I don't know. That's a terrific offer. I should tough it out. But let me have a rain check."

Michael nodded. As if by agreement, they ambled toward the parking lot.

"The Mustang looks terrific," Halberstam said, appraising the convertible. The top was down and the buckskin boot was snapped over it. "You must have spent more restoring this car than it cost new."

"Twice as much, actually. You're looking at the vessel of all the unrequited fantasies of my adolescence."

"That's a heavy load to put on a car."

"Why not? It's a national syndrome." He stuck out his hand to grip Halberstam's. "Don't hesitate to call. Or just show up on my doorstep."

Halberstam nodded, and once again Michael saw the quick flash of pain magnified by the eyeglasses. He gave Michael a quick, fierce hug and patted him on the back. There were very few male friends Michael felt comfortable hugging, but Halberstam was one.

He got in the car, but his friend absentmindedly kept his hand on the door, pondering.

"Mare Island. How did it get its name?" Halberstam asked.

"From a favorite horse of General Mariano Guadalupe Vallejo. A white mare's head is the emblem on the naval base's flag and publications. According to legend, the grandee's livestock was being ferried upriver when it was washed overboard in a squall. They later found the mare all by herself on the deserted island, which, of course, they christened Isla de la Yegua on the spot."

"Why did they translate the name?"

"Why not?"

He pointed to the hills south of them. "That's Palo Alto." His hand circled to the north. "The islands in the Bay are what? Buena Vista, Alcatraz, Tiburon. They are not called Pelican or Shark Island. The old Spanish names of places in California are not translated."

"You're making a point, Professor."

"Yeah, one that should fascinate you. The word *mare* has another, very old meaning in English. So old it's now obsolete, but it's the origin of the word *nightmare*."

"You're going to make me ask what it is."

"It's a monster or evil spirit that comes in the night."

"That's a terrific coincidence."

Halberstam shook his head. "One thing Freud and Jung agreed on is that coincidences are never accidental. Whatever is going on there has probably been going on for a long time. Take my advice, Mike. Stay away from there."

"I don't know if I can."

" 'From ghoulies and ghosties and long-legged beasties and things that go bump in the night, Good Lord deliver us,' " Halberstam intoned. He was quite serious.

Michael drove west to pick up the Junipero Serra Freeway, north to San Francisco. He still did not really believe that ghosts roamed the steel-walled caves and caverns of the *Santa Cruz*. Halberstam had simply presented the scientific possibilities, but he had proved nothing. Michael was still the doubting Thomas.

It was a pleasant, sun-spackled day, a day that denied the existence of another, darker world. It was for cheerful, glorious afternoons like this that Michael had bought and assiduously reconditioned the convertible. Ford had introduced the Mustang with a promotional blitz during Michael's first year at Berkeley. The automakers had pinpointed their market as the post-war baby boom now entering its late teens and twenties, and they had indeed hooked Michael. Struggling through college on budgeted handouts from his father, he had had to nurse an ailing, tanklike old Chevy sedan. But the striving adolescent who had ventured to California from New York nurtured his fantasies. In Vietnam and during the tortured depression that followed, they were the promise of life. Top down, a beautiful girl at his side, he wove along shining, precipitous sea cliffs to a hideaway in Mendocino. He rode through tree-columned country roads to a picnic and wine tasting in Napa. He raced flat-out on the coastal highway to the duney beach at Carmel. The car was tangible, definable in its 289-cubic-inch engine, four-speed transmission, metallic tan paint job. The image of the girl beside him, however, had always been elusive, the trials and errors of dating unsatisfying.

Driving through the rolling, wooded hills of the peninsula, top down, but the right seat empty, Michael thought of Suzanna Blackwell. He realized now what was the matter, what had always been the matter; she had, in a decade of dreams, always been the girl in the seat beside him.

He knew now he would never let her go. He was as obsessed as any ghost that might stalk the decks of the *Santa Cruz.*

26

FRIDAY AFTERNOON, AS SOON AS BLACKWELL
returned from his conferences in San Diego, he met
with investigators from the navy and the FBI.

"It has the signs of another freak accident," an FBI
man said.

"Another what?" Blackwell interrogated him. "What
are you talking about? Who besides Slade?" He noted
Bingham and the yard police chief glancing nervously
at one another.

"That television newscaster, sir," Bingham spoke up.
"Edward Riley. His body was found in the Bay. The
local police investigation turned up that he never left
the base here."

"Why wasn't I told about this before?"

"We just found out about it, sir. At first the police
believed he was killed in the East Bay area."

"But you're responsible for clearing civilians on and
off this base."

"Yes, sir, I know. I just got the FBI report yesterday.
I've been conducting an investigation—"

"We believe he was killed in the same immediate
area," the second FBI man interrupted, as if in a hurry.
"Possibly by the same cause."

"What was that?"

"We haven't pinpointed it yet. We're going to fly in

specialists in hazardous materials and have them go over the area."

"It happened the day of your change-of-command ceremony, sir," Bingham interjected.

Blackwell stared at the young marine as if there were some extraordinary significance to what he had just relayed, then listened very carefully to what each of the investigators said. He gradually realized that not one of them had the vaguest idea what the hell was going on. Neither did he, but he was gripped by a deep, chilling dread that he did not understand.

That evening Blackwell parked his car at the edge of the wharf, seized the flashlight lying on the passenger seat, and got out. His scanning eyes immediately focused on the silhouette and his heart stirred. *Santa Cruz* had been the ship of his dreams and the vessel of his nightmares.

Studying her across the dark tarn formed by the L-shaped pier, Blackwell thought she had never looked more potent. The rapier hull, the stepped turrets of long triple naval guns, the towering steel castle of the bridge. He remembered gazing at her in awe thirty years ago in Pearl Harbor. She had been his first ship.

She had been the first ship for most of them. They had, with few exceptions, all been about the same age—junior officers, petty officers, enlisted men. They had lived, worked, slept, eaten together aboard that ship for two years, except for the infrequent rowdy liberties in strange ports, which drew them even closer together. They had been lonely and terrified, fought raging battles, bled and died, made history aboard that ship. Never in life, either before or after, had he been as close to other men, loved them, as he had his shipmates aboard *Santa Cruz*.

How dare a neurotic like Lowenstein, who had pandered a confused, tragic war like Vietnam, how dare he judge what he, Blackwell, had done? *He had saved the ship.* For thirty years he had gone over and over and over that terrible day in his mind, until he began to view it with savage pride. He had had to make decisions that no man should ever have to make, and he had made them.

What the hell did Lowenstein or Suzanna know of the fanatic ferocity of those final battles? A kamikaze crashed into a port turret, and the impact catapulted the pilot out of the cockpit, his body demolishing a forty-millimeter battery as if, even in death, the Jap pilot had willed an extra act of destruction.

An explosion tore both legs off a twenty-millimeter gunner named Harris, but still he kept firing at the attacking suicide planes. Many insisted later that Harris had manned the gun even after he had bled to death.

To Blackwell's surprise, he found tears streaming down his face. Embarrassed, he hurriedly wiped his eyes and cheeks with a handkerchief and then marched briskly onto the darkening pier.

A loud, desolate moan suddenly froze him. It came from high in the spires of the old warship to his left, reverberating like a wail of mourning. It took a moment for it to register as one of the horned owls. The recognition gave Blackwell little comfort after the horror of Chief Slade. That morning on the pier, the line between Blackwell's life and the nightmares that had tormented him for thirty years had vanished.

It was noticeably darker. The ships along the pier were black, spiky shapes. Another owl shrieked and cackled like a possessed crone somewhere in the shadows. In the Bible studies of Blackwell's youth, owls inhabited the old ruins of Israel. They were the birds of desolation and destruction, spitting up the bones of their prey.

Blackwell did not know what had killed Slade. But the revelation that afternoon that the TV newsman, Riley, had also mysteriously died on this pier had profoundly shaken Blackwell. He alone at that meeting had known of Riley's connection to *Santa Cruz*. And for Captain John T. Blackwell, USN, Annapolis class of '43, that knowledge clearly defined his duty.

Whatever danger there was aboard *Santa Cruz*, it was his to discover. He could not honorably send other men aboard to face what he himself was unwilling to face. He would not be responsible for another man's death.

From a purely practical point of view, if there were hazards aboard—unventilated pockets of gas, the discarded, unstable explosives of a long-ago war—no one would be more familiar with them than he.

There was, of course, something else. It revealed itself only in his jumbled nightmares. But it waited for him in the deep crypts of *Santa Cruz*.

He stopped on the foot of the ship's gangway. The sloshing water below was as opaque as a tar pit. It threw back a grim, blackened mirror image of himself, as though signaling that *here* there were no illusions about the darkness of his deeds.

Blackwell climbed up the old cruiser's gangway, and for the first time in thirty years he stepped onto the quarterdeck of *Santa Cruz*. In a gesture that held no mockery he turned to the stern and saluted a pennant that had not flown in three decades. Then he turned back to the quarterdeck, half expecting a ghostly officer of the deck to greet him.

There was nothing but the dark emptiness. From the steeple of radar above Blackwell, an unseen owl emitted a brief, chilling, sepulchral laugh and then was suddenly silent.

Directly ahead of him loomed a blackness deeper

than the other shadows. He clicked on his flashlight.
The steel door leading to the ship's interior was open.
It should have been shut and dogged down to keep the
ship airtight. Perhaps Slade had opened it.

He crept forward cautiously, sniffing for fumes or
the telltale smell of cordite. At the hatch opening he
flashed the light about the inner compartment. It was
empty except for the dehumidifying machine. It was
about the size of a house-hold clothes dryer and vented
to an outside porthole. He sniffed again. The air was
fresh and odorless.

He clicked on the light switch, and the compartment
and the adjacent passageway were illuminated in cre-
puscular light. Blackwell took a deep breath and stepped
through the hatch.

Nothing happened, but then he did not know what
he had expected to occur. A steel ladder descended to
the main living compartments below. Blackwell shone
his light down it and then back to the lighting panel by
the door. The switches were labeled and he turned on
the lights for the area immediately below him.

He was, he realized, testing himself, seeing how far
he would go, like a child giving himself a dare. Would
he dare go back down into the after engine room and
the magazines?

What was there to stop him? Ghosts, perhaps.

There were always rumors about the mothballed ships
being haunted. Only a man totally barren of imagination could look at the hulks without having the specula-
tion cross his mind. But it was not bogeymen that
rooted his feet to the deck and chilled him. It was his
own sense of guilt. That was the hobgoblin he had
never really faced all these years. Blackwell sprang down
the ladder into the cave of the corridor below.

He hesitated a moment at the bottom of the ladder,
then turned toward the after sections. The layout of

the ship all came back to him, a blueprint forever engraved on his memory. His footfalls echoed with a hollow metallic sound through the empty caverns. Dimly lit passages branched off to the right and left of him. The separate compartments to each side were unlit, as dark as caves. The lights overhead suddenly dimmed.

Blackwell stopped dead in his tracks. The lights came back up. The level seemed dimmer, but he could not be sure. What had caused that?

His mind raced through the possibilities. There had been a sudden load on the circuit. Perhaps the ship's cathodic terminals or dehumidifier. The mechanical explanation satisfied Blackwell. He moved on, searching for the hatch to the engineering spaces below. There was a sudden whirl and hum in the air.

Blackwell literally jumped a foot, his heart freezing. The sound continued as a low throbbing that emanated from the bulkheads and ceilings. It took Blackwell a moment to identify the noise. It was the dehumidifier. It cut in automatically when the relative humidity in the air reached forty percent, and blew hot, dry air through the ventilation ducts.

The sound was comforting to Blackwell. It was reminiscent of the constant sound of the blowers aboard an active ship. The total silence before had been unnatural to his ear, unnerving. He found the hatch leading below to the next level and climbed down it.

At the bottom a watertight door, now dogged open, led to the after engine room. Blackwell touched the steel hatch with a trembling hand. This had been the first door he had shut.

He stared at it intently, as if there were some message inscribed on it. There was only the merciless steel and the screw locks. His eyes sought to pierce the blackness inside the engine room, but he could make out nothing. He stepped through the hatchway.

With his flashlight he searched nervously for the main switch. He found it and flipped it on. A few unseen bulbs broke up the stygian darkness, but most of the lights were out, leaving the vast cavern of the engine room unlit, hidden in shadows.

The dehumidifier suddenly cut out. Blackwell told himself that this was normal. The machine only ran five percent of the time. That was an engineer's statistic. But no comforting mathematics defined the unnatural silence that followed, as if it had been deliberately arranged to underscore his entrance.

If there was a seat of horror aboard *Santa Cruz*, this was it. Tons of water had poured in; the high-pressure steam lines had burst, scalding and boiling men to death.

At Ulithi they had not been able to repair the great hole in the ship's side. The ship had wallowed across the Pacific, this compartment still sealed and flooded, the dead trapped within.

That son of a bitch Lowenstein had nailed him on that point. He had left ship on leave the day they docked at Mare Island. He had been anxious for new orders, eager to woo Grace. He was not aboard when they had removed the bodies. Except in his nightmares, he had never confronted the rotted, pestilent corpses of the men he had trapped.

The dead had been gone now for thirty years. He was not sure what he had expected to find here. If not absolution, then perhaps his penance. Blackwell shivered. It was terribly cold, practically freezing. He wanted desperately to flee, but instead he willed himself to step down the ladder. His footsteps rang and echoed on the steel grating, as if he were being followed step by step. When he reached the main deck of the engine room, he stood there frozen, expectant.

For several heartbeats there was nothing but the oppressive silence. His nostrils twitched. There was a

sweet, gagging stink to the air. The foul smell of putre-
fied flesh.

Then, from far away, somewhere in the upper distant spaces of the ship, he heard a faint booming sound.
Then another, closer. And another, closer yet. The
sound, like the thudding footfalls of a giant, seemed to
start amidships, approaching on the upper deck through
which he had just passed. The booming became louder
and closer. He heard the heavy, resonant clang somewhere directly above him, and he then recognized the
noise with a paralyzing stab of fear.

It was the sound of watertight steel doors closing.
Each hatch through which he had passed a few minutes
before was now shutting behind him in sequence. Above
him, the door to the engine room slammed with a final,
dooming clangor.

Blackwell jumped up and spun about. A tall, lean
figure, his face hidden in shadows, stood at the top of
the stairs. He started down toward Blackwell. The de-
scending feet made no sound on the metal steps.

Blackwell stared in terror as the man, wearing a
chief's uniform, came down into an area of dim light. It
was Chief Slade.

Blackwell staggered back. Out of the corner of his
eye he saw movement and spun to face it. The figures
of other men, a score of them, emerged from the
shadows of the heavy machinery. They whispered his
name from unseen lips, the sound like a curse.

He shook violently, uncontrollably, unable to move.
The figures moved closer, heaving toward him on sham-
bling legs. The nauseating stench struck Blackwell, just
as they shuffled awkwardly into the light and he saw
their decomposed, skeletal faces.

He whirled to flee back up the steps and confronted
Slade's bloody, half-eaten face, the accusing death's head
of that awful morning. Blackwell screamed and bolted
to the rear of the engine room.

The corpses half encircled him like snarling beasts, his name a growl through teeth bared by decayed lips. He slammed against the bulkhead. At his back he felt the ladder going straight up to an escape hatch far above him in the high ceiling. He scrambled up it.

It was a long, difficult climb even for a young man, but blind terror drove Blackwell. His heart pounded as if it were about to burst through his chest. Each breath was an inflamed gasp. He collapsed against the rungs and peered down. A horror of rotted flesh and bared bones was right behind him, clawing its way up the ladder.

Desperately Blackwell struggled up, pushing his exhausted, trembling arms and legs. He reached the hatch. It would not open. An icy, damp hand grasped his leg from below.

He screamed and kicked out viciously, striking the demon again and again in its putrid face. It fell back several rungs, tangling with the creature below it.

Blackwell frantically reached again for the hatch. It was screwed down by a wheel. He heaved furiously at the wheel and lost his foothold, dangling out over the steel deck and groping monsters far below.

He clawed back onto the ladder. He shoved again at the hatch. It broke free, but it was too heavy to lift. He climbed up and threw his arms, head, and shoulders at the hatch. It lifted, and he dragged and twisted his body halfway through. He felt icy hands tearing at his legs and feet. He squirmed and wrestled through the hatch. The steel cover immediately began to lift open after him.

With a wail, he threw his body across it, weighting it down. He worked the wheel in a frenzy to screw the lid shut, and then searched about him. He located a dogging wrench in a bracket on the wall and jammed it through the spokes of the wheel, locking it down.

He lay panting on the deck. He was in an amidships corridor. It was obscured by smoke. There was a fire somewhere. He rose to his feet with great effort and staggered down the passage toward the port side of the ship.

The smoke became heavier, choking and blinding. He tripped over something thick, and fell on a blackened, charred corpse. He cried out and rolled away from it. The corpse rose up on its elbows, leered with white, sightless eyes, and grasped at him.

Blackwell scampered away on all fours. He was suddenly in the midst of a murky passageway clogged with wounded, burnt, and mutilated men. Their pleas, cries for help, tortured moans hammered at him. The smoke and heat were suffocating. Choking on the hot, poisonous smoke, he crawled through the litter of the dead and dying, ignoring the hands that reached out to him. Flames licked out through ruptures in the warped bulkheads. Blackwell stumbled through a hatchway, seized the heavy metal door, and threw his weight against it to shut it behind him.

A great explosion blasted the door open, hurling Blackwell down the corridor like rags on a hurricane. He was flung in a heap on the steel deck. Dazed, he looked up and saw a sailor crushed and flattened against the steel bulkhead, impaled there by the impact of the explosion. The bloody head turned to him and whispered, "Help me, Mr. Blackwell. Help me."

He tried to crawl away, but his legs would not move. He looked down and saw the jagged end of a bone protruding from his thigh. Using the strength of his arms, he lifted himself into a sitting position. Then he saw the burning fuel oil. It flowed down the corridor from the direction of the explosion. He watched helplessly as the burning oil consumed the shrieking, writhing bodies behind him.

Dragging the shattered leg, he started crawling, each movement sending a paralyzing bolt of pain through him, making him gasp. He was not fast enough. The flames reached him, burning his foot, then crept up his leg in a searing agony that wiped all other pain from his mind.

He clawed at the raised frame of a hatchway and, with an agonized surge, pulled himself over. The raised sill held back the burning oil. He beat out the flames with his bare hands, ripped away his pants, sacrificing his flesh for continued life. The fumes and smoke from the corridor choked him, and with his last strength he slammed the hatch and twisted it shut.

He sprawled on the deck, panting for breath. If he did not move, the agony in his leg lessened somewhat. There was a dim red battle light in the compartment. With wonder he inspected the jagged bone piercing the flesh of his thigh, and the scorched meat of his legs, arms, and hands. Shock was setting in, numbing the pain. But then he was suddenly pummeled by a torrent of water, rousing him to his agony.

A water pipe above him had burst. The compartment was flooding rapidly. He struggled up to open the hatch and allow the water to escape. The wheel twisted out of his hand, rotated in the opposite direction by someone outside, screwing the door watertight.

He clawed at the door, then pounded on it to open. It did not budge. The water rose rapidly to his chest. He struggled to stay up, the water now supporting the weight of his shattered leg.

He was trapped. In that moment of utter hopelessness, as the water rose to his chin, Blackwell knew a moment of desolate peace. Death was his redemption. There was no other price that was just and right.

He coughed for air. Then he smelled it, that rotten

garbage stench. A corpse rose from the black water. It wrapped loathsome arms about his face to embrace him. Blackwell's scream was drowned in the rush of water that burst into his throat and lungs.

27

RITA HAD NEVER BEFORE SEEN AN AURA LIKE that surrounding Michael. It was so intense that it crackled with energy. Zigzagging, smoky bolts of fear encircled him. Yet the fear was contained, encased in vibrant blood-red bands of courage. And all about Michael was the rosy, sensual emanation of a man in love. His passion created a field of force that shot out and charged those red bands of courage.

Rita studied her nephew intently. It would be futile to attempt to warn him. Those jagged gray shards of fear announced all too loudly that he already knew great danger was gathering about him. What more could Rita tell him? She could describe her terrifying dreams and flashes of visions and feed Michael's own fears until they shattered the fragile bands of courage that held them in check. Better to say nothing.

But there was still a *mitzvah* to perform. Perhaps she could strengthen Michael with her own love and her devotion. It couldn't hurt.

"So," Michael exclaimed, "suddenly you've got religion." He smiled at her, a crooked, slightly sardonic twist of the mouth that was his father's legacy. There was a dull yellow corona about Michael's head. He was still in strong control mentally.

It was Friday evening. Rita had invited Michael to

celebrate the traditional Sabbath dinner. It was something neither had done since her mother, Michael's maternal grandmother, had died.

Rita shrugged and put her hand on her daughter's shoulder. "Bridget and I have been discussing the possibility of her being bas mitzvahed. She should know something of her heritage. A little about who and what she is. I don't want her to grow up in a religious vacuum just because of her mother's marital mishmash."

"There's nothing wrong with her being a *shiksa*." Michael bent and kissed Bridget on the cheek. "Some of my favorite ladies are *shiksas*."

Rita watched the waves of affection radiate between Michael and his young cousin. "You still remember how to say *Shabbas*?" Rita inquired.

Michael nodded. "It's something you don't forget." He suddenly spotted the silver candlesticks and the *kiddush* cup on the table and fell silent.

Bridget followed his eyes. "My grandmother gave the candlesticks to my mother. And her mother gave them to my grandmother. And her mother before that," she recited in a voice hushed with awe.

Michael gently touched the base of the *kiddush* cup and Rita saw a faint blue flame, little more than a spark, jump from the cup to Michael's fingertips and then go out. "How long have you had these?" Michael asked quietly.

"For a while," Rita said vaguely.

The slender silver *kiddush* cup had belonged to her father, Michael's grandfather. Michael's own father had not been an observant Jew. But during the period that Michael had studied for his bar mitzvah, the family had gathered regularly for the Friday-night Sabbath dinner. Michael had been called on to make the blessings. Rita would remember to the day she died how, when the thirteen-year-old had lifted his grandfather's cup, the glow of the old man's pride had illuminated the entire dining room.

Sam Cohen had not had a son to whom to leave his *kiddush* cup. Michael, like his father, had never been an observant Jew. Yet it had always been understood that the grail was his to claim.

Michael picked up the bottle of sacramental wine, an Israeli wine. He studied the label a moment, then shook his head. "In five thousand years, you'd think the rabbinate would learn how to make a decent vintage."

"The sweetness of the wine is the sweetness of God's love," Rita said with some heat. She took a breath. "Please, Michael, a favor. Tonight, don't be the gourmet. No comments on the wine or food. It was all made with love."

"Mom and I made the gefilte fish ourselves," Bridget offered. "It's not from a Manischewitz jar."

"Terrific," Michael exclaimed. He looked from Bridget to Rita, nodding solemnly, and there was not the usual hint of amusement in his eyes.

Rita brought out the appetizer of chilled gefilte fish. The table was set. Everything was ready. Outside the bay window, a flaming orange sun had already dropped behind the Golden Gate Bridge into the sea, transforming the billowing clouds into pastel purple, pink, and tangerine heaps.

Michael and Bridget looked at Rita expectantly, their sense of anticipation creating a breathless hush in the room. Rita was nervous. She had memorized and rehearsed the ritual very carefully. It was, at this point, all she could give Michael.

She covered her head with the stiff lace handkerchief, took a deep breath, then picked up the match and struck it. She lit one candle, then the other, snuffed out the match, and began the invocation. "Blessed art Thou, O Lord, our God, King of the Universe, who hast sanctified us by Thy laws and commanded us to kindle the Sabbath light."

Rita slowly circled her hands above the candles, as if

sweeping in the holy warmth of their flames and gathering it in toward her breast.

> *"May the Lord bless us with Sabbath joy.*
> *May the Lord bless us with Sabbath holiness.*
> *May the Lord bless us with Sabbath peace."*

Rita felt that peace settle over her, a breathless calm of crystalline blue that permeated the room. She placed her fingertips on her brow and covered her eyes in the ancient gesture hallowed by her mother and her mother's mother through the ages. She prayed silently:

> *Light is the symbol of the divine. The Lord is my light and*
>   *my salvation.*
> *Light is the symbol of the divine in man. The spirit of*
>   *man is the light of the Lord.*
> *Light is the symbol of the divine law. For the*
>   *commandment is a lamp and the law is a light.*

Through her closed eyelids Rita saw the candle flames transform from yellow to blue and then deepen to a radiant violet that spiraled up and encircled the room as a hovering Presence.

"May our home be consecrated, O God, by Thy light. May it shine upon us in blessing as the light of love and truth, the light of peace and goodwill. Amen."

Rita opened her eyes and looked at Michael and Bridget. They stared at her, silent, glassy-eyed, and awed as she had once stared at her own mother, transformed and beautiful in the candlelight, as she had invoked, however briefly, the presence of God on earth, the *Shekinah.*

Rita smiled and nodded at Michael.

Michael hesitated, then poured the sacramental wine into the silver *kiddush* cup and raised it for the sanctification. "Praised be Thou, O Lord our God, King of the Universe, who hast created the fruit of the vine."

He then chanted the *kiddush* in Hebrew, in a voice that was deep, resonant, and charged with emotions that were, perhaps, untapped since his adolescence.

In Rita's eyes, the blood red of the wine became radiant and then transformed into violet, then blue. As Michael sipped the wine, the vibrant blue color flowed into him and infused his own aura.

He passed the cup to Rita. She sipped. The wine was sweet, strong, musky. It was a wine that was by nature deliberately rich and overpowering, a sacrament one should not drink too quickly, but taste and savor.

Rita in turn handed the cup to Bridget with an encouraging nod. Bridget beamed, her eyes wide with shining excitement, and she tentatively tasted the wine. Her aura was a radiant flux of deep blue religious awe and rosy glee.

The cup was returned to Michael. He then lifted the white linen from the loaf of *challah*. He broke off a hunk of the crusty egg bread. "Praised be Thou, O Lord our God, King of the Universe, who causest the earth to yield food for all." Again he recited the prayer in the same stirring, resonant Hebrew. The color of the bread shifted from its pale yellow to a clear white to a faint blue. Michael partook of the *challah*.

Then he broke off two more hunks from the braided loaf and passed them to Rita and Bridget. Bridget nibbled at the *challah* with the same shy tentativeness with which she had sipped the wine.

"When I was your age," Michael said to her, "my grandfather, your grandfather too, would put his hands on my head at this point and make a blessing in this deep, accented voice."

Michael gently cradled the girl's face in his hands and looked into her eyes. "He'd say, 'May the God of our fathers bless you. May He who has guided us unto this day lead you to be an honor to our family. May He who has protected us from all evil make you a blessing to Israel and all mankind.' "

"Are you blessing me?" Bridget asked in a very quiet voice, but her colors fluxed in an excited confusion. Even Michael could see the flush in her cheeks.

Michael shook his head. "I don't have that kind of power. Even my father didn't. But our grandfather did. At least I thought he did when I was a kid." Rita watched the pale blue spiritual aura that had enveloped Michael suddenly fade, veiled by a gray screen of doubt.

"You have that power," Rita declared with passion. "But you have to believe in it and practice it."

"Right now I feel in need of blessing, not empowered to bless."

"You have been blessed, Michael," Rita insisted.

He stared at her, then broke off and gazed down at the table, at the heirloom candlesticks, the *kiddush* cup, the broken loaf of *challah*. Once again a fluid blue aura swirled about him as he silently acknowledged and accepted the ancient communion.

Rita brought out the tureen of chicken soup. The rest of the dinner was quiet, pleasant, with a loving rosy aura investing the room. For that Rita was grateful.

Michael talked briefly about work. He told of meeting an old Berkeley classmate, a physicist who was now into psychic research. He did not mention Suzanna.

"So, your beautiful girlfriend, Suzanna. How is she?"

Michael shrugged. "We've had a temporary estrangement."

"Oh?"

"Her father and I refought World War II and Vietnam."

"*Oy*. You didn't battle your own father enough. Now you have to take on hers."

"It's a little more involved than that."

It certainly was. In spite of what Michael was holding back, Rita doubted that he knew just how dangerous and complicated it really was. But what did *she* know? She saw auras, read tarot cards, and had terrifying nightmares.

The nightmares were not the usual forgettable Freudian montages. They recurred night after night, and their vividness, emotional power, and sense of oppression were undeniable premonitions. It was as if Hell itself were about to open its maw and swallow Michael and Suzanna.

But that made no sense. What could she possibly tell Michael? A lot of *bobbe myses.* Grandmother's tales.

Rita played with her coffee. "Tell me, Michael, you still believe in premonitions?"

He looked warily at her, then nodded. It was a moment before he spoke. "I believe you can look at a man before a battle or patrol and know he's going to die."

"How can you tell that?" Bridget asked eagerly.

"His face becomes kind of blank, soft. It's as if part of him has already taken off."

"Do you ever tell them?"

"Never."

"Can anyone else see it?"

"If they know what they're looking for. My soundman in Vietnam—he was Vietnamese—he could see it. And I've met other men, ones who'd been in combat too long, they could see it too."

"Did they ever tell?" Bridget interrogated him.

"Never."

"Were they always right?"

Michael shook his head and said softly, "No."

Michael very rarely talked about Vietnam. Rita was sharply aware of how little she really knew about what Michael had experienced there. This was Michael's way of telling her that whatever she saw or knew, he did not want to know. He overestimated her "gift."

After dinner, Rita pressed a big bowl of pot roast and a bag of the dessert strudel on Michael to take home.

"I'll live on this for a week," Michael exclaimed with gratitude.

"Look, I'm a working woman. When I cook it's an occasion, so I make enough to live on for a week. It's no more trouble."

At the door, Michael still had a faint bluish-purple glow about him. He had had his spiritual communion, and the bands of courage that held his fear in bounds were strengthened. Rita was grateful she was able to do that. She had never seen it before, but she sensed that she was looking at the aura of a warrior about to go into battle. But with a heart that trembled, she realized that it would not be enough to shield him.

Michael kissed her and left quickly, without lingering, as if deliberately breaking off anything further she might say.

Rita went back into the dining room and hugged her daughter. "Please, darling, would you clean up in the kitchen? I'd like a moment alone."

"Sure, Mom." But her daughter looked at her strangely.

Rita knelt before the Sabbath candles, the mystical candelabrum that brought the light of the upper world into this profane and dangerous one.

She prayed. She invoked a sixteenth-century Kabalistic Sabbath prayer, one to chain the demons threatening Michael. She whispered fervently, "Weakened and cast out are the impure powers, the menacing demons are now in fetters."

She felt hollow-stomached, as though she hadn't eaten in two days. There was nothing more she could do.

28

*T*HE RED LIGHT·FLASHED ON THE ANSWERING machine.

"Mr. Lowenstein. This is Special Agent Frank Cooper. I'm with the San Francisco FBI office. It's very important that we talk to you right away. It concerns the death of your associate, Edward Riley. I'll be working late tonight. Please give me a call as soon as you get in." He gave his office phone number and hung up.

Michael wondered what the hell the emergency was. Riley had been dead for more than two weeks now.

He dialed the number. Cooper answered the phone himself. He sounded very young.

"Hey, thanks for getting back. We had some questions concerning Mr. Riley's death that we wanted to go over with you. You may have already covered this ground with the police, but it's not in the report we got from the sheriff's department." There was the casual flavor of the Midwest in the FBI man's voice. He was polite, slightly apologetic. Michael was, after all, media.

"What can I help you with?"

"Well, we understand you last saw Mr. Riley on the dock where the mothball fleet is moored."

"That's right."

"Would he have any reason to go back aboard any of the old ships?

314

"Yes, the *Santa Cruz*. An old cruiser there."

"*What?*"

"The *Santa Cruz*. He had been aboard it during World War II. He had exciting memories of it."

"*Bingo!*" Cooper exclaimed. Michael heard him shout excitedly to someone in the office, "It's the *Santa Cruz*."

"What's the *Santa Cruz*? What the hell's happening?"

Cooper came back on the phone. "Thank you, Mr. Lowenstein. I can't tell you how much time and trouble you've probably saved us. I thought we were going to have to crawl through every old ship in that fleet."

"Why? What for?" What did they know?

"We're not quite sure yet. We suspect old ammo or perhaps leaky fuel. The ships are supposed to be clean but, well, hell, I guess they mothballed thousands of them in a rush right after World War II. Procedures were kind of catch-as-catch-can. There's no telling what was left aboard some of them."

"You'd be amazed," Michael said grimly.

"No doubt. But we don't want any more accidents."

The plural alerted Michael. "*Accidents?* Did something else happen?"

"A chief named Slade was killed there the other night. An old-timer in charge of the maintenance crews."

"What killed him?"

"We don't know yet. That's what we're looking into. The body was found Wednesday morning on the pier. Right near that old battlewagon you mentioned."

"This chief, did he have any connection with the ship?"

"Well, as I said, he supervised the maintenance crews."

"No," Michael interrupted impatiently. "I mean was he ever a member of the ship's crew?"

"Well, I don't know whether he was or wasn't."

"Do you have a service record or personnel file on him?"

"Yeah, as a matter of fact."

"Please, look it up," Michael insisted.

"It will take a while to look through."

"No. It'll be right in the beginning. World War II."

The line was silent for a while, and Michael monitored the FBI man's breath, a deep hushing sound over the phone.

There was a rustle of papers and then a sudden exclamation.

"Goddamn. There it is. He was a damage-control petty officer aboard the *Santa Cruz.* How'd you know that?"

"I'm psychic," Michael said. "That ship is haunted, you know."

"I believe it," Cooper said easily. "They're spookier'n hell, those old ships. If any place is haunted, they sure are."

"Anything else?"

"No, but I sure want to thank you. You've made our job a lot easier."

Michael hung up and sat staring at the phone. He felt as if he were encased in ice.

He was a damage-control petty officer aboard the Santa Cruz.

Michael bolted out of his apartment, took the stairs two at a time, and jumped into his car. Traffic on the Golden Gate was light by the time Michael hit the bridge. The commuters were already firing up the barbecue pits of Marin, and he barreled up Highway 101, making good time. But to his right he could see the dense, woolly blanket of fog already smothering the Bay, and he cursed it.

Michael's comment to the FBI man about the *Santa Cruz* being haunted had been a macabre joke. But Michael did not have to believe in ghosts to know there was a madness that enshrouded that ship like a poisonous cloud.

He did not know who or what had killed Riley and

Chief Slade, but in the bloody chambers of his heart and mind, Michael recognized the rage that had killed them. In Vietnam he had seen it too often in the living, or rather the survivors.

Fear and pain and the doomed feeling of having been betrayed infected an outfit like an icy hysteria until life was defined as *us* against *them*. And *them* was the rest of the world, not just the declared enemy. The eyes of eighteen-year-olds became as shining and terrible as serpents. Distrusted or just unpopular officers and noncoms were fragged and shot in the back. And correspondents were not exonerated.

Michael would never forget the look on the faces of several grunts, the tight, mirthless smiles, when he had had to leave an area just before a shitstorm hit. Their hands trembled and they fingered their M-16s as he scrambled for the chopper. He had to cover a story elsewhere, but they itched to blow him away for deserting them as they were about to die.

The madness recognized no rationale but *them* and *us*. It exploded without sparks. Old men, women, children might be massacred or totally ignored.

Unless, of course, they were young women. In Hue, women had been raped by the North Vietnamese because they were the enemy, and then in turn had been raped by their liberators because they had been sexually used by the North Vietnamese.

That was the type of murderous rage and insanity that festered in the sealed Gehenna of the *Santa Cruz*. It threatened special atrocities to the daughter of John Blackwell, the officer who had sacrificed his own shipmates.

He had to convince Suzanna that she was in terrible danger. Whether ghosts or madmen, they had already murdered two men. There was no point in calling ahead. Suzanna and her father would think it was just a demented ruse to see her again.

He was speeding past the entrance to Hamilton Field, when it suddenly struck him that he had no pass to get on the base. He would have to call Suzanna. He careened into the next gas station and stopped two inches short of splintering the phone booth.

"Hello."

"Suzanna."

"*Michael.* Oh, my God." She immediately recognized his voice, and the alarm in hers unsettled him.

"I have to talk to you and your father."

"My father's not here." There was a moment of silence, and Michael was afraid she was going to hang up. Then her voice came back in a frantic rush. "Michael, I'm terrified. I just called his office. He left word with the duty officer that he was going down to the inactive ship facility. He was going aboard his old cruiser there."

"Suzanna, he can't. That ship's dangerous. There's something insane aboard it. Please, believe me."

"You *know* about the ghosts?" Suzanna asked it so matter-of-factly that Michael was momentarily stunned.

"Whatever is there, it—or they—killed Riley. And they killed an old chief there three nights ago."

"My God, I've got to get my father away from there."

"Suzanna, don't go near there. Wait for me."

"I can't. I've got to help him."

"You can't do it. They'll eat you alive."

"No, the ghosts won't hurt me. I have power with them."

She was not making any sense. She was excited and babbling. "Suzanna, you don't know what you're getting into. You've got to wait for me."

"I can't. My father."

She hung up, and the high-pitched buzz of the phone cut right through Michael. It was the most chilling sound he had ever heard in his life.

29

SUZANNA RACED FROM THE HOUSE IN THE MERcury she fumbled with her keys, dropping them once on the floor, before she finally stabbed the right key into the ignition. The starter whined rather than turned over, and she immediately shut it off.

She tried it again. This time it turned over with a harsh, grating noise, as if the battery were almost dead. She clicked it off again.

She sat a moment, breathing deeply to calm herself, her panic mounting. The benighted street was hazy with fog, and the house lights about her were ringed with rainbows. The moisture was probably shorting out the starter.

She tried once again, turning the key with a quick, desperate twist. The starter churned over, the engine coughed, then caught and roared with the excess of gasoline.

She sped straight down Walnut Avenue until she came to the fence delimiting the north end of the base, and spun east toward the river. She turned so sharply that for a moment she lost control of the car and ricocheted off the curb.

The car screeched to a stop at the end of the asphalt parking pad. The gray official navy sedan that her father drove was parked at the water's edge. It was empty. She stared fearfully at the convoy of forsaken warships. A sheet of summer lightning somewhere inland briefly silhouetted the steepled and spiky shapes and then they dissolved back into the darkness and fog.

Suzanna was very frightened. She knew now that she had some strange power. All that day she had wandered about the empty house, exhausted, half conscious, still stunned by the previous night's encounter, yet feeling as if she had been liberated from some undefined thralldom.

Doug Kennedy was gone. Gone to Arcturus, the Elysian Fields, or heaven itself. She did not know exactly where. Her passion had somehow released him. She knew that with the same certainty that she had known, at eighteen, on the night she had left Grey Knolls for college, that she would never see her mother's ghost again.

But her mother's ghost had really existed.

And Doug Kennedy had really materialized before her and held her in his arms. It had admittedly been a weird, kinky, neurotic love affair, because it had not been her own. She had been the medium of her mother's thwarted passion, implanted in Suzanna's psyche for thirty years, ticking there like a proximity fuse waiting for detonation. Now that it had finally exploded, she herself had somehow also been blown free.

At the dock, Suzanna did not stop. She ran down the pier, stumbling over unseen ropes, cables, and boxes that snatched at her legs from the ground. The ghosts of her mother and Doug Kennedy had demonstrated that she could safely converse with the spirits of the dead. Suzanna's love and fear for her father now forged the hope that she might intervene and save him from their wrath.

At the gangway of the *Santa Cruz*, she stopped and leaned on the railing for breath. The massive black structure, looming over her like an evil castle, suddenly intimidated her. Her father was somewhere in the maw of this ship, confronting God knows what. She took a deep breath to quell her heart, now surging to her throat, and strode up the gangway onto the quarter-deck of the *Santa Cruz.*

The hatch was open and she stuck her head into the dark compartment and shouted, "Daddy. Daddy. Captain Blackwell. It's Suzanna. Please answer me."

There was no reply. She repeated her call. Still there was silence.

She spotted a battle lantern on the wall. She clicked it on, and a strong yellow beam shot across the empty space to a staircase leading below. She unhooked the battery-powered light, shone it down the stairwell, and called out a third time, again without receiving a reply. She took another deep breath to allay the fear that was threatening to gallop away with her wits at any moment, and ventured down into the labyrinth below.

From all her visits aboard navy ships, she knew the wardroom, lounges, and officers' staterooms were at this level. At the foot of the stairs she paused to get her bearings. The corridor was very cold, a deep chill that sent spasms of shivers through her. She noticed a dim glow ahead in the passageway. Hesitantly she moved toward it on her tiptoes. Then she realized that she could not hide from whatever was aboard the *Santa Cruz.*

"Captain Blackwell. Where are you?" In a quieter, more timid voice she called, "Daddy. Are you here? Daddy."

The eternal chill was like being in the underground catacombs of Saint Callisto in Rome. The narrow passageways and gloomy recesses on either side of her held the secrets of the dead. She was an intruder here. She was suddenly terrified of becoming lost, stumbling into dark warrens filled with corpses, slowly going mad trying to find a way out of this maze of the dead.

The corridor ahead appeared to open into a larger space from which the glow emanated. The air was freezing, a fierce, unnatural cold that drew the heat from her flesh like the touch of icy metal. She instinctively moved faster, breaking into a hurried run, and burst into a large mess hall. Scores of spectral figures sprawled on the benches and tables.

The phantasma were like the light play of an old black-and-white movie on an invisible screen. Suzanna gasped in amazement. At the sound, the apparitions all turned toward her. Their manner was shy, hesitant, as though awed by her presence.

As they became aware of her, they appeared to shift into sharper focus, their faces and bodies taking on a solidity they had not had a moment before. Each seemed wounded, disfigured in some terrible, fatal way.

"Daddy, are you there?" she whispered, her voice tremulous and hardly audible.

The ghosts rose and came toward her, drifting rather than ambulating on weightless legs. She was paralyzed with terror, one so deep and primal that her limbs went numb. Her brain stormed with confused thoughts and emotions.

They were all so young and they had all died so agonizingly. There was a flash of pity so sharp it made tears surge, only to be quashed in an instant by the pain of the next thought. Her father had been responsible for their deaths. He had never denied it, he had only sought to justify it. She was his daughter and she loved and honored him. She could not judge him for something that had happened in the fury of a war at another time and place before she was born.

But Suzanna saw now, and understood, the horror of what he had done. In some blood reckoning, she felt she shared the guilt for it.

A ghastly change took place in each of the specters as he appeared to recognize her. Their expressions transformed, and she saw in their faces something uglier, obscene, a lust that craved to devour her.

At the touch of dank, icy fingers on her face, she shrieked and broke down the passageway. An anguished howl exploded behind her.

She raced down the corridor. From compartments ahead of her, hideous figures materialized, blocking her way. She stopped dead in her tracks. The wail behind her came from throats that sounded half human, half wolf.

She fled into a side passage. But that way was immediately choked off by other demons. She was trapped. There was no escape.

She pressed against the wall, cringing. She shut her eyes against the approaching horror. Her legs gave out and she slid down the wall and curled tightly into a fetal position. Icy hands brutally pulled and clawed at her. She heard herself whimper involuntarily from fear and the intense cold that permeated her body.

She fought to withdraw into herself, seeking some safe spot deep within, where these demons of the past could never touch her. *She would never surrender to them.*

She was so cold, she felt herself going numb. Phalluses of ice violated her, and other glacial tentacles invaded every orifice and pore, sucking heat and life from her flesh.

She felt that strings were being pulled from her as though she were a cloth doll being unraveled thread by thread. She retreated deeper and deeper, plunging into herself as if into a bottomless pool. And then she was falling into an abyss where there was no sound or light, but only the sensation of falling.

It was a fall into blackness without beginning or end.

30

THE YOUNG MARINE GUARD CONFRONTING MI-chael greedily eyed the Mustang as he stepped from the gatehouse. "Boss wheels," he said admiringly.

Michael flashed a police press card that resembled a military ID, and palmed it before the marine had a good look. "I'm Major Lowenstein. Captain Bingham is meeting me at the O-club." His tone was peremptory; it precluded challenge.

The marine snapped to attention and saluted. "Yes, sir, Major." He pointed to his right. "The corporal should have a pass for you at the office. You can park right there, sir."

Michael nodded and eased ahead. Instead of turning right, however, he kept on straight ahead, his foot increasingly heavy on the accelerator. He heard a shout behind him. Without obviously peeling rubber, the Mustang was going sixty when it hurtled onto the causeway.

Michael gambled that no one was going to shoot him for apparently misunderstanding directions. The major part of the island was not a high-security area. Wives and kids lived in the dependent housing. Girlfriends and "pass-around Pattys" casually visited the servicemen's clubs on the base. The marines would send out a patrol to track down Michael, but there would be no great alarm as long as he stayed away from the fenced-in areas where nuclear subs were built or missile warfare plotted.

He sped over the causeway. The ghost fleet was a black mass on the water to the north. At the first turnoff, Railroad Avenue, he wheeled sharply to the right, tires squealing. His only thought was to intercept Suzanna.

As he raced onto the tarmac, his headlights picked up her car. He braked to a jolting stop alongside it. "Goddamn her. Damn her," he shouted and pounded the steering wheel in fury.

He stepped on the accelerator, and his car bounced over a concrete curb and onto the finger pier. It swerved, threatening to plunge into the water, before Michael straightened the wheel and roared down the narrow pier. A sawhorse and a barrel in his way were knocked into oblivion.

He jammed to a stop at the gangway and jumped out, looking about frantically. Suzanna was nowhere in sight. Michael stared fearfully up the gangplanks leading aboard the ship.

The *Santa Cruz*, the fleet, the river were all shrouded in a weeping fog that closed out the rest of the world. Somewhere to the northwest there was a flash of lightning, and during the time it took the thunder to reach him, Michael stood transfixed with fear, staring up at the black, brooding towers above him.

In those moments Michael believed in the ghosts of the *Santa Cruz*.

Outlined in lightning, the great rods and disks of antennas pointed at the stratosphere, as though drawing in the wandering lost souls of its dead. Their outrage, their lust for revenge, had been a psychic spark smoldering all these years in the empty steel chambers of the ship, the energy building up steadily, as in a powerful condenser.

It was not just his life or his sanity for which Michael

now feared, but that deathless part of him, his soul,
which might be forever lost to these ghosts. Suzanna
also had claim to his soul, and she was aboard the *Santa
Cruz.*

Michael turned back to the car. He grabbed the keys
from the ignition, then moved around to the trunk. His
movements were hurried yet deliberate, as though he
had done this before. He kept his camera equipment in
the trunk, and he pulled out the thick battery belt and
strapped it on. He shoved it down on his hips, as if
consciously girding his loins.

Next he uncased the Sun Gun—a high-intensity, tungsten lamp—plugged it in, and checked the battery gauge.
The charge was low. He would have to conserve his
power. He switched on the lamp, and holding it by the
pistol grip, he swept the decks of the *Santa Cruz.*

It appeared empty. He stepped onto the gangplank.
At that instant there was an unearthly scream, and a
great black apparition with hideous yellow eyes pounced
on him.

Michael threw his arms in front of his face. Something slashed through the cloth of his jacket and raked
his arm. There was an explosion of air about him, a
loud beating. Michael fell back, and in the aura of his
light he caught sight of an enormous owl, five feet in
wingspan, soaring away.

He examined his arm with apprehension. His jacket
was ripped open, and there were three distinct gashes
on his forearm. He watched them ooze blood. The
wounds were not deep; the heavy cloth of his coat had
blunted the talons. If he had been an instant slower, his
face would have been shredded instead.

His light caught something white bobbing in the water below him. He leaned over the railing and shone
the light directly down. Captain John Blackwell, his
sightless eyes staring straight at Michael, floated face
up in the water.

Michael took no more than an instant to register Blackwell's body. He charged aboard the *Santa Cruz*.

"Suzanna!" he bellowed.

He plunged through the open door and down the stairs to the lower level, holding the blazing light ahead of him. At the bottom he suddenly froze to a stop. His breath turned to ice within him. They were all about him. The dead of his nightmares.

They encircled him, staying in the shadows just out of the direct beam of his light. Michael was awed as much as frightened. They existed. *They really existed.* They had form and substance—a gray, semiluminous, ghastly substance.

Michael constantly turned around, and they retreated before the light, wary of it, like primitive creatures afraid of fire. There was a primordial pattern to their cautious circling that gave Michael a strange confidence.

"Suzanna!" he cried out again, and he heard the name echo through hollow corridors, as if picked up and repeated by other voices, fleshless voices.

"Suzanna!" Michael moved down the passageway, holding the demons at bay with his light. They were all about him. The terror he felt was almost paralyzing. Only his greater fear for Suzanna kept him moving deeper into the ship.

He threw the light in every open compartment and connecting passage. Other specters scurried out of its beam, and the harsh, glaring white light cast dreadful shadows, the black outlines of monsters upon the walls. "Suzanna!"

The pack about him thickened, seething with a burning, demented rage. The fierceness of the cold drained Michael's strength, making him pant for breath. He felt weak, as if his legs might give way at any moment, dropping him in a helpless stupor.

It was not just the cold that ate away at his will to ward off the demons. In the phosphorescent glow of faces that stalked him, Michael recognized the rictus and mangled features of every dead eighteen-year-old grunt he had ever filmed.

These ghosts had a claim on him. He had lived too long among them and used their suffering and death for his own profit. That it had been a different time and place made no difference. Their agony and anger transcended time and space. It was not words that streamed through Michael's consciousness, but a recognition that flashed between him and the tortured spirits surrounding him. With it he felt his knees buckle and he lowered the light.

The falling beam of light shone down a side passage. "Suzanna!"

She lay in a lifeless ball on the floor, her body twisted into an agonized fetal position.

He sprang to her and dropped beside her body. Her skin was white and bloodless. She felt cold. He was totally absorbed in Suzanna, forgetting for a moment the furies about him. He suddenly felt cold, dank, reeking hands on him.

He whirled on his attacker, swinging the arc lamp like a pistol. For an instant the light illuminated a burnt, disfigured face and gaping mouth. Then the apparition's arms flung out as if crucified. The face became a blur, melting away like that of a wax doll in a hot fire. The nose, mouth, and jaw collapsed into one another. The eyes sank in their sockets and the frontal bone caved in.

The creature's legs gave way and he sank lower and lower, like a statue crumbling. In a few moments there was nothing but his ruined, liquescent head on the deck, then only a heap of soiled cloth, which disappeared with a whisk, as if a hand had pulled it after him.

Michael stared at the spot on which the phantom had stood. But his concern for Suzanna was stronger than his amazement. He sprang back to her. She did not seem to be breathing. He bent to lift her. To his horror, he discovered that she felt no heavier than a child.

He whirled on the ghosts with a fury. *"Give her back to me!"* he howled.

He flipped the Sun Gun to full power, and the entire corridor was flooded with a blinding incandescent light. The demons were frozen where they stood, poised to pounce on him, and then, like the previous effigy, they quickly melted and collapsed.

A luminous mist swirled about Michael and Suzanna. Before he comprehended what was happening, the mist concentrated about Suzanna in a rush, as if condensing on her, and evaporated. Suzanna writhed, as though wracked by some great pain. Her convulsion continued for several seconds, while Michael watched helplessly. Then the spasms quieted and she became deadly still. She did not appear to be breathing.

Michael frantically hoisted her in his arms, and with Hell at his heels, he careened down the passageway.

31

SUDDENLY, IN THE BLACKNESS AND SILENCE, there was pain. Pain was the color of blood and the shrieking of a thousand voices. Suzanna felt her body as an agonized open wound, writhing in chaos. She blacked out totally.

The next sensation of which she was sentient was a heavy pressure on her chest. It came and went with a heavy, throbbing persistence, like a slow flurry of blows. Air was being forced into her mouth. The air was warm, moist, with a sweet winey taste. It was not unpleasant to just allow the air to come in as her own breath, but the blows on her chest ached.

Her hand unconsciously drifted up to stop whatever was causing them.

"Suzanna!" a voice called across a great distance. It was a cry of great urgency. "Can you hear me? Are you all right?"

She recognized Michael's voice. He was very near. Her eyes fluttered open.

She saw his shape hovering over her. There was an incandescent mist all about, enveloping them like a shining nimbus. For a moment or two she thought they were dead. Then she felt the chill and the hard, brutal concrete on which she was lying. "I'm so cold," she whimpered.

"Thank God," Michael whispered. He hugged her and kissed her on the face several times. Then he lifted her. It hurt to be lifted and carried. She had no idea where she was.

Michael deposited her roughly in the front seat of a car, hurriedly shoved her legs in, and slammed the door. She gazed bewildered at the dazzling fog all about her. There was a very bright light on the ground in front of the car. It rested on the edge of a ship's gangway, shining up it. With a stab of terror, Suzanna recognized where she was.

Michael jumped into the seat next to her. The engine exploded into power, and the car backed up with a lurch.

"I can't see a damn thing," Michael swore. The pier was too narrow to turn around. Michael backed up at high speed, half hanging out the window. The headlights shining into the fog in their wake created a blinding glare. Suzanna could see nothing of the *Santa Cruz* or the other hulks they passed. Neither of them spoke. Michael suddenly slammed on the brakes.

The finger pier ended abruptly in an L-bend. There appeared to be a wider area in which to turn about, but the fog distorted perception, concealed the drop into the water. Michael made the turn in dangerously fast cuts, as though crashing into the water were the least of the evils that might befall them.

"The lights are blinding you," Suzanna advised. "Turn them down."

"No!" Michael shouted, and glared at her with wild eyes.

A few seconds later they were off the pier and on the road to Suzanna's home.

"Who are you?" Michael suddenly asked her.

"What?"

"Who are you? What's your name?" he asked again in a brutal voice.

"I'm Suzanna Blackwell. Who the hell are you?"

"I was so scared," he said in a much gentler tone. "You weren't breathing. I couldn't find a pulse. I gave you CPR right there on the dock. I didn't know what or who was going to come back in your body. I'm still a little crazy. How do you feel?"

"Like someone's been whipping me all over. I'm so cold," she whimpered. She touched Michael. He felt warm. She snuggled against him and buried her face in the warm, fragrant flesh and hair of his neck.

"My father," she cried out, suddenly remembering.

"I'm sorry. There's nothing we can do now."

"We've got to. We can't leave him there."

"He's dead, Suzanna. I'm sorry. I saw him back there when I went after you."

Suzanna moaned. She was still in shock. She would feel the grief and loss later. At the moment her wonder at being alive was only increased.

The car pulled up to the curb and stopped. They were at her house. To her great relief, she saw through the mist that she had left the lights on in her rush.

"My God, Michael, how did you ever get me out of there?"

"I don't know. It had something to do with light. Bright light. They're afraid of the light. It totally disintegrates them."

Suzanna did not understand what he was saying. The impact of what had happened was just beginning to break through the cocoon that shock had spun about her memory. Michael had come after her and carried her out from Hell itself. It seemed inconceivable to her that he had done that.

He put his arms about her. "Oh, God, I was so terrified of losing you, I was crazier than the ghosts."

She clung desperately to him, savoring the warmth and solidity of his flesh and bones. "I don't understand what they want with us. My father's dead."

"They want to destroy us, as they've been destroyed."

"My God, why?"

"You've got to have been there."

"Been *where*?"

"Where men have gone mad with pain and terror."

Suzanna shuddered and hugged Michael fiercely to smother her trembling in his body.

"Can you walk?" he asked.

"I don't know. I think so."

He helped her out of the car and to her feet. "A little shaky, but the patient will walk again," Suzanna announced. She held onto his arm.

She managed the steps to the veranda, though she felt very weak. Once inside the house, she lay down on the couch in the living room, while Michael scurried about, turning on every light in the house.

"Michael, we have to do something about that ship."

"We're going to take care of you first."

"I'm very hungry," she declared, as if the fact amazed her.

"That's a healthy sign."

"It's a sign I haven't eaten all day."

Michael went off to forage in the cupboard. "Campbell's chicken soup," he shouted from the kitchen. "A great cure for everything from postnasal drip to vampire bites."

While Michael was heating the chicken soup, Suzanna limped into the downstairs bathroom to examine herself. She felt as if she had been beaten and ravished. There were bruises and small hemorrhages on her neck, shoulders, breasts, stomach, and loins. Her mouth, vagina, and anus felt raw. There were traces of blood.

"I look like I played sixty minutes of football or worse," she told Michael as she came into the dining room. "I should see a doctor."

"We'll go right to an emergency clinic."

"What'll I tell them?"

"I don't know. Say anything. You fainted. You don't know what happened. Let them figure it out. We'll make sure you get a complete examination."

"What if we tell them the truth?"

"They'll put you in a psycho ward. And me too."

"My father?"

"Another freak accident."

Suzanna felt like weeping, but she held on to herself. As long as she was on Mare Island, she did not feel safe. But there was one more thing she had to do. "Before we leave here, I have to go to the chapel and pray for my father. He's among the war dead now. They have him."

Michael nodded solemnly and said nothing.

There was a flash of lightning, and almost immediately a great peal of thunder shook the house.

"Jesus, what freaky weather."

Michael shook his head. "A typical Bay area summer. There's a saying: If you don't like the weather where you are, go over the next hill and you'll find something different."

Michael's assurances did not ease her nervousness. She ate her soup in silence. They sat at the dining room table. It was another of her mother's grandiose antiques, a six-foot-wide, nine-foot-long monument of mahogany.

"You're right about chicken soup," she said, smiling. "I feel better already." She sipped a glass of wine Michael had poured. "I want to drink a bottle of wine and curl up and go to sleep for a week. But not here. Not in this house."

The lights suddenly went out. A moment later there was an appalling clap of thunder.

"What happened?" Suzanna cried out in alarm.

"The lightning struck a transformer," Michael said. "The goddamn lightning always finds a transformer." There was something ominous in his voice, frightened.

"I'll get the candles." There were candles and matches in the drawer just behind her. She groped about nervously and found them, lit one, handed it to Michael, and lit another. The harsh, flickering light was ghastly. It made Michael look ghoulish, terrifyingly reminiscent of the demons she had just escaped.

In a panic she lit one candle after another, thrusting them into glasses, cups, and cream pitchers. The room was illuminated by a dozen flickering lights, each throwing black, dancing shadows on the walls and ceiling.

"The light's too red," Michael said in an odd voice.

She felt a sudden chill, a gust of frozen air as if, in winter, a storm window had crashed open. "Michael, I'm cold," she announced in a trembling voice.

Her chair abruptly slid back from the table, and before she could cry out, it rose about a foot in the air. Then the chair dropped out from under her to the floor and Suzanna simply floated up to the ceiling.

The ascent was gradual and steady, as if she were a balloon. She felt no perceptible sensation other than feeling lighter than air. There was no pressure on any part of her body. Then she was gently lowered right back into her chair. She was entranced rather than frightened. She noticed that all but three of the candles were out.

Michael stared at her, dumbfounded. A large globe of light appeared to Suzanna's left. It sailed up over the dining table between her and Michael, at the level of their faces, and then vanished. It was followed immediately by one on her right side, which also rose up and vanished.

In a moment, from the same spots above the table, a multitude of small bright lights appeared—solid, luminous objects that floated about the room. One drifted into Suzanna's shoulder, and the feathery, chilling touch was as though a large firefly had settled there.

These too dissolved into thin air, but they were followed by a misty white cloud, about the size and color of a dirty sailor's cap, that floated between herself and the window. The cloud rapidly elongated into a fleecy pillar and then transformed, condensing upon an invisible body, concentrating into the figure of a sailor.

The ghastly seaman rose up from the floor onto the far end of the table and glided toward Suzanna on the mahogany surface. His eyes were veiled, not completely materialized.

Suzanna was faint, as if she had lost control of her limbs. She felt as if spiderwebs were being woven about her face and hands. The ghosts were using her, somehow feeding from her. She felt herself being drained.

"No, stop it!" she shrieked. "No, no, no!"

The pale, ghastly face contorted with anger. The body began to melt quickly away from the feet upward, until only the head, with its enraged expression, remained on the table. Then this too grew less and less and became only a white spot, which quivered for a moment on the dark surface and then also disappeared.

Suzanna looked at Michael. He sat, hands pressed to the table, staring as if hypnotized at that spot.

"Michael," she whispered.

He turned to her, and his eyes were glazed. Red lines broke out on his forehead, as if an unseen pen were scratching letters in blood: *Bitch.*

"Michael!"

On his left hand the blood letters spelled out *Cunt.*

Then on his right hand appeared *Whore.*

"Fight them, Michael," Suzanna cried to him. "You can fight them. Don't let them use you. They have no power in the house unless we give it to them. That's why they're playing tricks. To get control of us."

Michael threw his head back in an anguished movement. "I've been fighting them for so long," he wailed in a voice that had no strength in it, only sorrow and exhaustion.

Suzanna reached out to him across the table. "Together we're stronger than they are."

Sledgehammer blows suddenly smote the heavy mahogany boards, threatening to smash them to pieces. The fury of the blows shook the whole room.

They stopped and the massive table began to quake, quivering as if in an earthquake. The vibrating increased in intensity. The table rocked and swayed on its huge pillarlike legs. Alarmed, Michael moved toward Suzanna. The table rose up several inches from the floor and rammed forward, pinning Michael against the wall.

Suzanna threw herself at the table, but she could not budge it an inch. Michael shoved frantically at it, but he was like a large bug impaled against the wall, waving his arms and legs futilely.

Half-crazed, Suzanna threw herself against the table at the same instant Michael heaved. Working together, they dislodged it several inches. It was enough for Michael to squeeze down beneath it and scramble out from under. He shoved Suzanna ahead of him out of the dining room and they ran through to the front hall. A large globe of light suddenly materialized between them and the door.

Inside the light an arm and a hand formed. The fingers clenched into a fist and shot out and slugged Michael in the face, knocking him against the stair railing.

The disembodied hand then lashed out and seized Suzanna by the hair. It yanked her almost off her feet, dragging her powerfully back into the living room.

Michael bounced off the railing and grabbed her about the waist, fiercely tugging her to the door. She felt as if she were being ripped apart by wild forces, her head rent from her neck, her hair from her scalp. She grabbed at her hair, twisted around, and dug her heels in.

As she and Michael pulled together, their combined strength broke her free. He threw open the door and they fled outside into the fog.

"My car!" Michael yelled.

The moment they turned to it, the car burst into flames, then exploded. The heat drove them into the street.

"The Mustang," he whispered in a strickened voice. He stood transfixed, staring at the pyre.

"Forget the damn car," Suzanna shouted, pulling at his arm. "Let's get the hell out of here."

He turned a bewildered face to her.

"Come on!" She had to drag him several steps before he followed her.

"Where?"

"Just run," she ordered, grabbing his hand.

They sprinted blindly through the fog. Overhead, lightning flared, but the flashes were diffused through the mist, giving it unearthly brilliance. In the darkness between flares, disembodied faces materialized about them. They screamed silent obscenities in their rage, but Michael and Suzanna were able to dodge them. The specters abruptly appeared and disappeared, as though here, out in the open, they had only fleeting power.

"Where are we going?" Michael demanded.

"It's here, somewhere," Suzanna gasped.

"What is?"

"The chapel."

The block they ran seemed endless, an eternity in a nightmarish cloud. They must be lost, Suzanna thought in a panic. They were frantically running around in circles in the fog. When she and Michael were exhausted, the horrors about them would swoop in and overpower them.

Then the outline of a building finally emerged through the mist. The hope of deliverance gave Suzanna a surge of strength, and she pulled Michael up onto the porch, through the vestibule, and into the darkened chapel.

There was a dim glow through the stained-glass windows, but it was not enough light to distinguish the iconic figures that bordered the nave with an eerie, multicolored luminance.

Michael was rooted in the aisle, reluctant to go further. She could not see his face, but she felt the resistance in his body. "Michael, please. We'll be safe here."

She took him by the hand and led him quickly down the aisle, through the chancel gates, to the sanctuary. There all her strength suddenly deserted her, and her legs collapsed. Michael hugged her to him, and she felt him shiver.

"Whatever happens," he whispered, "I want you to know that I love you."

"I love you—" Her voice cut off abruptly.

They surged through the door. The horribly mutilated spirits of the *Santa Cruz* glutted the aisle and crawled over the backs of the wooden benches, as if ravenous to get at her and Michael. Their luminous bodies lit up the surrounding plaques and tablets memorializing the dead, as though some uncanny power passed from one to the other.

This chapel was their place, Suzanna realized in a flash of dreadful insight. The dead had power here. There was no sanctuary for the living. She had doomed Michael and herself by fleeing here.

But before the demons reached the sanctuary, they stopped. Their rage appeared to dissipate into bewilderment as they sensed for the first time exactly where they were. They peered about, and rather than drawing their rabid strength from the memorials surrounding them, they were confused. In their disfigured faces, Suzanna sensed the stunning realization that they too were now among the honored dead. It came to them as an epiphany.

There was a sheet of lightning somewhere outside, beyond the stained-glass windows. The ranks of archangels, saints, prophets, shepherds, knights, and madonnas flanking Suzanna burst into light, transmitting a radiance of their own. Above the altar, the ascending figure of the Holy Ghost hovered, his arms outstretched, his white robes and corona incandescent.

There was another burst of lightning outside, this one nearer the chapel. The thunder exploded and resonated in the peaked rafters.

A third sheet of lightning, following rapidly, totally enveloped the chapel, filling it with dazzling light, the brilliance of heaven and its saints in flux with the preternatural phosphorescence of the unholy ghosts of the *Santa Cruz*.

The tortured figures were limned in radiant light. The glare of it was searing.

Through her tears, Suzanna had a glimpse of the torn and burned bodies as they were transfigured. They were made whole and clean. They shimmered for an instant or two in glory and then melted into the streams of light that inundated the chapel from above and all sides. Suzanna could not open her eyes. It was too bright, too luminous.

The light intensified and surged about her as a roaring river, blinding and deafening her. Suzanna was forced to cover and avert her face.

Overwhelmed, she lost track of time. Gradually, through her tightly closed eyelids and hands, she sensed the light and thunder ebbing and fading. She opened her eyes.

The chapel was empty, dark again, with only the muted colored lights through the stained windows.

She turned to Michael and he stared at her with eyes wide with awe.

"I think it's over," she whispered.

He nodded, then whispered back, "If it's all the same to you, I would just as soon stay here till morning."

32

RITA SAT OUTSIDE MICHAEL'S APARTMENT ON the cold, bare stone of the stoop, hugging herself and rocking slightly, like a mourner.

A cab pulled up right in front of her, and she glanced up, startled. When Michael and Suzanna emerged from the cab, Rita rose slowly, hesitantly, as if she were somehow afraid of them.

The sun had just broken over the East Bay hills, and even in the soft, diffuse light, Rita looked haggard, as if she had aged ten years since the previous night's dinner. Her skin was drawn and bloodless, her eyes hollowed and darkly shadowed by a tortured night of nightmares, irrational fear, and tears.

She studied Michael anxiously, as if counting eyes, ears, and limbs, then intently searched Suzanna's face. Suzanna shuddered and began shaking uncontrollably, as though gripped by a sudden seizure. At that, Rita sprang forward and unhesitantly embraced the girl in a comforting maternal hug.

Suzanna collapsed into her arms and, for the first time since the night's horror had begun, gave way to wracking sobs.

At first Suzanna and Michael told no one else what had happened.

Blackwell, like Riley, had left a will requesting that he be cremated and his ashes cast upon the sea. Not being buried next to her mother was perhaps his way of finally ending the marriage, Suzanna told Michael.

The funeral was held in St. Peter's Chapel. There was no way Suzanna and Michael could avoid this final ceremony. They approached the dark gothic chapel with trepidation.

But the morning sunlight that splashed the building through the trembling eucalyptus and touched the packed pews of uniformed men who came to honor the memory of John Blackwell seemed to forbid the entry of any sinister spirits. The same chaplain who had given the invocation at her father's taking-of-command only weeks earlier now called out, "The Lord lift up his countenance, and give peace, to the souls of the faithful departed."

Suzanna wept bitterly.

The prayers, psalms, and hymns she had long dismissed as babble now seemed revelations. She prayed fervently for her father's soul.

Suzanna stayed with Michael. During the weeks of mourning, they clung to each other at night, but they did not make love. It was as though they were afraid they might again arouse wrathful spirits. No ghosts or *ignis fatuus* came to haunt them.

But Seymour Halberstam did. He had read of Blackwell's death in the *San Francisco Chronicle* and immediately suspected there was more than a "freak accident" involved. He eventually persuaded Michael and Suzanna each to tape their stories, with the agreement that all the tapes would be locked away until a time when what had happened to them might be scientifically accepted. The long, searching interviews were, in a way, a release for both of them. They had each had a need to tell somebody else, somebody who would believe them, in order to put it all behind them.

They continued to live together. "Perhaps it would be more convenient if I got an apartment of my own," Suzanna volunteered one evening several days after Halberstam completed his interviews.

"Not for me, it wouldn't," Michael said. Then he added, in a voice strained with emotion, "I don't want you to leave."

"Then I won't, because I don't want to go either."

They sat in the bay window seat of Michael's apartment, watching the sunset, sipping the '70 cabernet to which Michael had once referred as "my blood." Suzanna studied the play of colors on the protean clouds, and the fog seeping into the already darkening corners of the bay.

Above the mist, the stars would soon slowly appear, first one at a time, then in clusters and galaxies, as though they were a nightly reminder—before Suzanna slipped into dreams and nightmares—that there was an infinity of suns and worlds out there, beyond her time and touch.

The universe was infinitely more spectacular, more terrifying than Suzanna had ever imagined as a child. And with that thought came a surge of emotion that was very much like joy, and she knew that she wanted to paint again.

She turned to Michael, who she discovered was studying her as intently as she had been watching the panorama of light and darkness below. He had an oddly expectant expression, and appeared embarrassed at having been caught watching her.

"You know, Picasso once asked Aragon—the French poet, novelist, and journalist—how he could always stay in love with the same woman," Michael said in a strange voice.

"And what did Aragon say?"

"He said, 'I like to see her change.' That was his answer."

"That's a lovely answer."

Michael nodded. Then, taking a deep breath, he raised his glass.

"*L'chayim!*" he toasted, making a rasping sound in the back of his throat. He uttered it with intensity, as if it were a vow, and Suzanna was moved to ask, "What does it mean?"

"It's the oldest toast I know. Perhaps the oldest toast there is. *To life.*"

Suzanna touched his glass. "*L'chayim!*" she repeated.

"Look, I have this terrific idea I've given a lot of thought," he suddenly exclaimed. He held up the bottle. "Let's put up two cases of this. And every year on this date, we'll open a bottle. And this will be the test. You taste it and decide whether I've improved as much as the wine. If I haven't, it's grounds for divorce. I figure two cases will see the kids through college. After that we can coast."

He looked straight into her eyes, and there was no mockery or amusement in his expression, just a searching question.

Suzanna started to laugh, but then tears sprang from nowhere and coursed down her cheeks. She shook her head vigorously.

"What's the matter?" he asked in a strickened voice.

"You're cheating on me."

"What . . . what are you talking about?"

"This wine. You know goddamn well it'll start turning to vinegar before we finish the first case. We'll be using it for salad dressing." She wiped her cheeks with the back of her hand.

"A case of wine and then two cases of brandy,"

she bargained. "One of your raw California spirits that'll get smoother over the years but still stay potent."

"Christ, give me a break," Michael pleaded.

"Never," Suzanna vowed.

EPILOGUE

*I*N 1976 THE NAVY DECLARED THE WARSHIPS mothballed at Mare Island obsolete. By the end of the year, the last of them—several cruisers and an aircraft carrier—had been towed away by tugs, sold for scrap iron, and cut into scraps.

The great horned owls were dispossessed. At first they flew over the hills of Vallejo to the adjacent Suisun Bay, where a merchant marine fleet of some two hundred old freighters, troop carriers, and Victory ships from World War II, Korea, and Vietnam were mothballed.

But this fleet was already inhabited by its own fierce owls, and with snapping mandibles and vicious hisses, they drove off the birds of Mare Island.

Like great dark spirits, the horned owls wandered on the wind, scattering over the brooding mountains, the stark sea cliffs, and the towering groves of ancient sequoias. Each sought out a bleak, windswept, secret perch where it could hide during the day and then wing off at nightfall to prey on the hapless creatures of the light.

University Research Institute
Palo Alto, California

November 1, 1976

THE ATTACHED VIDEOTAPE is the only record of recent psychic manifestations aboard the warships of the Pacific Reserve Fleet "mothballed" at Mare Island in San Francisco Bay.

The accompanying audio tapes contain extensive interviews with the survivors of these extraordinary *psi* phenomena.

A consistent parallel between these phenomena and events reported in psychic literature should be noted. The hemorrhages and purpling bruises described in the medical report on Suzanna Blackwell (Appendix D) are very similar to those reported by Arthur Conan Doyle, M.D., on mediums he personally examined.[1]

The violent dematerialization of physical entities described by Michael Lowenstein in the presence of a strong light are almost identical to those detailed in the experiments conducted by the eminent physicist Sir William Crookes.[2] In the earlier case, the light source was gas burners turned up full rather than the high intensity tungsten lamp Lowenstein employed.

A more itemized analysis of the Mare Island phenomena and their correlation with those in the literature is listed in Appendix C. There is at present no scientifically accepted index of such events, and the list is based on this investigator's random reading.

[1] A. C. Doyle, *The History of Spiritualism*, Vol. II, p. 126
[2] In F. Marryat, *There Is No Death*, p. 143

At our present stage of knowledge, it would be rather fatuous to formulate an "explanation" of these events, let alone attempt to abstract a hypothesis or mathematical model. I leave that second stage of research for the future.

However, there are notable analogs in this researcher's discipline of subatomic physics that may be worth exploring. It is an axiom of quantum theory that the human observer is a necessary link in the chain of events. We are always an integral part of the process being observed. For example, if a researcher acts as if an electron is a particle, the electron will perform and give data indicating it is indeed a particle. But if the scientist asks a very different question, one that concerns electromagnetic waves, using different apparatus, the electron will behave as if it were a wave.

All light and matter, at their most elementary level, exhibit this strange property.

Everyone who reviews the events on Mare Island must question from the vantage point of his or her own discipline and life experiences how the witnesses and victims of these phenomena may have influenced and even created them.

The interviews are by design romantic, sexually explicit, and horrifying accounts. As a research scientist I make no apology for this.

This investigator's minor role during these events is detailed in the taped interview with Michael Lowenstein.

At the subatomic level we cannot prove with certainty that the most elementary particles that make up matter even exist. We say instead that they have a "tendency to exist." Things do not happen at definite times and in definite ways, but instead have a "tendency to occur."

This, ultimately, is the nature of the supposedly "solid" world we inhabit and grasp in our hands every day. Should we expect the ultimate essence of man—his soul, his holy and unholy ghosts—to be any less elusive?

—*Seymour C. Halberstam, Ph.D.*

Great Horror Fiction from SIGNET

*Prices slightly higher in Canada
†Not available in Canada

**Buy them at your local
bookstore or use coupon
on next page for ordering.**

Thrilling Reading from SIGNET

(0451)

- ☐ **ON WINGS OF EAGLES** by Ken Follett. (131517—$4.50)*
- ☐ **THE MAN FROM ST. PETERSBURG** by Ken Follett. (124383—$3.95)*
- ☐ **EYE OF THE NEEDLE** by Ken Follett. (124308—$3.95)*
- ☐ **TRIPLE** by Ken Follett. (127900—$3.95)*
- ☐ **THE KEY TO REBECCA** by Ken Follett. (127889—$3.95)*
- ☐ **EXOCET** by Jack Higgins. (130448—$3.95)†
- ☐ **DARK SIDE OF THE STREET** by Jack Higgins. (128613—$2.95)†
- ☐ **TOUCH THE DEVIL** by Jack Higgins. (124685—$3.95)†
- ☐ **THE TEARS OF AUTUMN** by Charles McCarry. (131282—$3.95)*
- ☐ **THE LAST SUPPER** by Charles McCarry. (128575—$3.50)*
- ☐ **FAMILY TRADE** by James Carroll. (123255—$3.95)*

*Prices slightly higher in Canada
†Not available in Canada

Buy them at your local bookstore or use this convenient coupon for ordering.

NEW AMERICAN LIBRARY,
P.O. Box 699, Bergenfield, New Jersey 07621

Please send me the books I have checked above. I am enclosing $_____
(please add $1.00 to this order to cover postage and handling). Send check
or money order—no cash or C.O.D.'s. Prices and numbers are subject to change
without notice.

Name_____

Address_____

City_____State_____Zip Code_____
Allow 4-6 weeks for delivery.
This offer is subject to withdrawal without notice.